M. Joseph

THE STONES

OF

CREATION

M. Joseph

THE STONES

OF

CREATION

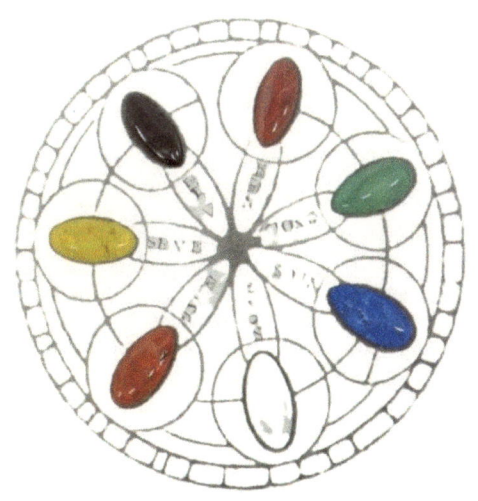

© 2024 M. Joseph
Publisher: BoD • Books on Demand GmbH, In de Tarpen 42, 22848 Norderstedt
Print: Libri Plureos GmbH, Friedensallee 273, 22763 Hamburg
ISBN: 978-3-7597-9543-4

1

In the autumn of the year 887 of the Third Age in the new reckoning, a girl named Marániel was born in the opulent port city of Dinambad, a renowned seat of the Princes of Miénast for generations. To those around her, she was known simply as Mara. At first glance, she seemed entirely ordinary, a fourth child overshadowed by three elder brothers, destined for a life of little consequence within the family's history. Yet, there was an undeniable sense, a subtle but palpable aura, that marked her as something exceptional, as though destiny itself had woven her into a tapestry of singular importance.

The names of her brothers were Enwir, the eldest, who was the heir to their father, the Prince of Dinambad; Anwar, the second-born, a station that bore little honor; and Diam, the third son. Each of the Prince's children was graced with hair of remarkable smoothness and beauty, though - except for Enwir, whose locks shone with threads of golden-blonde - they were distinguished by tresses of deep, almost raven-black hue. In this, they mirrored their father, Prince Ráhad, who was not only the ruler of Dinambad but also the brother-in-law of Dinhad II, the Warlord of Miénast, having wed Ráhad's elder sister, Aminas. All bore the same striking eyes, gray with a subtle glimmer of blue, as if the very essence of the ocean's waves had been ensnared within their gaze.

Ráhad's beloved wife, Iornieth, was taken by a swift and merciless fever in the very hour of their daughter's birth. Thus, Mara became the only child who would never behold her mother's face, while her brothers, mere children themselves at the time, soon let slip from memory the gentle visage of the one who had borne them. Only Prince Ráhad remained haunted by the beauty of Iornieth. Though he might have longed to relinquish such bittersweet remembrances, her enchanting smile - so full of life and love - clung to his mind, ever beyond the reach of forgetfulness.

Yet, despite their loss, the children of Prince Ráhad wanted for nothing. Ráhad, a man of immense wealth, had been beloved by the proud and willful people of the grand port city since his earliest years. And as a father, he spared neither expense nor effort in his unrelenting desire to surround his children with every comfort and joy that his vast fortune could provide, determined to fill their lives with happiness in whatever way he could.

On the very day Mara entered the world, and only hours after her mother's life had been claimed by fever, a young and mysterious stranger arrived at the gates of the city. She sought an audience with the grieving, clearly overwhelmed Prince, offering her services to tend to the newborn child. Her name was Adraéth. Though she wore her hair skillfully braided, concealing the pointed tips of her ears, it did not take long for the townsfolk to recognize her for what she was - one of the Immortal Folk, the Aedan. Whispers soon spread through the streets. What business could such a being have in their land? And why did she remain so faithfully by Mara's side? Some, in their ignorance and fear, even muttered dark suspicions, claiming she might be a witch, with sinister designs on the child, using her for purposes only the shadows could know.

Yet any lingering suspicions soon faded like mist in the morning sun, for Adraéth proved herself over the years to be a devoted guardian. She tended to Mara with unmatched care, and, from the moment she first cradled the infant in her arms, she loved her as though she were her own. Like a mother full of tenderness and devotion, she wrapped Mara in the warmth of her heart, dispelling the fears of all who had once doubted her intentions.

It was on a warm afternoon, as Mara, now a young child, sat by the well in the palace gardens, that Adraéth began one of her tales. Her eyes sparkled as she spoke, her voice carrying a soft lilt of enchantment. "On a vast island, once barren and deserted, nature showed kindness to the few survivors of a mighty wave that had swallowed the island of Tanuhal, their former home. As they landed on the shores of this new land, the untouched fields bloomed, plants sprang from the earth, and clear, drinkable streams gushed from springs high in the mountains, winding their way through the unspoiled landscape."

Mara, perched on the stone bench beside her, listened with wide-eyed wonder as Adraéth continued, "King Manardur II, one of the last of the Haládan bloodline, settled with his loyal followers on the westernmost coast of this great island, naming it Farham – Distant Home in Haldron. There, they built a grand harbor city of white marble and bright stones, calling it Dinambad. For many years, ships sailed from its docks, searching the vast unknown world for other survivors. But their efforts were in vain. Rarely did the sailors return, and those who did came back with empty hands and heavy hearts. Many were lost forever, swallowed by the endless sea. The few who made it back seemed reluctant to speak of what they had encountered, as if the great expanse of Ymbsetta, the encircling sea, hid secrets too dreadful to reveal. Their only answer was always the same: *There is nothing out there.*"

Adraéth paused, casting a lingering gaze upon the girl, as if weighing her next words carefully. "But the ships only ever sailed west and south. Never had they ventured to the north or the east. Farham may be vast, but do you know what lies to the east of this world?"

Startled, Mara lifted her head. "That's not part of the story."

"Every day you ask me to tell you more of this world, and yet you always return to this same tale."

"Because you've never told me how it ends."

"For good reason," Adraéth said gravely. "For the story has no end - not yet. So, can you answer my question?"

Mara blushed, lowering her head in embarrassment. "No, I cannot. But I don't believe the east is only water. That's what lies in the west and south. And what's in the north? Will you tell me?"

"When the time is right," Adraéth replied gently. "But not yet. Now, let me continue: After King Fheran, Manardur's great-grandson, ventured further east into Farham and reached the silver forest of Faldar, he encountered other inhabitants for the first time. A strange unease settled over him, and he began to worry for his people and their ancestral treasures. He ordered the construction of a grand fortress in the foothills of the greatest gray mountain of the Tin Uael, called the Mâhl. This fortress was surrounded by three massive walls of stone and an enormous crescent-shaped rampart. Once completed, Fheran moved there and named it Mahlrit, making it the new capital of the Kingdom of Miénast. Though the people of Faldar were peaceful and had no ill will toward the newcomers, Fheran never fully trusted them and kept them at arm's length.

What he did not know, however, was that long before the dawn of men, centuries before the Firstborn of Haládan saw the light of day, the Aedan had already walked the lands of Farham. They were tall and slender, their hair golden and smooth, their eyes the color of the sky. Their pointed ears marked them unmistakably as different from men. Among them, the highest of their kind - only seven in total - were crowned with snow-white hair. The Aedan were immortal, having lived since the dawn of creation of Sedäa, the Aerin name for Farham. Though they could not die from age, their hearts were not beyond breaking. Their fate was to love but once, for eternity. Should their beloved perish, their hearts would shatter, and many who could not bear the grief chose to end their lives, hoping to be reunited in the sacred halls of the First Mother, high above in the Mencael, the eternal heavens."

Adraéth took a deep breath, her eyes clouded with memory. "The High Aedin Mylias ruled over Faldar. She was kin to Elfor, Lord of Dunhir to the north, and Thergil, leader of the Aedan in the forest of Thrad. Together, they were the last of the seven High Aedan on all of Sedäa.

In his fear and greed, King Fheran fell ill and died without an heir at the age of 21. His younger sister, Fhara, was crowned as the first Queen of Miénast, moving her seat to the splendid gardens of Folares in the northwestern foothills of Tin Uael.

Nearly three hundred years later, King Mandir, the ninth ruler, had two sons, Miendir and Andor. A petty quarrel divided them, splitting the Haládan people in two. Miendir, as the firstborn, ruled Miénast from Mahlrit, while Andor, along with a few loyal followers, settled on the northeastern side of Tin Uael. There, amid fertile lands and flowing streams, he built the city of Suthawen and encircled it with wooden palisades. This small, unassuming village quickly grew into the capital of the newly formed Kingdom of Anros. Though the land was rich and fertile, it was also wild and dangerous, earning its reputation as the Wilderness.

Taladan, Miendir's grandson and the son of Taradan, who was slain by a monstrous creature, was-"

Mara sighed. "Do you expect me to remember all of this?"

Adraéth smiled faintly. "If my stories bore you, all you have to do is say so, and I will hold my tongue."

"No!" The girl sat up, startled. "Please, continue! I want to hear the whole story."

Adraéth's smile softened. She took another breath and continued, "Taladan was one of the first rulers of the divided kingdoms to face war. Far to the northeast, beyond Tin Elwech, beyond any lands men had ever dared to explore, protected by the impenetrable Iron Cage - a towering mountain range forming a massive ring with only one narrow southern entrance - a shadow rose, unnoticed. The land, known as Um-Atra, or Dead Land, was encircled by the Iron Mountains. There, in secret, a dark sorcerer had long been breeding an army of terrible creatures. He called the smaller ones Celkûn, twisted humanoid figures with hunched backs, brown skin, sharp claws, and two long, deadly tails. The larger beasts he named Nemar, their gray, scaly skin leathery and nearly impenetrable, their misshapen claws bearing only four fingers each.'

Adraéth hesitated, her words growing heavier with each passing breath. "The sorcerer who led them, more powerful than anything before him, was named Urehel. He was the Master of Darkness and Despair. Once, he had been one of the Firstborn, one of the seven High Aedan, who had descended to this young world along with his brothers and sisters. Together, they had shaped the mainland of Sedäa, with its vast lakes, towering mountains, and lush forests, a gift bestowed upon them by their creators in Mencael."

Adraéth paused again, her gaze piercing into Mara's. "Do you remember the names of the High Aedan?"

Mara frowned in concentration. "There were seven, right? Laeva and Argeniel, who created all plants and animals. Thergil, who shaped the waters with rivers and lakes, and now dwells in the forest of Thrad, watching the sea. Elfor, Lord of Life after Death, who lives in Dunhir in the northern peaks of Tin Elwech. Mylias of Faldar, the Lady of Love and Kindness. The mightiest was Vaago, who commanded the light that shined upon all worlds. And the one who is no longer counted among them, the one who turned against his own kind, seeking to rule them all but who must not be forgotten, was Urehel." Mara looked up at Adraéth with wide eyes. "Will you tell me about the Battle of a Thousand Deaths that took place before the gates of Um-Atra, where the Sea of Shed Tears now lies?"

Adraéth sighed with weariness in her voice. "Not tonight, my dear. It is already late. Perhaps tomorrow, if time permits." Her expression was troubled, but the reason for her unease remained a mystery, even to Mara. "But we are far from that part of the tale, for it was not Urehel who met his end there."

"Then who?"

Adraéth's eyes darkened as she gazed down at the girl. "If you wish to hear the whole story, you must learn patience, child."

Ô

Many days had passed since that time, yet Adraéth had found no further moments to share with Mara the tales of the ancient ages, for as the years slipped by and Mara grew older, her nights became haunted by ever more dreadful dreams.

"Is it the shadow again?" Adraéth asked gently, cradling the weeping girl in her arms.

Mara was silent for a long time, her tears flowing freely. It was rare for her to speak of her dreams, for she could not make sense of them herself, and so she kept them locked away, unspoken.

But on this day, something shifted, and she found the courage to speak. "It's growing," she whispered, her voice trembling. "Like a tree or a flower, but it needs no light. It feeds on the darkness, as if the shadows alone give it strength. In the north - far to the north - hidden behind the Iron Mountains, beneath the black clouds... it's there, growing." As she spoke, her gray eyes widened with terror. "I cannot see it, not really. For it has no form - not like us. But I can feel it, so close, and it hurts me." Her sobs came faster, her breath shallow. "It knows my name. It calls to me, again and again, until I see it - the shadow." Her body began to shake uncontrollably, curling in on itself with fear.

Adraéth held the trembling girl close, her heart aching as she watched Mara suffer under the weight of these relentless nightmares. "It will be alright, my child," she murmured softly, though the words rang hollow, as if she were trying to soothe her own growing dread. "It was only a dream. The shadow cannot touch you here. In Dinambad, you are safe - no matter what comes, I will always protect you."

Yet that day, as those words left her lips, there was a trace of doubt in her voice, a silent fear that perhaps even her strength might not be enough to shield the girl from the darkness that seemed to be reaching for her from the north.

ᕼ

As the dreadful nightmares persisted night after night, growing ever more harrowing, Adraéth knew she had to act swiftly. For the first time since her arrival, she departed Dinambad, vanishing for several days, and returned with an elderly man. Where she had ventured during her absence remained shrouded in mystery, for Adraéth revealed nothing, as though she had never been gone.

Her companion was clad in a long, dark brown cloak, beneath which he wore a similarly colored, flowing robe secured with a weathered leather belt at his waist. His chestnut beard, cascading down to his knees, was intricately braided to manage its length, though streaks of gray were evident, marking the passage of time. His piercing gray eyes, set beneath thick, dark brows, had the uncanny ability to penetrate the most obstinate of minds, guiding them with a wisdom that seemed both ancient and profound.

"You should have come to me sooner," he murmured to Adraéth as he knelt swiftly beside Mara's bed. The girl, her eyes clouded with confusion, glanced up at him. "Do not be afraid, my child," he said, his voice like a warm breeze after a storm. As he smiled, a gentle light seemed to fill the room, washing over every corner. "I am Dartur, one of the three wizards. I've come to lift the burden that weighs upon your heart."

"I'm not afraid." Mara shook her head, a sparkle of joy returning to her eyes. She sat up eagerly, wanting to study the old man more closely. "You don't look like someone who means me any harm. You're really a wizard? Can you show me a spell, or something magical? I'd love to see that."

Dartur chuckled softly. "Another time, perhaps," he replied swiftly. "I didn't come all this way to dazzle you with magic tricks."

"That's a pity," Mara sighed, lowering her head in disappointment. "But how will you help me, then? Can you stop the nightmares? Please." Her voice cracked with sorrow as her wide, tear-filled eyes searched his face. "They hurt so much, and I'm always tired. I'm afraid to sleep anymore. Please, make them stop!"

Dartur's gaze softened. "I will do all that I can, Maràniel, though I can make no promises. It grieves me to say that even my powers may not be enough. But before I can help, I must first see what you see." His voice grew firm, carrying a subtle weight of command. "Close your eyes, child!" He placed his open hand gently on her forehead, as though to measure her fever, though the gesture was filled with something deeper, a quiet magic that thrummed beneath his touch.

Trembling with a mix of fear and anticipation, the girl hesitated before finally closing her eyes. Though she wanted to fight against it, some unseen force held her captive. The mere touch of the wizard seemed to press her gently yet firmly back into the bed. Her voice wavered as tears slipped down her flushed cheeks. "I lied before," she whispered, her words heavy with emotion. "I am afraid."

"You have nothing to fear," Dartur murmured softly, though his brow furrowed in concentration. With eyes tightly shut, he began to whisper strange, melodic words - an ancient tongue, foreign and haunting, more like a song carried on a forgotten wind than simple speech.

As the spell unfolded, Mara's forehead heated as if touched by a fever, her body trembling uncontrollably beneath his hand. And then, in the depths of the spell, Dartur's vision opened. A shadowy figure appeared, distant yet unmistakable, coiling around a jagged, pitch-black fortress with many spires, like an immense serpent crawling its way upward. His gaze followed its ascent, spiraling toward the tower's peak, where the darkness gathered thick and heavy, swirling ominously around the highest spire.

And then he heard it - clear and terrible - a voice deep and maddening, a sound that clawed at the edges of reason. It called out the girl's name in twisted, nightmarish syllables, as if each utterance was designed to shatter the spirit.

Mara writhed in agony, her face contorted as if her very flesh was on fire. "It hurts," she gasped, her voice thin and trembling, "It hurts so much. He's hurting me. Please, make it stop."

Dartur's brow furrowed as he fought to remain focused, his gaze steady despite the girl's torment. "What does he say?" he pressed gently, though the weight of her suffering tugged at him. "What words does he speak to you?"

"Strange things," Mara whispered, her voice barely audible as she hesitated. "He speaks my name... over and over. Every time he does, the pain is worse." She swallowed, her throat tight with fear. "He says he knows me - he knows what I've done. And he's trying to stop it from happening again." A sharp cry escaped her as she convulsed, her body wracked with feverish tremors. "Please. Make it stop. Make it stop!"

The wizard's expression shifted, his eyes becoming distant, as though his mind had drifted far away. His lips moved, muttering words in an ancient, labyrinthine tongue - so old and arcane that even Adraéth could not decipher their meaning. But despite the strangeness of his incantation, the air around them began to hum with power, and his cryptic utterances stirred the very fabric of the room. At last, something in his words took hold, and the shadow began to waver.

Mara's eyes flew open, wide with wonder, and she looked up at the wizard. A soft laugh of relief bubbled from her lips, and she flung her arms around his neck, clinging to him in joy. "Thank you," she whispered, tears still streaming down her flushed cheeks - tears of joy this time. "It's gone. The pain is gone."

Dartur nodded, his own relief evident. "Good. Now rest, child. You need your strength. I will return in a few days to check on you." He rose slowly, his movements heavy with age, and made his way toward the door, his back slightly bent. Adraéth, her face clouded with concern, followed close behind him.

Mara, too weary to fight the pull of sleep, was quickly overwhelmed by a long-awaited and deep exhaustion. Before she could even process what had happened, she drifted into the first peaceful sleep she had known in what felt like an eternity.

Outside in the hallway, Adraéth caught up with Dartur, her voice low and urgent. "What does this mean?" she asked, stopping him with a hand on his arm. "You've seen it now - what torments her. Is it what I feared? Is it HIM?" Her voice trembled with barely contained dread. "And if it is, what does HE want with her? With Mara? She's nothing more than an innocent child."

"All of your fears have been confirmed," Dartur muttered, his breath ragged with fatigue. "Every single one of them, without exception. It was wise to call me, for what I saw answered many of my questions - questions that, sadly, have little to do with the innocent girl herself. But your Lady was right; she saw the truth. There can be no doubt now: she is the one." He sighed, the weight of his words heavy on his heart. "Shield her from the details. Say nothing of this to her - not yet! She will learn soon enough what awaits her. But for now, while she is still a child, let her remain one."

"So, it is true? Everything Lady Mylias told me?" Adraéth's voice wavered, her expression troubled. "You can imagine how this brings me no comfort. The poor child has already borne more than her share of suffering. Is it not unjust that she should be the one to walk this path? Why must it be her? I would take her place without hesitation."

"Believe me, I know," Dartur said, his voice tinged with sorrow. "I would do the same if I could, to spare such a delicate, innocent soul from bearing this burden. But this is beyond both of us. We cannot change what has been decreed. Her fate is sealed. All we can do is prepare her as best we can. But do not frighten her with the full truth - let her hold on to her innocence a little longer."

"I don't like deceiving her," Adraéth said softly, her eyes clouded with worry, "but I know well enough that the truth would only cause her harm. Wouldn't it be better, Dartur, if you stayed here a little longer? These nightmares might return to torment her again."

"They won't - not for a while, at least," the man replied, though there was a shadow of doubt in his voice. He swallowed, the weight of other concerns pressing on him. "Besides, there are other matters that trouble me. Here, in Dinambad, I've uncovered answers to many questions that have plagued me for some time, though I never intended to find them. But Mara, even as a child, seems to possess a powerful magic. I will return, but do not wait for me - when I shall come again, I cannot say. First, I must go to Dunhir to share what I have learned with Elfor. Then my journey will continue. I hope to reach Menyána swiftly, for I must speak with the guardians of the order. If I arrive too late, they may set out without me, heading northwest in an attempt to reclaim Nyardin."

He sighed, the weariness of his burdens heavy on his shoulders. "Several years ago, wild men from the Cûmeri tribe appeared in that region, scavenging what remains. I suspect they're searching for the Staff of Nyardin. Thankfully, after the fall of the northern kingdom of Nyarost, the staff was taken to Dunhir for safekeeping. But it seems the raiders are unaware of this, which may work to our advantage."

"If they're searching for something in a place where it doesn't exist, why not let them continue their blind quest? They're doing no harm in the old ruins."

"If only it were that simple," Dartur replied grimly. "Their search doesn't end with the ruins. They raid the surrounding villages and attack the nearby towns, leaving nothing but ashes in their wake. Ruthlessly, they burn everything to the ground, killing anyone who dares cross their path - man or woman, it makes no difference to them. They slaughter even the children, without a moment's hesitation. It's clear we cannot allow this to continue. The guardians must act swiftly, and I must reach them faster still."

He turned to leave, then paused, his gaze softening. "Farewell, my loyal friend. We will meet again soon. And take great care of Mara. Her path is not an easy one."

With these final words, the wizard hurried off, his cloak trailing behind him like the whisper of a fading storm.

2

The years that followed slipped by with alarming speed - too swiftly for Adraéth's liking, as she watched Mara grow older with each passing day. The girl's curiosity bloomed like a fire, her mind brimming with questions that grew more urgent as time marched on.

Dartur, once a frequent and welcome visitor to Dinambad, had initially come every three months without fail. But as time wore on, his visits grew sporadic, until, at last, he had been gone for four long years. Whispers spread through the city like wildfire. People began to wonder if the wizard would ever return.

"It must be tied to that dreadful shadow in the north," some speculated, their voices hushed.

"Nonsense," others dismissed. "It's just a storm brewing on the horizon, nothing more."

"And even if it is more than that," a few muttered darkly, "the old wizard likely meddled in affairs too grand for him and ended up in trouble. His wisdom isn't always as infallible as he thinks. Othorin, as we call him, can't possibly know everything."

"He never claimed to know everything," Adraéth shot back, her voice firm, cutting through the gossip. "But Dartur knows more than any of you could even begin to fathom, and that alone is far more than all of you put together. So, stop speaking ill of him. He has never abandoned us in our time of need, and his counsel has never been anything but sound and wise."

Silenced by her words, none dared to argue further. Over the years, Adraéth had earned the love and trust of the people, and whatever she said, they believed without question.

Yet even as she defended him, a seed of doubt had taken root in Adraéth's heart. It was unusual - far too unusual - that Dartur had been gone so long without a word. Still, she kept her misgivings to herself, unwilling to extinguish the faint spark of hope that perhaps, just perhaps, the old wizard would return.

Little did Adraéth comprehend the true reasons behind Dartur's absence. Yet far to the north, nestled among the quiet, mist-laden hills of Nanglorin, near the ancient and forbidding peaks of Tin Nangroth, lay the small and unremarkable village of Cottingen. It was there, in that remote and forgotten corner of the world, that a curious event was about to unfold - a deed, so seemingly insignificant at the time, but one that would ripple through the ages with far-reaching consequences.

In Cottingen, a small Wusel - one of those peculiar folk known for their diminutive stature, childlike height, noses sharp and keen like a hedgehog's snout, and bodies covered in thick, wiry hair - was about to make a choice. This creature, driven by an innocent curiosity, unknowingly set in motion a chain of events that would change the fate of Sedäa. And though his heart had been pure, the Wusel would soon wish that his hands had never touched what lay hidden in the shadows of his quiet world.

When Mara reached the age of maturity, her father spared no expense in throwing a grand celebration in her honor. Friends and family from across the lands traveled far and wide to attend, eager to offer their congratulations and present her with gifts fit for a princess. Throughout the day, the palace buzzed with merriment - tables laden with sumptuous feasts and the finest wines flowed freely. The revelry stretched long into the night, laughter and music filling the air. Mara, surrounded by guests, was kept busy unwrapping an endless array of presents. Silks and velvets of the finest weave, shimmering jewels of gold and silver, and even the rarest diamonds mined from the deepest caverns of the mountains adorned her hands. Wealth and opulence poured in from every corner, yet despite the outward appearance of joy, a quiet unease gnawed at her. She smiled gracefully, hiding the growing dread in her heart. It had been nearly five years since Dartur's last visit, and the weight of his absence pressed heavily on her.

But then, one gift caught her eye, and for a fleeting moment, all her worries vanished. With a delighted gasp, Mara sprang to her feet, her sudden movement causing the entire hall to fall silent. All eyes turned toward her as she stood, the joy in her eyes unmistakable. She gazed at her father, her hands clasping the hilt of an exquisitely crafted sword. The hilt, carved from shimmering pearls, was shaped like a graceful white swan with wings outstretched, as if about to take flight. The blade, though slender, gleamed with an uncommon sharpness, hinting at its deadly precision.

For that moment, as the sword glinted in the light of the grand hall, Mara's heart soared, and her fear seemed to fade into the shadows.

"There are only four such swords in all of Farham," Prince Ráhad said as he approached his daughter, his voice filled with pride. "And each one is worth more than all my treasures combined. When each of your brothers came of age, they received one of these swords, and now, so do you - though you are not a man. Still, I fervently hope you will never need to wield it, but should the day come, it will serve you well."

Mara was at a loss for words, her heart brimming with joy. The overwhelming sense of pride and belonging washed over her, as she realized, at last, she was being treated as an equal to her brothers. And not just in private - but before the eyes of all the gathered guests. With a cry of delight, she threw herself into her father's arms, her heart full of gratitude.

The other gifts, though beautiful and priceless, paled in comparison to the swan-sword. No jeweled trinket or finely woven garment could match the significance of the sword now resting in her hands. But as she turned back to the mound of unopened presents, her thoughts drifted – unbidden - back to Dartur. His absence had been felt more keenly than ever. The old wizard had not set foot in Dinambad for quite a time, and the ache of worry grew stronger each day. From the moment he had first visited, he had found a place in her heart, and now, as her fears mounted, she missed him deeply.

All day long, from the first pale rays of the sun creeping behind the mountains through the veil of dark clouds, she had held on to the hope that he would come - if only to celebrate her birthday.

But he did not come.

And the void left by his absence weighed heavier than all the riches she had been given.

When the final guests had departed, leaving only her family and a handful of women and young girls from the city, a deep sorrow settled over Mara. Despite the festivities, a growing sense of despair gnawed at her heart. She feared that something terrible had befallen the wizard, or perhaps, even worse, that he had simply lost interest in her entirely. The thought was too painful to bear.

Without a word, Mara quietly retreated from the gathering, slipping away unnoticed. She left behind the piles of extravagant gifts - once a source of joy, now meaningless. Tears filled her eyes as she climbed into her bed, pulling the covers tightly over her head, as though shielding herself from the weight of the day's disappointments. As the night deepened, all she wished for was that this day, which had begun in celebration, would be forgotten entirely, along with the emptiness it left in her heart.

6

Three knocks echoed through the room.

Silence followed.

Mara stirred and sat up, her heart pounding. The candle on the wooden dresser beside her bed had burned halfway down, marking the passage of at least six hours. Confusion clouded her thoughts as she glanced around. The night still held sway over the world outside, but the hour was a mystery to her.

She was just about to lay back down, dismissing the sound as part of a dream, when the knocking came again - louder this time, more urgent.

"Who's there?" she called, her voice trembling in the heavy silence. "And why do you disturb me at such a late hour?"

"It is an old friend," came the reply, the voice deep and commanding, filling the space with a warmth that ignited hope like a flame in the cold darkness. "And as for why I am here so late, I will not answer, for truly, I am here quite early - earlier than I intended. But since I've arrived, I ask you, Marániel, open the door and let me in, that we might speak without hindrance. It is rather unpleasant to hold a conversation through a closed door."

Mara's heart leaped with joy. She sprang from her bed, rushing to the door. With a swift motion, she flung it open and fell into the arms of the man standing on the threshold.

"Am I too late to wish you a happy birthday?" the old man asked, his eyes twinkling.

"You could never be late," Mara replied with a smile, her heart lifting.

Dartur laughed, the sound warm and full of joy. "Well then, a very happy birthday to you." He wrapped her in a gentle embrace before stepping into the room, sitting beside her on the edge of the bed. "How have you been, my dear? Adraéth told me your nightmares have returned. Is that true?"

Mara hesitated, searching for the right words. "In a way," she began slowly. "But this time, it's different. The pain is gone, but in its place, I feel an overwhelming fear and sadness. The shadow – HE - he's still there, always in my mind. And I can't stop wondering what he wants from me. Adraéth won't give me any answers. She dodges all my questions, as if she's hiding something from me on purpose. Can *you* give me the answers? Or will you just lie to me like everyone else?" Her voice wavered with frustration and longing, her eyes searching Dartur's face for any sign of truth.

"Adraéth has never lied to you," he began in a steady, calming voice. "Believe me, I would know if she had. She has only withheld parts of the truth, and that is a very different thing. And even then, she did so at my request. Before you grow angry, understand this - sometimes it is a mercy not to know everything. Ignorance can shield us from unbearable pain. But I can see from the sorrow etched across your face that you are no longer as unaware as you once were. The burden of your knowledge is heavy. So, I must ask - how did you come by this information, and just how much do you know now?"

"Why does that matter to you?" Mara demanded, rising to her feet, her gaze fierce as she faced the wizard. "You've been gone for nearly five years. In that time, everything has changed. *I* have changed. And before I reveal what I know, I insist that you tell me what *you* know - about me and about that terrible shadow!"

"There is not as much to tell as you might think," Dartur replied calmly, his tone unwavering. "Why he haunts your dreams isn't entirely clear, even to me. It would only make sense if he knew who you truly are, but I am certain he does not. He may only suspect, but his suspicions aren't enough. As long as he remains unsure, no harm will come to you. However, the reason you can see him so vividly in your dreams - so clearly, as if he stands before you - has far more to do with *you* than with him."

Mara's frustration hung in the air, but Dartur's calm presence soothed the edges of her anger, even as questions churned in her heart.

"Are you telling me that I can see him because *I* want to?" Mara asked, her voice tight with confusion and frustration. "Why would I ever want that? There is nothing more terrifying in this world than what I see when he appears. Why him, of all things?" She shook her head vehemently. "No, Dartur, I do not choose this. If I had my way, I'd never lay eyes on him again."

"This isn't a matter of choice, at least not consciously," Dartur replied, his tone soothing but firm. "You are not doing this willingly. But something deep within you compels you to see him. Sometimes, without realizing it, we keep our enemies close because it serves a purpose. And because of that - through you - I have found many valuable answers over the years."

"But why me?" she asked, her voice softening, a hint of sorrow creeping in. "Who am I, Dartur? What did you mean when you said, *who I really am*? Why can I see him? I'm just a human, a simple mortal... and still half a child - nothing more."

Dartur rose to his feet and gently rested a hand on her slender shoulder, his eyes filled with quiet understanding. "You are much more than that, Mara. And very soon, you will begin to see just how much more. I wish I could give you the answers you seek, but I cannot - at least not yet. Do not let this trouble you, for it would be in vain. In time, everything will be revealed to you. All the answers you long for will come, but for now, I can say no more."

His words were heavy with unspoken truths, but his touch was gentle, a reminder that even in the unknown, she was not alone.

"Then why are you here, Dartur?" Mara's voice trembled with frustration. "Have you come again just to wring more details from my dreams, like always? I feel like a piece of fruit - squeezed of every drop and then discarded. But if you insist on hearing what I saw, then fine." She inhaled deeply, steadying herself. "I saw dark, twisting caves and tunnels, buried deep beneath a massive mountain range. Most of the tunnels had collapsed, blocked off and impassable, but some remained open. In those passages, I heard a sound - something between a wail and a cry for help. Or maybe it was just the wind howling through the cracks in the stone."

She turned her gaze directly on the old wizard, her eyes sharp and questioning. "I wandered through those tunnels, as though I were really there, though I couldn't tell you where it was. I wasn't walking - I was running, as if something was chasing me. But there was no one there, no one except... this *thing*." Mara hesitated, her voice growing quieter as she glanced up at Dartur before continuing. "It was black, round and I held it so tightly between my fingers, as if I feared it would be stolen from me. What was it? A coin? A ring, perhaps? The old stories speak of enchanted rings - could it have been one of those? Or was it a gemstone? It was certainly large enough."

Her gaze searched Dartur's face, seeking answers. "Is *this* why you've been away for so long? Is this what's been keeping you from us? Ever since that dark shadow from the north began creeping across the land, strange things have started happening. It's as if HE's reaching out, searching for something. I know now that it's not *me* he's after. But what is it then? Could it be that object I saw in my hands? Could there actually be some truth to all the ridiculous gossip?"

She stared at him, her eyes filled with doubt and frustration. "You used to be much better at hiding your concerns. Or have there been so many now that they're starting to overwhelm you? I see something in your eyes - a flicker of regret, something that weighs heavily on you. But what is it? I can't make it out. Your advice has always been wise, even if stubborn at times, but it has never led us astray. So, tell me, what is it that you regret so deeply that it's beginning to consume you?"

Dartur paced a few steps away, his back to Mara, his shoulders heavy with the weight of unspoken truths. "You see much, more than most - more than those rare few who possess the gift of foresight and can peer decades into the future. But what you've glimpsed, as powerful as it seems, is no longer as crucial as it once was." Slowly, he turned to face her, his expression somber. "But yes, I regret it - deeply. Every single day."

For a moment, he was lost in his own thoughts, the silence between them thick with unspoken history. "What you saw in those dark tunnels was not yourself, for you've never set foot in such a place, and I pray you never will. It was Haradan, son of Huandar, the last king's heir. He was there, holding that... object."

Dartur sighed, the sound filled with the weight of years. "It was no ring. The tales of magic rings are nothing more than old fables. You shouldn't believe everything whispered in the dark. Most of it is nothing but fairy tales and legends. But the stories of the seven stones - the *Alyarel* - those are real. And what you saw was one of them."

"The *Alyarel*?" Mara's eyes widened, a mix of fear and fascination gleaming within them. "Which one? There are only three left in Farham, aren't there? Mylias's red stone, Elfor's brown stone and Thergil's green one. I know nothing of the others. Could it really be one of those?"

Dartur's gaze darkened, a storm of memories flashing in his eyes. "The Alyarel are far more dangerous than any tale would have you believe. The stone you saw... it holds a power far greater than you realize. And it may be one of the three that remain - or something far worse. I can't say with certainty." Dartur's voice was tinged with a distant uncertainty. "It may not be one of those stones at all - it could be something else entirely."

Mara took a step back, fear creeping into her heart. "But what could it be, then? Could it be the stone everyone believed was lost in the boundless depths of Ymbsetta?" The few tales Adraéth had shared with her about this ancient artifact were enough to make Mara's blood run cold.

"It's possible." Dartur paused, his thoughts momentarily clouded. "In fact, it's highly likely. But I'm not entirely sure yet. One last test must be completed before we can know for certain. However, that's a story for another time, one I won't burden you with."

"Not even if it's exactly what I wish to know?" Mara pressed.

"No, not even then," Dartur said with a knowing smile. "And besides, you already know more than most - far more than is good for you. But that's not the reason I came all this way to see you. There's still time before we need to discuss such things. What concerns me most is *you*,

23

and I must admit, my worries have only grown. The fact that you can see things - glimpses of events - confirms all of my biggest fears. A great destiny awaits you, Mara. And you won't have to wait much longer to see it unfold."

He stepped closer, his gaze warm but serious. "You are no ordinary mortal. You are something more, something greater. Your gifts surpass even those of the Children of Ahar. The yearning in your heart to do something, to make a difference in these dark days - it will be realized sooner than you think. But I can't tell you much more than that."

With a heavy sigh, Dartur turned toward the door, his movements slow and deliberate. As he reached for the handle, he looked back at her. "I must leave you again, but this time, I promise it won't be five years before we meet again. There are things I must attend to - urgent matters that cannot be delayed any longer, things you may never hear of. For now, I leave you in Adraéth's care."

He opened the door, his words hanging in the air. "Don't burden yourself with too many questions. Before the end, everything will become clear." And with that, he stepped outside, leaving Mara standing in the quiet room, her heart filled with a mixture of dread and anticipation.

"Which end, Dartur?" Mara followed him into the hallway, her eyes brimming with tears. "Ours?"

The wizard stopped abruptly, turning back to her with a look of deep contemplation and sorrow.

"I don't want to die," Mara confessed, her voice breaking with anguish. "I don't fear death itself - at least not my own - but I cannot bear the thought of losing my family. I've already endured more suffering than I can handle. If you know that we will all fail and die, why do you continue to strive so hard? Isn't it all utterly pointless?"

Dartur stepped closer, his presence both comforting and somber. He gently placed his hand on her shoulder, his touch warm and reassuring. "If even a single person is willing to fight for what is good, it is not futile - no matter how great or foolish that person may be. No, it is never, ever futile, because hope still exists. It may not be much, but it is enough to take the risk. You will still be able to live in peace here for a long time, and perhaps the impending war will never reach as far west as Dinambad."

He paused, softening his tone. "Don't take all my gloomy words so seriously! I am an old, weary fool, and sometimes I speak too pessimistically without even realizing it. But if it comforts and soothes you, I still hold onto the hope that we will achieve a good ending. And as long as this hope remains, you need not live in fear." His sigh was heavy with both resignation and enduring optimism. "So farewell, for now. May we meet again in the near future." With that, he swiftly turned and walked away, leaving Mara standing alone in the hallway. Her heart ached with fear and uncertainty, yet a flicker of hope kindled by Dartur's words provided a small measure of solace.

She stood motionless for quite some time, reflecting on his words, but soon fatigue began to overpower her thoughts. It felt as if an unseen force was guiding her, compelling her to return to bed. To her own surprise, she fell asleep almost immediately.

For a few hours, her sleep was restful and pleasant, but as dawn approached, it was abruptly shattered by a nightmarish vision far more painful and brutal than any she had experienced before.

She found herself gazing upon the stone city of Mahlrit. Though it was day, the sky was shrouded in dense, dark clouds, casting a gloomy, pallid light over the capital. Countless armored creatures lined the sprawling fields before the city walls, with the once-green land completely obscured. Here and there, monstrous siege engines - such as battering rams, catapults, and massive siege towers - were scattered about, operated by enormous, thick-skinned figures far larger and bulkier than any other on the field.

Screams tore through the air, piercing the ominous silence, as though the horror had just begun. A bloody battle erupted with terrifying suddenness. The mighty gates of the city creaked open just a fraction, and out charged a host of regal horsemen, surging into the chaos like a swift ship cutting through storm-tossed seas. At the head of the charge rode a young woman, her short golden curls glinting like a beacon in the gloom. Mara's heart sank - she knew her at once. It was her cousin Fria, Dinhad's youngest child. Though Fria rode with valor and defiance, the battle was swiftly turning against her and her men. Enemy forces overwhelmed them, toppling each rider in brutal succession - until Fria herself was thrown to the ground.

Mara's soul cried out in desperation, her instinct to scream tearing at her throat, but her voice was swallowed by the deafening roar of combat. Blinded by the anguish of the nightmare, she could only watch in horror as her cousin was struck by an unseen, ferocious force, flinging her body against the impenetrable gates of the city with crushing finality.

But then, something shifted in Mara's dream. As if another vision were fighting its way into her mind, she felt an eerie sensation, as though two realities were overlapping. She glimpsed a figure - perhaps King Huandar - riding along a worn path beside a river, a company of mounted men following close behind. But before she could grasp more, the scene blurred, dissolving into a haze. Deep waters and thick, impenetrable mist rose up around her, swirling and encircling her, until she felt herself lifted from the earth, as though she were weightless, drifting.

For what felt like an eternity, there was only darkness. Slowly, as if emerging from the depths of her mind, she saw the figure of a man clad in regal armor, a magnificently adorned sword held firmly in his hands. He stood tall, his stature noble and commanding, his hair dark and tightly curled. Yet Mara could see no more. It was as if she were being offered just a fleeting glimpse - an omen of the future.

And then, a deep, ominous voice echoed through the void, calling the name Ealdur with a tone laced with fear, as if the name itself carried great power. In that instant, Mara understood - this was none other than Huandar's heir, the rightful King of Miénast.

Suddenly, her vision was engulfed by a roaring inferno, the flames steadily consuming everything around her as though intent on devouring the very world. All that remained was fire - blazing, relentless, until it seemed nothing else could exist. And then, as before, the dark shadow emerged - its form barely more than a silhouette - and bellowed her name with such monstrous fury, she felt as though her very soul was being set ablaze, burning from within.

With a blood-curdling scream, Mara jolted awake, her body trembling violently as she sat upright in her bed. She was drenched in cold sweat, her skin ghostly pale. Her breath came in shallow, panicked gasps, and her limbs quivered uncontrollably beneath the weight of terror.

Within moments, Adraéth burst into the room, her face etched with worry as she rushed to Mara's side. "What happened?" she asked, her voice urgent. "Was it the same dream again, the one with the mountains?"

"No," Mara whispered, shaking her head, utterly drained. "I saw Mahlrit. The capital was under siege... attacked by countless horrific creatures, and massive, towering monsters." She paused, her breath ragged, struggling to calm the storm within. "And I saw Fria... she fell before the gates." Tears filled her eyes, spilling over as she broke down, her sobs wracking her fragile frame with grief.

Adraéth gently cradled Mara in her arms, her embrace tender yet firm, as though trying to shield the young girl from the horrors that haunted her. "It was only a dream," she whispered soothingly. "Fria will not fall, and Mahlrit will never be besieged. What you saw is not destined to happen."

Mara's tear-filled eyes met Adraéth's, her heart aching with doubt. "But what if it does?" she asked, her voice trembling with a mixture of fear and pain. "It wasn't me I saw in those cursed caves - it was Haradan, Huandar's son. Dartur told me about him. And the thing he clutched in his hands - it could have been one of those strange stones, or something even darker. Dartur believes, as I do, that it was the Black Stone, Haradan's curse. Urehel's stone."

"Do *not* speak his name!" Adraéth's voice rose, sharp and fierce, as though even the mere utterance could summon something dreadful. "It is dangerous enough that he torments you in your sleep, but to speak his name aloud invites disaster beyond imagination."

"I'm not afraid of him," Mara insisted, her voice laced with defiance. "No matter how powerful he once was, now he's nothing more than a shadow - formless and without true power. I have no fear of him. He cannot harm me."

"For now, perhaps." Adraéth's tone was softening, though it carried a warning. "But do not be so quick to dismiss him. His power, though diminished, is vast. And his allies - many of them - are not mere shadows. They are creatures of flesh and bone, and they *can* hurt you." A weary sigh escaped her, as though the weight of the world rested on her shoulders. "I don't know what foolish ideas Dartur has placed in your mind, but I do not like hearing you speak with such recklessness. You do not yet comprehend the full scale of the threat that looms from the north. Until you do, it would be wise to guard your words, lest they invite more danger than you realize."

"I've been silent for far too long," Mara declared, her voice filled with a newfound resolve. "That time is over. I won't sit here quietly any longer, waiting for fate to strike." Without hesitation, she leapt from her bed and hurried to the door. "Is Dartur still here? I must speak with him - he needs to know what I've seen."

"He's already gone," Adraéth replied, her tone gentle but firm. "By now, he must be many hours ahead of us."

Mara turned sharply, stepping closer to Adraéth. "I need to speak with him. It's urgent."

"Do you intend to chase after him?" Adraéth asked, her voice filled with incredulity. "What has Dartur said to you that has stirred this fire in you? I've never seen you like this before."

"It's not what he *said* that changed me," Mara replied, her eyes intense. "It's what he *didn't* say. Please, I need your help. I must follow him. If I leave now, I can catch up to him."

"Catch up?" Adraéth stood, staring at her as though she'd lost her senses. "You don't even know where he's going, or where he might be heading. How could you possibly find him? No, I won't help you in this madness."

"I *do* know where he's going," Mara countered, her voice steady and determined. "Dartur spoke of a final test, a way to confirm that the object is what he believes it to be. And I know where this object is - it's with the Halfmen of Nanglorin. As much as I've doubted the stories whispered in the city, I know this much to be true. I saw the boy in the dark caves as well, just once, and I saw him take the object. From the rumors on the streets, I've learned where these strange people dwell." Her eyes bore into Adraéth's with desperate conviction. "You don't have to come with me. I'll ride swiftly and in disguise - no one will recognize me if I don't want them to. But I need you to tell my father and brothers, should they ask - because they will - that I've gone to Mahlrit to visit my uncle and cousins. That will keep them from worrying. My father has urged me many times to visit the capital and see our family again. That's all I ask of you. I promise, I'll return before they ever suspect the truth."

"Do you really think I'm just going to let you walk away like this? I'm here to take care of you. How can I do that if you're not here?"

"You know better than anyone that I'm not what everyone thinks I am," Mara replied. "I am so much more than that. So don't worry about me. I'm old enough to look after myself. Nothing will happen to me. But the longer you hold me back, the further I'll have to go to catch up with Dartur. Please, let me go!"

Adraéth sighed in resignation. "Fine, if you're determined to go, then go! It's pointless to try and stop you - you're far too stubborn for that. I'll do what you're asking, but don't think for a moment that I'm happy about it. I'd rather want you stay here. But it seems that no matter what I say, it's like speaking to a wall. So go and be careful!"

Grateful, Mara embraced her briefly before dashing off.

3)

At the break of dawn, long before the first light kissed the horizon, Mara slipped out of the stables on a powerful gray steed. Cloaked and hooded, her identity was hidden beneath layers of disguise, making her completely unrecognizable. Without looking back, she sped away from the harbor city, riding swiftly and with purpose. The old main road led her east, toward Mahlrit, the great capital nestled safely between the imposing spurs of the Tin Uael. Above it all, the snow-capped Mâhl loomed like a massive, ancient sentinel watching over the land. From there, she followed the winding trade road south, which hugged the banks of the Uael River for hours, linking Mahlrit with the distant city of Suthawen.

Her journey was far longer and more grueling than she had anticipated. Days passed, and Mara found herself deep within the lands of Anros, yet still, there was no sign of the old wizard. Despite her growing weariness, turning back was no longer an option. Driven by a mix of youthful defiance and reckless determination, she made a bold decision - to ride north and find the boy herself. Surely Dartur had gone there, or so she believed.

Day after day, night after night, she pressed forward, the weight of her mission propelling her ever closer to the unknown. As she approached the gates of Anros, the distant peaks of the Tin Elwech loomed on the northern horizon, their snowy slopes stretching far into the sky, like a haunting promise of the challenges yet to come.

"I've never ventured this far - far enough to see the Sun Mountain with my own eyes," Mara mused as her gaze stretched toward the distant horizon. Yet the peaks remained hidden, veiled by thick mist and brooding clouds. A strange, unsettling chill ran through her as her mind wandered back to the dark caves and tunnels from her nightmares, though she knew they lay in a different mountain range altogether.

Urging her horse onward, she entered a broad, flat plain that seemed desolate at first, lifeless beneath the dull sky. But scattered across the land, barely noticeable, were small wooden huts - silent and solitary, like forgotten sentinels in a vast, lonely expanse.

At midday on the tenth day of her journey, Mara finally arrived at the city of Rist. Once, the northern region between the Tin Uael and the Tin Elwech had been thriving, with Rist at its heart, a bustling center of trade and commerce. Now, however, the vast plains that stretched before her were barren and desolate, shrouded in an air of decay and abandonment. It was no wonder the land had come to be known as the *Abandoned Lands*.

Yet, within the city walls, life persisted. The people there were descendants of those who had long ago migrated from the fallen kingdom Nyarost. A nearly 3-meter-high wall, constructed from rough-hewn gray stones, encircled the tightly clustered houses, perched on a rise near the edge of the mountain. Four massive gates, each fitted with a drawbridge that spanned a wide, circular river running along the base of the walls, faced the cardinal points. Wide roads passed through these gates, splitting into narrow alleys and side streets that wound their way into the town's heart, where a grand fountain dominated the expansive marketplace. The fountain stood just west of the mayor's residence, the largest and most imposing structure in the entire city.

Mara passed through the eastern gate of the city and dismounted gracefully, her boots crunching softly on the cobbled street as she led her horse, Celegrin, beside her. The city, though somber and weathered by time, was still alive with whispers of the past. Her gaze settled on the fountain ahead, its presence commanding the heart of the square.

Encircling the fountain were seven great oval stones, each towering higher than the tallest man. At the base of each stone sat a carved figure of a child, fashioned from stone so pure and white that it gleamed brighter than the finest marble. Each child's eyes were lifted toward the heavens, their faces serene and timeless. The fountain, known as the *Fountain of the Seven Children* or the *Lay of the Seven Stones*, was a tribute to the seven High Aedan, who had once shaped Farham into existence.

Though in the southern reaches of Miénast, and even parts of Anros, the Aedan were regarded with fear and superstition, here in the northern lands - once the proud kingdom of Nyarost - they were honored, almost worshipped as creators.

As Mara drew closer, her fingers lightly brushed the smooth stone, and she spotted a delicate inscription etched with precision, its lines fine and graceful, hinting at ancient wisdom hidden in plain sight.

bharan an Ahar,
umbetta tira neynnar, aurae vel, ehr e lica,
decere craer, cler e varca.

bharan an Ahar,
neynnanwen ar Sirdar. tharneyn sean terlae,
olyenna man e irjae.

bharan an Ahar,
termen neyn en majnar, ar Sirdar, tala aurae,
en armaren lara verae.

bharan an Ahar,
sech ienna mar anadar ach disna etir archat,
nim lewin athare hat

bharan an Ahar,
termen neyn en manyar.

The remaining words were too worn and faded to make out.

Mara gazed at the inscription in awe. The poem was written in Aerin, the ancient and near-forgotten language of the High-Aedan - a tongue that few, if any, could still speak, especially among mortals. Mara had been taught this rare language by Adraéth, yet she knew of no other soul who could understand it. The more she pondered it, the more her curiosity grew. Who could have built this fountain, and who had the skill to carve such intricate lines into the pure white stone? Certainly, no human hand could have etched such precise, elegant letters.

And then, as if stirred by some unseen force, a strange and unbidden feeling came upon her—a sense of fate yet unwoven, a destiny long veiled in shadow, lying dormant beneath the very stones of the ancient well. It was as though the earth itself whispered secrets, forgotten by time, beckoning her to uncover what had been buried in darkness, waiting to be revealed.

As the questions swirled in her mind, Mara shook her head, deciding not to dwell on the mystery. Instead, she turned her attention to the poem itself, carefully translating the ancient words into the common tongue, her lips moving softly as she pieced together the forgotten verse.

The Children of Ahar, all seven,
descended from the heights of heaven.
They crafted grass, forests, and seas,
and banished darkness, cold, and disease.

The Children of Ahar, all seven,
remained on Sedäa, beneath the heavens.
Now from below they gaze afar,
up to the sky, to moon and star.

The Children of Ahar, all seven,
oh, if only they had never been driven
From Sedäa, the world they had made,
but their mothers called them home, dismayed.

The Children of Ahar, all seven,
now only six remain in heaven.
For one was cruel, twisted, and torn,
and left all life shattered, forlorn.

The Children of Ahar, all seven,
oh, if only they had never been driven.

This was an ancient ballad, long forgotten in the southern lands, for Mara had never heard it before. Yet it resonated with her, and she found herself enjoying the verses. She wished she had time to encipher and read the rest, but the hours were slipping away, and she couldn't afford to linger at the fountain. Reluctantly, she moved on, deliberately ignoring the wary glances cast at her from every direction. Occasionally, her eyes would meet those of the townsfolk, their faces marked by confusion and curiosity. It was clear that a woman traveling alone - especially one so young and unaccompanied - was a rare sight in these parts.

As she passed a rowdy inn, from which loud shouts and raucous laughter spilled into the street, carried on the thick haze of pipe smoke and the stale scent of old beer, she noticed a young man nearby. He stood by a feeding trough, a wooden pitchfork in his hands, scooping sweet-smelling hay with practiced ease.

Mara approached him directly. "Good day," she greeted as she stopped in front of him. "A few days ago, did you happen to see an old man? He's dressed in brown robes and has a long brown beard with white streaks."

"If you're referring to the wizard Dartur, then yes. If not, then no," the man replied breathlessly, leaving his pitchfork stuck in the nearby haystack.

"Yes, that's him," Mara said, her relief palpable. Her hunches had indeed led her to the right place. "Is he still here?"

"No. Dartur stayed only a single night. He arrived late in the evening and left early the next morning." The young man pondered for a moment. "I believe it's been three days now." He eyed Mara with curiosity. "Isn't it dangerous to travel alone? You must have come from very far, as you look quite tired, and your face is unfamiliar. What exactly do you want with the old wizard?"

"I need to speak with him," she replied hastily, sidestepping his other questions. "Do you at least know where he went?"

"Went, you say?" The young man flushed with anger. "He rode off, actually. He stole our best and fastest horse - Ninwrith, the mayor's steed - without so much as a word. And then they blamed me for it." He furiously shoveled hay back into the trough, wielding the wooden pitchfork with a frustrated flair. "Now I have to handle all this and clean out the stables like some lowly apprentice. I have no idea where the old fool went, but he took the northern road. He left with one of those guardians of the order who had been waiting for him in town."

"Guardians? What sort of beings are they? And what is this order?"

Calming slightly, the man replied, "They are the last survivors of the Haládan, who came from the distant south. The order seems to be named after their ancestral homeland. I believe it was called Tanuhal. The order has always served as the personal guard of the Haládan king. They are skilled hunters, moving unseen through the forests and hunting all manner of creatures. Arwin, my younger brother, even claimed he saw one of them while searching for mushrooms in the Darkwood. He said this guardian brought down a massive troll - three times my size - with a single arrow." He shook his head. "But who knows if any of that is true? Arwin is not exactly a reliable source on such matters."

"Where can I find him?" Mara asked.

"Find who? My brother?" The young man laughed. "Why? Don't tell me you believe his stories? Trolls don't exist, as my wise old father always says. And Arwin is just a child. Who knows what parts of his tales are true and what's invented?"

"I'm not concerned about trolls or whether they exist. It's the guardians who interest me. If your brother knows where I might find them, I would be very grateful."

"I don't see why I should help a stranger," the man scoffed, wrinkling his nose. "Helping others has only ever brought me trouble."

"What if I were to offer you something in return? I can pay you well."

"No, no, no." He shook his head vehemently. "Your money's no good to me here." His eyes drifted toward her horse, and they widened with unmistakable greed. "But that fine steed... I want him."

Mara instinctively pulled Celegrin back a step. "No! I won't give him up. He's one of the horses of the Lords of Dinambad. Noble blood runs through his veins. He's far too valuable to me. There's no horse faster or more loyal than Celegrin."

"Too bad," the man said, turning back to his work. "Then I can't tell you where my brother is."

Mara hesitated, torn by the decision. It took every ounce of her resolve to even consider parting with her beloved horse, but she had to find Dartur - no matter the cost, and as quickly as possible. "Fine," she said, her voice breaking, as she reluctantly held out the reins, her heart heavy with the decision. "You can have him."

"Wonderful," the man exclaimed, eagerly taking the reins from her hand. "You won't regret it. This magnificent creature will be in good hands with me." He stroked Celegrin's coat with greedy fingers. "Arwin's with the neighbor's children, the gardener's lot, down in the south district behind the old tannery." He pointed southward with an outstretched arm. "Just follow the road. You'll hear him before you see him, I guarantee it."

"Thank you." Mara glanced wistfully at her loyal horse. Then she made her way down the road leading south, which brought her into a dilapidated district where many houses stood empty, some already in ruins.

It wasn't long before she could hear the deafening shouts of several children playing in a large yard behind an abandoned building. Mara stopped by the roadside and watched them thoughtfully.

"Uargh! I'm a troll! Uargh! I'll crush you all!" one of them shouted, lumbering toward the other children in a grey burlap sack as if he were enormous and heavy. The others fled, calling for help.

Then another boy jumped down from a wooden barrel at the side. He wore a dark brown cloak that was far too large and trailed behind him on the ground, and his oversized hood was pulled down over his head so that he could barely see. With a toy bow and a slender stick, presumably meant to represent an arrow, he aimed at the troll.

"Watch out!" he called. "I'm a guardian of the order, and I'll shoot you if you don't surrender."

"Uargh!" roared the other. "A troll never surrenders! Uargh! Never! And I am a troll!"

"Then your fate is settled." The armed boy drew the stick back in the bow - barely more than a simple string tied at both ends - and hurled it at the other.

"Uargh!" groaned the troll, clutching his shoulder where he had been struck, before collapsing to the ground in an exaggerated display of defeat.

The other children erupted in cheers, dancing in a circle around the fallen troll and his vanquisher. But when they suddenly noticed the unfamiliar onlooker, they all froze in place, staring at Mara as if they had turned to stone.

The woman couldn't help but laugh, her amusement bubbling up.

"Why are you laughing?" asked the boy with the bow, pulling back his oversized hood to get a better look at her. "It's not funny. Trolls are very dangerous."

"They are, indeed," Mara replied, a smile playing on her lips. "But not during the day. In sunlight, trolls turn into trees." The children's eyes grew wide with amazement, a mix of fascination and fear flickering across their faces as they stared at Mara.

"How do you know that?" the boy asked, his curiosity piqued. "Have you seen one before?"

"No, not quite," Mara said, her tone playful. "But I've heard stories. And I've also heard that one of you here has seen a troll. I'm guessing that's you, young guardian."

"Yes, that's right." The boy straightened up, standing as tall as he could, clearly trying to appear more impressive than his small stature allowed - though even then, he still couldn't surpass Mara's height, despite her being rather short for her age. "Did my brother send you?" His shoulders slumped, his voice filled with disappointment. "Astuil doesn't believe me. But I'm telling the truth. I *did* see a troll with my own eyes."

"I believe you," Mara said, her voice reassuring. "Would you mind telling me more about it? That's the whole reason I came to find you - and I had to pay a steep price just to get your brother to tell me where you were. But I'd prefer we speak about this in private, if that's alright with you."

The boy briefly glanced back at the other children. "Excuse me, but duty calls," he said with pride, and walked up the street with Mara. "I knew something like this would eventually happen. Still, I never imagined a woman would come asking me about what I saw. But anyway, what would you like to hear? Oh, wait!" He suddenly stopped, looking alarmed. "I don't even know your name. I can't tell a stranger anything."

"My name is Mara, daughter of Ráhad, the prince of Dinambad."

"Dinambad?" The boy's eyes widened in surprise. "That's ages away! You've really traveled a long distance. When I grow up, I want to do that too. I want to explore every city, every mountain, every stream, and every forest, traveling farther than anyone before me. Well then, Mara, daughter of Prince Ráhad, I'm Arwin, son of Solwid. Now that we're no longer strangers, I'll tell you everything you want to know." They continued on their way.

"Did you also see the guardian?" Mara inquired, her curiosity piqued. "I know about the troll you saw, but it's the man who was with him that interests me more. What can you tell me about the guardians of the order?"

"Oh, I saw him. I even talked to him. His name's Arahael, and he's a real hero - he saved my life. But honestly, I don't know much about the guardians, except where their camp is hidden. It's deep in the Dark-wood, clinging to the mountains. They call it Menyána. My father says it means *The Last Refuge* or something like that. There are countless legends about the place, mostly because no one's ever found it, and those who've gone looking for it never came back. That's why my father forbids me from entering the Darkwood - he thinks the forest devours anyone who steps inside. And it's not just him - everyone around here steers clear of the forest, even the Halfmen from Nanglorin. They'd ra-ther cross the great northern sea, the Nyar, by ferry - even though they can't swim - than risk the forest. But, well, the biggest and most deli-cious mushrooms grow there, so I couldn't resist sneaking in. Besides, the forest doesn't swallow everyone. Dartur, the old wizard - if you know him - comes and goes as he pleases, completely fearless. If I had his kind of magic, I wouldn't fear anything either."

Mara smiled faintly. "I believe you. And yes, I know Dartur. Actu-ally, I'm looking for him. I was hoping to find out where he's headed next."

"What a coincidence," Arwin said, his eyes widening in surprise. "Dartur was here just three days ago. I gave him Ninwrith because he was in such a hurry, but the mayor wasn't too happy about it. He pun-ished my brother, Astuil, and now he's furious with me. I only wanted to help, and Dartur promised - swore, in fact - that he'd bring Ninwrith back."

"He will," Mara reassured him gently. "Dartur always keeps his word. But can you tell me where he was headed?"

"Of course." A grin spread across his face. "He was heading to Me-nyána, the guardians' stronghold. I can show you where it is, because on your own, you might never find it."

"No, that's too much to ask," Mara said, stopping near the northern gate. "You've already done more than enough to help me. The rest, I must discover on my own."

"You're only saying that because I'm still a kid, right? You think I'm too young for this, or maybe it's too dangerous, isn't it?"

Mara knelt beside him, her expression softening as she placed a gentle hand on his shoulder. "I'd never say that. I've heard those same words too many times myself." Reaching into her cloak, she drew out a small, elegant dagger. The hilt was carved from shimmering pearls, shaped into the form of a swan with its wings raised toward the blade. She placed it carefully in Arwin's hand. As she gazed into his eyes, she saw herself in the boy - a reflection of her own struggles - and with that came a bittersweet sadness. She now understood him deeply, but in that moment, she also began to grasp her father's constant worry for her.

"This dagger belonged to my great-grandfather, Prince Deluin," she explained. "He used it to slay a terrible Nemar. It's precious to me, not just because of its history, but because it's always made me feel safe. They say that Deluin's spirit dwells within the blade, guarding anyone who carries it. Now, I'm giving it to you, Arwin. I think you may need it soon. The days are growing darker, and not just because of the turning seasons - you can sense it too, I'm sure."

She paused, taking a deep breath before continuing. "That's why I want you to stay here. Stay and protect your family. Whether you're still a boy or not doesn't matter - you're brave, and you have a good heart. You'll be far more valuable here in Rist, guarding those you love, than traveling with me - though I would very much enjoy your company." She smiled softly. "But you must stay."

Arwin's eyes gleamed with wonder as he stared at the knife, almost too stunned to speak. His hands trembled slightly as he held the pristine blade, afraid to even move it, as if doing so would break the spell and reveal it all to be a dream.

Mara crouched to meet his gaze, her expression serious yet kind. "Promise me that you'll stay here and stand your ground."

A smile of pride spread across Arwin's face. "I promise," he said, his voice filled with quiet determination.

"Good." Mara rose to her feet. "Now, tell me - where should I go to find Menyána?"

"Take the road north until you reach a crossroad," Arwin began, his voice steady with newfound confidence. "From there, turn right. That path will lead you into the Darkwood. Once you reach a clearing by the Great Oak - it's the largest oak in the entire forest - you'll need to leave the path and head east, toward the mountains. Hidden on the mountainside, among the trees, is a narrow tunnel. It'll take you straight to the guardians' camp. Just stay close to the base of the mountain - you'll find the entrance."

Mara smiled warmly. "Thank you, Arwin. Farewell. And don't forget - keep your promise!"

"I won't!" the boy called out, his voice bright with joy as he waved her off. As Mara passed through the gate, she turned back one last time, catching a glimpse of the young boy standing tall, clutching the dagger, before she disappeared into the distance.

And yet, as if stirred by some unseen hand of fate, a deep sense of certainty overcame her - an unshakable feeling that her path would soon cross once more with that brave boy. It was as though the threads of their destinies were woven together, bound to meet again in the tapestry of time, and that reunion, she felt, was not far distant.

4

On foot, Mara trudged northward up the rising road, which gradually ascended in height. She marched for three full days, resting only briefly at night, so that by the morning of the fourth day since her departure from Rist, she reached the edge of the Darkwood.

By day, the forest seemed not very menacing - at least from the outside. But as Mara stepped into the woods, a dark cloud seemed to descend upon her, cloaking her mood in a heavy, black shroud. With each step deeper into the forest, her fear grew, and her heart felt increasingly uneasy.

After hours of walking in a large clearing before her stood a colossal, ancient oak, its gnarled branches stretching out like a multitude of long arms in every direction, and its thick roots clawing their way to the surface, almost claiming the entire ground. The leaves rustled in the wind as if welcoming Mara, and through the gentle breeze, she thought she heard someone singing from afar. It was more of a hum than actual words, but carried by a beautiful melody that captivated Mara, making her feel as though she was rooting herself to the spot.

Only when the first stars began to appear under the clear night sky did the singing cease, and Mara realized she didn't know how long she had stood there, entranced. "What a strange forest," she thought, "where the trees seem to sing. It's both frightening and somehow mesmerizing." Regaining her composure, she left the road and wandered through the underbrush eastward toward the mountain, whose bare cliff face loomed threateningly behind the forest.

After several hours of navigating in near-total darkness, she reached a low hill and looked down from its crest. She yawned, stretched out wearily, and decided to rest there for a while.

But before she could lie down, she heard a dissonant rumble, as if something gigantic was rolling toward her. Then came the desperate cries of several men pleading for help. As the sounds drew nearer, Mara sprang up urgently.

The moon now cast a pale blue glow through the trees, illuminating the forest floor so clearly that almost everything around the hill could be seen in the dim light. A group of about twenty men, cloaked in long, dark robes with hoods pulled low, armed with swords and bows, ran along the base of the hill. They were pursued by eight towering creatures, massive and lumbering, trampling the thick roots underfoot with every heavy step, the crack of breaking wood echoing through the night. Every so often, one of the men would turn and fire an arrow at their colossal pursuers.

Mara quickly rummaged through her belongings and pulled out a bow made from sturdy black oak. She grabbed an arrow from the leather quiver beside her, slung it over her shoulder, and notched the arrow to the string. Taking a deep breath, she aimed briefly, then released. The arrow flew with deadly speed, striking one of the giant creatures squarely between the eyes. With a thunderous crash, it toppled forward, its enormous body hitting the ground.

Without hesitation, Mara gathered her belongings and sprinted after the men and the monstrous creatures. As she ran, she shot another arrow, this time hitting a second beast through the ear. It collapsed instantly, like a sack of stones, crumpling to the forest floor.

Ahead of the fleeing group, an impenetrable wall of trees suddenly loomed before them. The branches were so tightly interwoven that they formed a natural barricade, blocking their path and leaving them with no way forward.

"Have courage!" shouted one of the men, turning with a long sword gripped tightly in his hands to face their pursuers. "Do not give up now, friends! We can still prevail if we stand together!" He raised his sword high. "For the Order!" he cried, charging headlong at the enemies. "For Ealdir!"

"For the Order! For Ealdir!" the others echoed, their courage reignited as they followed him into the fray.

A brutal battle erupted, and many of the men met a grim and agonizing fate. Blood stained the ground as swords clashed, and the air was thick with the scent of death.

Mara didn't hesitate for even a moment. She threw herself into the chaos, fighting alongside them as best she could. As she unsheathed her sword and raised it high, it flashed brightly in the moonlight, momentarily blinding their monstrous foes. But even with her unexpected help, they were unable to defeat all of the towering creatures. In the end, only three of them, including Mara, remained alive, while three massive trolls still loomed before them.

At that moment, as the last survivors were cornered and hope seemed to drain from their hearts, a sudden volley of arrows came from behind the trolls, raining down like a fierce storm. The arrows struck their enemies with deadly precision, and one by one, the trolls fell.

When the last of the trolls had been slain, more than thirty archers, also clad in long dark cloaks, emerged from the trees and halted before the few remaining survivors. One of them stepped forward, his gaze fixed suspiciously on Mara. "Who are you, and what business do you have in the Aterhain?" he demanded sharply.

"I don't reveal my name to a stranger who hides his own," Mara replied fearlessly, meeting his gaze.

In unison, the archers around them drew arrows and aimed their bows directly at the young woman.

"Continue to speak in that arrogant tone, child, and you won't live to see the dawn," the man warned coldly. "Give us your name, or you will die."

"First, tell me yours," she responded, completely unshaken. "If it pleases me, then I'll consider sharing mine."

Before the archers could lose their arrows, one of the remaining survivors hurriedly stepped between Mara and the man, pushing the latter away from her. "Calm down, Arahael! She's not our enemy. In fact, she tried to help us."

"What?" Arahael exclaimed in disbelief, gesturing for his men to lower their weapons. "A woman? That's absurd." He eyed Mara with suspicion. "And she's barely more than a child. For all we know, she could be a spy from the Black North. Just look at her - she's clearly not from these lands."

"I am no spy," Mara said quickly, her voice steady. "I swear it to you."

"Whether your words hold any value remains to be seen before I can believe you." Arahael paused, studying her closely. "Whose side are you on?"

"Side?" Mara blinked in confusion. "I'm on no side - at least, not knowingly. I don't even understand what you mean by that. Are we at war? And if so, against whom? The only thing I know is that if I had to choose a side, it would be against the looming shadow from the North. For me, there are only two sides: those who fight the darkness and those who serve it."

Arahael's tense posture softened, and he stepped back. The other man, turning toward Mara, introduced himself. "I am Faran," he said, "and this here is Arahael, my loyal companion. We are the Haládan, the last remaining guardians of the order."

Mara observed the man thoughtfully, noticing a silver ring on his index finger. The ring bore the image of a sailing ship, with a red ruby nestled in a wreath adorned with intricate floral designs. "Faran? The Traveler," she translated, recognizing the word from the ancient language of the Aedan. "A rather curious name, especially for the wearer of such a valuable ring. It seems to me this isn't your true name, but at least you've given me one. In return, I shall give you mine - whether it's real or not is for me to know, just as that ring's secret remains yours." She took a breath. "I am Mara, from Dinambad."

"Dinambad is very far from here," Faran remarked, studying her with interest. "What brings you to us, and why now, of all times? These lands have never been more dangerous."

"An old friend led me here. And as for the danger of this place, it concerns me little, as you can see," Mara replied, a hint of defiance in her tone. "A far greater threat lies ahead - one that will affect all of us in the end. The man I seek is an old wizard. In my homeland and among the Aedan, he is known as Othorin the Timeless. He has many names, and which of them is the truest, I cannot say. But to me, he is Dartur, for that is how he introduced himself to me."

"We call him the same here," Faran said, glancing around cautiously. "Come with us, Mara. Even if the danger out here doesn't trouble you, it's unwise to linger any longer. And neither should we." He turned to the other men. "We return to Menyána!" Then, facing Mara once more, he added, "Come with us, and we can speak in peace. Since you seek Dartur, there are things I must tell you - and warnings I must offer in his stead."

ó

In a small chamber, lit only by a narrow window through which a sliver of the rising sunlight filtered in, stood a long wooden table surrounded by several chairs. Mara and Faran sat across from each other at the far end of the table. Arahael remained by the door, his piercing gaze fixed on the young woman, never letting her out of his sight for even a second.

"The last time I met with Dartur, which was about three days ago, he told me he was returning from Dinambad," Faran began, his tone steady but probing. "I assume I'm not mistaken in thinking that he was with you before he arrived here. So, having already spoken with him not long ago, I find it curious that you're still searching for him, especially in such dark and dangerous times. What is it you seek from him?"

Mara met his gaze, unflinching. "That, I cannot say - neither to you nor anyone else here. Only Dartur would fully understand my words. What do the guardians of the order know, after all, of the growing shadow in Um-Atra?"

Faran's eyes narrowed, his stare sharp and unwavering. "Far more than you might think," he replied sternly, "though perhaps not enough to offer us much comfort. But we know enough to recognize the enormous threat it poses. Dartur has been a trusted friend and mentor to me and my companions for years. We've faced many trials together and have journeyed far in search of answers about this shadow in the North. That's why I bear the name *The Traveler* - a name that seemed strange to you. Dartur himself gave it to me many years ago, and I've carried it ever since as if it were my true name."

"Then tell me," Mara pressed, her voice steady but insistent, "do you know where *it* is? The thing - whether stone or something else - that Dartur seeks? Because wherever it lies, that's where he'll be. If I know him as well as I think, and if he's shared his knowledge with you, then surely you must know where he's gone."

Faran leaned closer across the table, lowering his voice so that Arahael could no longer hear what he was saying. "No, he's not there yet - at least, not for the moment. But soon he will have to go, whether he wishes to or not, to finally set his long-laid plans into motion before it's too late."

Mara remained silent for a moment, studying the man in front of her, her gaze briefly falling once more on his ring. "What surprises me," she began quietly, "is that you don't seem to question how I even know about this thing. I fear it's the very stone stolen from Um-Atra long ago - Haradan's Curse, as we call it in Miénast, though few dare speak its name. It has faded into legend, a tale most believe to be nothing more than a myth, told to children at bedtime. Those who remember the Battle of a Thousand Deaths and the downfall of King Huandar think the stone was swept away by the currents of the Uael River, carried into the encircling sea of Ymbsetta, lost to Farham forever. Only a few know the truth - people like me. But Dartur didn't tell me this. I've seen it for myself, in a way. Much of what the wizard knows, he learned through me. Though he visited me often throughout my childhood to ease the torment of my nightmares, it seemed, over time, that he was using my knowledge for his own purposes. Isn't it only fair that I now seek to know what he plans to do with it?"

Faran's expression darkened, burdened with a deep sense of unease. "It's understandable," he replied, "but it wasn't wise to leave the safety of your home because of it." He sighed heavily. "In recent years, Dartur began speaking to me about you - about your dreams. In fact, he's spent much of his travels trying to uncover why you, of all people, are able to see these things. He often sought counsel in Faldar, the Forest of silver trees, with the High Aedin Mylias. The wise lady had been expecting him - she knew of you long before you were even born. Unfortunately, I know little more than this: that you are destined to achieve something of great significance in this age."

Mara looked at him in confusion, uncertain what to make of his words. But at least what he said aligned with what Dartur had told her. "This High Aedin knows something about me? Then perhaps it would be wiser to seek her help, and not the wizard's. Could she rid me of all this?" Desperation was written across her face. "It torments me, draining my strength. I long to do something, anything, to face the threat in the north, but how can I accomplish that when I'm left with no energy to fight?"

She paused, her gaze once again falling on Faran's ring. "You don't know the answer, do you? Or perhaps you do, but I don't want to hear it," she said with a weary sigh. "After all, I'm just a simple, weak girl who ran away from home, hoping to do more than just stand by and watch. Who would believe that someone like me could make a difference in these dark times? Only a fool would think so. And even the wisest fool remains a fool in the end." She raised her head, meeting Faran's eyes. "Dartur isn't here, as I can see, and I fear he won't return anytime soon. I had hoped to leave with more knowledge, but it seems I'll be going back with nothing. What a pity."

Clearing her throat, she straightened her posture. "That's not to say, Lord Faran, that I don't appreciate your company. But it seems neither of us will gain anything from this. If only I could remember where I've seen that ring on your finger before - I'm certain I've laid eyes on it once. But where, I cannot recall. Still, I know this precious token didn't end up in the hands of a guardian of the order with such a curious name by chance. Its bearer must be a man of great importance. And that you surely are, even if you won't reveal your true name to me."

"You see much and know even more," the man remarked, clearly impressed. "It's fascinating to hear such words from a young woman of Miénast, a stranger who lays eyes on me for the first time today. And yes, unfortunately, it's true - Dartur is gone. When he plans to return, I cannot say. It might be years before we see him again. But since he isn't here to speak with you, I must do so in his stead. He suspected that someone might come seeking him, and if that truly is the case, he left specific words for me to pass on to you: Turn back - return home as swiftly as you can. There are dangers lurking beyond the safety of your city walls, waiting for the chance to seize you. If that ever happens, Dartur's plans will be rendered meaningless. You may not see it now, and you might not wish to believe it, but there is far more to you than meets the eye. You have the ability to see things hidden from the rest of us - perhaps more than you're willing to admit. You may conceal this from others, but I can tell something is deeply troubling you - something you've seen in your recent dreams. If you wish, you can share it with me - as you would with Dartur - because I believe it is important you speak of it with someone. Whom you choose is, of course, entirely up to you."

Mara studied him closely, her brow furrowed. "The more I speak with you, the more I realize you are far more than just a simple guardian. As for turning back, though I know it would be the wiser choice, it seems I'm not wise enough to do so. Could I not, at least, stay in Menyána for a few days, to learn more about your friendship with the old wizard?"

"You know as well as I do that this cannot be, Mara. Do I really need to explain why?" Faran's voice softened. "It's not because you're a woman or too young, no. It's because your time has not yet come. But when it does, you must be ready - for a perilous journey, with an uncertain destination, that only you can find."

"Without a doubt, you are a friend of Dartur," Mara said with a hint of frustration. "You speak in the same riddles he does, as if the two of you were the same person. I wish I knew what this journey you speak of entails, but I suppose I'll find out soon enough. And yes, you were right - it weighs on me heavily, even though I'm not entirely sure what to make of it."

She paused and glanced at Arahael, who still stood near the door, watching her with an unyielding, stone-like gaze. Only when Faran gave him a subtle nod did he reluctantly leave the room without a word. Once he was gone, Mara continued, her voice more subdued. "In my last dream, which was far more intense and painful than any before it, I saw a great battle raging before the gates of Mahlrit. Tens of thousands of Celkûn and wild men, massive monsters, towering siege engines, and catapults filled the field. I saw my cousin Fria, leading far too few men into the fray, trying desperately to hold off the enemy. But they were all slain... including her."

She swallowed hard, fighting the burning pain that arose from merely speaking the words aloud. "Dartur believed that war would come to our land, but he also thought Dinambad might be spared. That, however, is pure nonsense. If Mahlrit was ever under attack, Dinambad would rush to its aid without hesitation. No one would be spared from the devastation of such a battle, should it come to pass."

Mara's eyes shifted slightly as she continued, her voice growing more intense. "But that wasn't all I saw. I had almost forgotten, dismissing it as unimportant compared to the rest - until I saw your ring. I thought I glimpsed Haradan, son of Huandar, standing before me as if he were truly there. But all I saw were disjointed images and fragmented visions, making little sense. The man in my vision was tall, of noble lineage, but his face remained hidden. Still, I knew in my heart it wasn't

Haradan I saw, but his heir - the rightful King of Miénast and Nyarost who is meant to rebuild the fallen kingdom and unite its people."

She paused, watching Faran for any sign of reaction, but his face remained expressionless, as if carved from stone, listening intently to her every word.

"The royal line isn't extinct, as so many feared," she pressed on. "This is what I intended to tell Dartur. He must find him. Miénast needs its king, or we are all lost. His true name and face were hidden from me, but not the name foretold for him - the Uniter King. Ealdur, in the old tongue. If Dartur cannot find him, then I will take up that task in his stead."

Faran smiled kindly. "I sincerely hope that one day you will find him, but here in Menyána, your search will be in vain. I suggest you try in Anros - rumor has it that he is on his way there, making his way towards Miénast. Since you no longer have a horse, I will provide you with one of ours, so that you can travel swiftly and perhaps catch up to him. However, we have a pressing task ourselves, one that Dartur has entrusted to us. The borders of Nanglorin must be secured against the enemy to ensure the safety of the stone and its young bearer. You should set out on your journey now. Whether it leads you to Anros or back home is not for me to know - that choice lies solely with you. In the end, you know best what is right for you."

Faran stood, his movements graceful but firm. "Arahael will escort you southward to the gates of Anros, if that suits you. I want to ensure you reach safety, at least that far. I wish I could send him further with you, but his duties here are too important to spare him any longer. Farewell, Mara of Dinambad." He bowed deeply, a gesture filled with respect. "Or should I call you by your true and full name, Princess Maraniel?"

Faran smiled gently, then cleared his throat as if he had lost the perfect tone for his words and needed to quickly recover it. "May we meet again, under brighter skies."

With that, he turned and left through the door. A moment later, Arahael entered, his stern gaze and slightly hunched posture signaling his impatience. He said nothing, but the look in his eyes made it clear - he was ready to leave, and he expected her to follow.

Ó

"Forgive my rude words from last night," Arahael said, riding along-side Mara on the road south, just outside the dark forest. "But a woman, armed and traveling alone in these times, is highly unusual." He tucked a lock of his shoulder-length, curly dark hair behind his ear and cast her a respectful glance with his chestnut-brown eyes. "Even for me, and I've seen quite a bit."

"You are forgiven," Mara replied, though her mind was elsewhere. She couldn't shake off the image of the ring on Faran's finger. "Tell me, how well do you know this Faran? And why does he bear such an odd name?"

"I know him better than any of the guardians of the order. Faran has always been our leader, and in many ways, he's both wise and cun-ning. His name isn't what you might think - he has many names, Faran is merely one of them. But that's all I can say."

"And what of his ring?"

Arahael's breath caught, his gaze drifting into the distance. "I can't tell you anything of significance about it - my apologies." He sighed heavily. "I can see how much you long for answers, but I cannot give them to you. Not about that. All I can say is that I would follow Lord Faran into the deepest shadows, even to my own end - no matter how grim - without hesitation."

"But what if your leader isn't who he believes himself to be?"

Arahael exhaled sharply, almost mockingly. "You're speaking non-sense, child. Faran is who he is, and nothing more. He can be no greater than the fearless leader he already is in these dark times."

Mara studied the man intently, and though a part of her wished to share her thoughts, trust had not yet fully formed between them, so she chose silence instead.

The remainder of their journey, which took them far beyond Rist and lasted several days, passed with only sparse conversation. Each of them was weighed down by their own worries, lost in private thoughts that swirled relentlessly in their minds.

When they finally passed through the gates of Anros, they halted briefly. Arahael bid her a hurried and uneasy farewell, as though the thought of leaving her alone troubled him deeply. It was clear he had no desire to know what fate might await her, and without another word, he turned his horse and rode swiftly back north.

Once again, Mara found herself completely alone. A sense of unease crept over her as she continued on, pulling her dark blue cloak tightly around her, as if to shield herself from the uncertainty that now lay ahead.

5

A dark shadow settled over the land, and the knee-high shrubs of the once vibrant green fields were swallowed by an unsettling darkness. The days seemed to grow shorter and more foreboding with each passing moment. Though the harvest fields of Westlad - one of the provinces of Anros - were renowned for their colorful splendor and well-kept cultivation, that evening, only a long, eerie veil stretched silently over the land, swallowing everything beneath it.

A lone rider approached along the road, halting atop a hill, straining to peer into the twilight distance. He rode a tall, majestic black horse, its bridle adorned in silver and gray. The rider himself was cloaked in a dark blue mantle, the hood pulled low over his head, concealing his face. Yet, even beneath the broad cloak, his frame was slender for a man of his stature. He gazed westward, scanning the hills and fields that slowly disappeared into the growing darkness, as though impatiently searching for something.

But his search proved futile. The sharp scent of smoke filled the horse's nostrils, causing it to whinny and prance anxiously. Turning his gaze to the north, the rider spotted a massive plume of smoke rising into the sky. And now he could hear the terrible cries of people fighting desperately for their lives in a nearby village, not far from where he stood.

Without hesitation, the rider spurred his horse onward, galloping straight toward the flames. As he neared the burning village, a sense of dread crept over him, for what lay before his eyes was nothing short of a battlefield. Enormous flames devoured the ripened fields and consumed house after house; piles of straw and wood blazed fiercely in the deepening night. Through the acrid smoke, the rider spotted numerous creatures, hunched and grotesque, wielding torches and rusted swords as they rampaged through the streets, setting every last building ablaze. Celkûn. They let out horrific war cries, striking down the brave villagers one after another with cruel savagery.

The rider's grip tightened around the hilt of his sharp sword as he unsheathed it. With his blade raised high, he charged fearlessly into the fray, cutting through the marauding creatures like a relentless tide. The long sword's edge gleamed brilliantly in the firelight, as though it carried its own glow in the darkness, and its swift, powerful strokes nearly drowned out the ghastly screams of the Celkûn.

"Get to safety!" the mysterious rider commanded the few remaining villagers, who looked at him with a mixture of hope and uncertainty. They stood frozen in place, realizing from that voice that this mysterious savior, their rescuer in their hour of need, was not a man but a woman. She called out again, her voice now sharp and commanding: "Get to safety!"

At last, spurred by the authority in her tone, the villagers obeyed. With reverence, they fled from the Celkûn, taking refuge in the few stone houses that had yet to catch fire.

But in a fleeting moment of distraction, a Celek managed to strike her with a swift blow, knocking her from her saddle. She tumbled to the cold, churned earth, her gleaming, razor-sharp sword slipping from her grasp into the darkness.

Her horse, now riderless and panicked by the flames, galloped wildly in every direction, as if the fire had encircled it. Its desperate whinny echoed across the burning plains, then vanished into the night.

The woman had little time to retrieve her sword, but amidst the rubble and the thick, choking smoke, it was lost to her. As a group of four Celkûn charged toward her with triumphant, mocking cries, she was forced to arm herself with a rusty sword and a battered wooden shield that lay nearby.

The smoke thickened, the flames roared higher, the streets grew hotter, and the night itself seemed to grow darker, almost blacker than it should have been. It wasn't just the sky that had dimmed; the spirits of the remaining villagers had darkened as well, their faint hopes dwindling into nothingness. A heavy, impenetrable shroud of fear and sorrow hung over the burning village, and it soon ensnared the woman too. Without her sword, her confidence faltered, and exhaustion crept in. She had traveled far, with too few moments of rest, never imagining that her journey to Anros would lead her into the midst of a battle.

She was acutely aware of the slim chances of victory, yet she couldn't abandon the suffering, defenseless villagers to their fate. Cowardice had never been in her nature, and this wasn't the first seemingly hopeless fight she had faced in her young life.

Through the dense smoke and rising flames, her vision grew dim, though just enough remained to spot her countless foes approaching. Yet the stifling heat and choking smoke swiftly worsened her perception, while her growing exhaustion only deepened her disorientation. She knew then, with painful certainty, that any hope of victory had slipped away. When a large group of Celkûn charged at her like an impenetrable wall, she lost her footing and nearly fell beneath their trampling feet. At the last moment, she managed to slip into the shelter of the smoke, finding refuge in the shadowed corner behind a house. Gasping for breath, she quickly surveyed the battlefield.

But the more she took in, the more the scene filled her with dread. Chaos ruled - wild, mindless destruction spreading unchecked. Tears welled in her eyes as the crushing weight of failure settled over her. There was nothing left to do but await the inevitable - her own death.

Suddenly, in the distance, a horn sounded. Faint but clear, its signal pierced the night. For a brief moment, silence fell over the battlefield, an unsettling pause broken only by the restless shuffling of the Celkûn, who looked about in confusion. Then, the horn echoed again, this time much louder and closer. It was approaching, fast.

She felt it now - a low rumble beneath her feet, like distant thunder, growing louder with each passing second, though no storm gathered in the sky. It took her a moment to realize what the sound truly was, but at last, she could make it out - the pounding hooves of at least a hundred horses galloping toward the battle.

Once more, the horn blared, a deafening blast that reverberated across the plains, shaking the very heart of the battlefield. The Celkûn froze in terror, turning their gaze westward, straining to see what force was barreling toward them from the darkness.

With a surge of renewed hope, the woman gripped a rusted sword and charged back into the fray.

Like a tidal wave crashing upon the shore, a glorious cavalry stormed onto the battlefield - riders clad in gleaming armor, their spears raised high, bows drawn, and helmets crowned with white plumes. They struck the Celkûn down one by one, their advance swift and powerful.

But the battle was far from won. The Celkûn, recovering from their shock, regrouped with ferocious speed. With a savage roar, they launched a counterattack, hurling themselves at the mounted warriors. Some riders were thrown from their mighty steeds, dragged down into the chaos below as the clash of steel and cries of battle filled the night.

On the broad road, a fierce battle raged between the Celkûn and the foreign cavalry, with the young woman fighting bravely amidst the fray. She stood her ground beside the still-strong riders, but for every Celkûn that fell, a man from their ranks also dropped, and the once-great army quickly dwindled, as did the forces of their enemies.

Before her, a man with dark brown hair and a gleaming, brown-tinted armor fought fiercely against four Celkûn. He was surrounded, but with his strong arm and swift movements, he cut down all four in rapid succession. However, two more enemies rushed at him from behind, intent on bringing him down.

"My lord!" one of the men shouted. "Behind you!"

But he could not react in time. Seeing the danger, the young woman quickly grabbed a fallen bow from the ground, seized two arrows, and nocked them in a single motion. She aimed swiftly and, with a single shot, struck both Celkûn - one through his left eye, the other in the throat. By the time the man turned to face his would-be attackers, he could only watch as they collapsed, near death. He glanced around and saw his savior. He nodded to her in gratitude before resuming his relentless battle against the enemy, his mind haunted by the feeling that he had seen this woman somewhere before. Even as he struck down foe after foe with powerful, rapid blows, the thought lingered.

Slowly, rain began to fall. The droplets pelted the blazing fires, gradually extinguishing them. The acrid smoke was driven away by the fresh air the heavy rain brought with it, and the fighters inhaled deeply, feeling renewed. With fresh hope, the soldiers mustered their remaining strength and launched a final, desperate charge against their enemies.

Side by side, the young woman now fought alongside the man whose life she had saved earlier, and the closer she was to him, the safer she felt. He radiated hope and confidence, and it was clear he was determined to protect her. It did not escape her notice that he made every effort to remain by her side, as if he sensed that her strength was waning. She was deeply grateful for his presence, as he gave her the courage she desperately needed after the exhausting hours of battle. But despite his support, she felt her legs growing heavier, her head throbbing as though struck by a hammer, and her reflexes slowing.

One of the Celkûn seized the opportunity and lunged at her from the side, catching her off guard. But the man quickly intervened, pulling her away with a strong tug just in time, causing the enemy's blow to land in empty air. He pressed her against a wall behind them, shielding her from further attacks. In that moment, he was so close to her that, for a fleeting second, he seemed to forget everything happening around them.

The woman felt his warm, almost intoxicating breath on her skin and looked up at him gratefully. But as her gaze met his - eyes clouded and weary from battle - her breath caught, and the chaotic roar of the ongoing fight seemed to fade into distant silence.

Their brief moment was abruptly shattered by the approach of the remaining enemies, and with a swift motion, they both plunged back into the fray with a newfound strength. As the rain ceased and the sun began to rise, their long-awaited victory was finally within reach.

The man gently stroked the dark brown coat of his exhausted horse, carefully checking it for injuries. But once again, his attention was drawn to the strange woman who wandered through the streets, where tendrils of smoke still rose into the gray morning sky. She moved as though searching, her gaze fixed on the ground. In the daylight, he could now see her long jet-black hair, hastily braided into a single plait, and her smooth, flawless skin, which shimmered faintly in the sunlight as if draped in silk. Even though the man had not met every woman in Anros - there were many - he was certain that this one did not belong to them.

"You're not from around here, are you?" He followed her through the streets.

"I can hardly deny it, now that the light of day reveals my true appearance." She glanced at him briefly before returning her focus to the ground, continuing to walk through the ruined village.

"What are you looking for?"

"My sword," she replied without looking at him. "It's very valuable. Losing it was an unforgivable mistake on my part."

Before the man could ask further about this weapon, one of the riders approached him, holding a silvery sword that gleamed in the sunlight.

"Look, my lord!" said the rider, offering him the blade. "I found this among the bodies of the fallen."

The man took the elegant sword, marveling at its craftsmanship. The hilt was made of smooth, pearlescent material, and at its head was a magnificent silver swan, wings proudly outstretched on either side. The blade itself was long, slender, etched with fine lines, and unusually sharp - sharper than any weapon forged in Anros. It felt light and balanced in his hand, yet also incredibly strong.

The woman stepped closer, her eyes fixing on the sword as the man admired it.

"That's it," she said, stretching out her hand toward him.

"This precious blade is yours?" The man pulled it back, keeping it out of her reach, and eyed her with suspicion. "How did you come by such a rare and noble weapon? It must be from the fiefs of Miénast, likely from one of the western harbor cities, for I recognize the sign of the swan from there. If you came from that far, it would have been quite a long journey."

"A journey far too long in these dangerous times," she said, her gaze growing somber. "I barely survived the night, thanks only to you and your riders. I owe you my gratitude, my lord. And no, I didn't steal the sword, if that's what you're thinking. It was a gift, crafted specifically for me. That's why it's lighter and narrower than your own blade. Please, return it to me! I am in haste and should already be much farther to the southwest by this hour."

"What troubles your mind?" He noticed the worry in her eyes and, without further resistance, placed the sword back in her hands.

"If only I knew," she said, as she sheathed the precious blade at her side. "Lately, so much forces me into deep thought - so many fears, so much grief. And no matter what I try, I cannot seem to do anything against the looming shadow in the black north."

"Whatever weighs on you, noble lady, know that last night, you saved many lives among our people. They are deeply grateful to you."

"I did only what anyone would have done. Handling a sword and bow are two of the few things I am skilled at, though they are not talents often expected from a woman of my standing. But I never hesitate to use them when the need arises. I simply did my duty, nothing more."

"What you did far surpassed mere duty. If even half of my riders had your courage, I would worry far less about the safety of Anros. Don't diminish your actions! Anyone else in your situation would have fled the battlefield without a second thought."

"Fleeing has never been my way," she said, taking a few steps to the side to lean against a half-burnt fence. Only now did she realize how weak and drained she truly was. Pain wracked her body, but she kept it to herself. "And yet, I have fled."

The man immediately noticed how unsteady she was on her feet and how her face had grown increasingly pale. He stepped closer, concern etched into his expression. "From where you have fled?"

"From my own home," she murmured, her voice barely audible from the suffering she endured. "I am not what I may appear to be to you. My ragged, dirty clothes hide who I truly am."

"Who are you? Tell me your name. Your face seems familiar to me."

"Knowing my name in these ever-darkening times is dangerous. Besides, I cannot reveal it to a man whose name I also do not know."

"Forgive me," he said, taken aback. "I am called Aric, son of Arid and Fasa."

"You are King Henric's nephew?" The woman smiled at him kindly, a trace of relief crossing her face. "Well, under these circumstances, I suppose I can tell you my name. But I must ask that you do not share it with anyone else. I do not want my father to know where I truly am."

"Please, tell me your name! I swear to keep it secret, as one would guard a great mystery, never to be revealed unless you wish it so."

"Very well. My name is Maràniel, but you may call me Mara. And my father is Prince Ráhad of Dinambad, a close friend of your uncle."

When Aric finally heard her name and realized her true identity, he was struck with shock. Never had he expected to meet her, of all people, in his homeland. He recalled how his uncle had often spoken of her incomparable beauty, urging him time and again to visit Dinambad with him. Now, seeing the lovely princess before him with his own eyes, even in her worn, dirty clothes stained with mud and blood, he thought his uncle had greatly understated her charms. Never in his life had Aric seen a more beautiful, flawless creature than Princess Marániel, who now stood before him. Stunned and overwhelmed by her grace, he dropped to his knees in the dirt, for an honorable princess stood before a mere soldier.

"Please, stand up!" she pleaded hastily, praying that no one else had noticed.

"Forgive me," Aric said humbly as he rose. "It's not often we receive such noble company here, though I must admit, one wouldn't easily recognize your rank at first glance."

"That's intentional," she replied. "Besides, here in the kingdom of Anros, the homeland of King Henric, I am no one. I dressed this way precisely so that I wouldn't be recognized."

"It wasn't a *no one* who saved so many men, women, and children from a cruel death today. You deserve great gratitude, princess or not."

Mara gave him a soft smile, understanding his kindness. But shortly after, her expression tightened as a sharp pain shot through her abdomen. She pressed her hand against it and realized she was badly injured, bleeding profusely.

"Are you alright?" Aric asked, his concern deepening as he noticed her obvious distress.

She tried to straighten up to respond, but all that escaped her lips was a pained groan before she collapsed in one swift motion.

Aric acted quickly, catching her gently in his arms. In her semi-conscious state, he pushed her cloak aside slightly and saw a deep, bleeding wound in her side. With urgency, he lifted the young woman and carried her across the street to his horse. Mounting swiftly, he cradled her in his arms as he rode, followed by the remaining riders, heading swiftly toward his home city of Suthawen, which wasn't far from the village.

As he held the princess close, fear for her well-being gripped him. Yet, at the same time, he felt something entirely new - an unfamiliar warmth spreading through his body, from head to toe, filling him with a profound sense of light and comfort.

Mara awoke with a start, her chest heaving with labored breaths, as though she had been pulled from the depths of a dark and endless dream. She sat upright, disoriented, the weight of some forgotten vision lingering in her mind. The stillness around her gave no hint of how much time had slipped away into the unknown. As her vision sharpened, she realized she was in a room where walls, ceiling, and floor were all made entirely out of wood. Even the bed, the narrow, elongated table, and the nearby chair were crafted from the same material. A door on the right stood wide open, revealing a long, high corridor beyond. Another door, directly in front of the bed, provided light from a candle on the table and led out to a broad balcony.

She tried to stand, pressing her hand against the wound on her abdomen while pulling herself up using the edge of the bed. Despite the pain, she managed to rise and felt the warm wooden floor beneath her bare feet, which was surprisingly soothing. She stood up slowly and stretched as best as she could. Looking down, she noticed she was wearing a loose white dress resembling one of her nightgowns. Although made from a less luxurious fabric, it had its own unique and flawless beauty. She then lifted her head, gazed out at the balcony, and made her way toward it.

Outside, she looked down from a high vantage point at a small town surrounded by a sturdy wooden palisade. Beyond the town lay a thinning forest, and in the near distance, she saw a large farm where several men and women were harvesting their fields. Beyond that, the land faded into a misty haze, with only a blurred, rugged landscape visible in the distance. To the left and right, the towering spires of Tin Uael rose into the sky. The town nestled in a small depression between the majestic mountains that shielded it from behind and both sides. A solitary path, appearing as a faint line in the plain, led up to the town, merging into a cobblestone street that climbed to the steps leading to the giant mead hall, from which Mara looked down.

The city below bustled with activity, and despite the growing peril in the north, the people appeared peaceful and serene, as though nothing could disturb their thoughts. As the princess, accustomed to the harsh sights of Dinambad, looked down at the tranquil city from the balcony, her heart warmed. She felt a deep longing to stay here forever, for peace and calm still reigned despite the horrors of the present days.

Yet, a pang of nostalgia hit her; she couldn't help but think of her father and brothers, who were undoubtedly worried about her since she had hastily left her safe hometown one early morning.

Aric entered the room with a cup of water in his hand, surprised to find the bed empty. Stepping out onto the balcony, he joined the young woman in her radiant white gown and jet-black hair. He observed her in silence as she looked out over the town, and he thought he could detect a strange, joyful sparkle in her eyes.

"Here." He carefully handed her the cup. "You should drink something."

Mara clasped it with both hands, nodded in thanks, and took a sip. Then she gazed back down at the town. "I've always preferred the warmth of natural wood to the cold hardness of stone, but I never realized you could build nearly an entire town from it." Her eyes sparkled with admiration.

"My home, Suthawen, was built long ago, when the world was still young. King Andor, who left Miénast after a dispute with his brother, founded the city; it used to be the capital of Anros, far grander than it is now, long before Westhawen and the King's Hall were built. It was once a magnificent place, but now my hometown is old."

"It may be old, but it remains timelessly beautiful." She looked directly at Aric. "In my homeland, everything is made of stone, metal, and iron - cold and unfeeling, just like the hearts of many of my people. All those harsh stones in Dinambad make me feel trapped, like I can't breathe. But here, I feel free, and I can sense nature's beauty in all its vibrant forms."

Aric listened, captivated by her words and the sweetness of her voice. Gradually, without realizing it, his affection for her grew boundless. Her beauty and enchanting words held him in a powerful spell. He nearly lost himself, overcome with a sudden desire to pull her close and kiss her; but shame quickly followed, for how foolish it was to think a woman as noble and lovely as she could ever love someone as unworthy as him.

"I would give anything to stay here in your homeland - right here." She gave him a heartwarming smile. "I've never seen a more beautiful place, and I fear that if I leave now, my heart will break from longing for it."

"I'm certain your homeland is just as beautiful as this, if not a thousand times more so. Surely, it's filled with splendor and wealth, as befits someone like you. Unlike here, where we have little." Aric fought against the deep ache of falling hopelessly and painfully in love with the woman beside him, knowing he could never be worthy of her.

"That's not what I want. No splendor, no wealth." She saw the anguish in his eyes. "Princess or not, I don't want a king or some high nobleman who desires me only because I am a princess of great standing. I don't want a man who doesn't truly love me, nor would I value his kingdom if it were mine. It would mean nothing to me. But someone who owns little can give much, and that is the kind of man I long for. His heart and his boundless love are all I desire - not his possessions."

Aric's heart swelled with new hope at her words, and an inner warmth filled him as it seemed she was speaking of him. Pure happiness surged within him, yet the persistent doubt lingered - was he truly worthy of her, no matter how deeply he loved her? He struggled to keep his feelings hidden, for her sweet smile was weakening his resolve. Still, he held firm and said nothing.

In their quiet, comfortable yet uncertain moment together, they were so engrossed in each other that they didn't notice a group of riders from Anros, weary and battered from battle, making their way up the long path to the city. They dismounted near the castle and climbed the steps on foot, entering the fortress until they reached the room where Aric and Mara stood on the balcony. For a moment, the riders simply watched them in silence, unsure whether to speak.

"Lord Aric," one of them finally stepped forward, breaking the stillness. It was only when the young captain turned to face him, and Mara did the same, that he continued, "Forgive the interruption, but we bring troubling news from the camps deep in the Eastlands. The Celkûn have set them ablaze and are now moving north. If we ride swiftly, we can intercept them before midday."

Aric paused, clearly contemplating his next move. He hesitated, torn between duty and something else. Glancing at Mara, it was as though he sought guidance from her without speaking.

"Why do you look at me so?" she asked, puzzled. "I am not the leader of your soldiers - you are, Aric. You already know what you must do; it's in your blood. But I sense you fear hurting me by leaving me behind. I assure you, it would pain me more if you neglected your duty because of what you think I might feel. Please, do what you would normally do!"

"And what if you're not here when I return?" Aric asked, uncertain. "What if all of this is just a brief, beautiful dream? I don't want to wake and find that you've gone."

"I'll still be here," Mara promised gently, offering him a reassuring smile. "Don't worry. Now go."

Aric bowed deeply, grateful for her understanding, and hurried outside with his men. From the balcony, Mara watched as the young captain shouted commands through the town, calling his riders to gather. A great band of horsemen, already mounted and ready, rushed through the streets and assembled near the castle. Aric mounted his gray warhorse, casting a brief glance up at Mara on the balcony before letting out a powerful shout. With him at the front, the company surged forward, riding out of the city. They headed northeast, soon disappearing behind the towering cliffs of the mountain, vanishing from sight entirely.

Mara stood on the balcony for quite some time, gazing out over the vast landscape until she spotted a lone figure on the horizon. A single rider galloped swiftly up the wide road, and soon she could see him more clearly. His magnificent armor looked expensive, adorned with ornate and gilded patterns on the breastplate. It wasn't until he rode through the city gates that Mara realized who the rider truly was - far from a stranger to her. Instantly, she turned around, making her way slowly but in a hurry through the corridor of the mead hall and down the stairs, until she stepped outside to wait by the doors, watching with curiosity.

The rider dismounted and, as he ascended the steps to the fortress, removed his gleaming silver helmet with its long, snow-white plume. Beneath it, dark brown, shoulder-length curls were revealed, belonging to a woman.

"Are my eyes deceiving me, or is it truly you, Mara?" the rider asked, pausing midway up the steps when she saw the young woman standing before her.

"Your eyes are perfectly fine, Fala," Mara replied.

The rider ascended the rest of the stairs and embraced Mara warmly in greeting. "What are you doing here in Suthawen, and where is my cousin Aric?"

"A camp in the Eastlands was set ablaze by the Celkûn. Aric is pursuing the enemies with his riders. You've just missed him. As for me, I was caught in a battle not far from here a few nights ago and was wounded. If Aric hadn't come to my aid, I'd be dead now."

"It's extremely dangerous here in the wilds of Anros. You know that. Have you been traveling alone, without an escort?"

"Yes, and I've been on the road for several weeks now."

"But what brings you here?"

"I've been searching for a man from the north. I heard he passed through Anros a few days ago and might still be nearby."

"Does this man have a name? He must be someone of great importance if the noble princess of Dinambad is willing to face such dangers just to find him."

"His name is Tharon, son of Erchad. He is a descendant of Ealdir and thus the rightful king of Miénast and Nyarost."

Fala's eyes widened in shock. "Haradan's heir?" she asked, her curiosity piqued. "Tell me, did you find him?"

Mara lowered her head in dismay. "No. It seems as though he doesn't wish to be found."

"The king of both Miénast and Nyarost could restore the hope that people have lost during the long, dark years under the keepers of the crown. In these terrifying days, which are nearly as dark as the nights that follow, he would be a beacon of light on this shadowy horizon - even for the people of Anros."

"I fear Tharon believes he might fail, and that no one would follow him. But that's not true. My uncle Dinhad is a great fool. Placing him at the head of our kingdom has brought nothing but ruin. In his blind stubbornness, he poisons the minds of the people, weakens them, and drains them of whatever hope they have left. He knows full well about the looming threat growing deep in the north, beneath the shadow, and yet he does nothing to stop it. He's convinced that no one can defeat the Dark Lord of Um-Atra, so he doesn't even try. The result of his folly will be the downfall of Miénast, Anros, and eventually all of Farham, which would bring an end to all life on this world. But if Tharon returns, we still have some hope - not much, but just enough to make us want to keep fighting."

"Convincing the rightful heir to take charge of a kingdom on the brink of destruction will not be easy, even for you. Your words alone can inspire such confidence and faith that even the smallest army could stand against the greatest of foes. But Tharon must decide for himself, of his own free will, to claim the crown. Only he can make that choice - no one else, not even you."

"But I can't just stand by and watch as my homeland slowly falls into darkness, while our only remaining hope does nothing to stop it. How can he be indifferent to the fate of all of Farham?"

"I'm sure he's not indifferent," Fala replied. "But perhaps there's something he must do first. I don't know this Tharon, but I am certain he isn't sitting idle, waiting for it all to be over just so he doesn't have to fight. I truly believe he will return soon. And I long for the day when I can stand by his side in battle against the Black Shadow. But that day will likely take some time to come. Your search for him seems pointless, my dear friend. If he were still in the wilderness, I would know it. Nothing escapes our eyes, and no stranger passes through Anros without the king's permission. So, it's a great mystery to me how you managed to travel through my homeland unnoticed, without my knowing. But now that this has changed, I ask you to come with me to Westhawen and greet my father. He would be delighted to see you, and I know he would be disappointed if he learned you passed through the wilderness without paying him a visit. Of all the children of his dear friend from Dinambad, you are his favorite, and he holds you in great esteem. Your presence would bring him hope and joy in these troubled times."

"It would never cross my mind to offend your father in any way. Had I remained unnoticed, he would know nothing of my stay in Anros. But since that is no longer the case, I will have to change my plans, for no friend of Anros would refuse a visit to its king. However, I will go nowhere without Aric. I promised him I would wait for his return, and usually I tend to keep my promises."

"And you should by no means break it," Fala replied, noticing a certain sparkle in the young princess's eyes as she spoke of Aric. She smiled knowingly. "If I know my dear cousin well, he won't take long to return. But I must admit, though I came here for him, I nearly forgot about it because of you. Come, let's walk through the city and talk until he returns. There is so much I wish to know in these dark times, and I hope you can enlighten me."

They strolled side by side through the streets of the ancient capital of Anros, where remnants of its long-lost grandeur still lingered here and there. The townsfolk who passed by bowed deeply to the daughter of their beloved king and to the mysterious woman beside her, whose presence exuded a quiet power. Walking with the heir to the throne, Mara was seen as someone of great importance.

As they wandered, Mara shared with Fala the many different speculations circulating in Miénast about the growing shadow in the north. They spoke of days long past, when they were younger, and the world was a better place.

"Do you remember the days when we played among the gravestones near my home?" Fala asked with a distant smirk, her voice softened by the weight of remembrance.

Marániel nodded, her lips curving into a gentle smile. "I do. I miss those days more than words can say. We had such joy then. Finian - oh, he was always so swift. No one could catch him. He won every time, as if some secret magic guided his steps."

"Perhaps he cheated," Fala murmured, but the smirk on her face faltered. Her heart, once filled with fondness for those memories, now ached with a sharper pain. She came to a sudden stop, and her voice grew faint. "I wish... I wish he had never left us. That he still walked this earth." Her eyes grew distant as she sighed in agony. "I would give anything, anything to see him again."

Marániel, sensing the sorrow that clung to her friend like the cold of a forgotten winter, gently laid a hand upon her shoulder. "I know," she said softly. "I grieve with you. Your loss is a heavy one, and no words can truly heal it."

A mournful silence descended upon them, as though the very heavens paused in their turning to mourn the passing of a brother, a prince. It was a silence so deep that even the winds dared not stir.

After what felt like an eternity, Fala drew in a deep breath, summoning strength from the very depths of her soul. "But we cannot linger in the shadow of those lost days," she said, her voice resolute. "My dear brother has been gone from this world for too long. We honor him by carrying forward, by seeking the light of tomorrow, not by dwelling in the darkness of yesterday."

With those words, the sky seemed to stir once more, and a faint light, almost imperceptible, touched the horizon.

6

The great mead hall in Westhawen, the newly founded capital of Anros, was adorned with splendid and colorful banners and tapestries in deep red, dark blue, gray, and forest green. Massive wooden pillars rose to the high, multi-leveled ceiling, intricately carved with delicate patterns and sweeping designs.

King Henric, dressed in his regal red-and-blue robe with golden embroidery, stood tall and upright at the base of three steps leading to his grand wooden throne. He was speaking with one of his advisors, who, in stark contrast to his festivity, was cloaked in a dark, almost black, long and plain mantle, as if trying to disappear within it.

Fala approached slowly with Aric and Mara, and the king finally turned his gaze towards them. For a moment, it seemed as though he could hardly believe what he saw.

"My eyes must be deceiving me - though they've seen much in their years - yet to see Princess Marániel, daughter of Prince Ráhad, standing here in Westhawen before me, surely this is but an illusion conjured by my aging senses."

"Your eyes deceive you not, and they are far from old. But if they were to lead you astray, then they have fooled everyone here, for I truly stand before you, King Henric," Mara replied with a smile.

The king, overjoyed, embraced the young woman and immediately ordered a grand feast to be prepared in honor of his unexpected guest. After all, King Henric was renowned for his boundless hospitality, and once again, he lived up to his esteemed reputation.

In just a few minutes, a grand table was laid out with an array of dishes - fruits, meats, salty, bitter, and sweet delights, from appetizers to main courses, all the way to mouth-watering desserts. Beverages of every kind - freshly pressed juices, crystal-clear spring water, and spicy brews and fermented delicacies - were served. The royal chefs worked their magic, crafting a hearty and bountiful meal in record time. The aroma of grilled, roasted, and braised meats in all varieties, alongside roasted and boiled potatoes, filled the hall. Fresh salads, warm, fragrant bread straight from the oven, still soft and hot on the inside, added the final touch of perfection. Of course, one of the finest and most exquisite bottles of Mársala wine, reserved only for such special occasions, was brought out. The sight of the lavishly laden table was enough to make anyone's mouth water, and the heavenly scents wafting through the air could lift the darkest of moods, no matter how troubled the heart.

One by one, Henric took his place in the center, with his daughter Fala seated on his left and his niece Aasa to his right. Across from the king sat Aric and Mara, side by side.

However, the king's advisor, dressed in a brown robe, remained standing nearby, leaning against one of the wooden pillars, casting a suspicious gaze in Mara's direction.

"Forgive my question," Mara began cautiously, "but is it not permitted for your advisors to step into the sun now and then? This one looks so pale, as though an incurable illness has taken hold of her. She doesn't seem to be from here. Her expression is as grim as that of some men from the wilds, yet she feels out of place to me."

"Ah," the king chuckled, amused. "You're speaking of Nariya." He took a hearty bite of tender meat. "She is indeed from here, though she may appear strange to some. As an advisor, she serves me well, and I'm glad to have her by my side. Not only for her loyalty, but also because she was my son's dearest and most loyal friend when they were both children."

Mara fell silent, feeling somewhat uneasy. Nariya's piercing gaze and strange demeanor made her feel thoroughly unwelcome. Everything about Nariya's presence disturbed her, but not wanting to forget her manners, Mara swallowed her dark thoughts and took a bite of the meat, deliberately turning her gaze away from the unsettling advisor. Her eyes now swept the table, and she noticed Aasa, nervously tucking her shoulder-length, dark blonde curls behind her delicate ears, staring at her with almost overwhelming curiosity.

"If a question lingers on your tongue, Aasa, I urge you to ask it," Mara said with a slight smile. "For as impressive as your eyes may be, they cannot read my thoughts."

Aasa flushed red, embarrassed at having been caught staring so blatantly, but her boundless, almost childlike curiosity quickly overcame her shame. "The days grow ever darker," she began. "I can sense it in the mood of the people here. They are becoming restless and fearful. It feels as though something is brewing in the northeast, far beyond the mountains. You've traveled quite a distance, and you've just come from the north. I wondered what you might have seen there?"

"Not much more than what you see here in Anros," Mara replied. "But in Menyána, I saw even thicker clouds of darkness. Nothing but impenetrable, looming shadows and veils of mist gathering for weeks - no, for months now. They are forming a storm, one that will likely be fiercer than any we have ever witnessed. This is what the people in Mahlrit speak of - merely a storm in the far north. But it is much more than that. My uncle Dinhad, the warlord of Miénast and keeper of the crown, sits far from the shadow, yet it clouds his heart and mind as though it were right beside him. It is a growing threat, rising slowly beyond the Tin Ferrior. He knows it too, yet he stands paralyzed, doing nothing. The day is coming when it will be too late. The darkness is already at our gates, knocking on the stone walls of the capital. Dinhad will lead Miénast to ruin unless someone stops him."

"I've heard the heir to the throne has been found - one of the Halá-dan," Aasa said thoughtfully. "But he's hiding among the guardians in the forests of the north."

"Then he is a coward," Aric said grimly, taking a hearty swig of the sweet Mársala wine.

"Would you want to rule a kingdom doomed to collapse, where all hope is already lost?" Mara asked sharply, meeting his gaze.

Aric swallowed a large bite of meat before replying in his cautious, skeptical manner. "That's not my choice to make. I'm a simple soldier, not a king - and I have no desire to be one. As a warrior, I know how to wield a sharp spear and swing a keen sword. I know how to ride my faithful warhorse into battle. But I am no leader of men, nor do I aspire to be. I follow orders; I don't give them."

"And how can you call Haradan's heir a coward when you yourself wouldn't want to be king?" Mara pressed.

"Because if I were in his place, I would act differently," Aric responded, his tone steady but firm. "Even though I would rather remain who I am, as I have always been, if it meant saving my people, I would face what I feared most. I would do whatever it took to protect my people. Even if that meant trying to save a kingdom destined to fall - even if it meant my death."

Mara was deeply impressed by Aric's words. Despite his modesty and seemingly simple nature, his qualities and strengths were clear to her. She realized now that Aric would likely make a far better king than many of his ancestors, especially because he had no desire for the throne, unlike so many who came before him.

"What do they say of this threat in your homeland, Mara?" Fala asked. "You mentioned that in Mahlrit, people think it's just a storm. But what's being said in Dinambad?"

"Sadly, not enough," Mara replied. "Though my father and brothers aren't as blind as my uncle, they still underestimate what's coming for us all. They speak optimistically in front of me, trying to soothe my worries. But no words in the world can make this looming darkness sound less threatening. They think they must shield me from what they can't see, but I see far more than all of them combined. In my homeland, I feel trapped in a cage, unable to move, and I just want to be free."

At that moment, Nariya approached with a dark expression, a sinister grin spreading across her face. "Ah, so you've escaped your cage, have you?" she began in an exaggerated, theatrical tone. "Like a small, naive bird that's been locked away all its life, now finally catching its first glimpse of sunlight and fresh air. But are you not aware of how dangerous it was to flee that cage? It wasn't built for nothing, after all, to protect your delicate beauty. In the wild lands of Anros, wolves, bears, and darker creatures lurk, caring nothing for your noble lineage. To them, you are nothing but easy prey, no matter how high your birth. I can only imagine the worry your father must be feeling right now. It was a foolish mistake to flee your safe cage. Can you truly bear the thought of the pain your father must be enduring for your sake? Was it worth it? Such selfishness, thinking only of yourself."

"Silence!" Aric roared, rising to his feet in fury.

But unlike him, Mara remained calm and gently pulled him back down onto the bench beside her. "Perhaps it was selfish," she said evenly to Nariya, "but I do not owe you an explanation for it. I answer only to my father. And when he learns the true reason behind all of this, he will understand why I had to leave Dinambad."

"Did such an important reason bring you here?" Henric asked.

"The name of that one guardian from the north is Tharon. He is the last living descendant of Ealdir in the direct line and therefore the rightful king of Miénast and the fallen kingdom Nyarost

. One of the main reasons for my journey - though at first unknown to me - was to find him and make him understand the gravity of our situation before it's too late."

"As if the heir to the throne would listen to the words from your inexperienced mouth," Nariya interjected with disdain.

"Nariya!" Henric shouted angrily. "That's enough!" He gestured for his advisor to leave at once.

Nariya, now intimidated, left the room, suddenly appearing much smaller than before.

"Forgive her words," Henric apologized politely. "She often struggles with strangers."

"Please don't apologize, King Henric. Her harsh words don't trouble me."

"But you are my guest, and I am truly delighted to see you. You are the most beloved child of my dearest and most loyal friend. Over the years, I have come to love you almost as a daughter, and I will not tolerate anyone treating you poorly in my own house. You've always been far ahead of your brothers in so many things. Even as a child, your words were wiser than those of many of our counselors. You could always hear better and see further than anyone I know - myself included. You did not deserve to be spoken to by Nariya in such a way."

"No words of hers could offend me, no matter how painful. I am far too pleased to be a guest in your splendid capital, and it saddens me that I cannot visit your kingdom more often. There is nowhere else where the fields grow greener and the flowers bloom more vibrantly than in Anros. My eyes have seen nothing more beautiful than your grand homes and halls, adorned with intricate carvings and decorations. Nowhere else do people live in such harmony with nature as they do here in Anros. No human-built city can rival the beauty of Suthawen and Westhawen, and I have seen many cities."

"It brings me great joy to hear that you love our homeland, especially as such words rarely - if ever - come from someone of Miénast. In your homeland, people see us as nothing more than wild and primitive people who dwell in dark caves. They call us grim and uneducated re-cluses." Henric found it difficult to hide his wounded pride.

"Don't believe them!" Mara offered him a warm smile. "Many of Miénast's people are spoiled and blinded by the splendor and wealth of their grand cities. They boast of the flawless cold stone from which they've built their metropolises, yet overlook the true beauty in the plants and animals around them. If it were up to me, I would never leave Anros again. Your homeland is every bit as noble and magnificent as the deluded people of Miénast claim their capital, Mahlrit, to be. They simply cannot see it because they have closed their eyes to the true gran-deur of nature and would rather live in cities built of cold, hard stone. Do not hold it against them; they simply do not know better."

"You truly should stay here. In Anros, you will always be welcome, as if you were one of us. You may stay as long as you like."

"I thank you for your generous hospitality. But sadly, this is not my decision to make - not yet, at least." She sighed. "It is only a matter of time before my brothers, who have likely been searching for me for days, eventually find me. Whether I want to or not, I must return with them. The small window of time I was granted is nearly up. It's a shame because I could not find Tharon. Yet, my journey wasn't entirely in vain or without purpose." She glanced briefly at Aric. "Something was given to me, without taking anything from anyone else."

Fala and Aasa were the only ones who noticed how Mara had looked at Aric. And now, even though his expression was still as stern as always, they both seemed to recognize that something had changed in him.

"And moreover, by chance rather than intention, I received a mes-sage from Dartur, the old wizard, in one of the villages near the gates of Anros," Mara continued, trying to ignore the piercingly curious gazes of the two women. "Whether he left the message for me deliberately or not, I do not know, for I don't understand all the things the old wizard plans and does. But he must have known about my journey and anticipated that I would take this path. In his message, he revealed important de-tails about Tharon, and also about one of the Halfmen who live far to the northwest at the foot of Tin Nangroth, in small hills and caves near the Nyar. They call their home Nanglorin, and by appearance, they are no taller than children; even dwarves would seem giants next to them. Dartur mentioned in his letter that one of them has found something that should have remained lost. He suspects it to be Haradan's Curse."

Henric and his entire family flinched, filled with fear and uncertainty.

"It was lost many years ago," Mara pressed on, undeterred. "Cast out into the surrounding sea, or so all the myths I know claim. Yet one of these Halfmen from Nanglorin, a young boy no less, retrieved it from somewhere unknown to me. Dartur will soon set out to find him."

"What happens then?" Aasa asked, tense with curiosity.

"I'm not sure. Dartur fears its power, just as I do, but he knows something must be done, and it must happen quickly. The growing threat from the iron north must not reclaim it."

"The stone of Urehel has been found," Henric said in shock, turning pale instantly. "Then our doom is sealed."

"No. Nothing is sealed or lost yet. But the Alyarel must be destroyed."

"No hammer is heavy enough to shatter it," Aric remarked suspiciously. "How does the old wizard plan to destroy something that is utterly indestructible?"

"He should use it," Fala said thoughtfully, her gaze distant, as if she could see something in the void that remained hidden to all others. "He should wield its great power against our enemy, defeating him with his own weapons."

"He would fail, as any of us would," Mara's voice was now bitter and full of despair. "The power of the Alyarel is so immense that only its true and rightful master can wield it. The black stone, like the others, has a will of its own, and it longs to return to its master. If Dartur were to use it, as you suggest, Fala, the stone would lead him straight into the hands of the Lord of Um-Atra without him even realizing it."

"But how will he destroy it, then?" Aasa asked, looking at her in hopelessness.

Mara shrugged helplessly. She had no answer for that, though she wished she did.

◌

The evening had already fallen, and the darkness of night enveloped the capital of Anros in an impenetrable black shroud. From some houses, candlelight could still be seen, and here and there, a torch burned. In some places, a few townsfolk stood outside their homes, conversing with their neighbors.

Mara emerged from the King's hall and stopped at the natural stone steps. Motionless, she gazed up at the sky, catching sight of a few twinkling stars for a brief moment before thick, dark clouds swelled up and obscured them. Then she sat down at the top of the long stone staircase, which led from the city, winding up the hill to the elevated hall of the King.

She observed the beauty of the landscape, which, even in this dark hour, had not entirely faded. She could also hear snatches of conversation from the villagers outside their homes, as if they were speaking right beside her; Mara caught fragments of their words - though much of it was idle chatter. Nevertheless, in her silence and isolation, she tried to sift through their words, searching for a glimmer of truth. But her brief moment of solitude was soon interrupted.

"You may approach, Aasa," she called out, her eyes still fixed on the scattered lights of the city.

"How did you hear me?" Aric's sister asked, bewildered, as she stepped closer.

The princess glanced back at her briefly. "I have very keen hearing, better than most. Your uncle mentioned it earlier. Though you were quieter than most who try to sneak up on me, I could clearly hear you trying to steady your nervous breathing."

Aasa sat down beside her on the top step, following Mara's calm gaze over the city. "I often sit here, just like this, in the recent days and nights, thinking about all that weighs on my mind."

"This is a beautiful and peaceful place to gather your thoughts. Back home, I sometimes go to Tan Altusôl and climb the steps all the way to the top. There used to be guards stationed there who would ring a bell and light a great fire in bad weather to warn incoming ships of the dangerous cliffs. But now, few ships pass by, and the old watchtower is slowly crumbling. No one but me goes up there anymore, as it's due to be torn down. But I love being up there, for in that solitude, I can think clearly. Most of the time, I simply enjoy the silence, which at least gives me a fleeting sense of freedom."

"I understand that well. I, too, feel trapped here, like a bird in a cage, forced to stay behind while my loved ones fight for peace and freedom in our land. But I am no longer a little girl - I know how to wield a sword. And I am no less strong or courageous than any of the riders from the wilds."

"I don't doubt that for a moment." Mara smiled briefly. "But your uncle would never let you go into battle. The loss would be too great for him to bear, no matter how brave you are, Aasa. Don't be reckless - heed the wishes of your king. Do not follow my example; it is not wise. Believe me when I tell you that the time will come when you will have the chance to show your great strengths. Until then, stay by Henric's side, even if you long for freedom - after all, that was one of the reasons I fled. Perhaps Nariya was not entirely wrong." She sighed, feeling guilty. "I was certain from the start that I would never find Tharon, at least not here in Anros. But I was granted a few days of freedom, though they were not as I imagined. Only now do I realize that I was running from myself. But when your brother brought me to Suthawen, I no longer wanted to flee. Now, here I am, filled with newfound hope, knowing that among the children of Andor, the tamers of the wild, there are kindred spirits. It is a relief to speak with someone who does not turn a blind eye to the looming threat but addresses it openly, unafraid to name the dark lord. I would worry less if only a few people from Miénast were as brave as you here. No one in Anros fears Urehel - except for Nariya, who wears her fear plainly on her face. But I fear her anxiety is not about Urehel. You are so far from Um-Atra that you should be safe for some time, yet bands of Celkûn are already roaming your lands and burning your villages. Forgive me for suspecting that Nariya has something to do with this." Mara took a breath. "No matter how far Urehel's reach may extend, it cannot reach here yet. I sense that he is not our only enemy. I feel another danger that many overlook, though I cannot say what it is - not even here among you." She looked directly at Aasa. "I fear greatly for the well-being of your king."

"I will keep a close eye on Nariya," Aasa said, clearly understanding Mara's implications. "As best as I can. But she has always been my uncle's most trusted advisor, and she often speaks with him alone. Who knows what dark thoughts she may be planting in the king's mind?"

"We cannot let that continue!" Mara replied sharply. "Henric must stay strong! Only then will his people remain brave, for their loyalty alone can either lead to victory or bring about their downfall."

"Then help us!" Aasa's eyes filled with tears, glimmering in the light of the dying torches. "Don't leave! Convince my uncle that Nariya's words bring only danger and ruin! He no longer listens to me, but it seems your words still hold value for him."

"Nothing would please me more than to stay here and help you and your kingdom. I've never set foot in a more beautiful land, and I have seen many grand places and cities. I would gladly try to aid you all. But I cannot. Ever since I left Dinambad too many days ago, I know my brothers have been searching for me - I can feel it. I cannot hide from them any longer. I don't want to cause my beloved father, already burdened by life, any more needless worry in these dark days." Mara sighed, her heart heavy. "I cannot help you, Aasa, no matter how much I wish I could. But trust your instincts. They will guide you on the right path."

"So, you are going to leave us alone? That will surely mean the end of our beloved homeland."

"You are not alone. Even if it seems that way now. You have many allies in Miénast and in other regions of Farham. Help will surely come to you, and I hope it will not be too late. But you are not alone."

"Our allies will come too late, if they come at all. Anros has already fought many battles and suffered great losses without their aid. Miénast never came. Why should they come now? You yourself said that the commander of Miénast cannot even see the danger at his door. How can he help us? No, Mara, we are truly alone."

"And yet, we have always triumphed," came Aric's rough voice as he approached, standing a few steps behind the women.

Aasa and Mara turned to look at him, and they saw anger, pain, and a flicker of fear in his grim expression.

"We don't need Miénast's help," he continued gruffly. "We've done just fine without them so far. And we don't need your help either. In the end, you're just a weak woman. You wouldn't survive long in the harsh wilderness. What can a delicate princess do in our rugged, untamed land?"

"Perhaps nothing," Mara replied calmly, turning her gaze back to the small lights of the city below. "I didn't come to offer help where it's not needed. You're right; I am just a simple, weak woman. There's nothing I can do to ease the great suffering that plagues your beautiful land. But I cannot flee either. That's not in my nature."

Aric stepped closer, towering over her with an expression filled with rage, as if possessed by some demon, wiping away all his memories and emotions. "Then tell me, what is in your nature?"

Mara looked up at him, her gaze meeting his furious, glowing eyes, and for the first time, she felt true fear of him.

Aasa, too, glanced at her brother, then stood. She stared into his darkened face, hoping he would calm down. But he remained unmoved, like a statue, so she silently passed by him and left the two of them alone.

"What can Miénast do that we cannot?" he asked once Aasa was gone. "Build houses from cold stone and forged iron? Pave the earth with rough rocks and hide like scared children in their impenetrable fortresses surrounded by three walls, while their loyal allies are attacked from all sides? The people of Miénast are all the same. And you, woman, pretty or not, are no different. You're all cowardly and foolish."

Aasa lingered behind the corner, hiding in the shadows of the wall, listening with horror to Aric's words. She had never heard her brother speak with such bitterness and malice, though he had been moody and irritable of late.

Mara stood up hastily, deeply hurt by his cruel words and angered by his foolishness, and faced him. "Go ahead, lump everyone together and blame the brave among my people for the cowardice of the few! That's what you here in the wildlands do best. Stubborn and thickheaded, I'm not surprised your people are seen as backward cave dwellers with no manners." She exhaled sharply. "I understand your anger, I truly do. But do not direct it at me, for I did not hide. I fought for the people of Anros, neither cowardly nor foolish. And my father and brothers would have done the same had they been here. Don't blame the loyal people for the failings of one man. Dinambad would have come to your aid without hesitation, had the messages from Anros reached our lands. My father would have done anything to help King Henric's people - you know that full well. So, call my uncle Dinhad a coward and a fool, and I won't disagree. But mind your tongue when it comes to my family. And don't speak of things you know nothing about, proud warrior. For we, too, have fought great battles with even greater losses. And, like you, we fought alone. But our army was half the size of yours, though our enemies were no fewer. Bandits have plundered the southern villages and encircle our land. Libentya has been overrun by Celkûn and other dark creatures, and our guards dwindle too quickly. And yet, despite all of this, Dinambad would have come to Anros' aid without question, if only we had known."

Aric's anger faded, replaced by a quiet remorse, though he feared to apologize. He didn't want to show that he, too, was a weak man like any other. Especially not in front of her - he wanted her to see his strength and courage, not his fears and weaknesses.

But he didn't need to say anything. She could read the bitter regret clearly in his eyes.

"Did you truly think you would find Haradan's heir here in Anros?"

"I hoped so," she replied calmly, "but my chances were always slim."

"Then why are you here?"

"There came a point when I grew tired of watching strong armies return, one after another, defeated and reduced to just a handful of men. I spent long enough tending to the soldiers' wounds, seeing the fear in their eyes as they gradually lost hope. I could heal their physical wounds and ease their pain, but I couldn't mend the torment gnawing at their souls. Nothing can heal the shadow that haunts them. And perhaps I am only a simple, weak woman, as you said, but that no longer matters to me. I want to do more! I cannot just sit behind closed gates, waiting for the day when my father and brothers also fall in battle. I don't want to bury them knowing they gave everything while I did nothing. Behind Dinambad's walls, I am no help to anyone. And soon, those walls will not be as secure as they are now. I am young, strong, and courageous. And though I may not be a great warrior like you, I have just as much right to fight for those I love."

"I must take back my earlier words. I don't know many people from Miénast, and most of those I do know are as cowardly as Dinhad. But you, Mara, are nothing like them. You are indeed brave and strong - more so than I am. But your death would be a far greater loss than mine ever could be. I was born a soldier; when my father died, I took his place as the commander of Suthwand, but in the end, I am nothing more than a simple warrior of Anros. My death would soon be forgotten. You, however, are far from an ordinary woman. No, you are much more than that. Please forgive my harsh words, for you are a noble princess of high birth, whose beauty knows no bounds. Your death would plunge an entire city into despair. But above all, it would shatter the heart of a simple, stubborn man, as if his heart were made of thin glass, dropped from the heavens onto a cold, unfeeling stone floor. Each of its countless shards would only be a small fraction of his endless grief. So, you must never go into battle. His... *my* heart could not bear the thought of never seeing you again. You are courageous and strong, but your words carry far more power. You bring hope where there was none, light where darkness reigned, and love and trust where once there was only sorrow and despair."

Aric stepped closer to Mara, gazing lovingly into her eyes.

"You are mistaken," Mara replied, her eyes shining. "Your death would not be forgotten quickly. Many people of Anros look up to you, for you, too, give them hope where there was none. And far away in Dinambad, in the westernmost lands of Miénast, I would grieve for you. Even beyond the end of my days, I would never stop mourning your loss. For you are far greater than you realize, Aric. With your death, my life would also end."

"You light up my weary, burdened heart," Aric said with a soft smile. "I have lost so much in recent years, but you make me forget my pain and allow me to embrace the happiness you bring. Yet fear fills me when I think of what people might say about us. *'Look there,'* they'll call out from their grand houses of stone and iron, *'the fairest lady of Miénast has taken the side of a foolish, wild man. She has followed him into his lowly and wretched homeland, where filthy peasants and savage cave-dwellers reside. Soon, her once-unreachable beauty will fade among the rough, backward people of this forsaken land, and her radiance will be lost forever. What a tragic waste of such perfection.'*"

"Let them talk." Mara smiled kindly at Aric. "Their words - no matter how loudly they shout - will never reach as far as Anros. And even if they did, I wouldn't care. For no prince or king from Miénast, or anywhere else, could be as honorable to me as you are. So don't let them speak ill of you or your loyal people!" She stepped closer to him. "I don't want gold, gems, or grand palaces - only the love of one man. And though he may be a simple warrior - or even less - it matters not, for he is the only one in this world who can make me truly happy with just a few words." She smiled warmly. "I don't care that you're not a king, for true greatness is not measured by wealth or power, but by the size of a man's heart. And yours is boundless. To me, you are worth more than all the kings, princes, and noblemen in Farham combined. I don't want to be a princess with you; I just want to be by your side until the end of our days - and I hope that end is far away."

They said no more, simply gazing into each other's eyes, both fearing this might all be just a fleeting, beautiful dream. Hesitant, but with a steady hand, Aric reached for hers, gently wrapping her delicate fingers in his rough, battle-worn hands.

But even in this bittersweet moment, they could not forget the looming danger rising from the dark north. As long as that threat remained undefeated, they could not fully declare their love for each other. And so, they kept their thoughts and feelings to themselves, clinging to the hope that one day they could be together, free from the shadow of fear. Without needing to speak, they both longed for that day - a day when the promise of a brighter future would give them the strength and hope to endure the dark times ahead.

7

As the sun rose, the dew that lay upon the fields of Anros melted away, and the frost dissolved with the first rays of sunlight, gently warming the cool earth. The new day brought fresh hope to the hearts of the loyal people of Anros, yet it also marked the swift end of a journey that had lasted far longer than intended.

A company of nearly one hundred riders rode steadily along the road, led by three tall men clad in gleaming silver armor, pointed helmets, and dark blue cloaks. At the front, another man, dressed in simpler yet equally well-crafted armor, bore a banner. With both hands, he held it high - a gold-framed banner that fluttered majestically in the wind, displaying a white swan with wings spread wide against a deep ocean-blue background. As the riders approached, the farmers who were already up and on their way to the fields marveled at the sight of the emblem - the proud symbol of none other than the port city of Dinambad, now appearing before them on the roads of Anros.

Without slowing, the procession rode directly toward Westhawen, passing through the city gates one by one. The riders carried themselves with dignity, their horses bearing them up to the steps of the stone staircase that led to the king's hall. Only there did the three leading men dismount - one with golden locks and the other two with black hair, just like Maraniel - commanding the rest of the company to wait. As they hastened up the steps, they ignored the curious and scrutinizing gazes of Westhawen's townsfolk. The demeanor of these men seemed cold and selfish, and it was hard for the people of Anros to believe that the kind and gentle princess Mara could hail from the same homeland as these three heartless men.

In truth, however, they were her older brothers - Enwir, Anwar and Diam - who had been searching for their sister for nearly an entire moon. They had scoured every corner of Miénast and Anros, finding nothing. Now, certain that she was here in Westhawen, they entered the last place they had yet to search in all of Anros.

As they stepped into the great hall of the king, they paid no mind to the elaborate tapestries or the intricate carvings on the wooden pillars.

Their focus was entirely on reaching the front, where they saw king Henric speaking with his daughter Fala and a strange, pale woman standing beside him. Without hesitation, they approached and stopped just short of the group.

"We greet you, Henric, King of the Wildlands!" the three brothers said in unison, bowing courteously before him.

"Welcome, Enwir, Anwar and Diam of Dinambad. Though I am not pleased by the reason, I must admit I expected you. It would have been more joyous had your visit been under different circumstances."

"We regret to disappoint," Enwir replied, "but we have spent nearly thirty days searching in vain for our sister, Maràniel. This is the only place left where she could be."

"She is indeed here," said the pale stranger beside the king, a sly grin on her face. "I will fetch her for you at once." She moved to leave quickly.

"That's not necessary," said Aric, appearing at that moment with Mara beside him, walking toward the group from one of the rear corridors. Together, they stood between the king and the three brothers, who were strangers to Aric.

"Mara!" Anwar called out when he saw his sister, rushing to embrace her. "We were sick with worry. You can't imagine how much our father has fretted over your wellbeing. Why are you here and not home where you'd be safe?"

"I had my reasons," she replied.

"Foolish and selfish reasons," Nariya sneered, a malicious grin on her face.

"Silence!" Enwir barked harshly at the pale woman. "Who are you, some wildling without title or name, lacking even a shred of proper decorum and color in your face, to judge the actions of our sister? Speak out of turn again, and I'll tear your vile tongue in two!"

Anwar placed a calming hand on his older brother's shoulder, offering him a gentle look of restraint.

"What reasons could possibly excuse what you've done, sister?" Diam asked, his tone harsh with judgment. "Was it worth the pain you've caused our father and us?"

Mara looked down at the floor, guilt weighing heavily on her. She felt the weight of her actions and the needless suffering she had caused her family. Her shame grew so great that she couldn't think of anything else but her foolishness. There was so much she wanted to say to her brothers, but her voice failed her, and she remained silent, burdened with guilt.

"She brought us vital news," Aric spoke up, unable to bear seeing her in such distress any longer.

"Hopeful news, which we needed desperately in these dark times," added Fala.

"Your sister, with courage and selflessness, sought Haradan's heir alone," Aric continued, standing tall before the three brothers. "She fought fearlessly in more than one battle, saving the lives of many people of the Wildlands. You should be ashamed to wound her with your ignorant and callous words and belittle her brave deeds with accusations of guilt."

"I won't be lectured by a mere wildling," Enwir spat bitterly. "You may be the king's nephew, but your words carry no more weight than those of a simple stable boy."

"Enough, Enwir!" Mara stepped between her brother and Aric. "You are angry with me, and rightfully so, but don't take it out on him or anyone else here. If it weren't for Aric, I wouldn't be standing here after all. I owe him my life and more. I forbid you to speak ill of him or his family, for to insult him would also be an insult to the king of Anros. I advise you, dear brother, to watch your tongue. King Henric has always been a loyal friend and ally to us, a generous and kind leader unlike any other. Control your anger before you say something foolish that you can't take back."

"You've been here in the wilderness too long," Enwir replied, his tone quieter but still condescending. "Don't forget who you are. Come home with us now! This is no place for a girl of your standing. Your home is in Dinambad, and that's where you should stay. To leave you here in the wild, untamed lands of Anros would be an irreparable waste. You belong in a grand palace, not in a stable - and certainly not by the side of that lowly soldier."

"I would rather live in a stable than in the palaces you would choose for me," Mara replied firmly. "And while you may not see the worth of the man standing here beside me, I do. Neither he nor I will be hurt by your cruel words." She took a deep breath. "Though I knew you would come for me, and I had intended to return with you, I've changed my mind. Your cold and heartless words toward the people who saved my life have made that decision clear for me. The three of you can return to our father and tell him that you failed to bring me back, thanks to your own behavior."

"We will not leave without you," Anwar said, his tone firm but respectful. "I have no intention of speaking ill of Anros, but I don't want my dear sister living in such a harsh and dangerous land. It's called the Wildlands for a reason. You'd be safer behind the walls of Dinambad. I wouldn't sleep soundly knowing you were here, surrounded by fierce and merciless creatures. This is not the place for you. Please, come home with us, and we'll forget everything that's happened."

"But I don't want to leave," Mara replied, her voice steady. "Anros may seem rough and dangerous at first, but it's also a place where nature thrives more beautifully than anywhere else. The people here are kinder and warmer than anyone I've ever met. I'm staying."

Aric, speaking carefully so as not to hurt her, said, "It's true that Anros is dangerous, and things will likely get worse. This is no place for a princess of your rank. You would be far safer in Dinambad. Though it pains me to see you go, you'll soon realize it's the only right decision."

"You want me to leave?" Mara looked at him, hurt and shocked. "Do you not care that it would break my heart? Were all your words just lies to deceive me?"

Aric gently took her hand, ignoring the watchful eyes of those around them. He gazed deeply into her eyes. "Everything I said to you was true and came from my heart. But you mustn't forget who you are - and who I am. This land isn't safe for you, not while the dark shadows of the iron North still loom. It's better for you to return home, where you belong."

Mara was speechless. His words stung deeply, for they echoed exactly what her brothers had said: that Anros was beneath her, unworthy of her presence. She had thought that Aric, at least, would think differently and that he wouldn't care where she came from, just as she didn't care about his origins. Why couldn't he let go of his reservations and embrace his feelings? Had his words been nothing but lies? Questions flooded her mind, but instead of speaking, she remained silent. She had no more words for Aric, feeling that any expression of her feelings would be futile.

Dejected, she turned to the king, bowing respectfully. "Please forgive the rude behavior and poor manners of my brothers. They are blinded by the years and can no longer see true beauty and splendor, even when it stands right before them. Forget their foolish words, for one day, Miénast will come to Anros for aid, and without your support, it will fall. Not all in Miénast are like my brothers. You know my father, and you know me. We are different, as are many others in my homeland. It breaks my heart to leave, for no place have I ever loved as much as I love Anros, but your nephew is no fool. So, I will heed his advice, though it pains me greatly."

"My dear Mara," Henric said with a kind smile. "You will always be welcome here in Westhawen, no matter what the future holds. But I cannot offer you the safety that your father can in Dinambad. So, go home now, and return when these looming shadows have passed. You may stay as long as you wish then, even forever. The doors of my house will always be open to you and your father. But as for your brothers, you'd better leave them at home." He sighed. "It's a mystery to me how the same blood runs through your veins, yet you are so different in nature. But one thing I do know: your true home is in the Wildlands. That's where your heart belongs, and that's where you will find happiness. Farewell, Mara, and send my regards to your father. I look forward to the day when he and I ride side by side into battle again."

"I will pass on your greetings," Mara said with a smile. "And he will be glad to hear them. Please also give my regards to Aasa. It saddens me that I must leave without saying goodbye to her, for in the short time I've been here, she has become like a sister to me. I hope to see her again soon. Now, farewell." With that, she turned and left.

As her brothers closed in around her, escorting her out into the morning light, Mara's mood darkened with sorrow. She glanced at the faces of Westhawen's people and saw confusion and fading hope. The further she walked from the city, the more she realized that leaving Anros was a terrible mistake. But what choice did she have? What could she - a young, weak girl - do to change anything? To spare her father from further worry, she had to return home. She also needed distance from Aric, who, it seemed, was not the man she had thought him to be. Yet, despite her decision, she felt a deeper sense of guilt as she left Westhawen, thinking of Aasa and the doubt and fear that plagued the people of Anros - for she knew that Miénast would not come to their aid.

6

Burdened by his self-imposed guilt, Aric trudged aimlessly down the corridor toward his chamber in Suthawen. Though he had only returned from the capital, he looked as though he had fought a fierce battle. And indeed, he had - a battle within himself. His feelings of guilt were overwhelming, yet he knew he had made the only right decision. All he wanted was to know that the woman who had stolen his heart was safe. But even that did little to ease the pain, for with Mara's departure, a part of him had vanished from Anros as well.

"You return alone?" Aasa's voice called out suddenly from behind him.

Tired and defeated, he turned to face her, noticing the growing fear in her emerald-green eyes.

"Where is Mara? Is she still in Westhawen, where it's safer? I hoped to speak with her. Will she come back? If not, I must go to Westhawen."

So many questions, so many words, but only one answer echoed in his mind. Yet Aric couldn't bring himself to say it aloud.

"Why aren't you answering me?" Aasa asked, her concern deepening. "Are you alright? You look pale and exhausted."

Without responding, Aric turned abruptly and continued down the corridor.

Aasa grew increasingly anxious. Even a blind man could see that something was wrong with her brother, so she hurried after him. "Did something happen in Westhawen? Something with Mara? Is that why she didn't return with you? Please tell me she's safe!"

As Aric entered his chamber, a bitter anger began to rise within him. The torment of his own guilt was bad enough, and now his curious little sister was bombarding him with relentless, torturous questions.

But she persisted, following him into the room where her brother stood motionless, his back turned to her, as still as a statue. "Say something! Anything. Please, Aric, just tell me what happened!"

"She's gone." His voice was hollow and broken, yet he didn't move an inch. "Her brothers came this morning and took her back home."

"No..." Aasa recoiled in dismay. "So, she's left us, too. I never had much hope, but now it's completely gone. Mara's insight and her wise words could have given us the confidence we so desperately need. But now we're left with nothing but this growing shadow, and it just keeps getting darker. How could she return home in these bleak days, leaving us to face our hopeless fate alone? Without her, we're lost."

Finally, Aric turned to face his sister, and the fury in his eyes made her tremble with fear. "Be silent, foolish girl! You have no idea what you're talking about. It was obvious from the start that a princess from the oh-so-noble and pretentious land of stone couldn't stay in our unforgiving home. You think she could have helped us?" His gaze was sharp and bitter. "With what, exactly? Mara is still just a woman. What could she have truly accomplished? Beauty and wise words won't defeat the enemy." He sighed heavily. "We've always been on our own, and we've managed well enough. We don't need some naive princess here, no matter how charming she may be. Women don't belong on the battlefield."

"And where do we belong, then?" Aasa challenged, her voice defiant. "I know you think we're weak and foolish. I've long understood your narrow view of us, but it's not very helpful. Mara has fought in battles before, and she survived them, didn't she?"

"She survived because I saved her," Aric snapped. "She's just as stubborn and naive as you are, and it will lead both of you to your deaths one day. I won't always be there to save you."

"I never asked for your help, and I'm sure Mara didn't either. Why does it anger you so much that we only want to fight for our families, to defend them instead of sitting idly by as they are attacked or even killed? Why do you even care what we want?"

"I will not bury my own sister. But if you want to die so badly, do as you please. If you don't understand why I'm angry, then you don't know me at all. Men fight wars and battles to ensure the safety of their wives and children."

"Yet far too often, men die, leaving their wives and children to grieve without end." Aasa sighed. "Or have you forgotten how it was for our mother?"

Aric's anger began to cool, and he pondered her words. "She didn't want to leave," he said quietly. "Mara fought so hard against her brothers that they became quite rude. But still, she didn't want to go with them."

"Then why did she change her mind in the end?"

"She didn't. Not really. But I asked her to." His voice faltered.

"Why?"

"Her father was sick with worry. She's far safer in Dinambad than she could ever be here. That's why I want you to pack only your essentials and ride to Westhawen. You'll be safer in the capital than here."

"But I don't want to leave. This is my home."

"Don't forget what you promised Mara. How can you keep an eye on Nariya if you stay here? Go now. I'll escort you north later."

Aasa turned to leave but paused in the corridor, glancing back at her brother. "You should never underestimate women, Aric. After all, we will soon have a woman as our queen."

"Fala is Henric's last remaining child. He has no choice." Aric's voice was steady but resigned. "Finian's death was premature, not intended."

"Not intended?" Aasa looked at him, confused. "He died of fever, Aric, when he was just a child. Fala has been Henric's heir for many years now. You should come to terms with it."

"I have. Fala is a good leader and an excellent warrior."

"But she's a woman."

"I'm the commander of Anros. My duty is to protect the king and his heirs, no matter who they are."

"And I'm sure you'll do so to her utmost satisfaction. But Fala will one day be your queen. You won't be able to simply send her away to keep her safe. If a battle comes, she'll be fighting at the front."

Aasa studied her brother for a long moment. "She's not Mara. Fala is a born warrior. And warriors, as you know, die eventually. But you don't seem to fear her death, do you? It's Mara you're truly worried about." Aasa sighed. "If you send away everyone you love, Aric, you'll end up dying alone." Without waiting for his response, she walked away, troubled.

"I haven't forgotten what happened," he said softly, his voice cracked with pain, stopping his sister in her tracks. "I was there, Aasa. I saw mother's unbearable grief, and though I tried everything, I couldn't ease her pain. No power in this world could heal her broken heart." He exhaled heavily. "You might think I'm bitter and heartless, but you didn't see what I saw, little sister."

Tears welled up in Aasa's eyes, and she turned back, rushing toward her brother. Without a word, she threw her arms around him, sobbing into his chest.

8

After several days on horseback, it was a relief to finally feel solid ground beneath her feet again. Lord Ráhad's sons, along with their sister and an entourage of a hundred men, passed through the southern gate of the city. The townspeople who caught sight of the princess cheered and called her name, their hearts filled with hope as she finally returned home.

But to Mara, this no longer felt like home. Returning to Dinambad felt like arriving in a place foreign to her, strange and distant, even though it had once been her sanctuary. Now, it wasn't. Surrounded by her brothers, who left no room for escape, she ascended the broad stone steps leading to the palace, and with each step toward her father, her apprehension grew.

"If only I had stayed in Westhawen," she thought nervously, feeling her heart pound faster and louder, as if it might burst from her chest and flee. More than ever, she longed to escape. But there was no turning back now.

Two men of the prince's guard silently opened the grand door, allowing them to enter before closing it behind them.

Mara kept her gaze fixed on the sea-blue carpet that stretched across the white marble floor. In the background, she could hear the gentle splashing of water from four towering fountains adorned with grand stone sculptures of swans, two on each side of the grand hall. The high arching windows were lined with vibrant stained glass depicting the great voyages of past ages across the vast seas.

In the center of the long hall, Mara halted, too afraid to take another step. At the far end of the hall, her father stood atop a raised platform, reached by seven wide steps, where a grand stone chair, adorned with flowers and elegant ribbons, sat in the middle. At that moment, the prince noticed her.

"Come closer, my child," the man said gently, offering her a warm smile. "You have no reason to fear me."

Her usually talkative brothers stood in respectful silence, watching with curiosity to see what would unfold.

Hesitantly, Mara approached her father, looking into his kind face. When she finally stood before him, laden with guilt, he descended the steps and lovingly embraced her. "Surely I don't need to tell you how happy I am that no harm has come to you?" Ráhad gazed at her with his ocean-gray eyes, scrutinizing yet still smiling. "Why did you leave, my dear? Did I upset you? Did someone else here wrong you? Whoever dared to harm my beloved daughter will face a just punishment."

"No one has hurt me, least of all you, father." Her voice almost failed her, choked by guilt. "I didn't mean to cause you worry. Please forgive me. But I didn't leave without purpose. I was searching for someone."

"The enemy is advancing on our lands in great numbers, and at such a time, you chose to leave the impenetrable walls of Dinambad? What could be so important, so urgent, that my daughter would risk her precious life for it?"

"Not what, but who," she said, looking at him with a grave expression. "The heir to the throne of Miénast and Nyarost." For a brief moment, her eyes glimmered with hope. "Tharon, son of Erchad and descendant of Huandar. Dartur told me he would be in Anros."

"Dartur?" Ráhad frowned disapprovingly. "You mean the old wizard Othorin. Only in the far west and the wilderness is he called Dartur. It seems you've spent a bit too much time in Anros." He then smiled kindly. "At least, did you meet with king Henric?"

"I did," Mara's face brightened. "And he sends his greetings to you. He is a loyal friend, and his hospitality is as grand as his kind heart. But although he is not blind or naive to his enemies, like some, my hope darkens at the thought that someone within his own house might betray him."

"What are you talking about, my child?" her father asked.

"One of his advisors - her name is Nariya. It seems to me that not everyone there trusts her. And rightfully so, for her words are often poisonous and dangerous."

Diam stepped closer to them. "Indeed, she is an odd figure. She doesn't seem to fit in with the people of Anros - so pale, so frail and hunched. But she stinks just like the others, of horse, manure, and stables."

"I don't trust her," Mara said firmly.

"This is not your concern, my child," Ráhad responded gently. "King Henric knows best what he needs to do. I am certain of that. If this advisor intended to betray him, Henric would have surely sensed it by now. Leave that matter alone - there are other things for you to attend to."

Curiosity and confusion swirled in her mind as she looked up at her father. Deep within her, a restless longing for adventure ignited once again. She began to wonder what task he might have for her, even as she secretly feared it would be some tedious chore or punishment for her recent actions.

"You have a visitor," Ráhad said, his voice tinged with concern. "He's been waiting for you for two days now, in the guest chambers. He knows you've returned, and it has only made him more impatient than usual. Making a wizard wait is never wise, especially one who has traveled a long way. But he insisted on speaking with you personally and wouldn't be turned away."

Ó

The young princess hurried down the stone corridor, her footsteps echoing off the walls, until she reached the eastern wing of the grand palace and finally burst into the guest chamber, where the door stood wide open.

"Dartur!" she called out, her voice filled with relief and joy as she spotted the old wizard. He was draped in a long, brown cloak, seated on a stone bench by the window, his gaze searching the endless horizon of the sea.

Resting his large hands on the bench, the elderly man rose to his full, imposing height, momentarily darkening the room with his towering presence as he stepped aside from the window. He cast a skeptical glance down at her, as if he hardly recognized the young woman before him. Gone was the delicate princess he remembered, always adorned in elegant, regal attire. Instead, a warrior stood before him, her hair disheveled, her clothing stained from travel - this was no longer the Mara of his memory.

"You're quite late," he chided, his tone stern. "By now, I could have passed the gates of Anros already, perhaps even returned to Aterhain."

"Forgive me!" she pleaded, bowing her head. "I didn't know you were coming."

He smiled warmly, his previous harshness melting away. "Did you at least receive my message?"

"I did. But why are you here? Shouldn't you be with those Halfmen in Nanglorin?"

"I should be," Dartur sighed, "two days ahead of schedule, in fact. But my journey brought me here first, so I could give you something." He rummaged through the deep folds of his cloak and pulled out a silver necklace, adorned with a small, dark-blue gemstone. Gently, he placed it in Mara's delicate hand.

"A necklace?" She gazed at him in confusion. "Just a simple necklace, albeit with a beautiful gemstone - is this what kept you waiting for me?"

"It's not a simple necklace," Dartur chuckled. "I'm no foolish peddler of trinkets. This blue gemstone is called *Alarmár*, among other names, and it has the power to shed light even in the deepest darkness. According to ancient tales, it was washed from the heart of Tin Elwech in the north, carried down the Areglos River to the Sea of Areglin, where young King Andor of Anros retrieved it near the great falls. He fastened it to this chain as a symbol of the kings of Anros, and it was passed down to his heir, Irmen, who gave it to his son Urwen. But after Urwen's untimely death, the stone was lost in a land no living being had ever set foot in. Somehow, though, the Alarmár found its way to Faldar, to the High Aedin Mylias. She entrusted it to me, to give to you."

"Why would Lady Mylias give such a valuable gift to me? She never gives anything without a reason," Mara said, her voice tinged with disbelief.

"With her vast knowledge, she can see many things. And she has seen you. She asks that you prepare for a long journey. But be warned, it will not be an easy path."

"I've already been on many journeys," Mara said. "Where must I go?"

"You will find out soon enough, but not from me," Dartur replied. "Lady Mylias will guide you when the time comes." His gaze shifted back to the sea. "But there are other matters that must be attended to first." He looked at Mara again. "I must continue on my way to Nanglorin. The young boy I mentioned in my message to you - his name is Ardil. He, too, will soon have to embark on a great journey." Dartur sighed heavily. "And he has agreed to hand over the stone he - through some strange twist of fate - managed to find, so that it can be kept safe."

"There is no place in all of Farham where that stone could ever be safe, if it's truly the one," Mara said, her voice trembling with fear.

The wizard began to explain in great detail what he intended to do should the stone fall into his possession - though he neither hoped nor wished for it, as he feared it more than most things. Mara listened in silence, and a small spark of hope flickered in her heart.

"Elfor, Lord of Dunhir, is a wise man," Dartur said. "I will travel as quickly as I can to him with the boy and the stone. For in all the breadth of Sedäa, there is no sanctuary like Dunhir, where the Alyarel might find its truest haven. This mighty fortress, standing since time immemorial, remains unmatched in its grandeur and strength. No foe, however bold, has ever breached its towering walls, nor dared approach its gates. It is not by mortal hands alone that Dunhir stands invincible, but by an ancient power - the very essence of the brown Alyarel itself. This stone, bound to the fortress, weaves its strength into the very ground and mortar, forming a barrier of such impenetrable might that no force, neither of this world nor any other, can sunder. It is said that nothing under the heavens or within the deep can overcome the enchantments that guard it, for the Alyarel's magic endures beyond the strength of any mortal power. By the time we arrive there, I trust Elfor will have made a decision on how we should proceed. Word of the black stone's discovery has already spread to many lands - including Mahlrit. It's only a matter of time before your uncle sends an emissary to the northwest. Like all the uninformed, he will assume the stone is in Dunhir. Unfortunately, he will be right. And knowing Dinhad, that old fool, he'll likely send his son Torhael with the aim of seizing the stone for himself. But the Alyarel must never fall into his hands - if it does, Farham is lost." Dartur's expression grew grave. "That's why I want you to go to Dunhir and convince your cousin to see reason. He'll listen to you more than anyone else."

"You ask much of me, Dartur," Mara said, feeling slightly disheartened. "I'll do it, for the sake of my family's honor. But I want no part in dealing with the black stone itself. Its power and influence terrify me - I know I would not be able to resist it. The blood of humans flows through my veins, and we have always been weak. Haradan's curse must not become mine as well."

"It won't," Dartur reassured her. "Your role in Dunhir is to advise, not to act. And remember, not all humans are weak. Haradan may have failed long ago, but Tharon, his heir, will not."

"Will he be there?" Mara asked, her eyes gleaming with hope. "Have you found him?"

"Yes. I will meet him in Menyána with the stone. He too will come to Dunhir as a representative of the ancient kings." Dartur paused briefly. "It has been fifteen days since we parted ways. I wrote my message to you in his presence, so he knows you are coming. He is eager to speak with you."

"What could the rightful king of Miénast and Nyarost wish to speak with me about? There's nothing I could tell him that he doesn't already know. But I admit, my heart yearns to meet him. I've placed all my hope in his capable hands. He must return to Miénast as soon as possible to put an end to my foolish uncle's reign. Miénast needs its king."

"He will return," Dartur said, "for it is an inevitable part of his journey. Whatever you wish to tell him, he already knows. He always has. Tharon never fled or hid from his destiny - he had his reasons for waiting. When the time is right, Tharon will reveal himself as the rightful king of men and confront our enemy. Urehel does not know that he still lives, for if he did, we would know it. Urehel fears Tharon more than any other man in Farham, and I believe this will be his downfall in time."

"Why?" she asked, her voice filled with confusion. "Why does Urehel fear him?"

"Because of Haradan, his forefather," Dartur replied, his gaze heavy with the weight of ancient memory. "Haradan was not merely the first mortal to steal the black Alyarel from Urehel's grasp, he was the only one who ever wielded its dread power without being consumed by the shadow. It is said that Haradan, in his strength and courage, used the stone many times. With its dark might, he forged the kingdom of Nyarost and raised the great capital, Nyardin, in the north. In those days, he was unmatched in all of Farham, the most powerful being to walk its lands. And had he been wiser, had he not been blinded by the terrible allure of that power, he might have ended Urehel's reign once and for all." Dartur sighed deeply, his voice growing wearier, the exhaustion of long years and longer journeys pressing upon him. "But he did not."

He paused for a moment, his words laden with the weight of lost opportunities. "The legends tell that Haradan met his end by the power of the stone itself, that the black Alyarel devoured him, as it does all who seek to wield it. But that is a falsehood - a lie spun to warn men of the stone's terrible danger. The truth is far more sorrowful. After his beloved wife, Nielas, was taken from him by a cruel fever when their son Haradil was but a boy of fifteen, Haradan's heart broke in two. It is said that the male heirs of Ealdir are cursed with undying love, and when they lose their heart's companion, they lose the will to live. Haradan, the great, the mighty, died not by the stone's hand, but by grief. His heart could bear no more. That is the truth of Haradan's curse."

Dartur's voice softened with sorrow, as though he too had walked that path of endless loss. "And with the death of him, the black Alyarel vanished from the world, lost to time and legend, its power hidden - waiting."

Dartur stretched, looking weary. "I am late. I must take my leave. Time waits for no one, and right now, it is working against me and my perilous task. Farewell, Mara. Take care of yourself. I hope we meet again soon in Dunhir, where we can decide the stone's fate."

With those words, Dartur strode out of the room, his heavy footsteps echoing in the corridor until he disappeared around the corner.

Mara stood there, lowering her head in sadness and fear. She felt unprepared for the task ahead of her. She couldn't understand why the wise Lady Mylias of Faldar had seen her in her visions. Were there not others more suited to this mission? Brave, strong men, rather than a doubtful and fragile woman like herself? Mara now hoped fervently that her journey from Dunhir would take her back to Dinambad, rather than leading her to Mylias in Faldar. She feared the great power of the high

Aedin and her ability to influence people's minds without uttering a single word.

A wave of guilt washed over Mara. She had always hoped to do more than simply tend to wounded soldiers returning from battle. But now that she was given the chance to make a real difference, fear had taken hold of her. No matter what she had experienced, she had never wanted to come into contact with the black stone of creation.

Her gaze fell on the blue Alarmár in her hand, and she couldn't help but think of Aric, whose homeland lay in King Andor's fortress. A heaviness settled over her heart as she realized how much she missed him. The anger she had once felt toward him had long since faded, and she now understood that he had acted in her best interest. It would have been foolish for him to let her stay, especially when Anros was far more dangerous than Dinambad.

Taking a deep breath, the princess returned to her chambers, where she sat at her desk, strewn with parchment and writing instruments. With renewed resolve, she began composing a long letter, which she would soon send by a swift messenger to Anros.

ᛟ

In the early morning, just after the sun had risen behind the mountains, a tall, stately man with shoulder-length, light blonde hair quickly left the Tower of Fheran in Mahlrit and headed toward the stables, where a mount had already been saddled for him. Torhael, Dinhad's firstborn son, dressed in his finest gilded armor with a deep blue cloak bearing the emblem of the stone city, walked down the cobbled road, greeting the townsfolk he passed with good spirits. But when a tall, slender woman with braided blonde hair, clad in gleaming armor reminiscent of the ancient Aedan warriors, approached him, he stopped abruptly and stared at her with uncertainty.

"The time has come, it seems," she said, stepping closer. "Your journey north begins, and its end remains hidden from me. Yet, I cannot and will not stop you."

Torhael gazed into her dark green, shimmering eyes. Gently, he touched her cheek with his hand. "Do not despair, dearest Aleth. I promise you, we will meet again soon. Perhaps not tomorrow, and perhaps not for some time, but when that day comes, the stone city will once again shine in its former glory, and its people will find joy once more. And I too will be joyful, knowing that you are by my side."

"Your words feel distant and unreal," Aleth replied softly, "yet I will believe in them, just as you do. I will wait for your return, my beloved Torhael, no matter how long it may take."

The man pulled her close and kissed her tenderly. "Farewell, my love," he smiled. "And look after my little sister Fria for me. She may be as capable a leader as I am, but she has always lived in my shadow." He caressed her cheek gently, kissed her again, and walked away.

Aleth stood in the street, watching him go. Though she possessed many gifts as an Aedin, she could not foresee Torhael's fate. All she could see for him in the near future was endless darkness, and this filled her with great concern, for it foretold nothing good. She remained there for a long time, even after Torhael and his small group of riders had left the stone city far behind and disappeared beyond the horizon.

Just as Aleth was about to leave, Fria appeared beside her. She wore the ancient armor of a city commander - a leather breastplate adorned with the white mountain and the three walls of Mahlrit, and a dark-blue cloak with a hood. She was armed with a sword at her side, arrows in a quiver, and a bow slung across her back. Though her armor was finely made, it seemed a little too large and loose on her.

"These are dark days," Fria said somberly. "And without my brother, they feel even darker. I wish he hadn't left."

"He had no choice," Aleth replied. "But I am as troubled by it as you are. I see no good ending for him, and I only hope my senses are mistaken." She then looked at the young woman beside her. "Where are you off to? You look as though you're about to head into battle."

"I hope not - at least, not yet," Fria smiled uncertainly. "But I am headed to Libentya. My men are waiting for me at the city gate. Scouts have spotted strange creatures in the forests near the Uael. We'll try to slay as many as we can." She looked at Aleth hopefully. "If you wish, you could join us. An extra sharp eye and a swift bow would be a great asset in those dense woods."

"I would love to help, but I must refuse your request. Another path lies before me. I'm riding to Dinambad. Though I hate to leave you, Fria, someone there needs my help even more urgently."

"I won't stop you." Fria nodded. "But when you reach Dinambad, please send my regards to my uncle, his sons, and especially to my dear cousin Mara. She has always been a loyal friend to me, visiting often after my mother passed away. Mara helped me through a difficult time, and I am forever grateful to her. But as the days have grown darker, she has not come to the capital, and I worry for her well-being." Fria paused. "I would have liked to have you by my side, but I won't divert you from your mission. Still, it diminishes what little hope I have left now that both you and my brother are gone. I stand alone now - without him and now without you, Aleth."

"You are not alone," Aleth said softly, offering a gentle smile. "You have many allies, and even your stubborn father will soon realize that you are a great leader."

"I'm afraid I can't fully believe that," Fria replied, her gaze darkening. "My father will likely never stop blaming me for Amras' and my mother's deaths. And just like him, I don't think I'll ever be able to see it any differently."

"It wasn't your fault. There was nothing you could have done to prevent what happened back then. Amras was never truly happy, not here or anywhere else. His death was tragic - I won't deny that - but for him, it may have been the only release. You have to let him go, Fria. He wouldn't have wanted you to suffer because of it."

"Then he shouldn't have killed himself." Fria swallowed her pain. "It feels like a part of me died with him when he leapt from the tower. The agony is unbearable. Tell me, since you can foresee so much - will this ever end?"

"It will," Aleth assured her with a compassionate smile. "But when that day will come, even I cannot say. Everyone mourns in their own way. Don't lose hope, Fria. The day will come when it won't torment you so deeply."

After several days, the mounted courier from Dinambad arrived in Westhawen by evening, riding as fast as he could. He entered the king's hall, clutching an important message in his hand. He hurried forward toward the lone woman standing before the steps of the empty throne, her gaze distant as if lost in thought.

"Greetings," the courier said in a respectful tone, though he had no idea who she was. "I bring an urgent message from Dinambad for Lord Aric."

At the mention of that name, the woman's eyes lit up with an eager gleam. She stepped closer to the courier. "For Aric, you say? I assume it's from Princess Mara, is that right?"

The courier nodded. "Yes, indeed. Where might I find him?"

The woman gave a sly smile. "Lord Aric is not here at the moment, and it will be a few hours yet before he returns. Hand the message to me, and I promise I will see that it reaches him as soon as he comes back. Princess Mara is a dear and trusted friend." Her grin widened. "She trusts me."

Hesitantly, the courier handed her the letter from Mara. "The Princess insists that Lord Aric receives this message as soon as possible."

"He will," the woman replied, her eyes now fixed intently on the letter in her hands. "I will personally ensure it."

"Then my duty is complete. Farewell." The courier hastily bowed before turning and leaving the grand hall.

Once he was gone, the woman began to laugh - a harsh, unsettling sound. The naive messenger from Dinambad had no idea that he had just handed Mara's letter for Aric to Nariya, the very woman who despised him. There was no way she intended to deliver that message. Instead, Nariya rushed to her small chamber behind the king's hall, locked the door behind her, and greedily tore open the envelope to read the letter.

Fascinated and even deeply moved, she devoured the heartfelt words that the young princess had written to the unsuspecting Aric, filled with love and hope. Nariya laughed aloud, fully aware that she now held something of great value in her hands. Consumed by greed, she hid the letter beneath her bed, confident that no one would ever find it there.

໐

Princess Mara rushed eagerly toward the returning courier, who was climbing the long steps to the palace after several days of travel.

"Well?" she asked with anticipation, stepping directly into his path. "Did you deliver the letter to Aric? Has he read it yet? What did he say? Did he send a message for me?"

The man bowed respectfully, his weary eyes meeting hers. "No, my lady. I did not meet Lord Aric. Instead, I handed the letter to a woman who told me she was a friend of yours."

"What was the name of this woman? Did she tell you?" Mara's voice grew cold.

"No, she did not." The courier suddenly remembered the woman's greedy smile.

"Was it Fala? The king's daughter herself?" Her voice hardened. "Speak!"

"It was not princess Fala, for she bore nothing regal about her. I would have recognized the king's daughter at once. This woman seemed somewhat unkempt and... strange."

"Nariya." Desperation flashed across Mara's face, quickly transforming into bitter anger. "How could you hand my letter to her?" she shouted, glaring at the clueless man. "Do you not know any better? You were always our fastest and most reliable messenger, but no longer! Nariya will never deliver that letter to Aric. She despises him. And me. She'll destroy it, and with it, she'll break my heart." Her fury deepened, and she fixed him with a scornful gaze. "Get out of my sight, you foolish wretch! If you value your life, leave this place and never set foot in my homeland or anywhere else I may be!"

Terrified, the poor man dared not speak or meet her eyes again. In shock, he quickly turned and hurried back down the long steps, fleeing the city as fast as he could.

"Wasn't that a bit harsh?" a tall, slender woman asked, approaching Mara. She wore a worn, dark blue gown, her long, white-blonde hair loosely braided to cover her pointed ears. "He didn't know any better. Anyone might have trusted a stranger claiming to be your friend. Even I would have."

Mara scoffed. "Then you're not much wiser than he is, Adraéth."

"Perhaps not. But I don't need to be wise to be a simple maid. Cooking and washing clothes are the only skills I need, and I do them well enough that your father hasn't sent me away." She paused for a moment. "Still, you should reflect on what just happened."

"I am," Mara snapped. "You don't know Nariya like I do. I met her in Westhawen. There's something deeply evil about her. Anyone who can't see that is not only blind but also remarkably foolish."

"Like many of us here," Adraéth replied calmly. "Your uncle is no better. Forget this woman and think of your future. She can't harm you here. Who knows? Perhaps everything will turn out fine, despite her meddling. Aric knows how you feel. Whether he gets your letter or not won't change that. Trust your heart and look forward, not back. These are dark times already, and I don't want to see you saddened by it."

"You're probably right," Mara said, her anger cooling. "Your advice has always been helpful, Adraéth. You may be a simple maid, but you're also a loyal friend." The princess smiled again, trying to push her anger over Nariya aside. She then walked with the Aedin back into the grand throne room of the palace.

9

Prince Ráhad stood by one of the grand fountains with his three sons, discussing matters with urgency.

"Father, we have little time before our stronghold in Libentya falls into enemy hands," said Anwar. "Fria has sent an urgent request for reinforcements. She needs every man we can spare."

"I will give you all the able-bodied soldiers I can," Ráhad responded firmly. "Libentya must not be lost."

"Torhael should never have left," Enwir remarked bitterly. "He abandoned us in our darkest hour, and no one even knows where he has gone."

"To Dunhir," Mara interjected, stepping closer as Adraéth stood aside with a group of women cleaning another fountain. "To the High Aedan, Elfor - though he's likely about to make a grave mistake, and he left too soon."

"Too soon?" Diam asked, confused. "How do you know this?"

"Because Mara is also bound for Dunhir, but not yet," Ráhad answered in a commanding tone. "She still has a few days left here in Dinambad."

"What use is the High Aedan in Dunhir?" Enwir scoffed. "No doubt he speaks in honeyed words and dazzling nonsense. I could never go to those people. They do not die as we do, and they outlast us all. But just as birth belongs to life, so does death. They lack that, and it shows - they are hollow, like wisps of fog drifting silently across the plains. But it's good that you go to them, little sister. It suits you better than it would me."

"All you know is how to fight in raging battles," a voice interrupted from behind, sharp and noble in tone. Then, out of the shadows, a tall figure emerged. "For subtlety and care, as we Aedan possess, are foreign to you. You are more like a jagged rock in the stormy sea - stubborn and rough." The woman, cloaked in dark green, pulled back her hood, revealing her shining blonde hair and piercing green eyes. "It wouldn't hurt you to be a little more cautious."

"Aleth!" Mara exclaimed joyfully, rushing to embrace her. "What brings you here?"

"I heard of grave dangers and great battles brewing, so I came to offer my battle-hardened hands to Prince Ráhad."

"And I gladly accept your offer," Ráhad said, smiling warmly. "May you bring us hope in these bleak times."

"You Aedan are truly peculiar," Enwir said, scrutinizing the delicate-looking woman with her impossibly long hair, taller than even him, though he was among the tallest in Dinambad. "You only come when there's danger."

"What help would I be if there was no need for it?" Aleth retorted, her gaze penetrating.

"Pay him no mind," Anwar interjected with a smile. "He doesn't know you well enough, nor your people. Though his words may sound harsh, I'm sure he's glad you're here to help. I know I am."

Aleth smiled at him, and in her eyes, he thought he caught a fleeting glimmer of affection.

"Time is short," Enwir interrupted, his tone cold and urgent. "We need to leave immediately."

"It won't do much good, brother," Diam said. "We are too few to make a real difference in Libentya."

"You have my bow," Aleth said, standing tall. "And it's swift and deadly, as if ten of my kind were fighting by your side."

"If Aleth goes, then so will I," Mara said, her spirit reignited. "My sword is sharp, and I am rested. I yearn to quench my thirst for battle in a great fight."

"No, my child, that would be foolish," Ráhad said, his voice heavy with concern. "Foolish even to consider, and it would be even more foolish for me to allow it."

"It would be foolish to leave me behind when every sword counts!" Mara pleaded. "Let me go with them! I am not a burden they must worry about - I never have been. You don't see it, Father. In Anros, my sword did not rest often. I felled many foes and saved the lives of countless people of the Wilds. Let me go with them!" She dropped to her knees before the prince, her voice desperate. "You taught me how to wield a sword yourself, saying that one day it would be useful to me. You also gifted me one of the four most precious swords in all of Miénast. I will not carry it as mere decoration."

"Stand up, child," Ráhad commanded, looking down at her sternly. Only when she rose to her feet did he continue, "I will not send my daughter into battle - not while I still have men who can fight."

"I was born a prince's daughter with three powerful brothers, but I am no less brave and strong than any of you, just because I am a woman."

Her father was silent for a moment, clearly battling with his thoughts. "I have said no. Your journey lies elsewhere."

Disheartened and humiliated, Mara turned on her heel and ran off.

"Can we go now?" Enwir snapped impatiently, and without waiting for an answer, he marched toward the gate.

As the others, Aleth included, prepared to follow, Adraéth stepped in their way. "Be careful, Aleth! In the ruins of Libentya, there are creatures worse than those you've faced before. Do not forget the influence of the dark shadow. The iron north and the south are more closely connected than you might think - you know this."

Aleth placed a hand on Adraéth's shoulder. "Do not worry, old friend. This is not my first battle."

"And hopefully not your last," Anwar added as he and Diam hurried after their older brother.

As Aleth eagerly moved to follow the others into battle, Adraéth grabbed her by the arm and pulled her back. "Be careful! Or something terrible will happen. In the Tower of Tin Iushvhatu sits one who was once among the mightiest of us, but has now succumbed to the dark shadow. He and his companions are not far from Libentya, and they will see you. Do not let them peer into your heart! Still, you must weaken them."

"How am I supposed to do that?" Aleth asked.

"The Black Lord of Iushvhatu wields a staff imbued with powerful magic, crafted for him by the enemy. The tip, a pale, black crystal, holds a significant part of the power of the lost Alyarel. Without it, his strength diminishes, and he and his followers can be defeated."

"I'll see what I can do," Aleth replied hastily, attempting to break free from Adraéth's grip and join Mara's brothers in battle.

But Adraéth tightened her hold, stepping closer and whispering in Aleth's ear, "Do not underestimate the danger posed by the Lord of Iushvhatu. He is Urehel's right hand, and if he gets hold of you, we are all doomed. Do not let what our Lady foresaw come to pass."

"What are you talking about?" Aleth demanded, confusion creeping into her voice.

"You have a long and treacherous path ahead, one that does not include Libentya. You will face a trial, and if you fail, we all fail. Sending you to Libentya may be a mistake, but you can use your proximity to the enemy to mislead them. You must not fail - otherwise, this will be our fate." As she spoke, Adraéth laid her outstretched hand on Aleth's chest.

Suddenly, Aleth's vision filled with disturbing and chaotic scenes that sent a chill down her spine. With a scream of terror, she pulled away, unable to bear the searing pain, staring helplessly at Adraéth.

"It doesn't have to happen," Adraéth said softly, knowing exactly what her friend had seen. "And it won't, as long as you don't fall into the hands of the enemy, or worse, into death. All our fates rest on your decisions now - whether you like it or not. If you go to Libentya, not only your life hangs in the balance."

Speechless, Aleth stared at Adraéth, unable to find words to respond. What she had just seen terrified her too much to form a reply. Instead, she wrenched herself free from Adraéth's grip and rushed outside in a panic. As she raced down the long steps, her mind was consumed by the horrifying vision, desperate to figure out how she could prevent what Adraéth had shown her.

"What did you show her?" Ráhad asked worriedly, having noticed how distressed Aleth had been when she left. After all, she had come to Dinambad to help them - not to meet her death.

"The same as I showed you, my lord. But only a small part of it. The full vision would be too much for her - it would only confuse her more."

"I hope I made the right decision," Ráhad said, his voice heavy with doubt.

"You did, my lord. Your sons are strong - and so is Aleth. Sending her to Libentya is no mistake. Much can be done there that will benefit us later."

"It seems unjust to risk such a valuable life," Ráhad muttered, lowering his head as he slowly walked away, his spirits sinking.

Adraéth turned back toward the now-closed gate, hoping she had made the right choice. The thought of sending her long-time friend to what seemed like certain death weighed heavily on her heart. Aleth's success was anything but certain, and it now seemed foolish to have sent her into battle. But Adraéth had only followed her Lady's command.

And Aleth would not be the only one facing an overwhelming task. Unbeknownst to her, on that very day, at nearly the same hour, a young and brave Wusel - a Halfman from Nanglorin, who had unexpectedly come into possession of something so powerful that the fate of all Farham rested in his small hands - was pondering similar worries. He, along with his friends and the wizard Dartur, had just embarked on a perilous journey.

6

Night had fallen, and a menacing darkness shrouded the ruins of the ancient city of Libentya. Once grand, its white walls adorned with silver and gold now lay shattered and crumbled, covered in moss and filth. In the dull moonlight, they cast a foreboding gray glow over the long-abandoned streets and paths. The city was empty - almost.

A horde of Celkûn, grotesquely deformed, human-like creatures from Um-Atra, climbed from their boats along the river, hunching as they made their way over the rubble toward the northwest. It was a small group by the standards of the Dark Land's forces, barely fifty strong.

Suddenly, an arrow shot through the air, striking the lead Celkûn square between the eyes. Without uttering a sound, the creature toppled over, lifeless.

Panic rippled through the horde. They halted, crowding together, frantically scanning their surroundings. Yet, even in the dark - where they could see better than any other living being in daylight - they saw nothing.

The captain of the Celkûn stepped forward, peering into the distance. "Show yourself, coward!" he bellowed. "Or we will scour this city until we find you, and then we'll torture and tear you apart."

For a moment, an unsettling silence filled the air. No one dared to move.

A figure appeared atop one of the walls high above them. The dim glow of a nearby torch cast shadowy outlines of their body into the night. In their left hand, they held a bow; in their right, an arrow.

"Who are you?" the captain demanded, squinting to see the stranger's face. But the faint light blurred his vision.

"I do not give my name to my enemies," the figure replied.

The captain let out a loud, mocking laugh, quickly echoed by the Celkûn around him.

"A woman?" he jeered. "A woman dares to stand in our way? And alone, no less?"

"Not alone." Her voice boomed like a wave, echoing menacingly through the ruins of the city.

In response, more figures emerged from the shadows, surrounding the horde, their bows drawn and torches held high. Eight in total, all with their faces concealed from the Celkûn's view.

Fear gripped the grotesque creatures as they huddled closer together. Even the captain felt a chill of terror as he stared up at the woman.

"It would have been wiser for you," she said, "to never cross the river and stay in your dark realm." She drew her bow, quickly aimed, and fired another arrow, striking down a Celkûn beside the captain.

Enraged, the captain drew his sword. "Kill them! Kill them all!" he roared.

But before they could react, nine arrows flew through the air, each finding its mark and felling a member of the horde.

However, the Celkûn's fear had turned to fury, and they scrambled up the crumbled walls from all sides, their spiked spears and jagged swords raised to attack the strangers.

A brutal battle erupted, filled with the agonizing screams of the wounded and the fierce roars of warriors, piercing the once silent night. Though the Celkûn far outnumbered their adversaries, they struggled to match the skill and precision of the nine masked figures who fought with lightning speed and flawless coordination. Each strike from the defenders was calculated, every move methodical, as they led the Celkûn into a series of deadly traps that had been carefully laid throughout the ruins of Libentya. One by one, the monstrous creatures fell, ensnared by the cunning strategies of their foes, until not a single one remained standing.

The Celkûn captain, the last of his kind, knelt on the cold ground, his head bowed in defeat. The eight masked warriors silently surrounded him, each with a bow drawn, arrows trained on his head. Moments later, the woman who had spoken to him earlier stepped through the circle and stood before him.

The captain looked up, his eyes meeting her now fully revealed face. As he realized who she was, a look of terror washed over him, draining the color from his face.

"Tell your master to beware!" she commanded, her voice cold and unyielding. "Though he seeks to spread fear among men and Aedan, and raze our cities to the ground, there are still some of us who will fight him to the last breath." Her gaze hardened, and her voice was edged with steel. "I did not walk through fire and ice only to be crushed by Urehel. Tell him his reign is coming to an end, for Huandar's heir is on the way. And if Urehel wishes to wage war against us, the heir to Miénast will stand at the forefront and bring an end to you all." Her piercing green eyes gleamed menacingly in the flickering torchlight. "Now rise and return to the dark hole from which you crawled. Tell your lord everything I have said here!"

The captain rose slowly, his eyes locked on her face, reluctant to look away.

"No power in this world can extinguish the hope of men and Aedan," she declared with defiant certainty.

Suddenly, the Celek grinned wickedly. "You're a fool," he hissed. "I know your face. I have seen it many times, in places far from here. When I return, my master will unleash his fury upon you and your people. The houses of your homeland will burn, and your kin will be slaughtered like animals. Your so-called powerful sorceress will be impaled on a spear, in front of the last of the living, to paralyze them with terror. And it will all be because of you. And then... you will die."

Fury flared within the woman. She seized the creature by the collar, her eyes burning with rage. "Then so be it, Celek. And may you return safely, so that all unfolds as you claim." She shoved the captain away, her face a mask of seething anger as she watched him slink eastward into the darkness, disappearing from sight.

From among the remaining eight defenders, another woman emerged and stood beside her. "Once he reaches Um-Atra and tells Urehel of this, we're all doomed. Aleth, our lives will end."

"It won't come to that," the Aedin said, her gaze fixed on the eastern horizon. "He's not heading to Um-Atra. I fear his master lies elsewhere. And he won't be traveling alone on his return. I will follow him unnoticed. I'll track him until he leads me to his true master."

The woman at her side gasped. She pulled back her hood, revealing none other than Fria herself. "That's pure madness! This is a mistake. You can't simply walk into the enemy's land. It's a death sentence."

"You may be right," Aleth replied calmly, "but someone has to take this path. And since you are all far too valuable to your families and friends, it falls to me. This was foretold to me long ago. It must happen."

"Will you return?" Anwar asked, stepping closer.

Aleth placed a gentle hand on his shoulder. "I do not know. Perhaps I will, perhaps I won't. My fate is now shrouded in uncertainty." She softly stroked his cheek, then vanished into the night.

"Trust her, Anwar," spoke another of the companions as he approached. He, too, removed his hood, revealing his identity - it was his brother Diam. "Without her, we wouldn't have survived this battle. As you can see, from what was once a large army, only nine remain. Without Aleth's leadership today, none of us would be heading home at all."

The rest of the group dispersed, leaving the two brothers alone.

"You speak so easily, brother," Anwar said, his tone heavy. "You're young, and your life still lies ahead of you. Mine, however, is already lost to dark paths, and I doubt I will ever find it again."

"Don't fool yourself. I have far more to lose than you realize. But I won't give my heart so freely to the first beautiful woman who crosses my path."

"Don't talk nonsense, little brother! I've seen the way you look at Adraéth." Anwar smiled, pleased for him. "You can't hide how you feel about her from me."

"Fine, I admit it," Diam sighed, "if it's so obvious. But keep your mouth shut! She mustn't know. I fear she may leave us soon."

"We should get moving," came Enwir's commanding voice as he rejoined his brothers. "We can still make it back safely under the cover of night."

The two younger brothers followed their eldest as they left the ruins of the deserted city of Libentya, where they regrouped with the others waiting by their horses outside the crumbled walls. Once Enwir mounted his grey-speckled horse, the others followed suit, including Fria and two of her soldiers. Together, they rode northwest along the South Road, which cut across the wide plains of Miénast and crossed the South Route near the Hávath Hills. From there, Enwir's group took a more westerly path, leading them swiftly back to the port city of Dinambad, while Fria and her companions returned to the stone capital of Mahlrit.

6

Silently and unnoticed, Aleth crept along a deserted path, her dark brown cloak blending with the shadows as she pursued the Celek captain eastward. As expected, he had taken the direct route toward Iushvhatu, from where he could easily reach the ancient tower in the mountains.

Iushvhatu had once been a great fortress, centuries ago, offering a vantage point from which one could see far across the plains of Vhatu. The land had once been covered by a magnificent and sprawling capital. But now, the entire region was drowned in swamps and marshlands. According to legends, the great city of Vhatu had sunk into the muck, swallowed whole by the earth as punishment from the Ahar for the sins and arrogance of its people.

As the night grew its darkest, the Celek captain carefully ascended the narrow steps carved into the rocky cliffside - steps so expertly hidden that they were nearly invisible to the untrained eye. Reaching the top, he beheld the fortress of Iushvhatu, its high black tower looming ominously, glowing a faint red in the night. He hesitated, frozen by a mixture of awe and fear.

Just as he was about to continue forward, Aleth sprang from the shadows, grabbing him by the collar with her left arm and pressing a silver dagger to his throat with her right. "Did you really think we'd let you escape so easily? You've led me here, to this hidden path, without realizing I was right behind you the whole time. That's the only reason you were spared."

"There is no going back from here." The Celek's eyes widened with terror as he stared at the looming fortress, its red glow pulsing in the darkness. "The Dark Lord has already sensed your presence - before you even set foot in his domain. He will not let you leave."

At that moment, the great spiked gates of the Iushvhatu tower creaked open, and five tall, black-clad figures emerged, their voices filled with torment as they screamed into the night, moving steadily toward them.

Aleth's grip faltered. Her silver dagger slipped from her grasp as she instinctively stepped back, fear overtaking her.

The Celek laughed cruelly. "Now, you will die." He darted forward.

But with swift precision, Aleth retrieved her fallen dagger and hurled it after him. It struck the Celek in the back of the head, and he crumpled lifelessly to the ground.

The dark figures encircled Aleth, drawing gleaming swords that glinted in the dim light. Their forms were hollow, as though filled only with a swirling, malevolent shadow. Clad in black armor, their hands encased in iron gauntlets, they were faceless, shrouded in long hoods, with nothing visible beneath but an impenetrable fog.

Aleth stood motionless, her eyes fixed on the creatures as they appeared to study her, though their faces were hidden. It was as if they were scrutinizing her, sensing her very essence.

One of the figures, towering above the rest and wielding a long iron staff, stepped forward. "What brings a woman of the blessed Firstborn to my realm?" His voice was raspy and harsh, as though speaking each word caused him great agony.

"I have come to deliver a message from the realm of men," Aleth declared, her voice unwavering. "The last stone of creation has been found, and it will soon seal the doom of your dark master."

"Why should we care?" the dark figure sneered. "Whether the humans have found it or not, it changes nothing. They are weak, easily swayed. All of you will be destroyed if you refuse to bend to Urehel's will."

"Urehel is nothing more than a servant of the shadows," Aleth replied with cold defiance. "The darkness existed long before Sedäa was ever formed, and it will persist long after Urehel is vanquished. But by then, it will no longer pose a threat."

"Silence!" he roared, raising his staff high, its dark crystal glinting ominously. "There is no escape for you. You must die. No mercy will be granted."

Unfazed, Aleth drew her sword and eyed the creatures surrounding her one by one. "You are no better than the others - slaughtering the descendants of your own kin. Once, you were all mighty warriors and lords of Tanuhal." Her gaze fixed on the towering figure before her. "And you, you are the worst of them. Once a great sorcerer, trusted by many. But you were weak, and in your failure, you submitted to your former enemies."

Enraged, the dark lord lunged at her with tremendous force, initiating a fierce duel. Time and again, Aleth was struck down, her body covered in dirt and grime. Yet, she accomplished what none had before. As she lay on the ground once more, she raised her sword for a final effort, slicing through the staff just below the black crystal. The sword shattered with a grinding noise, crumbling into dust.

The crystal fell to the earth and rolled to her feet. Quickly, Aleth snatched it up and rose to her feet.

The dark lord collapsed to his knees, his power significantly weakened. But his ghastly form remained unchanged, for he had served Urehel for far too long. His body and soul were bound, a mere puppet to his master. The staff's power had long since been irrelevant; the dark sorcerer's strength was too vast to be contained by such a tool.

Without looking back, Aleth fled in terror. She stumbled repeatedly over the jagged stones in her path, falling hard to the ground, but she never dared to turn around. Her fear of the lord of Iushvhatu was too great. Clutching the dark crystal tightly in her hand, she leaped down steep, rocky ledges until she finally reached level ground again.

As exhaustion threatened to overwhelm her, the first rays of sunlight broke over the mountains, slowly brightening the sky. Hope flared anew in Aleth's heart, and she pressed onward, running as far as her weary legs could carry her."

10

Princess Mara sat on a stone bench behind the palace in Dinambad, in the meticulously crafted gardens that, though unnatural, still radiated a breathtaking beauty. She gazed out over the cliffs toward the endless, open sea.

Enwir, who had returned from Libentya just a few hours earlier, approached and took a seat beside her on the bench. "Have you heard anything yet?" he asked.

"No, nothing," she replied, her eyes sorrowful and glistening with unshed tears. "Did we send her to her death?"

"In the end, it was her choice."

"Even so, someone else should have gone. Not her."

"You are not to blame, Mara. And she will return."

Mara remained silent for a moment. "Even if she does return and I am not to blame for Aleth's death, it won't change anything. For even if Urehel falls, and the last stone of creation is finally destroyed, there will always be someone possessed by evil. Whether the enemy from Um-Atra is defeated or not, the lies that he has sown into the hearts of the Aedan, men, and most of all, the dwarves, are a terrible seed. It will never fully die out, nor can it ever be completely destroyed. From time to time, it will sprout again, bearing its dark fruit until the very last day."

Enwir looked at his sister, her words filling him with sorrow and fear, for they made it painfully clear that peace and happiness would never truly last, even if Urehel was vanquished.

"Then what are we fighting for?" Mara's voice trembled as she turned her glassy gaze toward her brother.

"For *our* lives," Enwir responded firmly. "For the lives of our children. Even if your dark words are true, at least your life and mine will no longer be threatened once Urehel is overthrown. Let us fight so that we and our children might live in peace after our destined battles have been fought."

They both fell silent, the only sound the distant crash of the waves against the cliffs upon which the harbor city was built. The waves seemed to break and dissolve, as if they had never existed at all.

"The stone has been found," Mara murmured, her eyes fixed on the horizon as though hoping to catch a glimpse of the light of Mencael, which she longed to see more than ever.

Enwir said nothing, though her words shocked him. He kept his emotions tightly in check.

"For many years - perhaps decades - it remained hidden in the mountains, hoarded by the darkness itself in small caves and passages. But it was stolen from the dark by a child, one of the half-folk of the North. Dartur told me this just days ago, before he set off on his journey. He said he would try to destroy the stone's power, though he wasn't sure if he could succeed. I fear his path will lead him through great darkness, filled with pain, sorrow, and perhaps even death. I only wish I could have gone with him, to stand by his side and do whatever it takes to rid the world of that cursed object. It was the overwhelming allure of those stones of creation that turned Urehel into what he is now. He was once one of the seven High Aedan, more powerful and noble than any creature in all of Daraën. But the black light of the stone and the lies it brought into the world gradually darkened his heart until only his corrupted soul remained."

Mara took a deep breath. "I've given up hope of saving everyone from evil. Some are beyond redemption, no matter how carefully I choose my words. I once believed that no one was born evil. But now, I'm not so sure. In the eyes of the soldiers returning from battle, I've seen enough to know that no matter how hard we fight to make life worth living, in the end, we will all die. And with each passing day, as I sit behind Dinambad's mighty walls - safe, yet still trapped - watching the hope in people's hearts slowly fade, my own heart fills with sorrow. Soon, I fear, it will break entirely."

She sighed deeply. "And more than ever, I realize now that my place was never here in Dinambad. A powerful force is pulling me far away from here."

Enwir stared at his sister, unable to fully understand her words.

"Do you remember the capital of Anros?" she asked. "Westhawen. Such a beautiful, enchanting place. The intricate carvings in the wood, with symbols of mighty bulls, majestic horses, fantastic flowers, and other wondrous creatures. Or the vibrant, fragrant gardens of Suthawen? Have you ever seen them? Just once - one last time - I want to gaze upon the endless beauty of the wild gardens with my own eyes."

"It's been a while since we were last in Westhawen, long before the days grew as dark as they are now. Much has changed there since then. Still, I won't deny that Anros has its own kind of beauty. Yet I can't shake the feeling that the people of the Wildlands live more like peasants, simple folk without grandeur or real value."

"What good is this grandeur to us here?" Mara replied. "It only blinds us to what truly matters in life. Trust, loyalty, and love - these are everyday things in Anros, yet here, in the Land of Stone, you find little of them left. The people are afraid, but they do nothing about the growing, looming threat from Um-Atra. Soon it will be too late, and all of Miénast will fall. We live far too close to the enemy from both the north and south for anyone here to see what's really happening."

"Not all of us are blind," Enwir countered.

"But most are, and even that is too many."

"Are you truly planning to leave your home? To abandon your family? People here will call you a coward, accuse you of fleeing from the threat of Um-Atra. They'll lose all trust in you."

"You can't lose something you never had," Mara said, her voice steady. "And you know better than anyone that I'm no coward, nor am I running away. I'm simply trying to find the place where I truly belong. The cold, pale stone walls and paved streets of Dinambad smother all the beauty of nature that once filled this city. Iron and stone, as far as the eye can see. Only the endless expanse of the great sea remains, a reminder of the once vibrant and living city, though today, little of that is left. I feel trapped, as though I'm locked in a prison, unable to move, unable to feel free."

"The people here love the pristine white marble that covers the city. The iron and stone represent progress for our economy, and the walls protect us from the enemy. They are necessary." Enwir cast a glance across the cityscape. "To me, there is no place more beautiful than our home, Dinambad, the city of the snow-white swan, surrounded by the blue sea." He turned to his sister, studying her. "But is it really the city you're restless about, Mara? I see a longing in your eyes that nothing here can satisfy. What is it you truly desire, I wonder?"

But Mara dared not answer. She feared admitting the truth to her brother, the truth about what tugged at her heart.

Enwir, however, seemed to sense what she was thinking. "Don't forget where you belong, sister. You are the daughter of the Lord of Dinambad, from Miénast - not some lowly stable maid from Anros. Don't waste your beauty and noble bearing on those worthless peasants and filthy cave-dwellers! They are beneath you."

A terrible rage ignited within Mara, searing through her. Though she knew her brother held such views about the people of Anros, hearing them so blatantly from his lips filled her with fury. "What do you know?" she spat, leaping to her feet. Her fists clenched, nails digging painfully into her palms as she stared him down with blazing eyes. "You have no right to judge others, especially those you've never met. The people of Anros may be different from us, but they are not lesser. In fact, they treasure things that have long lost their worth here. Loyalty to their king, trust in one another - those things still mean something in Anros. But what value do they hold here?" Her voice shook with passion. "Where I'm drawn is none of your concern, and there's nothing you can do to change that - especially not when you speak so arrogantly about people who mean something to me."

"Forgive my choice of words, but it pains me to see my sister give her heart to a man who isn't worthy of her," Enwir said, his voice laced with frustration.

"How can you speak of him that way?" Mara's voice trembled with restrained anger. "Is the king of Anros just a simple man to you as well? I don't seek glory, wealth, or a life bathed in honor and prestige. I don't want an arrogant king by my side. I'd rather spend my life alone."

"What about Tharon, the heir to the throne?" Enwir pressed.

"I don't wish to be the wife of a king."

"And as the wife of a peasant, you'll starve and wither away," Enwir stood now, his stance rigid. "As the wife of a soldier, one day you'll receive word that your beloved husband has fallen in battle. Are you strong enough to bear that kind of pain?"

Mara turned away from him, her gaze fixed on the endless stretch of sea before her. She took a few steps forward, resting her arms on the stone railing as if it were the only thing anchoring her to the moment.

Enwir stood in silence for a moment, watching her with a deepening concern. "You'll neither find a home nor be welcomed in the land of the Wilds," he said softly, "because that's not where you belong. Don't forget where your place is."

"*Min ihrest varcu, tha mihrest cariaemna min avar,*" Mara whispered, her voice heavy with sorrow as she spoke in Aerin, the ancient language known by few in the cities of men.

Enwir stared at his sister, confused and thoughtful, unable to grasp the meaning of her words. He, too, had never mastered the language of the Aedan and had no idea what she had said.

Mara, sensing his bewilderment, translated the words for him. "My heart is empty, for it belongs forever to my father."

The weight of her words settled over Enwir like a dark cloud. Guilt began to creep into his mind, the painful realization that his harsh words had caused her more pain than he had intended. But his pride, stubborn as ever, refused to let him show it. In silence, he turned and walked away.

Mara was left standing alone. Tears welled in her eyes as she stared out over the sea, wishing more than ever that she could be someone else - someone for whom it didn't matter where her heart truly belonged.

☾

When Aleth finally awoke, it was already late afternoon, and the sun hung low in the western sky. It took her a moment to realize where she was, for this was not the place where she had expected to be. The Aedin lay on a simple bed within a small tent, alone. Exhausted from her long journey, she sat up slowly, casting a tired glance over herself.

Just then, a young woman, petite with dark blonde hair that bordered on brown, tied hastily into a loose braid, entered the tent. She pulled back her hood and looked down at Aleth with concern. "Finally, you're awake," she said softly.

"Fria," Aleth replied, both relieved and confused. "Where am I? How did I get here?"

"You're in a hunters' camp north of Libentya. Some of the men found you unconscious in an open field, covered in blood and dirt. They brought you here for safety." Fria sat down beside her on the edge of the bed. "What happened?"

Aleth's mind raced as she tried to piece together what had transpired. "I was heading east... further than any of us have ever gone. I saw the Lord of Iushvhatu, the Black Sorcerer. And I..." Her voice began to falter as the memory of the dark crystal surfaced. Almost instinctively, she reached into her pouch, desperately seeking its presence.

But the stone was gone.

"Where is it?" Aleth asked, panic creeping into her voice. "Where is it?"

Fria hesitated, then slowly withdrew something from her own pouch. She held it up for Aleth to see - a dark, shimmering crystal that seemed to pulse ominously in the dim light. "Is this what you're looking for?"

"Give it to me!" Aleth lunged forward, her hand outstretched.

But Fria swiftly closed her hand around the stone, stepping back in alarm. "Where did you get this thing?"

Aleth stammered, her thoughts disjointed, before she managed to speak clearly. "It's the Black Sorcerer's crystal. I took it from Iushvhatu."

"Have you used it?"

"No." Aleth shook her head frantically.

"Then why did you bring it with you? Why didn't you leave it where it belongs?"

"I couldn't." Aleth looked away in shame, her gaze falling again on the clenched fist in which Fria now held the crystal.

"It was a mistake," Fria said coldly as she turned her back to Aleth, opening her hand once more to gaze at the cursed stone. She seemed transfixed by it, as if an unseen voice were whispering softly in her ear. Aleth watched in horror as Fria's expression shifted, her eyes glazing over as though entranced by the stone's dark allure.

Aleth realized too late what Fria intended to do. Only when the young commander allowed the stone to rest flat in her palm, raising her other hand slowly above it, did Aleth fully grasp the gravity of the situation.

"Fria! No!" Aleth shouted, leaping forward and grabbing her friend by the shoulders, pulling her back before the dark power could be unleashed. "It's a mistake!"

Fria wrenched herself free, turning her back on Aleth. She clenched the stone tightly in her fist, her knuckles white with tension. Before Aleth could react, Fria disappeared entirely - the stone rendering her invisible. But its power extended far beyond mere concealment.

"Fria!" Aleth cried, now more fearful than angry. But there was no response.

Outside the tent, chaos erupted. Panic spread through the camp as hunters ran in every direction, their shouts and screams filled with terror.

Aleth hesitated, then stepped outside, scanning the scene in disbelief.

One of the hunters sprinted toward her, breathless and wild-eyed. "Run! They're here!" he gasped.

"Who?" Aleth demanded, but the hunter offered no answer. Instead, he gazed eastward with a look of abject horror.

Following his gaze, Aleth saw it - a dark, massive shadow advancing through the trees, like a tidal wave of destruction rolling through the forest. She stood frozen in place, paralyzed by fear.

As the darkness surged closer, the hunters fled, disappearing into the wilderness. Yet no one looked back for Aleth. She was left alone, her heart pounding as the shadow closed in around her.

☾

Lord Ráhad sat upon the throne in the hall of his forefathers, staring into the void with a distant, weary gaze. He looked older than his years, burdened and worn as though the weight of the world had settled upon his shoulders.

At that moment, Mara entered the hall, hesitating a few steps from the door, watching her father with concern.

"Come closer, my child," he beckoned, his voice heavy but gentle.

With some reluctance, she approached the throne, stopping before the narrow white steps. "You asked to speak with me, Father?"

Ráhad looked down at his daughter, his silence lingering before he finally spoke. "I received word from Dinhad of Mahlrit - word that the enemy's weapon has been found. The time has come for you to begin your journey to the far north." He paused, his gaze softening as it rested on her. "Though I wish with all my heart you could stay here, I know now I cannot shield you from your fate, no matter how much I try to keep you safe. The lives of many now rest in your hands. Do not fail them, for they place their trust in you - they would follow you anywhere, even into death, if need be."

He sighed deeply, a man wrestling with the weight of his decision. "I release you now from the chains I unwittingly placed upon you. You are free to act as you see fit. I will no longer stand in your way. Go now, and return to us soon."

His voice grew quieter, tinged with sorrow. "Do what you were born to do, *Althûbeael* - as Adraéth named you when she first laid eyes upon you. She taught me its meaning - 'Light of Hope' in our tongue. That name was given to you by the High Aedin, Mylias of Faldar. You were destined for greatness, my dear daughter. It's no coincidence you wear the powerful stone around your neck, gifted to you by Othorin."

A flicker of fear crossed Mara's face as she raised her gaze to meet his. "I am afraid, for in my heart I wished you would forbid this journey to Dunhir. But you have not. And yet, I am thankful you finally trust in my abilities. I will not fail anyone - least of all you."

At her words, Ráhad rose swiftly from his throne and descended the steps to her, his face filled with warmth. "You could never disappoint me." He smiled kindly. "Everything you do, no matter what it is, fills me with pride. You have shown me that of my four children, the youngest and seemingly most unassuming is the mightiest of them all." He embraced her tightly. "You are the greatest and most precious gift I have ever been given, and letting you go now is a trial for my patience. But I will endure it, for you were chosen for this, and in time, you will realize just how powerful you truly are, Mara."

He held her in his arms for a moment longer, then stepped back, his eyes glistening with emotion. "Farewell, my beloved daughter. May all the luck in the world be with you on the path ahead - and even more than that."

Ó

At dawn, Mara descended the long steps from the palace of the Lord of Dinambad, stopping before a well-armed and armored troop of fifty mounted soldiers. Her silver armor gleamed in the early morning light, adorned with the white swan and two crossed swords on a blue field - the emblem of Dinambad - emblazoned on her chest-plate. A long, dark blue cloak flowed behind her as she mounted her grey warhorse and placed a helm upon her head. Before riding off, she cast one final glance up the long stairs, where, in the shadows of the palace, a slender figure waved to her with a hint of sorrow. It was Adraéth, bidding her farewell. Mara smiled faintly, hoping this was not the last time she would see her trusted friend, for the long journey ahead filled her with dread.

But it was no longer her choice which path to follow - she would do what was required of her, as long as she had the strength to see it through. With a heavy heart, she looked to the sturdy riders around her and nodded to Finmar of Folares, her commander, signaling him to lead the way.

Finmar's powerful voice echoed across the plains as he called his men to move out. Slowly, the cavalry began their march. Mara, at the center, led them through Dinambad's grand gates, riding north along the harbor before turning eastward onto the main road that would take them toward Mahlrit. By evening, they reached the capital nestled at the foot of a towering mountain range. As the sun dipped below the horizon, its fading light bathed the ever-white mountain peaks in an ominous red glow, as though the very sky had been wounded, its blood staining the jagged summits.

Mara gazed southward with melancholy, where distant smoke once again rose from the ruins of Libentya, barely visible in the great expanse. Her heart grew heavy as her thoughts turned to her friend Aleth, uncertain whether she would ever see her again. Aleth's fate remained unknown, just as her own was clouded by uncertainty. Guilt gnawed at her, for she had wished to take Aleth's place on that perilous path, but that choice had been denied her. Now, she carried a burden that weighed heavily upon her.

6

Mahlrit, once only a great, impregnable fortress in the days when Dinambad was still the shining capital of Miénast, now sprawled around the Mâhl, the largest mountain of the range, connected to Tin Uael by two steep, saddle-like stone ridges. The city's three great walls, carved from the surrounding rock, blended seamlessly into the rugged mountains behind them. At the highest tier of the city stood Fheran's Tower - a solitary, grey spire that jutted starkly into the sky.

It was there that Dinhad often sat in his stubborn solitude. In the uppermost chamber of the tower, he had placed one of the seeing stones, ancient relics brought from Tanuhal by King Manardur II, which allowed him to glimpse events before they occurred. It was through this stone that he had seen Mara embarking on the same journey as his son, Torhael. But he had also glimpsed something else that piqued his interest even more - a dark blue stone hanging from a silver chain around Mara's neck, emanating a rare power.

Blinded by greed, Dinhad had scoured the ancient records of Farham, desperate to learn more about the mysterious stone. Though the writings revealed little, he had at least discovered its name: Alarmár, derived from the words *aláuma* and *márta,* meaning *Blessed Fortune.* In Miénast, it was known by this name, but in Anros and the northwestern lands, it was called *Bariltincu* - the *Blue Stone.* In the House of Andor, it had been the royal jewel, passed down with the crown since the founding of Anros, until the day Urwen, the son of Irmen, second king of Anros and grandson of Andor, faced a wild beast alone, the same beast that had claimed the lives of his sons, Aethain and Aelac. Urwen never took his rightful place on the throne in the newly built King's Hall in Westhawen, the legacy of his father. Nor did the Bariltincu, for it vanished with Urwen into the wild paths, never to be seen again.

The stone had long been thought lost, its memory fading with the years. But in his vision, Dinhad had seen Mara wearing the Bariltincu, a stone thought to be forever lost in the lairs of beasts where no man had ever returned. Now, fear gripped Dinhad, for he knew the dreadful tales of those untrodden paths high in the mountains, and none who ventured there had ever come back.

Despite this fear, Mara now bore the lost Bariltincu, unknowingly carrying a relic that tied her fate to the wilds and the horrors that lurked there. Her journey was not just one of destiny but also one of danger, fraught with the unknown and the ever-looming shadow of the past.

They rested only briefly in Mahlrit, for the road ahead was long and treacherous. As the sun disappeared behind the dark shadows of night, casting all of Miénast - the noble land of stone masons - into darkness, they rode onward. Their path led them onto the great trade road that connected the capitals of the two kingdoms, Miénast and Anros, winding around the vast foothills of the Tin Uael. They crossed the mighty river Uael, which flowed southward to the forests of Libentya before bending into the Areglin, and by dawn, they reached the ancient mountain settlement of Uswang, situated at the border of Anros. Without stopping, they passed through the old city gate, riding along the base of the snow-capped mountains until they finally entered the kingdom of Anros, the Wilds.

11

The hunters fled in panic from the camp north of Libentya, scattering deep into the dense woods, but no matter how fast they ran, they could not escape the terror that pursued them. Aleth ran amidst the group, weaving between the broad trees, the piercing screeches of the dark creatures from Iushvhatu closing in behind them. A shiver ran down her spine as she risked a glance over her shoulder, seeing the shadowy figures, cloaked in darkness, galloping towards them on black, spectral horses, mere meters away.

Near the old road that led directly to Mahlrit, the creatures managed to cut Aleth off from the other hunters, surrounding her. Gasping for breath, she stood trapped as the Lord of Iushvhatu dismounted his grey-black steed, followed by his dark followers. They formed a tight circle around her, drawing their long swords as they advanced slowly.

"Return what you have stolen!" the Dark Mage shrieked, thrusting his empty hand greedily forward.

"I don't have it," Aleth replied, meeting his gaze without fear.

The Lord of Iushvhatu let out a blood-curdling scream, so powerful it sent flocks of birds from the surrounding trees into the air, and Aleth, trembling, dropped to her knees in terror. Slowly, the dark lord raised his blade high, ready to strike her down. Aleth squeezed her eyes shut, bracing herself for the final blow, her heart pounding in despair as she awaited death.

But just as the blade was about to fall, something yanked her violently to the side, pulling her out of the deadly path. When she dared to open her eyes again, she found herself inside a cave, far from the shadowy figures. She was safe.

She looked up and saw Fria, crouched on a small rock, clutching the black gemstone in her hand. Fria stood and approached Aleth, her expression dark and heavy with sorrow. "I've seen terrible things," she said, her voice tinged with the weight of an overwhelming darkness.

Aleth, still shaken, gazed at her friend, noticing how much older and more worn Fria appeared in just a few short hours.

"Destroy it - or at least get rid of it!" Fria's voice was sharp, and her eyes burned with a cold, distant anger. "I'll never touch it again. The things I saw... they fill me with sorrow."

"What did you see?" Aleth asked, rising slowly, curiosity and dread battling within her.

Fria sighed deeply. "I saw Torhael, my brother... pierced by countless swords and spears." Her voice wavered. "I watched him die. I don't know if it has already happened or if it will, but I refuse to believe it. Perhaps it was just a cruel illusion, a lie meant to deceive me. No," she shouted, her voice breaking. "I won't believe it until I see it with my own eyes." She paused, her gaze shifting to the gemstone in her hand. "But there was more. I saw... him."

Her eyes widened with fear as she recalled the vision. "He spoke to me. Asked me questions, but I couldn't answer. I could only stare into his face, surrounded by shadows. I felt a darkness inside me, deeper than any night I've ever known." She looked back at Aleth, her voice shaking. "I never want to see that face again."

Fria dropped the gemstone as if it had suddenly become searing hot, and it rolled to Aleth's feet. "Take it. I want nothing to do with it. Destroy it while you still can. The power it holds is far beyond anything even your magic can withstand. I'm going to gather my men and return to Mahlrit. I don't care what you do next, Aleth, and I don't want to know. You've brought this danger here with your blindness to the darkness it carries, and now it's your responsibility to deal with it."

With those words, Fria turned and left the cave, disappearing into the trees without a backward glance.

Aleth remained behind, silent, staring down at the gemstone. Slowly, she bent and picked it up, holding it gingerly in her hand. Mesmerized, she stared into its depths, unable to tear her gaze away, as though caught in a spell.

6

After a wide turn toward the northwest, the group, led by Finmar with Mara close by his side, rode along the Great West Road. This route passed through the Suthwand, where the ancient capital Suthawen once stood, wound through the Westlad, near the royal seat of Westhawen, and finally led through the Gate of Anros - situated between the Tin Uael and Tin Elwech mountains - before joining the North-South Road into the old kingdom of Nyarost.

As they reached the border between Suthwand and Ostlad, in the vast plains of Elwech, they set up a small camp for the night, even though dawn was only a few hours away. Few among the riders found restful sleep. Most lay with their eyes closed, too troubled by fear to truly slumber. However, with less than two days to traverse the kingdom of Anros, this brief rest was a necessary reprieve, essential for the journey ahead.

Like Finmar, Mara could not sleep. She sat by a small campfire, adding wood to the warming flames, while her mind was restless. The proximity to Suthawen, the former capital, stirred memories of Aric that refused to let her find peace.

After a while, Finmar approached and sat beside her, weariness etched on his face. "Forgive my words, my lady," he said, looking at the princess with deep respect. "But isn't it unwise to undertake such a long journey in these dangerous times?"

"It is, indeed," Mara replied, her gaze fixed on the dancing flames. "But it must be done, Finmar. So commands my father, and his will is yours to follow."

"And do you not wish it yourself?" Finmar asked, sensing the despair hidden in her voice.

Mara glanced at him briefly. "What I wish is of no consequence. The days have grown dark, and they will grow darker still. Even the bravest warlord would know fear now, but I cannot dwell on that. A task lies before me, one with an uncertain end, and I cannot see far enough ahead to know what awaits us. Though part of me is glad to play a more important role in these troubled times, I am also afraid. I am not infallible, and there are many stronger and braver than I. Yet it is the hope for brighter days that gives me the strength to carry on through the darkest hours. One day, peace will come, and it will last long enough for the world to heal from all the suffering it has endured. People will be happy again, without fear or sorrow. That day is coming, I promise you. Even if I do not live to see it, my deeds will not be forgotten so easily."

"None will ever forget you," Finmar replied, his voice filled with admiration. "There is no woman in all of Farham more noble and wise than you. Braver and more just than all the men of Miénast combined, yet cautious and thoughtful. And your beauty, like the morning dew and the evening sunset entwined, rivals even the untarnished, radiant stars in their glory. It is not your fate to fall in battle. Such a loss would be immeasurable. If you were to die, so too would all our hopes. You are destined for far greater things - that much I can see, as if I were looking into the future. But it's enough for me to gaze upon that shining blue gemstone around your neck."

Mara glanced down at the stone hanging from her necklace, and for a moment, it seemed to glow faintly, as if a fire had ignited within its core. Yet, it remained cool to the touch. The young woman spent the remaining hours of her rest in silence, mesmerized by the strange light of the gemstone, as it flickered softly in the darkness.

6

The deafening roar of battle cries filled the night, underscored by the thunderous pounding of hooves and the fierce clash of swords. Fala and Aric fought side by side, leading their brave riders in what felt like a hopeless struggle against a much larger horde of Celkûn. They fought valiantly, mustering every ounce of courage they had, but the oppressive darkness of the night gave their enemies a deadly advantage. Things looked grim for the king's daughter and nephew, though the king himself had no idea of their peril. Once again, Fala and Aric had ridden out without the king's permission, seeking to push back the enemy forces at the southern and eastern borders. They might have succeeded if not for a hidden enemy battalion that ambushed them near their camp. From this trap, there was no escape.

The numbers of Anros' soldiers dwindled far too quickly, and soon only a handful remained, clustered with Fala and Aric as the Celkûn closed in around them. If no help arrived soon, the night would end in tragedy, claiming not only the king's only surviving child and heir but also his nephew - who had become as dear to him as his own son. With their deaths, Anros itself would fall. A kingdom without an heir is worth nothing, and Henric, old and weary, had few years left. Without his children, he would lose all hope and likely plunge into despair, seeking his own end. Fala and Aric knew this well, but now they could do nothing to change it. Their deaths seemed inevitable, and neither expected to see the dawn.

But then, through the suffocating darkness, they noticed something approaching from the south - hoofbeats pounding the earth in a rapid, growing rhythm. Soon, they saw the glint of silver in the moonlight, the flash of a sword leading a charge. And then they recognized the armor of the approaching riders, emblazoned with the white swan of Dinambad. Hope rekindled within them. The force from Miénast crashed into the Celkûn, felling many of the dark creatures, though they lost some of their own in the fierce combat. Yet the riders pressed on, driving the enemy back.

At the head of the charge was Mara, her silver armor gleaming as she fought her way through the chaos. She saw Aric surrounded by Celkûn and, for a moment, a horrible vision flashed before her eyes - a grim premonition of his fate. In that instant of distraction, a massive Celek warrior struck her with brutal force, knocking her from her horse. Mara and her steed fell to the ground, and she tumbled into a cluster of enemies who had been lurking in the shadows. She scrambled to her feet, her sword flashing like a beacon of fire in the dark, carving a path through her foes. She fought desperately to reach Aric and Fala, but the Celkûn pressed her back, driving her further away until she found herself at the edge of the Ghostwood. From there, she could no longer see the others.

A towering Celek captain, larger and broader than the rest, blocked her path. His greedy eyes locked onto the glowing blue stone hanging around her neck. With a wicked grin, he raised his weapon and struck at her with savage fury. Mara fought back with all her strength, but the captain's brute force was overwhelming. He slashed deep wounds into her, and she fell, weakened, her sword slipping from her grasp onto the churned earth.

The Celek captain laughed cruelly as he approached her. "You may be strong, woman, but not strong enough to stand against the united armies of Iushvhatu and Um-Atra," he sneered, his voice dripping with malice. Raising his jagged blade high, he prepared to deliver the final blow.

Mara raised her hand to shield herself, praying for salvation in her final moments. But no rescue came. She was alone, at the mercy of fate.

As the captain's sword came crashing down with enough force to cleave a boulder in two, the blade struck something unyielding. The Celek staggered back, astonished to see that his blow had been stopped by a radiant, blue-flaming light that enveloped the fallen woman. His strike had done nothing.

Mara opened her eyes, stunned to find herself still alive. Seizing the moment, she crawled toward the shadowy refuge of the Ghostwood. The Celek captain hesitated, unwilling to follow her into the haunted forest. She didn't look back, dragging herself deeper into the woods, where the trees and shadows offered protection from her enemies. In her desperation, she failed to notice the ominous atmosphere of the Ghostwood, the unnatural danger lurking in the twisted branches and undergrowth. She stumbled through the dense thicket, her strength rapidly fading, until she tripped over a large root and became entangled in the gnarled branches.

Unbeknownst to her, the chain of her necklace, with its glowing blue stone, caught on a low-hanging branch. She staggered a few more steps before collapsing, her wounds too severe, her energy utterly spent. In the thick, suffocating darkness of the Ghostwood, Mara's body crumpled to the forest floor, lost to the shadows."

The sun rose that morning, casting a dim, blood-red light across the sky, bringing no hope with its glow. Aric trudged across the battlefield, his mind distant, haunted by the strange blue light he had glimpsed the night before at the edge of the Ghostwood, a place no living soul dared to enter willingly. Fear gnawed at him, wondering what or who might have caused that eerie glow. But more than that, he was searching for something, driven by an obsession as he stepped over the lifeless bodies strewn across the desolate land. Finally, he stopped, staring in horror at the ground beneath him.

"Aric!" Fala's voice called out as she approached him, but he didn't respond.

He knelt in the dirt and reached down to pull a valuable sword from the earth. His hand trembled as he held it up, recognizing the weapon immediately. "No," he whispered, his voice choked with grief. He gazed upon the silver sword, its hilt adorned with the noble insignia of a swan and the rune-inscribed blade, now stained with blood and dulled by battle.

Fala came to stand beside her cousin, and as soon as her eyes fell upon the sword in Aric's hands, she too understood to whom it belonged. "Men!" she shouted, her voice sharp and laced with panic as she turned to the remaining riders of Anros, who were dragging the bodies of their fallen comrades from the field. "Find Princess Mara! She must be here somewhere!"

But Aric remained motionless, staring down at the sword in silence, his heart heavy with sorrow. Finmar, the captain of Mara's escort, approached with a downcast gaze, bowing respectfully before them. "She has fallen," he said, his voice strained and broken. "I saw her struck down by a great Celek, and I was powerless to stop it."

"What was she doing here?" Aric fought to control the anguish rising in his chest.

"She was not meant to be here," Finmar sighed, his words heavy with regret. "The princess was supposed to travel north to Dunhir. This was merely a stop on our journey."

Aric's gaze turned bitter as he looked at the captain. "Was there no other route from your lands to the north that didn't take her through this dangerous, deadly region? I warned her not to come. Anros is perilous - entering it was a grave mistake. And now..." His voice faltered, and he swallowed the pain. "Now she is lost forever." He stared into the void, his heart breaking.

Fala gently placed a comforting hand on his shoulder, her eyes filled with concern. "Do not despair, cousin. She has not been found yet, and until she is, we cannot say she has fallen."

"My lady," one of the riders called cautiously as he stepped closer to them. "We cannot find her. It's as if the earth itself opened up and swallowed her whole. Princess Mara is not here."

This revelation brought no comfort to Aric. The uncertainty gnawed at him, and the pain in his heart deepened, filled with the torment of not knowing her fate.

"Burn the remains of the creatures," Fala ordered her men before turning to Finmar. "Come with us to Westhawen. Many fell last night, but thanks to your aid, not all of us perished. My father will want to thank you and your men personally for saving his daughter and nephew."

Finmar's expression darkened with sorrow. "Our lady is gone. Without her, we cannot continue to Dunhir. We've traveled far with little rest, but duty compels me to return to Prince Ráhad and deliver the dreadful news of his daughter's loss, though the thought fills me with dread. He must be told immediately."

"Westhawen may not lie on your path home, but I ask you for just a short time. I wish to know more about what is happening in the north," Fala pleaded.

The captain nodded after a brief pause. "As the king's daughter and a loyal ally of our lord, I cannot refuse your request. But we can only stay briefly and share what we know. After that, we must return home as swiftly as we can."

6

At midday, the few remaining riders of Anros, accompanied by a small contingent of soldiers from Dinambad, returned to Westhawen. At the front rode Fala and Finmar, while Aric followed them silently, lost in thought. The exhausted men led their horses into the grand stables, where fresh, lush feed awaited. But the three leaders continued onward, riding up to the great hall of the king. As they ascended the steps, they were abruptly halted at the doors by Eruhad, captain of the king's guard, and Anlac, a sentry from Suthawen.

"What is the meaning of this?" Fala's voice flared with anger. "You dare to block the path of the king's daughter?"

"Not yours, my lady," Eruhad stammered. "You and Lord Aric may enter, of course, but not the outsider."

"Who gave you the right to decide that?" she demanded.

"The king himself," Anlac replied, his gaze shifting uneasily toward Aric. In the young commander's silent expression, he saw deep sorrow.

"I command you to let him through." Fala's eyes blazed as she stared down the guards. "This is Finmar, a great captain from Dinambad. His men saved both Aric's life and mine last night. For their bravery, they deserve honor, not banishment."

"You three do not look especially grateful, if I may say so," Anlac observed, his eyes falling on the gleaming silver sword in Aric's hands - the one with the swan-emblazoned hilt. His face paled, for he immediately knew whose sword it was.

"Many fell last night," Fala said sadly, glancing at her cousin. "Some losses are simply unbearable."

"Very well, enter," Eruhad said, stepping aside with Anlac to open the door for them. "You've suffered enough. But do not seek gratitude or forgiveness in the king's hall, for neither will be found here. Henric's mind is troubled, and he no longer knows what he speaks - if he speaks at all."

Confused by Eruhad's ominous words, Fala, Finmar, and finally Aric stepped into the king's hall. They walked toward the rear, where the wooden throne stood empty and forlorn, and found Nariya crouched beside it, her posture low and despondent.

"Where is my father?" Fala's voice was sharp with suspicion. "What has happened here?"

"King Henric was so consumed with worry over you, my lady, that he fell into a terrible fever," Nariya replied, her voice dripping with mock sympathy. "He is gravely ill now, all because of you."

"Silence, you wretched snake!" the princess spat, fury rising.

"Do you not see how your harsh and cruel words have wounded the king time and again?" Nariya straightened to her full height, towering over the princess. "Mind your tongue, or will you be the one to drive your poor father to his death?"

Fala, enraged, lunged at Nariya, intent on grabbing her, but Aric swiftly intervened, pulling her back without a word. "She's not worth it," he said quietly, his tone steady despite the tension in the room.

Nariya's sharp eyes fell upon the sword in Aric's hand, the one that unmistakably belonged to Princess Mara. Her interest was piqued, but before she could speak, Aasa rushed into the hall and stood between them. As her eyes landed on Mara's sword, her face shifted from hope to sorrow, her gaze heavy with grief.

"Tell me it's not true!" Aasa's voice trembled with desperation as she looked from Fala to Aric, her expression pleading.

Neither could find the words to respond. The weight of the truth was too much to bear, and speaking it aloud would only deepen their own suffering.

But Aasa didn't need them to say it. The anguish etched into Aric's face told her everything she needed to know. Tears streamed down her delicate cheeks, falling silently as she understood the terrible fate that had befallen her dear friend.

"She wanted to help us," Aric whispered in agony.

"Why did she come back?" Aasa asked, her voice trembling with emotion.

"The princess didn't return," Finmar replied, his voice heavy with grief. "She was merely passing through. My men and I were tasked with escorting her safely to Dunhir. But we failed miserably. The weight of our failure is unbearable, and the pain of her loss cuts deeper than we could have ever imagined."

"I need to see her!" Aasa demanded stubbornly. "I won't believe it otherwise."

"She's gone," the captain from Miénast said softly. "No one could find her after she was struck down by a giant Celek."

Aasa's heart darkened, and sorrow overwhelmed her. She had placed all her hopes in Mara - a woman so much like herself. She had always believed the princess was stronger, untouchable by any foe. But she had been wrong. Mara, like herself, was just a mortal. How could she have ever been the beacon of hope that Aasa had dreamed her to be?

In the throes of unspeakable grief, Aric silently began to walk away, seeking solitude. But Aasa, desperate, hurried after him, catching him at the door.

"Wait!" she called.

Aric turned to face her, his expression tortured, his eyes distant.

"I don't believe she's dead," Aasa said, her voice urgent. "My heart tells me she's still alive."

"No," Aric's voice cracked with anguish. "She's truly gone. If she were still alive, we would have found her. She's lost forever, and nothing will ease the pain her death has brought me."

"Your sorrow blinds you, brother, clouding your sharp mind. I won't believe it until I see her with my own eyes."

Aric showed no interest in her words, his gaze vacant as he continued walking away.

But Aasa grabbed his hand, clutching it tightly. "Before grief consumes you and you throw away her sword, give it to me," she pleaded. "I will keep it safe and guard it - though I won't use it unless you wish me to. Please, just let me have it! I have nothing else to remember her by. But you, you have her love. Nothing else she could have given would be more precious."

With a heavy heart, Aric loosened his grip on the blade, letting it fall into his sister's hands.

Aasa held it up reverently, a flicker of hope shining briefly in her eyes. But just then, Nariya approached them, stepping close with malicious intent. She was eager to deepen Aric's suffering, relishing the chance to twist the knife further.

"My deepest condolences, Aric," she said, her voice dripping with false sympathy. "Your pain must be unbearable. It's quite clear to me - and to many others - that you had a particular fondness for the princess."

An overwhelming rage erupted within Aric, and he seized Nariya roughly by the collar. "I don't want your sympathy! Don't you dare speak of her, you snake! Your venomous words have already caused enough harm." He shoved her away with force.

"Then perhaps you don't care that a messenger from her homeland, Dinambad, arrived here a few days ago." Nariya pulled out a letter, the one she had hidden for quite some time. "He carried this message, addressed to you, from Princess Mara herself."

Aric snatched the letter from her hand. "Why do you have this? Did you steal it?"

"No, my lord," Nariya replied, suddenly meek. "I swear, I found it."

"I don't believe you," Aasa interjected, her gaze piercing. "How would you know it was brought by a messenger from Dinambad if you merely 'found' it? You're lying. I saw the way you watched Mara with suspicion when she was a guest here. You feared her from the start. Admit you stole it."

"I didn't," Nariya insisted, though her growing nervousness betrayed her.

Aric pushed her away again, this time harder, sending her sprawling onto the cold floor. "You treacherous wretch!" he snarled, advancing slowly, as Nariya scrambled backward on all fours, whimpering. "I'll cut off your head for this."

But before he could draw his sword, Fala rushed between them, placing a calming hand on her cousin's chest. "Aric," she spoke softly, her voice steady. "You told me earlier she wasn't worth it. That still hasn't changed now." She then turned her gaze to Nariya, who was groaning as she struggled to stand. "If you value your life, snake, you'd better disappear this instant. Because I won't be able to hold Aric back much longer, and when I let him go, you'll lose that treacherous head of yours."

Nariya, now trembling, realized that not only Aric but also the king's daughter had become her enemies. She knew she had to find a way to rid herself of both, but for now, she retreated in silence, nursing her bruises, and wasn't seen again for the rest of the day.

Aric, still burning with anger and pain, looked down at the letter in his hand. The red wax seal, embossed with Dinambad's regal swan, had already been broken. Without waiting for anyone to follow him, he retreated to a small chamber behind the throne room and locked the door behind him. He sat down on a wooden bench, the letter heavy in his hand. His heart pounded violently in his chest as he carefully pulled out the parchment. For a moment, he hesitated, his breath shallow and filled with dread. Then, taking a deep breath, he unfolded the letter and began to read, bracing himself for the words within.

After a moment Aric let the letter fall onto his lap, his mind reeling with her words. The deep ache in his chest only grew sharper, more unbearable. It felt as if his heart, already bleeding from sorrow, would be better torn from his chest altogether, if only to end the torment coursing through him. In a surge of overwhelming rage, he leapt to his feet, fury burning through his veins. Anything within his reach met its end at his hands - vases shattered, chairs splintered, and objects smashed against the floor in a storm of destruction, scattering into thousands of pieces, just as his heart had been fractured into countless shards.

He let out a guttural scream of anguish, so fierce it seemed to shake his very soul, before collapsing to the floor, utterly drained. Exhausted, he lay there, consumed by the bitter grief of losing the most precious thing he had ever held in his life. Hot tears of despair rolled down his face as he mourned, knowing that no amount of rage or sorrow could undo the tragedy.

In the midst of his torment, the full weight of his mother's own sorrow struck him - her deep, endless grief from losing her beloved husband in battle. For the first time, Aric truly understood the boundless suffering she must have endured, and in that painful realization, his own heartbreak deepened further.

12

The light that gently filtered through a narrow window shimmered both silver and gold, warming Mara as it softly roused her from sleep. She opened her eyes. Still groggy from the events of the previous night, she glanced around in astonishment. The place where she now found herself was no longer the Ghostwood, which was her last memory. Curious and frightened, she looked in every direction, discovering that she was inside a modest tent. A glance through the tent's small opening revealed a glimmering forest, its colossal trees towering far above any she had ever seen before. Seated beside her on a simple wooden stool was a man with long golden-blonde hair, gray eyes, and strikingly smooth skin. His long, tapered ears peeked out from beneath his silky hair.

"Where am I?" Mara asked as she struggled to sit up.

"In Faldar," the man replied kindly. "I am Aranel." He smiled gently. "I found you far to the west, beyond the Aregnar River, in a place few dare to tread. You were lying still and bloodied among the roots and ominous branches of the Ghostwood, *Morabidan*. At first, I feared I had arrived too late. But I was wrong, and so I brought you here at once."

"But why am I here? I am expected in Dunhir. I don't wish to be late - there are some who eagerly await my arrival and wish to speak with me. I don't want to disappoint them. Please, give me a horse, for mine fled in fear, and let me be on my way."

"All in due time," Aranel said as he stood. "But first, the Lady Mylias wishes to speak with you. There are many things she must share and counsel you on before you continue your journey." He extended his hand to her. "Come, *Althûbeael*." With great care, he helped her from the makeshift bed.

"Why do you call me that?" she asked, confused, as they stepped outside into the twilight, walking together along a broad forest path.

"That name was given to you by the Lady of the Silver Wood herself. It suits you, though you may not see it yet."

Lanterns hung from the thick branches overhead, casting a warm glow on the path lined with vibrant flowers. The trail began to slope upwards, leading over a large root as wide as the path itself, then wound around the trunk of the largest tree in the entire forest. Carved into the wood around the tree were intricate archways, sheltering the stairs from the weather. They crossed a bridge high in the treetops, coming to a broad platform draped in silken cloths and fine carpets. Above them, a brilliant light gleamed - golden and silver in its radiance.

They paused at the foot of a long staircase, waiting in reverent silence. Aranel gazed up the steps, and Mara followed his gaze, her heart swelling with awe and curiosity.

Descending the stairs was a tall, graceful woman. She wore a gleaming silver gown, more radiant than freshly fallen snow, more beautiful than any flawless gemstone. Her long, snow-white hair fell in sleek waves down her back, and her deep blue eyes shimmered with an inner light. She stepped gracefully down the last stair, standing before them.

Though Mara did not know her, nor the immense power she possessed, she bowed low, unable to meet the woman's gaze.

"Rise," the Aedin spoke, her voice both kind and cold, gentle yet commanding.

Hesitantly, Mara stood and looked into her eyes, filled with awe and reverence.

"You have traveled far," the woman continued, "but the path ahead is much longer. You are late, however. I have awaited your arrival, and now, time presses upon us."

"Please forgive me!" Mara recoiled, her voice trembling with humility. "But I do not understand what you speak of. My path was meant to lead me to Dunhir - at least, that was my intention. I know of no other road."

"You know it," the Aedin replied, her smile gentle yet knowing. "But your fear has clouded your understanding. A great danger lies ahead, Althûbeael."

"What danger?" Mara asked, her voice laced with confusion. "Why have you chosen me, when there are surely others far better suited for this task? And why do you call me by this strange name? I know your language well enough, and yet I find no connection between myself and what you call the *Light of Hope*."

"Your name was bestowed upon you long before you were born into this world, for a great destiny was foretold for you. That is why I gave you the Bariltincu, the *Tear of Heaven*. Only one with a pure heart can bear it without succumbing to its torment. But I see with sorrow that you no longer carry it."

Startled, Mara's hand flew to her throat, where she had expected to feel the chain Dartur had gifted her. But the necklace was gone.

"Last night, you lost much - more than just the Alarmár, as the people of the West call it. And I fear you are unaware of the true extent of your loss. Your trusted sword is gone, your loyal horse fled. But most grievously, you have lost your heart."

At these words, Mara's thoughts turned to Aric, and a deep sorrow welled up inside her. She could not even imagine what he must now think, for she was far from his homeland, leaving behind only the haunting evidence of her absence - evidence that would surely lead him to believe she had perished. Here in Faldar, she was safe and alive, but unable to prove it to Aric or to anyone else. The thought of her family and friends suffering in anguish while she remained helpless in this distant land filled her with dread.

"Do not grieve," the Aedin's voice echoed in her mind, though her lips did not move. It was as if she had reached directly into Mara's thoughts, effortlessly unearthing the fears she had not dared to speak aloud. "The pain will fade, and soon you will have the chance to dispel the falsehoods that now cloud the hearts of your loved ones. But for now, there are greater matters at hand. What was found should have remained lost forever, and now it rests in the hands of a boy who does not yet comprehend the vast power of what he holds. For now, he seems immune to its dark influence, but that will not last. In a few weeks, I hope, he will arrive here. But his journey is long, and first, he must go to Dunhir."

"As must I," Mara replied softly. "Dartur awaits me there."

"And you shall go. But listen, Althûbeael, the sands of time have been against you since the moment you first left the safe walls of your city. Aranel will accompany you, but only as far as is necessary. When your task is done, return here, for there is much more we must discuss. But that can wait until we have more time."

Mara found herself unable to speak further, silenced by the weight of the Aedin's words. She looked into her glowing eyes and saw within them a light, bright and dazzling, as though the entire night sky had been captured in their depths. Though the woman had never revealed her name, Mara knew beyond doubt that this was no ordinary Aedin - this was the wise and powerful Lady Mylias herself.

6

The path along the Aregnar heading north was slow and treacherous. To the west, the mighty peak of Elwech, the tallest mountain in the range, loomed snow-covered, guiding the small group that had set out from Faldar just hours ago. They had taken the northern route over the Arensted, the Snow Pass, and though it was the dead of winter - January 12th - the mountains were blanketed in more snow than any had ever seen before. As they left the broader road and entered a narrow, rocky mountain trail, they were forced to dismount, leading their horses behind them. No beast could traverse the deep snow and jagged rocks hidden beneath it without risking injury or worse.

"So much snow," Mara murmured, gazing at the endless white veil draped ominously over the pass. "This can't be natural."

Aranel, walking beside her, nodded. "The Arensted is always buried in snow, year-round. No one has ever seen what lies beneath that frozen blanket. But this... this is more than unusual. Let us hope the weather does not turn against us, or we may have no choice but to turn back."

The higher they climbed, the thicker the clouds became, and the stronger the wind grew. By the time they reached the pass's summit, an icy storm had set in, the snowfall so fierce that visibility was nearly nonexistent. Though the Aedan among them seemed unaffected by the biting cold, their horses struggled through the blizzard.

Mara, however, found the harsh conditions nearly unbearable. Each step was a challenge, and soon she fell behind, barely able to keep up as the path finally began to descend. Every step was an agony, but the hope of meeting Huandar's heir in Dunhir gave her the strength to press on through the freezing gale.

As she fought to follow her companions through the blinding storm, a strange sound reached her ears. A deep voice, carried on the wind from the far north, echoed around her. Though it sounded like a cry for help, the words were too distant to make out. Yet she felt a shiver of recognition. She knew that voice.

"Torhael!" she cried out, halting suddenly. The voice was no longer distant - it rang clear in her ears as though the man stood just beyond her sight. Without hesitation, she turned to follow the sound, determined to find her cousin.

Aranel, who had heard the voice as well, rushed back to her, grabbing her arm and holding her back with great difficulty. "Do not listen!" he shouted over the storm.

"But that's my cousin!" she cried, struggling against him. "I have to help him!"

"You cannot," Aranel urged. "Every voice you hear screaming in these winds comes from beyond our world. Follow them, and you will perish too."

"Torhael..." Mara whimpered, collapsing to her knees, the weight of her helplessness crushing her spirit.

"Stand up!"

But the princess did not move. Her grief in that moment was overwhelming. Seeing this, Aranel grabbed her roughly by the arm and yanked her to her feet. "It's too late," he said urgently, pulling her forward. "We cannot stay here."

Shivering, Mara pulled her cloak tighter around her, trying to shield her neck from the bitter cold. Lost in thought, she trudged behind the Aedan, her mind consumed with worries about her cousin Torhael. She tortured herself with questions about what might have happened to him, hoping desperately that Fria had not yet heard of his fate. Another loss would be too much for her to bear.

As Aranel finally released his grip on her, Mara managed to keep pace for a while. But gradually, she began to lag behind again, struggling more with every step. Determined to focus on her own path rather than dwell on her cousin, she forced herself to catch up with the Aedan ahead of her. After a time, she fell into step behind them once more.

While walking, her gaze drifted to the west, where she spotted faint tracks in the snow. They couldn't have been more than half a day old.

She stopped and studied them, noticing that the tracks abruptly ended, leading back down into the valley as if someone had started to climb the pass but then turned back.

"Aranel," she called, waiting for him to return to her side. When he did, curiosity filled his eyes as she pointed to the tracks. "What does this mean?"

"It means we're not the only ones who've tried to cross this pass in this merciless weather," Aranel replied. "But it seems they turned back here, likely seeking another route. Whoever they were, unless they were light-footed Aedan or at least as hardy as you, they wouldn't have made it through the pass."

"But if they were trying to reach the other side, what other route could they have taken?"

"The West Road, through the Darkwood, around the entire mountain range, and through the Gate of Anros. The other route... well, no one would take that unless they had a death wish."

Mara's brow furrowed. "What is the other route? Where does it lead?"

"Through the East Road, straight into the land of Cûmer," Aranel said with a shiver. "But no one would willingly enter that treacherous region. It's been overrun by Cûmeri, Celkûn, and other creatures for a long time now. Humans and Aedan haven't lived there for ages, though it used to be a fertile land. It's also the fastest way to the other side." He shuddered again, visibly unnerved. "Come now, before the cold claims us!"

He hurried forward, and Mara followed quickly, every moment deepening her longing to leave the frozen mountain behind.

After another day of difficult travel, they finally crossed the Dark Chasm, which stretched far to the west along the mountain range. From there, they entered the rolling plains of Ahren, where they could at last ride their horses again. This allowed them to make swift progress as they followed the West Road, eventually arriving at the high ravine that led to Dunhir.

But just outside the gates of Elfor's homeland, the Aedan halted. One by one, they said their farewells to Mara, for she had reached a safe region and could now travel on her own. Aranel and his company turned back, disappearing swiftly into the ravine, leaving her alone to complete the final leg of her journey.

໐

By midday the next day, Mara rode up the narrow road toward Elfor's house. A small group of guards, clad in elegant armor gilded with gold, stood vigil before the large gate, each holding long, golden spears. When they saw the woman approaching, leading her horse beside her, they respectfully stepped aside and opened the gate for her. One of the guards took her horse to the nearby stables, allowing the weary animal to rest after the long and arduous journey, which had clearly taken its toll.

Inside the great hall, many Aedan - both men and women - stood gathered, dressed in splendid robes, speaking quietly amongst themselves. But when they noticed the unfamiliar woman entering, a heavy silence fell over them, and they looked at her with anxious eyes.

In that brief moment, Mara realized with a sinking heart that she had arrived too late. The stone - or whatever the object was - had surely been in Dunhir, she could see that much in their faces. But now it was gone, and no hope remained in their expressions. Still, she couldn't be certain. Perhaps she was mistaken, reading too much into the eyes of the immortal Aedan.

Feeling lost, she paused in the center of the hall, faintly hearing the distant strains of harps and flutes. She hesitated to approach any of the Aedan, sensing their unease with her presence as though she carried some great danger with her.

Then, a small figure hurried toward her with purpose, stopping before her. He was no taller than a child, with curly white hair streaked with a few threads of gray. Despite his apparent age, he moved with youthful energy. He had large, hairy ears and a small, upturned nose, making him resemble a cuddly creature more than a man, though he was indeed a human - albeit a rather small one.

"Welcome to Dunhir," he said with a warm smile. "Are you the woman from the Stone Lands in the south, the one whose arrival has been eagerly awaited?" He paused briefly, but didn't give her time to answer. "I am Albin, Albin Cottner. And I am a Halfman - a Wusel, as we are properly called - from the beautiful land of Nanglorin. Cottingen, to be exact, in case you were wondering. I'm certainly not a dwarf, nor am I a child. In fact, I'm one hundred and seven years old." He puffed up his chest, as if trying to make his impressive age more noticeable despite his small stature. "But enough about me. You're very late, human, and it's all the more important that you quickly see Lord Elfor. He must speak with you immediately. Come! I'll lead you to him."

Without waiting for a response, Albin turned and hurried toward the end of the hall, ascending the stairs to the upper floor with surprising speed.

Mara struggled to keep up with the small, old Wusel, who moved far more swiftly than she had expected. He led her all the way down the corridor to the very last door on the upper floor, where he stopped. "He's in here - Lord Elfor," the Wusel said, gesturing toward the white door adorned with intricate carvings. Then, with his task complete, he disappeared in a hurry.

The young woman hesitated, standing uncertainly before the door, wondering what awaited her on the other side. She didn't know the High-Aedan Elfor personally, nor had she ever seen him before. In fact, she had encountered very few Aedan in her life, as she had been confined to her home city of Dinambad for most of her youth. In Miénast, Aedan were rare, as most had retreated to the forests of Thrad or Faldar, or they resided in the northern lands beyond the Tin Elwech, in Dunhir. The only Aedin she had truly known until now was Adraéth, who worked as one of the many maids in the palace. Mara could no longer recall when or why Adraéth had come to Dinambad, as her homeland was in Faldar's woods, but Mara had been a mere infant at the time - less than six months old. All she knew was that Adraéth's arrival coincided with her mother's sudden death. And now, standing before this door, Mara found herself wondering why her mother had died at all, for she had been told the woman had been in perfect health until she was claimed by a sudden and fierce fever.

Shaking herself from her thoughts, Mara reminded herself that this was neither the time nor the place to dwell on her mother. After all, a powerful and influential leader of the Aedan was waiting for her.

With a flutter of anxiety in her chest, she opened the door and stepped inside. She entered a high, well-lit room, where shelves lined the walls, stretching all the way to the ceiling and filled to the brim with ancient books, scrolls, and documents. In the center of the room stood a long, dark oak table with two chairs beside it. Sitting in one of the chairs was a man dressed in a deep blue, almost black, robe that cascaded to the floor. His long, white hair was woven into intricate braids down the sides and back of his head. In his hands, he held a thick book bound in a fiery red cover.

As if sensing her presence, he suddenly looked up, as though she had spoken. He closed the book with a quiet thud, set it on the table, and rose to his feet, walking toward her with a graceful air.

"I welcome you to my home, Mara of Dinambad," he said, his voice warm yet commanding as he gazed down at her - he was nearly two heads taller than she. "I had hoped to greet you sooner, as Dartur intended, but I am well aware of the delays you encountered. It brings me great joy to see you arrive unharmed, even though you are late. Unfortunately, Dartur has already departed. He likely crossed the Arensted by now."

"The Arensted?" Mara repeated, distracted. Her mind flashed to the faint, snow-covered tracks she had noticed on the northern side of the pass. "That's where I've just come from. But there was no one on the pass except Aranel from Faldar, myself, and a group of other Aedan who accompanied us. It was a difficult crossing - the weather was dreadful, and I'm sure it still is. However, I did see some tracks in the snow, just below the highest point on the northern side. I almost missed them at first, but I noticed that they led up the mountain from one side, then back down again, heading off on a different path."

"A different path?" Elfor's expression grew tense. "Dartur wouldn't take the route through the Gate of Anros - too far a detour, and an unnecessary one at that. But what other way could he have gone? It concerns me."

"Then there's only one path left," Mara said with dread, recalling Aranel's words. "The East Road through Cûmer."

Elfor's face turned ashen at the mention of this route, for he knew all too well the dangers that lurked there. Far worse creatures than Celkûn roamed the desolate plains of Cûmer. "The group's fate now hangs by a thread," he said, his expression darkening.

"Group? Dartur isn't alone? Who else is with him? Has Tharon gone as well?"

"Yes," Elfor sighed. "The two of them set off together, determined to put an end to the looming threat. Along with them is one of the Half-men." He paused, as if the next words pained him too much to say. "And that one carries the Alyarel - the stone that was lost for a good reason."

"Is it the one who found it?" Mara asked, alarm creeping into her voice.

"No," Elfor said, managing a faint smile. "He merely carries it. The true finder of the stone has returned to Nanglorin. He's just a child - a Wusel, only twelve years old, which in human years is merely six. I believe you've already met his grandfather, the one who guided you here to me. Despite his advanced age, you wouldn't guess it - Albin Cottner is a lively little fellow. He's lived here in Dunhir for many years. As a young Wusel, he traveled widely, later often with his grandson. That's why he could never settle back in his homeland of Nanglorin." Elfor sighed deeply. "Now, although Ardil - the boy who found the stone - wasn't exposed to its dark power for long, I still fear greatly for his well-being. A handful of guardians from the Dark Forest are safely escorting him home, but I doubt he'll ever be the same. The stone has shown him many things - cruel, barbaric things. The torment that boy has endured will likely never leave him. I fear it may one day consume him from within."

"What can I do now, my lord?" Mara asked, her voice tinged with frustration. "Now that Dartur has already left, my presence here seems pointless. Yet I wish to follow him."

"I've heard that your pursuit of the old wizard has not been particularly fruitful," Elfor replied, with a hint of knowing in his tone. "Changing that would be of little use. Dartur is wise and powerful enough to face the dangers ahead. Tharon is a sufficient companion for him on that journey. No, Mara, I have a different task for you. Ride to Nanglorin and find the boy, Ardil. When he was here in my halls, I sensed a shadow creeping over his mind. This must not be his undoing. Go and speak with him!"

"But what am I to say to him? I can't find the right words to ease even a fraction of his suffering."

"You will find the right words, ones that will grant him the peace he deserves. You are wise, and though you may not yet realize it, you always know what to say when the moment calls for it. Go now! Return to me once the darkness has lifted from his soul!"

Mara bowed respectfully and made her way to the door. Then, as if seized by a thought, she paused, standing motionless for a moment. "How does Dartur intend to destroy the stone?" She turned back to face Elfor.

"He cannot. No one can - except perhaps the Highest Goddess, Iah herself. But that would bring about the end of us all. If even one of the seven Stones of Creation is destroyed, all that was brought into existence by it will collapse as well. And since the world cannot exist in imperfection, Sedäa and all life upon it would perish."

"But this stone brought forth darkness and everything that is dangerous and wicked. Wouldn't the world be better without all the evil it created?"

"The brightest light only holds its true power when it shines against darkness. Day and night follow each other in a cycle, allowing the world and its creatures to gather new energy during the night. The following morning brings them renewed hope. Not much of what Urehel created is good, but even it has a necessary place. The balance between light and dark, day and night, good and evil, must endure forever, or the world itself will break. If there were only eternal daylight, how could we ever long for the new morning filled with hope if it would never arrive? Without darkness, even the purest light would be powerless." He paused briefly. "I hope you now understand that the stone must not be destroyed. None of the Seven. Dartur must find another way to defeat the enemy."

"But if he tries to use the stone, it will betray him, won't it? Urehel's Alyarel has a will of its own and will surely resist any attempt to turn its power against its true master, no matter how powerful Dartur may be."

"I never said he would use it - or that he even could. But I admit, I don't know what Dartur intends. He has traveled far beyond my sight. However, he is mighty and wise, a great one among us - greater than most can fathom. Without doubt, he will find a way. But you needn't burden yourself with this any longer. The stone is far from here, held by someone who cannot use it to cause harm. Your journey is not the same as Dartur's. Even if you had arrived on time, I would not have sent you with him. It was his wish that you take this different path. Ride to Nanglorin, and do not let your thoughts dwell on the stone, Althûbeael! Farewell."

13

With an uneasy feeling, Mara rode along the wide coast of the Nyar River, following the ancient King's Road. After a few days, at the break of dawn, she reached the hill villages of Nanglorin. As she crossed the border, it felt as though she was entering a sea of peace, joy, and innocence.

Small folk who looked like children wandered along the paths or across the rolling grassy hills, singing, laughing, and whistling with such glee, as if no danger in the world could ever harm them.

Mara continued along a broad road heading west until, beyond a sparse woodland, she saw a few large hills. Upon them stood several small huts made of wood and straw, nestled closely together - this was Cottingen, home to the Cottners, Cottenfields, Cottenrivers and Cottenhills. They were all named so because they didn't live like most Wusel folk, who made their homes in deep underground burrows. Instead, these Wusel built houses with doors and windows like cottages, and some even had little vegetable gardens in front. Thanks to them, the Wusel were later called Halfmen, because they lived in houses like humans. And of course, they walked on two legs, though in appearance they resembled small gnomes or pixies. Their noses were small and round, their cheeks plump and soft, and their ears large and long. At first glance, they seemed like harmless, cuddly little creatures, whom even the fiercest enemy would hesitate to harm. Yet, there were mischievous Wusel among them - mostly the youngest ones, who often stole ripe vegetables from their neighbors' gardens with great intent, hoarding the spoils for themselves. For eating was their greatest passion, if not their absolute favorite pastime, though they'd never admit it.

Mara approached a low door set into a wide fence that surrounded a small wooden house and a winter-prepped garden. She dismounted her horse and entered the property alone.

From an open window next to the low-set entrance door, which was painted a bright yellow with blue cross stripes, soft music and singing floated out. Two male voices could be heard: one deep and old, the other high-pitched and young.

When Mara knocked on the door, the singing ceased. After a moment, she heard hushed, nervous whispering from inside. No one moved.

She knocked again.

Suddenly, a frightened cry rang out, and there was a loud crash as a stool toppled over.

"Who's there? We're not expecting any visitors!" called the older voice shakily through the open window.

"I've come from very far. I've traveled many days and nights, and faced great dangers to finally arrive here," Mara said.

"What dangers?" the younger voice asked, nearly bursting with curiosity.

"Quiet, boy!" the elder immediately scolded. "We don't know if the one outside is friend or foe. One can't be too careful these days."

"But what if she's the one Dartur told me about?"

"I am neither an enemy nor anyone who means you harm, nor anyone here. I come directly from Dunhir, with a request and an urgent task to meet the young halfman Ardil Cottner."

Once again, hurried whispers followed. Then, two small figures scurried to the door and opened it. Behind it stood two Wusel. One was gray-haired, old, and slightly plump, but with a serious expression. The other was small, with short, golden curls and curious bright blue eyes.

"Greetings," Mara said with a deep bow. "I am Mara of Miénast, Princess of Dinambad."

The old Wusel was visibly shaken and slapped his hands to his face in shock. "Oh dear! A princess knocking at my door, and I, a foolish old man, didn't even let her in! Please, forgive me!" He bowed low. "Come inside, please!" He then looked to the boy. "Ardil, show the lovely princess to the living room, would you?" He hurried down the hallway. "Would you like some tea or perhaps wine?" he asked as he disappeared around the next corner, mumbling something under his breath. In a flash, his head popped back around the corner, his wide eyes fixed on her. "You must be hungry after such a long journey. I have cookies - freshly baked, of course. Or perhaps some double-smoked bacon with herb-marinated goat cheese?"

Mara shook her head politely, smiling warmly. "Thank you, but no. I don't plan to stay long."

The old man vanished again. "I'll just set the water on for tea," they heard him say as he disappeared into the kitchen.

"Please, come in," the boy said, still awestruck by her beauty, his wide, curious eyes fixed on her.

Mara ducked slightly as she crossed over the low threshold.

Inside, the cottage was much larger and more spacious than it appeared from outside. Most of the rooms were dug deep underground in cellars, invisible from the outside. Wooden walls were nearly covered by an array of pictures of landscapes and ancestors. In every corner, stacks of crates were piled high, filled with old books, candlesticks, and cooking utensils. Here and there, large barrels stood against the walls, with half-empty sacks of flour, sugar, or potatoes leaning against them.

The boy led Mara around the second corner to the left, where they entered a tall, wide room bathed in the soft light of the early day, streaming through narrow windows. On the table in the center were several cups, pitchers, and plates, all piled high with cakes and cookies.

"Please, have a seat!" The old man entered through a second door on the other side, holding a steaming teapot in one hand and a plate of spiced bacon and flavored cheese in the other. After Mara had taken her seat at the table, he poured hot, reddish water into a cup before her. "Forest berry," he said as he placed the teapot on the table. "My favorite blend. I hope you'll enjoy it."

Mara nodded gratefully and cautiously took a sip from the hot cup. Immediately, her mouth was filled with the taste of berries and herbs, as though she were lying in a vast, blooming forest, rolling on its fragrant, mossy floor. It was an unusual flavor but remarkably pleasant. "Quite exquisite."

"Harvested and dried by hand," the old man said proudly. "The Cottner family is, by far, the best when it comes to making tea. We've been known as the Masters of Tea for generations." He sat down opposite her, with the boy beside him. "Ah, how rude of me!" He suddenly jumped up. "My name is Anfrid, and this is my great-grandson, Ardil. My son Albin and my grandson Aldur aren't here at the moment. But since you've come from Dunhir, perhaps you've met at least one of them? Do you know how they're doing? I haven't heard from them since they traveled east with Ardil."

"I believe they're doing well," Mara replied, waiting for the old Wusel to sit again. "I did meet Albin in Dunhir, though I didn't have much chance to speak with him. But he seems to be well cared for under Lord Elfor's watch."

"Oh, how good to hear! That eases my mind. Albin's always been an adventurous one, ever since he was little. Got him into all sorts of trouble. 'It's your own fault,' I used to say, 'You'd better stay home and help your old man in the garden.' Never worked, though. Not once did he listen to me. Well, it caught up with him eventually - he just can't sit still. Even now, in his old age." Anfrid sighed. "And my grandson Aldur is exactly the same. Off on adventures, the fool, and left poor Ardil here to come home alone, accompanied by some of those strange guardians. I'd love to know where he is now and what trouble he's gotten himself into this time."

"Oh, I'm sure he's fine," Ardil said. "Papa went with Dartur. He'll protect him. He promised me."

Mara's eyes widened in surprise. "Then does he have the stone?"

Ardil hesitated briefly. "No, he doesn't." He stood up, ran swiftly to a chest in the corner, and rummaged inside before pulling out a small object wrapped in a white cloth. Returning to the table, he sat down and placed the bundle before Mara. "I have it." He carefully unwrapped the cloth to reveal an oval-shaped, pitch-black gemstone, nearly the size of Mara's entire hand.

Mara stared into the dark depths of the stone and suddenly felt as though she could hear a deep, rasping voice speaking in a terrible, guttural language. For a moment, the young princess was frozen in place, unable to move, her gaze locked on the stone. Then, with great effort, she tore her eyes away from its hold and quickly wrapped the cloth back around it, so she wouldn't have to look at it anymore.

"How dreadful." Her whole body trembled with fear. "Why do you still have it? Dartur was supposed to take it away, wasn't he?"

"Well, that was the plan, at first," Ardil said. "But Dartur refused to take it. He said he feared it too much. He couldn't bring himself to do it."

"But what is your father carrying if that dreadful stone is still here?" Mara asked.

"A knife," Ardil replied simply.

"A knife?" she repeated, incredulous.

"Yes, of course. He needs to protect himself if danger comes," Ardil explained.

Mara furrowed her brow. She found it hard to believe that Aldur, the Wusel, was only armed with a simple knife. 'There has to be more to this,' she thought. 'Dartur would never bring one of these little folk along on such a dangerous journey with only a knife for protection. And besides, Lord Elfor said that Aldur had the stone. Strange. None of this adds up.'

As she eyed the young boy with suspicion, she saw only pure innocence reflected in his harmless gaze. It became clear to her that if something truly was amiss, the boy had no idea of it at all.

Ó

With overwhelming dread, Aleth returned to the white harbor city by evening, just as the sun threatened to disappear behind the horizon. As she entered the prince's palace, it felt as though she were stepping into a thick, impenetrable cloud of sorrow. Everyone in the grand hall - noble knights of the prince's guard and hardworking maids - stood in mournful silence, exchanging no words, their faces stricken with grief. For a moment, Aleth wondered what could have caused such suffering among the people and briefly feared that it might somehow be her fault. But she quickly pushed that terrible thought away and hurried to the far end of the great hall, where Prince Ráhad sat despondently on his throne. His three sons stood around him, and Adraéth knelt beside him, gently holding his hand. When Aleth met the prince's eyes, she felt his deep, burning pain as if it were her own, and in that instant, she knew that something terrible had happened to Mara.

"Greetings, my lord," she said in a loud voice, trying to mask her fear as she stopped before the steps leading up to the throne.

"What more do you want here, Aedin?" Enwir asked coldly, his gaze filled with grief and bitter anger. "Can you not see what has happened? Can you not leave us in our painful suffering and finally return to your carefree, otherworldly, ghostly homeland?"

Aleth then understood even more clearly what had transpired, as though she could read it from his eyes, and a deep sorrow filled her. Trembling, she stepped back, struggling to hold back her tears.

Adraéth stood up now, looking down at the Aedin with a piercing gaze. "You came too late, Aleth Deoricar. You should have gone with her, just as I told you. But instead, you chose another path, and now Mara is lost forever because of you."

Aleth lowered her gaze to the floor, overcome with a crushing sense of guilt, for the maid's words rang true. And now, in bitter clarity, she realized the weight of her actions.

"Perish in your grief, Dark-Singer," Adraéth continued, her voice sharp, "for soon that is all you will have left. Mara's fate was to drive out a darkness from this world - one that casts all other darkness that has ever existed into shadow. But now she is dead. And with her, our hope has died as well. Your folly and your blind greed have sealed all our ends, including your own."

"Silence!" Aleth snapped, her eyes glistening with unshed tears as she looked up. "It was not my fault. It wasn't I who sent Mara to her death, but you." A fierce, uncontrollable hatred flared within her. "The blood of the Aedan flows in your veins too. I only did what was commanded of me. I did not fail, even when I had to face a terrifying creature whose very sight would strike fear into the hearts of every one of you."

"Urehel's most powerful general. The Black Sorcerer and Lord of Iushvhatu. You ventured deep into Vhatu and learned nothing, nor did you change anything. The Lord of Iushvhatu and his chief marshals have crossed the Uael, despite your futile interference, and have ridden into the northwest. So, tell me, Nightingale, how exactly have you not failed in your task?"

A strange sensation came over Aleth, and she thought she heard a deep voice softly whispering to her. Unconsciously, her hand reached into her jacket pocket, and she began to fiddle with the sorcerer's stone hidden within.

"No," Adraéth continued scornfully. "You failed. And Mara only had to die because of your failure."

"Enough!" Ráhad's tortured voice filled the room, trembling with emotion. "I don't want to hear any more. It matters not who is to blame. It changes nothing - my daughter is gone." He then turned to his second-eldest son. "Ride to Anros! Let Finmar accompany you and show you the place where Mara fell. Find her! Find your sister and bring her home!"

Anwar nodded silently and swiftly departed.

"Let me go with them, my lord!" Aleth pleaded. "So, I can at least try to make amends for my failure."

"Your guilt will never be absolved," Enwir said bitterly, glaring at her. "Never will your conscience be clean again, witch."

Ráhad did not respond to his son's words and looked at her indifferently. "Do as you wish. And leave my home!"

Without hesitation, Aleth turned and hurried out of the hall, quickly following Anwar outside.

6

Around noon, Ardil and Mara sat on a small bench in the garden in front of the cottage, gazing down at the peaceful village nestled beneath the hills. They silently enjoyed the warming rays of the sun on this unusually pleasant winter day.

"Will Dartur succeed?" Ardil asked, staring pensively into the distance.

Mara looked down at him. "I can't say. I wish I could because then I'd feel at least a little relief. But I cannot predict the things yet to come."

"Dartur told me about you. He said you can see many things - in your dreams."

"That's true," Mara acknowledged, "but what I see doesn't always make sense, and not everything I dream of actually happens. It's uncertain what will come to pass and what won't. My gift, if you can call it that, is more of a curse than a useful ability. Because many times, what I see brings sadness, pain, and..." She fell silent, troubled.

"And death?"

Mara looked at him, both surprised and shocked.

"Ever since I've had the stone, I can see certain things too. A black shadow in a dark, tall tower behind an iron mountain. I see him often. He's tried to call me, but I think he doesn't know my name." As Ardil spoke, his expression grew darker. "I'm terrified of him - though I don't even know who or what he really is. But one thing I'm certain of, he brings great danger."

"He won't harm you. Don't worry," Mara reassured him, her voice firm. "I've seen him too. That's Urehel, the dark ruler from Um-Atra, shrouded within the Tin Ferrior, the iron mountains. He doesn't know where you are, and he doesn't know you. So don't fear him. Everything will be alright."

"I know." Ardil's voice took on a strange tone of hope. "Because now you're here. Dartur said you would come. And I haven't only seen that shadowy lord, I've seen you too. You saved us all."

Mara remained silent, not knowing how to respond. The idea that the boy had seen her through the stone's power unsettled her. But it also confirmed something she had suspected—that their fates were intertwined somehow. She too had seen him in her dreams.

"You bring us hope," Ardil said, his voice full of conviction.

"Not everything you see is how it will turn out in the end," Mara replied softly. "I don't know what kind of hope I could possibly bring. Ardil, I'm not who you think I am. I came here to talk to you, to lift the shadow from your soul. And although Lord Elfor said I would know exactly what to say, I find myself doubting that now. I desperately want to help you. I wish I could carry your heavy burdens and take on all your troubles. But I can't."

Suddenly, Ardil pulled the stone from his pocket and held it out to Mara, his hand trembling slightly as he extended it toward her. "Then take it! Please! I don't want it. I never did. It has already brought so much evil into the world. It has to stop. I can't bear to have it any longer."

Mara's gaze locked onto the stone, its infinite darkness drawing her in. Once again, she heard the spine-chilling voice, but this time, the words were clear. They echoed in Aerin, the ancient tongue she understood.

Seweth tincath, seweth ahnel,
seweth trakath, seweth calquél.

Calieyenna thrin umbetta,
velech nael a terramistretta.

Uhrath erst uhrath tira mestor,
athra el ûrch barast intu peritor.

Iech, thard lewin i craer,
test larvenn au bridale staer.

Seweth tincath, seweth trakath

Mara's hand reached out toward the dark stone. "Such a small, unassuming thing, yet filled with unimaginable power. What couldn't I do with it? I could make the world better, bring endless peace to it." Her eyes widened. "But it would darken my deeds, turn all my good actions into wicked ones. And I would not even realize it."

She gently placed her fingers over Ardil's hand, closing it softly around the stone. Then she looked into his eyes with compassion. "I cannot take it from you, Ardil, no matter how much I might want to. The stone would deceive me, and who knows what chaos I might bring upon us all. Don't ask me again, for I may not be able to resist its influence next time. There's a reason why the stone fell into your hands. I believe Dartur thinks the same. That's why you still have it. In anyone else's hands, it could bring great harm, but you seem completely immune to its dark will. That is a hopeful and encouraging sign. In your possession, it will never be a danger. Think of it as a gift, Ardil, not a burden, even though it may be painful to bear. One day, the shadow from the Iron North will be destroyed, and with it, the darkness on your soul will lift, and peace will return. Trust my words, for that's how it will be. Perhaps not today, and maybe not tomorrow, but one day. Perhaps very soon."

"I hope you're right," Ardil said as he tucked the stone back into his pocket. "But for now, I'd rather not worry about it. It's time for lunch!" He jumped up, suddenly full of energy. "Come on, Mara! I bet my great grandpa has already set the table." Before he even finished speaking, he was racing eagerly back toward the little cottage.

6

Anwar stood beside Finmar and two gray horses in front of the stables, ready to depart.

"Wait!" Aleth ran toward them. "I'm coming with you."

"She's not dead." Anwar looked directly at Aleth. "Because if she were, my grief would be far greater - greater than I could possibly bear. My little sister is still alive, no matter what the others say."

"I don't believe she's dead either," Aleth said with a confident smile. "Let's find her quickly and end this needless suffering before anything worse happens!"

14

Girded about her waist was the splendid swan-sword of Dinambad, its bright blade glimmering in the dim glow of the rising sun, as Aasa rode across the wide plains of Ostlad, her course set eastward, towards the Ghostwood that lay beyond her homeland.

A foul stench and a shroud of mist, thick with the vapours of decay, hung low over the battle-scarred fields at the forest's edge. A shudder of revulsion swept through the young woman as her gaze fell upon the charred remains of the Celkûn, whose smoldering corpses were the source of the wretched smell. Dismounting from her steed, Aasa approached the reeking mound with cautious steps. She pressed a hand to her nose to block out the stench, prodding at the blackened refuse with her foot. Yet nothing of note did she uncover - only dented armor, bloodstained axes, rusted swords, and bodies, burnt beyond recognition.

Bereft of the last spark of hope, Aasa cast her eyes upwards to the heavens, where the now bright sun bathed her in a soft, warming light. As she turned to leave, her gaze was caught by a sudden gleam - a flicker of light that dazzled her sight. Warily, she followed the shimmer, her steps leading her nearer to the dark verge of the Ghostwood. It was a curious blue glint that drew her in, captivating her eye. And despite the fear that tugged at her heart, she pressed on, driven by wonder, crossing into the ancient forest.

There, hanging from a slender branch, almost at eye level, was a silver chain. Suspended from it was a brilliant blue stone, radiant as if made from purest glass, with a flame of blue fire burning fiercely within its heart, trapped and flickering as though alive.

Aasa plucked the chain from the branch, holding the stone delicately in her open palm, her gaze fixed upon it with suspicion. As she studied it, the glimmering light within faded, and the stone darkened, changing in hue. A memory stirred within her, for it now resembled the boundless sea that lapped against the shores of Dinambad, encircling the very world itself. In her foolish hope - naive though she was - Aasa became convinced that this must be Mara's necklace, for Mara alone had been present at this place in the battle long past. No man of Anros would possess such a precious stone, least of all one that was surely more than a mere adornment.

Slowly, Aasa ventured deeper into the forest, seeking some further sign, or perhaps Mara herself. But all at once, the shadows thickened among the trees. A deep hum arose, and the ground beneath her feet began to tremble, as though the Morabidan - the ancient wood itself - would brook no intruders, least of all those who walked on two legs.

Fear seized the young woman, and she turned and fled, running back toward the light of day. Breathless, she emerged, gulping the fresh air, for it had felt as though the trees themselves had stolen her very breath within their gloom. Dazed, as if under a powerful spell, Aasa looked down at the stone still clasped in her hand. She gazed into it, deeper and deeper, for she believed she could make out something - or someone - within its depths.

A tall, slender figure, robed in radiant white and silver light, seemed to appear. In her growing excitement, Aasa was ready to call out Mara's name. But as the figure's face grew clear, her voice faltered. It was not the face she had expected, but that of a woman, unknown to her - long white hair cascading like moonlight, and eyes of piercing blue, within which the starlight of a clear night sky was mirrored.

"*Ûrechdil nîn, Auderiáre,*" the white-haired figure spoke, her voice deep and majestic, like the echo of forgotten ages. Aasa's fear surged, and she longed to drop the stone, but found herself unable to move, her gaze locked upon it. "Fear not, Aasa, maiden of Anros, land of the taciturn and stubborn folk who dwell in their royal mead-hall of Westhawen, descendant of the house of Andor the Kind. Your fate has led you to find the Bariltincu, and to return it to its rightful keeper."

"Who are you?" Aasa managed to ask, her voice trembling.

"A friend to one who is also your friend," the figure replied, her voice steady and calm. "Though many believe her lost to death, she lives still. Yet she now walks far from your homeland. It was truly fated that she should lose the blue stone, so that it might come into your hands. This stone will be a beacon of hope for your people, for you and your kin, Auderiáre. Return swiftly and bear this message with haste: Mara lives. But know this - she treads dangerous paths, and for you and yours, only hope remains. Hold to that hope, and much will soon turn for the better. But if hope is lost, Anros shall fall into shadow, and no future will remain for your people. Hope, Auderiáre!"

As the woman spoke her final words, her face began to fade, slowly dissolving until only the cold, bare stone remained.

Aasa stood for a time, staring at the now lifeless stone. No movement, no sign of the vision that had spoken to her remained within it. Lost in thought, she considered the words of the strange woman. Then, without delay, she mounted her horse and rode with all speed toward her home. But not to Westhawen did she go; instead, her path led to Suthawen, for it was her suffering brother who must first hear the message of hope she now carried.

Mara lives.

6

After a most splendid luncheon - a feast in its own right - the afternoon tea followed, accompanied by freshly baked cakes. And then came the grand evening meal. Yes, the Wuselfolk dearly loved their food, that much was plain to see.

"You've outdone yourself once again, Great-grandfather," said Ardil, patting his full belly with a look of satisfaction.

"It's a marvel to me how such small folk can devour what would satisfy a whole band of grown men," Mara remarked, casting a glance at the two Wusel who had consumed the lion's share of the many delicacies.

Anfrid chuckled. "Well, we do have a special appreciation for the finer things in life," he said, rising from his seat to begin clearing the table. With a few empty plates in hand, he made his way to the kitchen and disappeared into the adjoining room.

Mara stood as well, stepping over to the half-open window, where she paused to listen to the sounds of the outside world. She remained there for a long while, utterly still, as though lost in thought.

Meanwhile, Anfrid had almost cleared the entire dining table, which had been filled to the last inch with dishes of every kind. Ardil stretched, his eyelids heavy with weariness.

"Ah, now is the perfect time for a little nap. If you'll excuse me for a moment," he yawned loudly, rising from his seat and stretching his arms wide, preparing to leave the room.

"I fear your nap will have to wait a while longer," Mara said suddenly, her tone unusually stern. Ardil froze in place, turning to look at her, startled. "It seems Dartur feared this might happen."

"What do you mean? What's wrong?" he asked, concern creeping into his voice.

She turned to him, her face dark and grave. "He is here," she said, striding quickly towards Ardil. "Hide in the cellar, as deep as you can go! And take Anfrid with you! You must remain completely silent. Perhaps then, he won't sense your presence."

"Who is here? What's happening?" Ardil stammered, confusion swirling in his mind.

"Go now! Quickly!" she commanded.

"But-" Ardil stared at her, bewildered.

"Now!" Mara's voice rang out like steel, brooking no argument.

Shocked and utterly perplexed, the boy ran to the kitchen, calling out to his great-grandfather. "Hurry, Great-grandfather! We must get to the cellar at once!"

Meanwhile, Mara stepped out into the hallway and into the now dark and frosty night.

"But what are we supposed to do in the cellar?" Anfrid asked in confusion. "No, no, no, my boy. Later. We can play later. First, I must finish the washing up. Otherwise, I'll never get the fine porcelain gleaming again, and that would be a terrible shame. After all, I paid quite a bit for it - a lot, I tell you."

"Forget the dishes!" Ardil exclaimed. "There's no time for that. Danger is upon us. Someone is out there."

"Of course there's someone out there. Mara just stepped outside. You have no need to fear. It's only her."

Suddenly, both heard the unmistakable ring of Mara's sword - given to her by Lord Elford - as it was drawn from its scabbard.

"But she told us to go into the cellar. That's why she's outside. That's why she's here at all," Ardil urged, his voice growing frantic. "Now come on!" He grabbed his great-grandfather by the wrist, tugging him away from the sink and dragging him with great effort toward the stairs that led down into the cellar.

"Show yourself, creature of shadow!" they heard Mara shout. Her voice echoed through the cabin's hallway, bold and commanding, as the door to the outside stood wide open, letting a biting wind sweep into the warm and homely air.

"Hurry, hurry! And be quiet!" Ardil urged, pushing the old Wusel down the cellar stairs.

The two fled to the very bottom, descending into the seventh and final level of the cellar, where they hid themselves in the large store-room, cluttered with barrels, great sacks, and wooden crates. Behind a stack of the largest crates, they crouched, huddling in the corner, fear gripping their hearts.

"The stone!" came a bone-chilling screech from above, the voice shrill and piercing. The very ground beneath them trembled as the creature's voice reverberated through the cabin. "Give it to me, woman, or you shall die!"

"Never," Mara answered, her voice resolute. "I do not have it, and it is not here."

"That is a lie. A lie!" the creature bellowed. "I can smell it. I can feel its presence. It is close - so very close. Give it to me!"

"Begone, shadow-walker!" Mara commanded.

As the two Wusel cowered below, listening to the clash of words above, Ardil was suddenly seized by a strange sensation. An uncontrollable urge overtook him, and without realizing what he was doing, he reached into his pocket and drew forth the black stone, gripping it tightly in his hand.

A piercing scream echoed down from above, as though the enemy had finally sensed the stone's presence with unmistakable clarity.

"Stand back!" Mara's voice rang out, commanding and urgent.

"Out of my way, fool!" screeched the dark being, forcing its way into the cottage with unstoppable might. Wooden beams groaned and snapped in two, and the small door shattered into splinters. The terrible creature leapt over the threshold, and a pained gasp escaped from Mara's lips.

Ardil and Anfrid huddled closer together, trembling with fear. They heard the heavy thud of iron-shod boots descending the stairs, each step like a hammer striking the fragile remnants of their courage. Their hearts pounded in their chests as a deep, rasping breath echoed from the stranger who had entered the storeroom. It was as though he were scenting the air, searching for something with his nose, unable to see but guided by an unseen sense.

"*Seweth tincath,*" the creature's voice thundered, its words spoken in the ancient tongue of Aerin, yet twisted and vile upon its lips. "*Seweth ahnel. Seweth trakath, seweth calquél.* Come forth, come forth! I can smell you, half-blood. Come forth and show yourself! *Seweth tincath, seweth trakath.*"

With each monstrous word, the creature moved deeper into the room, the darkness cloaking him. Yet his voice filled the space like a looming shadow, suffocating and terrible. "The stone. Give it to me, for it is not yours to hold!"

Suddenly, Ardil stood up, his body moving against his will. It was as though the thing in his hand was guiding him, and no matter how hard he tried, he could not resist. Slowly, he stepped out from behind the crates, facing the dreadful creature, whose terrifying visage - thankfully for Ardil - remained hidden in the dark.

But the stranger saw him clearly, for his eyes, keen as those of a hunter at noon, pierced the gloom with ease. "The stone," he growled. "Give it to me! I command you!"

Without any power to resist, the boy's arm extended forward, his hand opening to reveal the stone to the enemy. The creature, consumed by greed, lunged for it, eager to seize it. But before its grasp could close upon the prize, Mara came rushing down the stairs and into the storeroom. Armed with a blazing torch, she sprang between Ardil and the dark foe, driving the creature back with the flame.

"Go! Quickly!" she shouted to Ardil and Anfrid, pushing the enemy away with the searing heat of the fire.

Without hesitation, the old Wusel grabbed his great-grandson by the shoulder and pulled him toward the exit. The moment Ardil was freed from the creature's spell, he bolted in terror, racing up the stairs and out of the house. As the two Wusel fled through the garden, they heard terrible screams rising from the cellar, followed by a thunderous crash.

As if struck by lightning, they halted in their tracks and turned to look. The left side of the cottage had collapsed entirely. Smoke was rising from some of the intact windows, swirling into the cold night air. They stood, horrified and uncertain of Mara's fate, staring at the ruins.

After what seemed like an eternity, as the smoke began to clear and snowflakes started to fall from the sky, something stirred beneath the rubble. Ardil made a move to run back and help Mara, but Anfrid caught his arm, holding him back. A deep, uneasy feeling rose in the old Wusel's heart, whispering to him that whatever was emerging from the wreckage was not Mara.

His instinct proved true.

From the debris, a shadowy figure emerged, rising like a towering, pitch-black void, its immense form striking terror into the hearts of the two Wusel. The creature stretched to its full height, a terrifying sight in the pale, falling snow.

"Run!" Anfrid shouted, and he darted across the fields, with his nimble great-grandson following close behind. They fled eastward, their path leading inevitably toward the Nyar, the vast northern sea.

Yet both knew the truth - they could not swim, as none of the Wusel-folk could. They had always feared and avoided the sea, its dark, endless depths a source of dread. But Anfrid clung to one desperate hope: that the cold would have frozen the waters, just as it had over seventy years ago during the harshest winter, when the entire sea had frozen solid and the Wusel had skated upon it well into May. Perhaps, he thought, the ice, even if thin, might bear their light, small bodies. It was their last hope.

As they ran, hearts heavy with the uncertainty of Mara's fate, Ardil's thoughts darkened. He feared that she had perished in the collapsed cellar, crushed beneath the weight of the ruined cottage. Yet even in the depths of their despair, both held onto a fragile hope - that somehow, Mara still lived, and that she might yet save them from the peril that pursued.

6

Aasa rushed into the ancient fortress of Suthawen, her childhood home, where she had once lived before her parents had died far too soon. She hurried to the far end of the former throne hall, which now felt desolate and dark, a shadow of its former glory. All the windows were shrouded with thick curtains and heavy drapes, allowing no light to penetrate the gloom.

She came to a halt before her brother, who sat slumped on the old throne of their ancestors. His head was bowed, his eyes bloodshot, and his face twisted with torment. Lost in his grief, he seemed oblivious to his sister's presence. He did not look up, his gaze fixed instead on the loose boards of the worn wooden floor beneath him.

"Aric, look at what I've found," Aasa said, pulling a silver necklace with a blue stone from her pocket. She held it out before her brother's face.

But he only stared at it in silence, showing no sign of interest, as though it meant nothing to him - neither what it was nor to whom it might belong.

"I found it where Mara vanished. She didn't fall, Aric. She's still alive."

"You can't know that." Aric's voice was low and broken. "Did you see her? I'm certain you didn't. Otherwise, she'd be here with you now, not just this worthless necklace."

"I did not see her," Aasa admitted, though her mind returned to the memory of the white-haired woman she had encountered. Her eyes filled with a reverence that mirrored her renewed hope. "But I saw someone else in her place. A tall woman, with long white hair, clothed in a gown as radiant as freshly fallen snow. Her eyes were light blue, shining like the stars in the night sky."

Aric furrowed his brow and looked at his sister with suspicion.

"She called me *Auderiáre* and spoke to me in the beautiful, melodic language of the Aedan," Aasa began, "though much of what she said was in our Common Tongue. I understood her words, but not fully their meaning. Yet she asked me to deliver a message."

"I want nothing to do with this dangerous Aedan sorcery," Aric snapped, rising to his feet. "Take that thing and remove it from my house!" He brushed past his sister, turning his back on her. "And keep your message to yourself, Aasa. I won't be bewitched by these ghostly immortals." With that, he strode away.

"Mara is still alive!" Aasa's voice rang through the hall, loud and unwavering in its conviction.

The words struck Aric like a blade to the heart. He stopped abruptly, his breath heavy and labored.

"She lives, and we must not lose hope," Aasa continued. "For hope may be the last thing left to us in these dark days. But as long as we still hold onto it, we are not lost."

Aric finally turned, his face twisted in bitter anger, and he walked back toward his sister. "What good is hope to me now, when I have already lost everything?" he spat. "No, Aasa, I can't cling to hope, nor can I believe what this spirit-woman has told you. If Mara truly lives, where is she? She would not have left us to suffer in this torment of uncertainty." His voice faltered, and he swallowed hard, as though trying to suppress the pain that threatened to overwhelm him. "She would not have abandoned me."

Gently, Aasa took his hand, placing the necklace with its blue stone into his palm. She closed his fingers around it. "Take it, and let it give you the hope you need, dear brother. It gave me hope, for I know now that it once belonged to Mara. Keep it, and perhaps it may soothe your pain as well."

Aric remained silent, his heart heavy with sorrow, struggling to understand why his sister was so unwavering in her hope.

"Trust me," Aasa said, her voice soft and full of kindness. She smiled gently. "Believe that she still lives! To see you suffering like this tears my heart apart and casts a shadow over my soul. I beg you, Aric! Don't follow the same tragic fate as Mother! I cannot bear to lose you as well." She hesitated for a moment. "And remember, you haven't lost everything. You still have me. You are the only one left to me, after all these years. Please, don't leave me alone in these dark times!" Her voice broke, and she could no longer hold back her tears.

Aric gently embraced her, holding her in silence. "Thank you, sister," he whispered. Slowly, a faint smile crept across his grief-stricken face. "Your words have lifted the thick, gray veil that clouded my mind and have given me new hope." He tucked the necklace into his pocket. "Come! We must return to Westhawen before something worse befalls us. I must speak with Fala urgently." Together, they made their way out of the hall.

"We must hurry now," Aasa urged. "I fear Fala is in grave danger. While you were away, Nariya's grim words drove her to fury, and I believe she now intends to march against the roving Celkûn near the Northern Wall, defying the king's orders."

"Quickly!" Aric exclaimed, his dread growing, quickening his pace. "Return to Westhawen and see to our uncle's safety! I will gather my riders and follow Fala northward. Perhaps it is not yet too late."

Ó

The night had grown terrifyingly dark, and the snowfall thickened with each passing moment, so dense that one could barely see their own hand before their eyes. Ardil and Anfrid stumbled across the snowy slope, making their way to the shore of the Nyar. In the darkness, they hurriedly hid behind a few sparse bushes and knelt on the snow-covered ground.

Limping, the black creature drew nearer to the water's edge, pausing for a moment. It crouched low, bending forward as it searched the ground for a trace, some sign of their presence.

"He'll find us here," Ardil whispered, fear gripping his voice. "We can't hide from him."

"No," Anfrid replied, though doubt clouded his words. "We only need to be very still." Yet even he did not truly believe it. His mind raced, seeking any way they might escape this terrible plight. After a time, the old Wusel placed a hand on Ardil's shoulder. "My boy, you know as well as I do that staying here will do us no good. It is pointless to wait any longer." He hesitated for a moment. "When I give the signal, you will run across the frozen sea. It will bear your weight, easily."

"I won't go without you, Great-grandpa. Please, come with me!" Ardil pleaded.

Anfrid sighed deeply, his eyes filled with both sorrow and love. "Ah, my dear little Ardil," he said softly. "Here, our paths must part - though I pray only for a time. That does not mean we shall not meet again. Run as fast as you can, and don't look back! Make your way to Dunhir - you know the way well enough by now. There, you'll be safe. You cannot stay here any longer. I'll draw his attention. That way, you can flee, and he will not pursue you further."

Anfrid rose to his feet, straightening his back despite his age. "Hey, you foul creature of shadow!" he shouted, his voice echoing through the dark. He waited until the enemy turned its gaze upon him. "I'm here, and I have your wretched stone. If you want it, you'll have to come and take it!" Then he glanced down at the boy. "Now, Ardil! Run!"

Without waiting for a reply, Anfrid bolted, racing not toward the sea but up the northern hills, away from the shore. The black creature let out a shrill, piercing screech and followed, leaving Ardil behind.

And so, the boy ran, his heart pounding, tears freezing on his cheeks, across the icy expanse toward the safety of Dunhir.

At first, Ardil remained crouched, frozen in place, watching helplessly as Anfrid and the dark creature vanished from sight. A heavy, gnawing guilt weighed upon him, twisting in his stomach. Slowly, he rose to his feet, stepping cautiously onto the vast sheet of ice that stretched across the great sea as far as the eye could see. Fearfully, he began to run, though he could no longer tell if he was heading south or east - the blinding snowstorm robbed him of all sense of direction. But in that moment, it mattered little to him.

Once again, a bone-chilling scream echoed through the storm, and Ardil, terrified, stumbled over his own feet and fell forward into the snow.

Suddenly, a sharp crack echoed beneath him. The ice groaned, beginning to give way, and a thick fissure split open directly beneath his legs.

Panic seized him. He scrambled to his feet and ran as fast as he could, his breath coming in ragged gasps. But he had barely made it a few meters when the ice shattered beneath his small, fur-covered feet. With a horrified cry, Ardil plunged into the frigid water below.

The shock of the icy depths paralyzed him, and try as he might, he could not fight his way back to the surface. The freezing cold sapped his strength with every passing second. Like a sack filled with heavy stones, he sank deeper into the seemingly endless black depths of the sea. The black stone, which he still clutched tightly in his hand, grew ever heavier, pulling him further into the abyss.

His senses began to blur, his vision clouding, as his lungs burned with desperate need for air. He could feel how close he was to the end, to the inescapable grip of death. Just as the freezing cold began to overwhelm him and consciousness faded, he glimpsed something above - through the pale light of the moon filtering down through the ice, the outline of a hand reached for him.

But whether it was a mere illusion or truly happening, Ardil could not tell, for in the next moment, all sensation left him, and darkness claimed him entirely.

6

When Aasa arrived in the capital, she was met with utter chaos. She sprinted up the stone steps toward the mead hall, only to be stopped by Eruhad and Anlac.

"What has happened?" she demanded.

"The king... he's been poisoned," Eruhad whimpered, pushing Anlac forward. "Take her to him!"

Anlac hurried inside the hall, with Aasa close by his side, as they raced up the stairs to the royal chambers on the upper floor. He led her into the king's bedchamber, where several healers and herbalists were gathered around the bed, leaning over their ailing lord. As Aasa and Anlac entered the room, the men stepped back, revealing the sight of her uncle.

His face was shockingly pale, his entire body drenched in sweat, as though he were burning with fever, despite the chill in the room. Aasa rushed to his side, falling to her knees beside him. Tears filled her eyes as she took his cold, trembling hand in hers.

"Aasa," Henric wheezed weakly.

"Uncle?" She crawled closer to him. "Who did this?"

"Nariya," the king whispered, his voice barely audible.

Aasa's gaze darkened with fury, and she turned sharply to Anlac. "Find Nariya! Find that traitor and kill her!"

Anlac nodded swiftly and disappeared from the chamber.

"Where is Fala?" Henric grimaced, his body wracked with pain. "Where is my child?"

"She is on her way, Uncle. Fala will be here soon," Aasa reassured him, gently stroking his hand. Seeing the agony etched across his face, she turned desperately to the healers. "Do something! Help him! Do anything!"

"Forgive us, my lady," one of the healers replied softly, "but we have done all we can. The poison of the Thorned Crown has no cure. King Henric will not survive."

"No," Aasa murmured, her voice breaking as she looked down at her uncle in despair.

Henric, with a frail smile, raised a trembling hand to caress his niece's cheek. "Do not weep for me, dear child. I am old, and even without this, I would not have had many years left."

But Aasa refused to accept his words. With tears streaming down her face, she laid her head on his chest, clutching the dying man as sobs wracked her body, unwilling to let him go.

6

"Come on," Mara called nervously, clutching the boy tightly, wrapping him securely in her cloak. "Wake up! Please, wake up!"

To Ardil, it felt like a long-forgotten dream - endless, dark, cold, and filled with unbearable pain. But suddenly, life surged back into him, and consciousness returned. He opened his eyes, coughing and gasping for breath, his body writhing in pain. When he looked up and saw Mara, the one he had feared lost to death, joy filled his heart. He threw himself into her arms.

"My great-grandpa," he said, his face paling. "Where is he? Is he safe?" He gazed up at her, desperate.

Mara shook her head sadly. "I don't know."

"We have to help him! That terrible creature is after him. It thinks he has the stone."

"I fear any aid may be beyond us now," Mara said, her concern clear as she stood. "We must move on, and we must go now."

"I won't go anywhere without my grandfather," Ardil insisted stubbornly. "I won't leave him behind! Not now, not ever."

"We cannot turn back, Ardil. To do so would mean your death. And mine too - I barely escaped my own fate in that cellar. His terrible power is far beyond me, and beyond you even more so. Your great-grandfather would never want you to run straight into death when you could flee. Now, come! We must go."

"Where? To Dunhir?" Ardil asked as he slowly stood, still wrapped in Mara's warm cloak. He looked up at her, doubt in his eyes. "We'll never make it."

Mara knelt beside him, looking him squarely in the eye. "Do you trust me?"

"Yes."

"Then we will make it." She stood again, though it was clear she was struggling to hide how the bitter cold was wearing her down. "We must hurry. If we are swift, we can reach the southern ferry before dawn. There, we'll cross the sea."

"But isn't that taking us further from Dunhir?"

"Precisely," Mara replied, already moving ahead with urgency.

Ardil scrambled after her, but despite his best efforts, he couldn't keep up. For a Wusel, he was quick, but Mara, even on foot, was extraordinarily fast. He struggled to match her pace. After a short distance, Mara paused, waiting for the breathless boy to catch up. When he finally did, she hoisted him onto her back, carrying him so they could move more swiftly.

And so, with renewed speed, they made their way through the night. By the time they reached the southern ferry, dawn had not yet broken, and under the cover of darkness, they crossed the water unseen, making their way to the other shore.

The sun slowly rose over the distant snow-capped peaks, casting a faint warmth upon the white-blanketed earth. Yet the frost seemed to grow fiercer still, for an icy wind swept across the land, chilling even the feeble rays of sunlight.

Ardil, exhausted, had fallen asleep, and Mara trudged onward, carrying him through the knee-deep snow with the last remnants of her strength. The little Wusel, still wrapped snugly in her warm cloak, slept soundly, while the young woman, exposed to the biting cold, was nearly frozen through, her entire body trembling. Each step grew heavier, her pace slowing as weakness crept into her limbs.

Suddenly, her legs gave way. She collapsed to her knees, her breath coming in labored gasps. She had no strength left to rise. Darkness closed in around her, and the piercing cold seemed to reach her very heart. With one final, faltering breath, Mara lifted her gaze to the heavens, hoping for some sign of aid, before her vision faded. She slumped forward, unconscious, into the snow's icy embrace.

15

With the tolling of bells, the new day began, yet it brought no hope. For King Henric had, in the dark of night, lost his bitter struggle against death.

Aasa, who had remained by his side through it all, was now the one tasked with delivering this sorrowful news, for none other of Henric's family were present. Fala and Aric had yet to return, and Aasa feared deeply that they too had met their end. Yet she clung to the last threads of hope, unwilling to yield entirely to despair.

The people of Westhawen had gathered in great numbers. They stood before the mead hall, waiting with heavy hearts for the word. When they saw the king's niece emerge, her face marked with deep sorrow, and watched as she stood at the top of the stone steps, a somber silence fell upon them all.

"At the early hour of this day, King Henric, son of Edric and Ranyariel, brother of Fasa, departed from us," Aasa began, her voice trembling with grief. She swallowed hard, forcing herself to continue. "In these last days, he endured much suffering, for he was poisoned by the Thorned Crown. But now, his soul has found peace, and the king rests with his ancestors."

She paused, stepping aside as the great doors of the mead hall swung open. Four men of the royal guard emerged, carrying the king's body upon a bier. They bore him down the steps with great care. As was custom, the king was dressed in his own armor, and his still-sharp sword lay across his chest.

Aasa followed behind them, her voice lifting in prayer. "O High Lady of the Heavens," she began. The gathered crowd joined her, their voices rising as one as they followed the solemn procession toward the crypt of the kings. "High Mother, be merciful to us and forgive our sins. Receive your son into your boundless realm and grant him life after death. Awaken him in your halls to endless life, that he may serve you as is your due."

And so, with heavy hearts and bowed heads, the people of West-hawen mourned their fallen king.

The gates of the stone crypt were opened by several men, allowing the king's procession to enter and lay his body to rest in its designated place of eternal peace. After the mourning ceremony, during which all the townsfolk had the chance to bid their final farewells, the crypt was sealed once more, with the hope that it would remain closed for many long years.

Aasa, without delay, returned to the mead hall. In Fala's absence - who was now, by right, Queen of Anros - Aasa had assumed command in the capital, though it was a burden she had never sought.

As she climbed the stone steps, a maidservant of about her own age, with dark, curly hair, hurried toward her and intercepted her midway up the stairs. "Please forgive me, my lady," the maid began, her voice trembling with distress. "I tried to stop her. But the traitor... she escaped."

Aasa regarded the young woman with a cold, indifferent gaze. "What is your name?"

"Rían," the maid replied, wiping tears from her eyes. "Forgive me! I could not stop her."

"You are forgiven, Rían," Aasa said, her voice flat and weary. "Nariya will face justice, sooner or later. And if I must see to it myself, I will. She will receive what she deserves. As will we all."

Rían nodded, her expression filled with awe. She stepped aside and then followed Aasa into the mead hall, like a lost and whimpering dog, unsure of its place but eager to serve.

6

Bright daylight streamed through a narrow window, flooding the room with almost blinding white light. The air was thick with the warm, comforting scent of hot pumpkin soup.

Mara slowly awoke and sat up in bed, glancing around with a sense of disorientation. She had no clear idea of where she was. The last thing she remembered was the frantic escape across the ferry. But how many days had passed since then? She had no way of knowing.

"Good morning, sleepyhead," came a cheerful voice. A young man entered the room, carrying a bowl of steaming soup. As Mara looked up, she recognized Astuil, who crouched down on a small stool beside the bed. "I feared you were a goner when I found you half-frozen in the snow. Well, actually, it was my little brother who found you while he was out riding with Celegrin, despite me strictly forbidding him. The boy's got no sense of propriety. Should be ashamed of himself, really. But at least he found you. If he hadn't, our father would've been beside himself with rage. So, in the end, we were lucky - if you can call it that."

"Where is Ardil?" Mara asked anxiously. "The boy who was with me - where is he?"

"Oh, you mean the half-human, the Wusel?" Astuil smiled, placing the bowl of soup on a low table beside her. "He's with Arwin somewhere in the south quarter. I tell you, those two are a perfect pair - both equally mad. But as long as they don't cause trouble, it's none of my concern. And if they do, well, I can punish two troublemakers in one go. But I do hope they don't have any mischief in mind - that could end badly."

Without paying much attention to his words or thinking on them further, Mara attempted to rise from the bed. A groan escaped her as she clutched her stomach, her body bending forward in pain. Her stomach growled fiercely, as though she hadn't eaten in over a year, and her weak frame seemed to confirm her desperate need for nourishment. With another sigh, she collapsed back onto the bed, breathing heavily as she looked at Astuil.

He chuckled softly, "Looks like you need a bit of rest and some soup before you go running off anywhere. Getting up right away is not such a good idea." Astuil's face filled with a smirk. "Of course, I would have told you, had you asked. You haven't eaten anything at all - not since you arrived here, at least. But how could you have? No one eats while asleep. That's simply impossible, isn't it?" He paused suddenly, realizing he had nearly forgotten something. Reaching for the bowl of soup, he handed it to Mara. "Here, eat! It's pumpkin soup. My dear mother made it to help you regain your strength. She said, 'Go quickly and bring it to her before the soup gets cold!' And I thought to myself, 'How is she supposed to eat when she's not awake?' I didn't want to wake you. But now that you're up, please, eat."

Without hesitation, Mara began to taste the soup, which was still quite hot and remarkably delicious.

"Well?" Astuil asked, his eyes wide with anticipation. "Is it good?"

Mara nodded, swallowing with satisfaction.

"Oh, how wonderful!" Astuil beamed with joy. "That will please my mother. She doesn't think much of her own cooking, though she's truly excellent at it. She always says, 'The greatest hunger is the best cook.' I've never quite understood what she means by that because, to me, she's the best cook there is. Well," he stammered slightly, "actually, she's the only cook I know, but that's beside the point. Absolutely beside it."

"You may tell your mother that she is indeed a fine cook, no matter what others - or even she herself - may say." Mara finished the bowl. "I have never tasted anything more delightful."

"How marvelous." He took the empty bowl from her and stood up. "Rest a little more! My mother says you should stay in bed for at least another full day."

"I can't," Mara replied, her tone growing serious. "If we stay here any longer, something terrible will happen, and I must prevent that at all costs." She glanced up at the young man, her thoughts racing. "What day is it?"

"Wednesday, the 24th of February." Astuil looked at her curiously. "What exactly are you worried about? You haven't done anything wrong and are now on the run because of it, are you?"

"No, not directly," Mara sighed. "At least, I haven't broken any laws. That much I can tell you, but no more."

"Fair enough. I'll trust you for now," Astuil said as he moved toward the door. "If you need anything, just call for me." And with that, he left the room.

Without stirring much, Mara rested for several more hours. It was only after midday had passed that she felt strong enough to stretch her legs a little. Rising from the bed, she left the small house, which stood just two streets below the grand inn of Rist, tucked away in a narrow side alley. She made her way leisurely toward the South Quarter, a path she had taken before, and soon found herself in the midst of a group of young children, laughing and playing with great noise and energy.

It wasn't long before she spotted Ardil and Arwin, surrounded by a circle of curious children who watched the Wusel with wide-eyed wonder as he regaled them with stories of his homeland. He spoke of their fine vegetable gardens, their often unusual baking skills, and, of course, the highly esteemed art of tea-making - a tradition in his family that had been perfected over two centuries. He went on to describe his little expeditions into the ancient mines of Tin Nangroth, where, he added with pride, he had discovered a very peculiar black stone.

"Enough stories for today," Mara interrupted hastily as she approached, for even these innocent, unknowing children could be endangered by learning too much about the stone.

The boys and girls groaned in disappointment. They had been eager to hear more from the strange newcomer.

But Ardil, seeing Mara, darted through the crowd of listeners and ran straight into her arms, his face alight with joy.

"How are you?" she asked, her voice laced with concern.

"Good. Much better than you," he replied cheerfully, though a shadow suddenly crossed his face. His joyful expression darkened into one of fear. "You slept for a long time - you had a terrible fever."

"Yes," Mara sighed, her brow furrowing. "Nine days is indeed a long time - especially when we should have been far from here by now."

"Where should you have gone?" Arwin, who had been listening closely, stepped forward. "To the Aedan in Dunhir? Ardil has told me a lot about them." The boy's eyes gleamed with excitement. "I'd give anything to see just one of them with my own eyes! That would be incredible!" With a determined look, he turned to Mara. "I want to come with you. May I?"

Mara regarded him with a mix of surprise and amusement, but also a hint of caution. "That is no simple request, Arwin. The journey we face is fraught with danger, and the Aedan are not beings to be approached lightly."

Arwin's face remained steadfast, brimming with youthful resolve. "I don't care about the dangers! I want to help! I want to see the world beyond this town."

She sighed, considering the boy's eagerness.

"I would allow it, were we traveling under different circumstances, and if we were truly going to Dunhir," Mara began gently, "but as it stands, I must forbid it, as much as it pains me. Please, do not be angry with me. Where Ardil and I must go, terrible and dark creatures lurk along the paths. I could never ask you to face such dangers."

"But Ardil gets to go, and he's much younger than I am!" Arwin protested, his disappointment clear.

"If I could, I wouldn't bring him either. I would go alone. But I cannot. Ardil is, in a way, indispensable. Anywhere else but where I must take him, he would be in grave and defenseless peril."

"Even here?" Arwin's eyes widened with fear.

"Sadly, yes," Mara replied, her voice heavy with concern. "Which is why we must leave as soon as possible. As long as we remain here, not only Ardil, but everyone else in this town is in great danger."

"Are you leaving right away?" Arwin asked.

"I don't think I've fully recovered just yet," Mara admitted. "The road ahead is long, and I need to regain my strength for the journey that lies ahead."

"Not if you don't go on foot. You can take Celegrin," Arwin offered.

"Oh no, I'm sure your brother wouldn't like that," Mara replied with a smile.

"Astuil is always finding reasons to be cross with me anyway. Besides, Celegrin isn't happy here - I can feel it. He misses you. It would be better if you took him with you."

"Thank you, Arwin," Mara said, her smile growing warmer. "But I'll speak with your brother first. I'm sure we can come to an agreement that will satisfy him, without putting you or anyone else in harm's way."

☾

On the evening of that same day, Mara decided it was finally time to leave the city of Rist behind. She had no way of knowing where the dark shadow now lingered, and she was not eager to encounter it again so soon. After some negotiation, she came to an agreement with Astuil, promising to send him a young and sturdy horse from her homeland once she returned there.

And so, before nightfall, she and Ardil set off, hoping to reach their destination in less than four days. Her farewell to Arwin was brief, for it pained her to leave the lively boy behind. He had grown dear to her from the start, and after all, it was thanks to him alone that both she and Ardil were still alive.

"I'll miss Arwin," Ardil said, sitting in the saddle on Celegrin before Mara. "He's clever and funny. In Cottingen and all of Nanglorin, there isn't a Wusel half as adventurous and brave as he is. Do you think we can visit him again someday?"

"I hope so," Mara replied as they rode along the North-South Road, heading toward the Gate of Anros, which lay between the two towering ridges of Tin Elwech to the north and Tin Uael to the south. "But it won't be anytime soon. Who knows what still lies ahead of us before we reach our final destination? Not even the wisest of all the wise can foresee that. I can promise nothing, but I have a feeling that this won't be the last time we see him."

"I'd feel a lot better if I knew where we're going," Ardil said, looking around with curiosity. "Everything here is so barren and empty, as if no one - neither man nor beast - has ever lived in this place. It feels desolate. Where are we exactly?"

"We are in the abandoned lands of Nyarost," Mara explained. "Long ago, many hundreds of years before now, when Nyarost and Anros were still part of Miénast and together with Ahren formed the vast and majestic kingdom of the West, this place was home to many people who lived in splendid cities. But that was so long ago that even the oldest of living creatures no longer remember what this land looked like in its days of glory and beauty." She pointed ahead, where the cobbled road stretched toward the horizon, and the mountain ranges of Tin Elwech and Tin Uael drew ever closer together until only a broad gate, seventy feet wide, separated the mountains. "That is the Gate of Anros."

"Anros?" Ardil furrowed his brow. "My Aunt Utilie told me about that place once. She said wild men live there - or, no, she said they 'dwell,' yes, 'dwell,' like untamed and ruthless beasts. And she said their homeland is incredibly dangerous and harsh."

Mara smiled faintly. "That is what some say, yes. But not all tales are true, Ardil. The people of Anros are hardy and fierce, yes, shaped by the rugged lands they call home. But there is more to them than mere savagery. Like all peoples, they have their own ways, their own strengths, and their own sorrows. You will see for yourself soon enough. And you shouldn't believe everything your aunt tells you. Anros is no more dangerous than anywhere else in these troubled times. I know some of the people here quite well. King Henric and his daughter Fala are longtime friends of my family. They are loyal allies, honest and grounded, with a deep love for nature and all that is beautiful and timeless."

Mara's thoughts inevitably turned to Aric, and a wave of sadness swept over her. She had to admit, though reluctantly, that she missed him dearly. But after a brief moment, she regained her composure, reminding herself of the task at hand and what lay ahead for her and Ardil. There was no room for a broken heart in the journey to come.

"Do not worry," she continued. "We won't stay in Anros for long. It will take us about four days to cross through the land - perhaps an extra day if we lose our way or rest too long. But we must avoid both. As long as I don't know what has become of the dark enemy that attacked us in your homeland, we must hurry. He may be close behind us, and we wouldn't even know. We are headed to Faldar, to the High Aedin Mylias. I visited her only a few weeks ago, and I must return. I also hope to find Dartur there, for I believe he too is on his way, unless something has hindered him. We must make haste now. Who knows if Dartur has already arrived, or if he ever did? But I fear we are being pursued."

Ardil's eyes widened in fear. "By whom? That terrible creature?"

"I don't know. I could be mistaken."

"Let's hope so. I never want to face that monster again. Not ever. What was it? And how did it know I had the stone?"

"You didn't tell anyone about it, did you?" Mara asked.

"No, I didn't - not directly, at least. I told the Aedan in Dunhir about it, and later I mentioned it to the children in Rist." Ardil sighed. "Oh, they were so curious."

"And your great-grandfather? You spoke of the stone to him as well, didn't you?"

"Yes, of course. I told him too. But no one else. So how did the dark shadow know?"

"The enemy has spies everywhere. In many places, he has eyes and ears, always listening, always watching, seeking out anything of interest to him. He has been searching for the stone you found for a long time.

But I do not wish to speak of him further. We should fall silent now. Who knows what ears are listening in this place? And when we reach Faldar, I want you to tell me exactly where and how you found that stone. Until then, we should speak little, if at all, and move swiftly."

6

On the morning of the twenty-eighth of February, Anwar and Aleth finally arrived in Westhawen, after being led by Finmar to the edge of the Morabidan Forest, where they had found nothing. Frustrated and despondent, Anwar had sent Finmar back to Dinambad, and, with no other course to follow, he and Aleth had ridden to Westhawen in search of answers.

Hastily, they climbed the steps to the mead hall, eager to inquire about Mara's whereabouts. However, their path was blocked by Eruhad and Anlac, members of the king's household guard.

"Forgive us, but we cannot allow anyone into the king's halls," said Anlac, his face etched with sorrow. "The land is in mourning."

"King Henric passed away a few days ago," Eruhad added, his voice strained with grief.

Anwar stepped back in shock, momentarily lost for words. The weight of the news stunned him, and he struggled to find a response.

Aleth, however, remained unmoved, standing like a pillar of stone before the guards, her face devoid of any emotion. She said nothing, but her presence was as cold and unyielding as the stone beneath their feet.

Anwar placed a hand over his heart, a gesture of sympathy and respect. "My deepest condolences," he said, drawing a deep breath. "We mean no intrusion. We seek word of my sister's fate. Her name is Mara, and many days ago, we received the dreadful news of her death." His voice faltered, burdened by sorrow. "My father sent me to bring her home, yet we have found no trace of her. I have searched far too long, and my hope of finding her alive dwindles with each passing day."

"You have our deepest sympathy, my lord," Eruhad replied, his gaze clouded with grief. "I was not present when she fell, nor when she bravely and without hesitation saved the lives of Princess Fala and her cousin Aric. I searched for her as well, many times. But your sister vanished, as though the earth itself had swallowed her whole."

"Utter nonsense!" Aleth suddenly erupted, fury bursting from her like a dam breaking under the weight of a flood. "Such things are impossible! You clearly did not search hard enough, you thick-headed, foul-smelling peasants! And now Princess Mara has become food for the wild wolves and other terrible creatures that haunt your merciless, frozen land. And it is all your fault!"

Her words were like venom, lashing out with the force of her pent-up anger.

"Calm yourself!" Anwar snapped at Aleth, raising his voice in a rare outburst of anger. Her tactless words had ignited his temper, but he quickly regained his composure. "I am certain the men of Anros have searched as thoroughly as we have."

"You have my word," Eruhad said, bowing respectfully. "And if King Henric still walked among us, you would have his as well."

"Very well. I trust your word," Anwar replied.

"And what good does that do us now?" Aleth interjected, her voice tense. "We still have not found Mara, and it seems less likely by the day that we ever will. While I regret the king's death - do not misunderstand me - our long search has brought us no closer to her."

Almost silently, Aasa stepped forward, her presence calm and grave. She carried a silver sword - the sword of the princess - in her hands. "You are searching for Mara?" she asked softly. "Though I cannot tell you where she is now, I can offer some relief: she is not dead."

"Mara lives?" Anwar's eyes filled with tears of hope.

Aasa handed him the Swan-sword and nodded. "Yes, I saw it in the blue stone."

Anwar took the sword, confusion clouding his face. Before he could speak, Aleth swiftly pulled both him and Aasa aside, away from the ears of the guards.

"What is this blue stone you speak of?" Anwar asked, perplexed.

"It is a powerful stone," Aleth replied, and there was a clear note of fear in her voice, something rare for her. "Othorin gave it to her long ago, well before she began her journey to Dunhir, shortly after she returned from Anros." She turned to Aasa with a sharp, probing gaze.

"You have Mara's sword and her necklace, but not her? That seems more than strange. Show me the stone, woman. I wish to see it."

"I do not have it," Aasa replied, her eyes dropping to the ground. A subtle tremor of fear crept into her voice. "I gave it to my brother, Aric."

"Why?" Anwar asked, his voice tinged with frustration, for he knew the name far too well. "Is it not enough that my sister chose your cold and rough land over our safe and beautiful city? Must I now hear that she entrusted him with something so precious?"

"Mara gave him the most valuable thing she could offer," Aleth said, her voice now calm. She placed a reassuring hand on Anwar's shoulder before turning back to Aasa. "Where is he? Bring him here."

"I don't know where my brother is," Aasa said, lowering her head once more. "He rode out with his men to pursue a group of enemies who burned one of the villages along the northern wall. Fala was chasing them, and Aric went to join her. I cannot say when he will return."

Aleth stepped closer to Aasa, her gaze piercing. "I see great fear in your eyes, much of it directed at me. Yet I am not the first of the Aedan you have encountered. You have looked into the blue stone, the Barilt-incu, as it was once called in your land long ago, and there you saw my lady, Mylias, the greatest and wisest of all the Aedan since the founding of Sedäa as it is today. But tell me, what did she say to you?"

"She told me that soon we would have nothing left but hope," Aasa replied, her voice trembling with the weight of her words. "But even my hope is fading now. My uncle, our king, is dead, and my cousin and my brother are somewhere in the wild. I cannot say for certain if they are even still alive." Her eyes darkened with fear. "And here I am, trapped - doomed to lead a land that stands utterly alone. All I can do is hope that somehow, things will turn for the better. Despite all my fears, the words of Lady Mylias gave me enough confidence to believe that, despite our grim prospects, we might yet be saved."

She hesitated, struggling to recall the exact words of the Aedin. "She called me Auderiáre. I would very much like to know what that means, for I do not understand your language, though it sounds beautiful, like soft music to my ears."

"It means, *'She who has the courage to fight when all hope is lost,'*" Aleth replied, her gaze hardening like stone. "It seems there is much still ahead for you, more than I can say." She then turned her eyes back to Anwar. "But it is clear we will find no answers here."

"What do you suggest then?" Anwar tore his disheartened gaze from his sister's splendid sword. "Return to Dinambad in failure? That would break my father's heart - and my brothers' as well. It would shatter mine, too. But I will not return home until I have found my sister, even if I must search for the rest of my life. Without Mara, I shall never set foot in Dinambad again, whether she be dead or alive." He took a labored breath. "Though alive, of course, would be far better. Thus, my fate is sealed. I beg you, Aleth." He sighed heavily. "We must find her, or my heart will surely break into a thousand pieces from this sorrow."

"Do not despair, Anwar!" Aleth smiled kindly at him. "We will find her. And I never said we should turn back or give up. No, I would never dare suggest such a thing - not even if it meant my own death. I will not return without my dear friend Mara, come what may. And as for Adraéth, that foolish maid, I will not be insulted by her baseless accusations. She will regret her words when we return with Mara, and her false claims will bring her bitter shame. No, we will not turn back - we will ride to Faldar. My lady possesses the gift of foresight, and in her visions, she can see much that happens around her. Trust me! She will guide us further."

"Then farewell, Aasa, Lady of Anros," Anwar said, and with Aleth, he departed swiftly.

Aasa remained behind, her heart weighed down with little hope. She stood overlooking the city, watching in silence as the two riders left the capital and hurried eastward. Her eyes followed them with a longing gaze until they were lost from sight, vanishing into the fading horizon, swallowed by the mists and shadows.

Fortunately, the rest of their journey passed without incident. On the evening of the 28th of February, Mara and Ardil reached the silver forests of Faldar, and they sought counsel from the High Lady of the Wood at once.

"Come closer, child," Mylias said gently, her gaze falling kindly upon Ardil. "Do not be afraid." Then her eyes turned to Mara. "Much have you risked to return here, and you bring with you a grave danger. You should have come alone. Why did you bring him?"

"We were attacked in his homeland, by a creature of shadow. Ardil is in great peril. I did not know where else to take him."

"The black Alyarel is not safe here either. There is no place where he can truly be safe as long as the Dark Lord in the North still endures. He may remain here unnoticed for a time, but not for long. The stone cannot stay here."

"What do you counsel me to do?" Mara asked, her voice filled with desperation. "I don't know the best course of action."

"I am reluctant to give you advice, Mara," Mylias replied, her voice soft but firm. "Though I wish to help you, my heart desires not to interfere in the affairs of others. Yet, I shall make a rare exception, for much has transpired in recent days, and many of these events are leading toward fateful outcomes." She took a deep breath. "I have seen Dartur. He and his companions are safe for now, but he walks a path that was not foreseen, though it has become necessary. He traveled through Cûmer, against the counsel of Elfor. Thankfully, the wizard and his companions passed through the ravaged lands unnoticed. Yet the Enemy has seen them - he knows now that the old wizard sought to deceive him. Because of this, both you and Ardil are in far greater danger than you realize."

Mylias' expression grew grave. "Dartur's path has led him to the northern wall of Anros, where he saved King Henric's daughter from a fate that seemed certain. Together, they now travel to Westhawen, where they will receive dreadful news: King Henric is dead, poisoned by his closest advisor."

Mara's heart sank at the news, her mind reeling with the weight of the danger they faced. She recoiled in shock, a sharp pain overwhelming her, forcing her to the ground as though a great weight had descended upon her. She struggled with all her strength not to collapse entirely.

"The death of the King of Anros changes much," Mylias continued, her voice grave. "It strikes a deep wound into proud people, whose aid Miénast will soon desperately need. In Henric's place, his daughter Fala will now rule, and may she lead the land back to strength." Mylias sighed deeply. "But now, to my counsel." Her gaze pierced Mara, steady and unwavering. "Many in your homeland suffer deeply from your absence, for they do not know you are still live. The word of your death has reached too many ears, and few now would dare to doubt it. Would you leave your family to their bitter grief? That would be a grave mistake. Consider how this irreplaceable loss will slowly drive your loved ones into despair. Grief weakens them, strips them of hope, until nothing remains but sorrow, misfortune, and emptiness. And from that emptiness follows, inevitably, a cruel and agonizing end. Do not let it come to that! Otherwise, all that has happened in these days, every sacrifice, no matter how painful, will have been in vain. Return to your homeland, and stay there until Dartur joins you! For now, there is nothing more you can do here. Go home, and let others carry this burden forward. For the time being, your journey has reached its end."

"I cannot return home," Mara protested. "Not while Ardil is still in danger. What will become of him? I will not leave him behind."

"Then take him with you!" Mylias said. "Here, I can only protect him for a short while, and even that would place my entire people at great risk. Moreover, I see clearly that your fates are intertwined. To separate you now would be most unwise. But tonight, you will be my guests. At least here, you may rest in peace and safety, without fear. Tomorrow, the world may appear different - perhaps more familiar, more secure. Rest now, and do not dwell on what is yet to come." Mylias then turned and departed.

"All the stars from the clear night sky seem to shine in her eyes," Ardil said in awe, turning to Mara. "What a magical and extraordinary being she is."

"What did she say to you?"

"She told me the stone is far more dangerous than I realize, that it manipulates anyone who carries it." Ardil's wide eyes filled with fear as he looked up. "Does it do that to me too?"

Mara knelt beside him, her expression softening into a kind smile. "No, it won't. Not with you, which is a mystery to me - but as I've said before, you seem to be immune to its influence. The stone will not harm you, so long as you never use it. Never! You must promise me that."

"I won't use it, I promise," Ardil said, standing up straight and puffing out his chest, trying to make himself look as tall and serious as possible.

Mara couldn't help but laugh at the sight of him, his effort to appear larger than he was both endearing and amusing. "Alright, I believe you."

As Aranel approached quietly, Mara rose to her feet. "We should get some sleep. It's late, and the night grows old."

"Follow me," Aranel said, gesturing for them to come. "I'll show you where you can rest in peace tonight."

He led them to a tent adorned with lanterns. Inside were two small beds, separated by a long wooden table with elegantly curved legs. Atop the table stood a large, cylindrical candle, recently lit, as the wax had only just begun to melt.

After Aranel left, both Mara and Ardil, weary from their travels, collapsed onto the comfortable beds.

"Will you tell me now how you came upon the stone?" Mara asked.

Ardil looked at her with a startled expression, as though feeling guilty about something. "Alright," he stammered, then began his tale somewhat hesitantly. "I used to explore the abandoned shafts and mines in the mountains of Tin Nangroth with my grandfather and my father. We found all sorts of things there - old oil lamps, some of which still worked, axes, shovels. Everything seemed to have been left behind, but nothing of real value. And we never went too deep, because my father always said it was too dangerous. Once, he even told me he thought someone else was down there with us, but we never saw anyone. Then, when rumors started about something dark stirring in the north, in Um-Atra, we stopped going altogether."

He paused briefly, then continued, "But I got bored, so one day I went back alone - just once more. I wandered into tunnels I'd never seen before, and it was dark, really eerie. I began to feel like I wasn't alone. I wanted to turn back, but then I found it. The stone. It was just lying there on the ground, as if it had been waiting for me all along. I wouldn't have even noticed it if I hadn't tripped and landed right in front of it. It was black, as dark as the night. And when I picked it up, it started glowing from within, like a flame was trapped inside. It felt as though it was calling to me, wanting me to take it - so I did."

"Why do you lie to me?" Mara's voice trembled, her eyes narrowed, questioning.

"What? How?" Ardil faltered, guilt weighing heavily on his words. He exhaled deeply. "Everyone else believed it. Why wouldn't you?"

"Because I am not like everyone else," Mara said, her gaze piercing. "And because now I understand why that foul creature pursued you in Nanglorin." She paused, her eyes darkening with remorse. "Urehel does not know about you. He sent the beast after me. It was my stone, the blue Alyarel, that he sought. I... I brought this peril upon you, Ardil, and for that, I beg your forgiveness. I did not know." Her voice softened, heavy with guilt. "Urehel still believes his stone to be lost. So, tell me the truth: how did you come to possess it?"

Ardil hesitated, his face pale. "I... I didn't find it. Somehow, it came to me."

Mara's brow furrowed. "What do you mean?"

"It... it was delivered, hidden in a wooden box, wrapped in cloth, left on our doorstep."

Her eyes widened. "Who could have placed it there?"

"I do not know," Ardil whispered, uncertainty filling his voice. "But whoever did... they made a grave mistake."

A gentle smile graced Mara's lips, tinged with sorrow. "I'm not so sure about that, Ardil. You've kept it safe all this time. And I think I know who gave it to you."

"Who?" The boy's eyes widened, eager for answers.

"Tharon," Mara whispered. "The heir to the throne of Miénast and Nyarost. I believe it was he who found the stone first."

Ardil blinked in confusion. "But why would he give it to me? It makes no sense."

Mara considered for a moment, her gaze distant. "At first, no. But perhaps Tharon foresaw something in you, something we cannot yet understand. Maybe he sought to deceive Urehel, making the Dark Lord believe that he still held the stone in his grasp."

The boy shook his head, doubt creeping in. "But I'm just a child."

Mara knelt beside him, her eyes soft with admiration. "You are a child, yes, Ardil. But you are also the bravest soul I have ever known."

"Fine." Stretching his arms and yawning, Ardil added, "I'm done talking for today and I'm really tired from the long ride."

"Then rest," Mara said, her voice gentle. "For now, I've heard enough. Lie down, and if I think of anything else to ask, we'll talk tomorrow or the days ahead. Sleep well - you'll need it."

The boy needed no further prompting. He wrapped himself snugly in the soft woolen blanket, turned over once, and was soon fast asleep, already lost in the realm of dreams.

Mara followed his example, lying down in her own bed, but sleep eluded her. Too many thoughts crowded her mind. 'Where is Dartur now, and why isn't he here? Surely, he knows that Aldur, Ardil's father, does not carry the stone. Of course, he knows... So why isn't he here when I need his counsel more than ever?' Her mind raced. 'If Dartur knew the stone was still with Ardil, what is the purpose of all this? What is he planning? He is powerful, yes, but is he truly a match for Urehel himself? I fear not. How does he plan to defeat him? It seems impossible. And what role do I play in this? Why was I sent to Dunhir and then to Nanglorin? For Ardil's sake? I don't understand. What do I have to do with him and the stone? Does Dartur truly expect me to protect Ardil at all costs? How does he imagine that to be possible? It's madness. How am I supposed to manage that? I nearly perished when we fled from that shadowed creature. The fact that we escaped at all, and that we both still live, is thanks more to luck than any skill of mine. Such fortune will not come to us again, I am certain. Oh, what am I to do? What can I do?'

Eventually, exhaustion took hold of her, and her eyelids grew heavy. Just as she was drifting into sleep, she heard a faint, dreadful sound - or at least, she thought she did. It could have been a dream. But then, the sound came again.

Startled awake, Mara sat bolt upright and listened more intently. It was unmistakable - a horrifying screech, like the one she had heard in Nanglorin. Quickly, she rose, slipping quietly out of the tent so as not to wake Ardil. The crescent moon shone brightly through the tall silver trees, and here and there, a few stars glimmered through the torn clouds.

At the far end of the street, near a small bridge that crossed a deep, empty trench—once a riverbed but now dry, covered with leaves, stones, and moss like a great fortress moat - stood Aranel, along with a few other Aedan. Mara hurried to them, studying their appearance carefully. All of them, including Aranel, wore ancient-looking armor with silver breastplates adorned with golden stripes. Over their armor, they wore dark green or perhaps brown cloaks - though in the dim light of the night, it was hard to tell. Each of them held a slender bow made of black wood in one hand and an arrow in the other, as though they were prepared for battle at any moment.

The air was tense, as if they awaited something - something dark and ominous.

"What was that?" Mara asked the men as they noticed her approach.

"We do not know," Aranel replied.

Again, the dreadful screech pierced the air, sending a shiver of fear through them all. Yet this time, it seemed more distant. Aranel signaled to the others, except for one, to follow the sound, and they swiftly disappeared into the tall trees.

"You were followed when you returned with the halfman," Aranel continued. "My brother, Rável, saw him."

"Like a shadowed figure, humanoid but without form, I saw it - or him," Rável added, his voice trembling with the memory. "Full of dread and terror, I beheld your pursuer, and a bitter cold ran through me. I did not know who or what it was at the time," he said, his pale blue eyes searching Mara's face. "At least, not until I came here."

"You know this terrible figure, don't you?" Aranel's gaze was sharp. "You have encountered it before, haven't you?"

"Yes," Mara admitted. "He attacked us in Nanglorin. We barely escaped with our lives, fleeing across the Nyar. I had hoped never to see it again. He is after the Alyarel. His power is terrible, and I came frighteningly close to death. But who or what he truly is, I cannot say for certain. What I do know is that he serves the Enemy - and he is one of the most fearsome servants at that. Whether he was sent from Um-Atra or from Iushvhatu, I cannot be sure."

"We suspect Iushvhatu," Aranel said, his voice steady. "Two days before your first visit here, word reached us that dark creatures from the south had begun to roam through Anros, making their way northwest. That is all we know."

"Othorin warned us about them," Rável added, "though he shared little, as is his way. He's never been one for lengthy explanations, and perhaps it is better that way. I want to know nothing more of them - the mere thought of those creatures fills me with enough dread."

"There are more of them?" A cold wave of fear surged through Mara.

"We cannot say for certain," Rável replied. "So far, we have only seen one of these creatures at a time. But it is, sadly, very likely."

"This knowledge cannot be ignored," Aranel said, sighing. "You must be extremely cautious when you leave Faldar. You are leaving, aren't you?"

Mara nodded, her mind reeling with the implications of their words. "Yes." Her expression was weighed down with sorrow. "The High Lady told me I should return to my homeland. A part of me - a very large part - wants that very much, but another part does not. Quite the opposite, in fact. What is *home* really? How can Dinambad still be my home after all that has happened? I fled from there, in a way, and now I am supposed to go back. Yet something deep in my heart tells me that my former home is no longer truly my place. I feel drawn away from it, as far as possible. And yet, I don't want to break my father's heart, nor my brothers', just because I no longer feel like Dinambad is my home." She sighed deeply. "*Tin barastmin mihrest, than armare eyn-minna maech dewienpela*."

"Oh," Rável exclaimed, his eyes widening in astonishment. "A mortal, speaking the language of the Immortals! And the words sound so beautiful from your lips. Tell me, how did you come to know our tongue? In the West and South, where men dwell, none speak it anymore, for your people fear us."

"Not all fear you," Mara replied gently. "I never have, nor will I. For as long as I can remember, one of your kind has lived in Dinambad - perhaps for my sake, or so I believe. She taught me these words, and much more. She told me of the creation of Sedäa and the rise of the seven High Aedan. She has been like an elder sister to me, a dear friend who cared for me with endless love. When I was young, she would tell me tales of the ancient ages. But there is one story she always withheld, as if she feared it above all others."

"The Battle of a Thousand Deaths at the iron gates of Um-Atra," Aranel said at once, a shadow of fear flickering in his eyes for the briefest of moments. Then, as though relieved by a sudden realization, he added, "So, she is truly there. Adraéth is in Dinambad; how wonderful." He smiled at his brother, then turned to Mara once more. "You should know, she is our sister, and we have missed her dearly since she left us. Though the short years of Men are but fleeting moments to us, it feels like an eternity since our little sister was last here. Although we three do not hail from Faldar, but from Thrad, where our father is one of the highest of all the Aedan, we often walked the same paths together. Her thoughts and journeys have often been a mystery, and she frequently traveled alone across the centuries. But this time, it was the will of the Wise Lady herself to send her into the realm of Men. The reason was never revealed to us, only that it had to do with one of the seven Alyarel."

He paused, eyes narrowing in thought. "We were puzzled by this. What business could one of the Stones of Creation, the tinca aurir, have among mortals? The stones have always belonged to the High Aedan, the Lords and Founders of the world, given to them as gifts by Iah, the One Goddess. Only one of the stones was lost during the Battle of a Thousand Deaths. Three of them remained in Sedäa: one in the hands of our father Thergil in Thrad, one with Lord Elfor in Dunhir, and the third with the Wise Lady Mylias here in Faldar. The remaining three vanished from the world, taken by Argeniel, who bore her own stone as well as the Alyarel of Laeva - which fell at Um-Atra by the hand of Urehel - and by Vaago, the eldest and mightiest of the Seven. Together, they left Sedäa, passing the world into the hands of the Men of Tanuhal. But it is said that one day they will return, when the Enemy in the North dares to rise again, to destroy him once and for all. And when that time comes, all things magical and immortal will fade and ascend to the Mencael, leaving Sedäa to the mortals. Then, even the silver forest will lose its beauty, withering with time until nothing of its grace or splendor remains."

"So, you do not wish for Urehel's death, so that your flawless homeland may endure?" Mara asked, her voice filled with both curiosity and sorrow.

"What we desire in the end has long ceased to hold any value," Rável replied. "For too many ages have we lived in this world as guests, untouched by the passing of a single day. The time of the Aedan is drawing to its close. It is inevitable that we will depart from here and return to our final home. For only there, in the Mencael, the heavens beyond the stars, where our fathers and mothers, the Ahar, dwell, can we truly be at peace. They await our return with great longing."

"But not all of us will leave," Aranel added, noticing the sorrow in Mara's eyes, as if she already felt the weight of saying farewell to Adraéth. "A few will remain, though the longing for Sedäa may break their hearts. Their love for what was created here binds them to this world, and to leave it behind would be their death. The moon has almost set, and the dawn of a new day is near." His gaze met Mara's with quiet intensity. "Go back now, and rest for the few hours that remain to you here in safety, before you must leave us again."

As Mara turned to return to the tent, Rável followed her and gently held her back for a moment longer. "Never lose hope," he said softly, "for love does not die, nor will it ever come to an end. I see in your eyes a yearning that grows with every passing moment, a longing that will never be satisfied in your homeland. Yet I tell you, hold fast to that love, for it will never fail you, though at times it may bring great pain."

With that, he released her, and Mara made her way back toward the tent, the first light of dawn beginning to creep into the sky.

16

The Silver Forest lived up to its name in full measure, for the towering trees glittered with a pure silvery light. The woods exuded a deep sense of peace, yet beneath that peace there lay an ancient, untamed power. Anwar and Aleth approached from the west, following the course of the Aregnar as it flowed through the Morabidan, eventually merging with the Areglos before reaching the Sea of Areglin. From there, it meandered southward, skirting the eastern borders of Vhatu and passing through the free lands, flowing ever onward until it emptied into the vast encircling ocean, carrying all that it swept away from Farham into the deep waters.

Just before the bridge that crossed the Aregnar at the pass leading into the heart of Faldar, Anwar and Aleth dismounted and continued on foot.

"There is something uncanny about this place," Anwar said, his voice low. "Uncannily beautiful. Nowhere else have I seen trees half as tall or shimmering with such purity. Now I understand why it is called the Silver Forest. But I don't understand how it can be both beautiful and unsettling at the same time. Your Lady must be truly powerful, Aleth, and now I fear meeting her. I've only heard of her in old tales - the Lady of the Silver Forest. They say that few escape her snares or the dangerous magic she weaves. What terrible thoughts will she plant in my mind, poisoning it with her enchantments?"

"She will give you hope, Anwar," Aleth said, quickening her pace. "At least, if that is what you seek. She will offer you confidence, comfort and trust, not ensnare your thoughts in venomous webs like a savage spider entangling its prey. Trust her, as you trust me - if you do indeed trust me." She stopped and looked back at the weary man, her gaze questioning.

"I do," Anwar replied. "Otherwise, I wouldn't be here in these woods, which is inhabited by those Firstborn of ages long past."

Aleth continued onward, and Anwar followed close behind her.

"Yet I am still afraid," he muttered under his breath.

In that very moment, nearly two dozen arrows, drawn on sleek black-ash bows, were aimed at them by several cloaked figures, forcing them to halt.

"And your fear is well-founded," one of the figures said, stepping forward. "The High Lady does not welcome strangers who trespass unbidden into her woods."

"I am no stranger," Aleth replied, stepping boldly in front of the masked figure. "I am well known among the folk of Faldar, for I am one of them. My name is Aleth, and I am kin to Lady Mylias herself. I am also called Deoricar, if that name pleases you more."

"Your many names are known to me," the figure responded coldly, "but none pleases me, for you are no longer welcome here, *Aelferme*, the Outcast. You bring great danger with you."

"If it is me you speak of," Anwar interjected, stepping beside Aleth to confront the stranger, "then let me assure you, I mean no harm to you or your Lady. And if by some unwitting act I bring danger, it is without knowledge or intent. I am Anwar, second son of Lord Ráhad of Dinambad, descendant and heir of the Aedan Rehuil. I seek no conflict, only aid. Desperation has driven me here, into your Silver Forest. For many days, even weeks now, I have searched, hoping to find a clue or an answer. I seek my sister, Mara, Princess of Dinambad. With deepest sorrow, I have searched for her, and she is nowhere to be found, as if she has vanished from existence. Yet I refuse to give up hope, and I still believe she lives."

"Oh, she lives indeed," said the stranger, pulling back his hood to reveal his fair Aedan face. It was Rável who stood before them. "Mara is alive, though in these past days, she has been far too near to death more than once. But come, I will not leave you standing here any longer, for she awaits you." He motioned to the other cloaked archers, signaling them to depart. They melted into the forest, leaving Rável with Anwar and Aleth. Without delay, he led them swiftly through the woods until they reached their destination.

Yet Anwar could find no peace, even as they walked. Rável's words about the danger that Aleth carried gnawed at his mind. What danger could she possibly bring, and why had it been hidden from him? His thoughts turned to the fact that she had ventured deep into Iushvhatu before returning to Dinambad. Could it be that she carried some dark shadow from that cursed place, one that only the keen eyes of an Aedan could perceive?

As Anwar and Aleth ascended the winding staircase that spiraled around the trunk of an immense tree, guided by Rável, the young man from Miénast felt his awe grow with every step. Never before had he seen a place so beautiful as the forests of Faldar, and within him, a longing awakened - a yearning that even the boundless beauty of the wide sea could no longer satisfy.

At last, they reached a high plateau where they stopped, gazing out over the shimmering treetops. To the west and east, the rivers Aregnar and Areglos flowed down from the northern mountains, flanking the Silver Forest before meeting in the south and emptying into the vast Sea of Areglin. A grey mist hung over the waters, and the farthest southern reaches were veiled in the haze of distance.

From the side, bathed in radiant light, came the noble Lady Mylias. Her long, snow-white hair flowed down to her feet, adorned with a few delicate braids, and she wore a gown as white as the winter moon. She approached and stood before the guests.

Anwar bowed deeply in reverence, and Aleth followed suit, though her bow was marked by a sense of shame.

"I have been expecting your arrival, Anwar, son of Ráhad from Dinambad," said Mylias with a gentle smile. But her expression darkened as she turned her gaze to Aleth, and though her lips moved not, her thoughts reached only Aleth's mind. "I did not expect you, Aelferme. You stand before me now as someone different than when you left. You wear the same form, but your heart has grown dark and burdened. You ventured deep into the shadow of Iushvhatu and faced the Black Sorcerer, just as I foretold. And you have proven all my fears true, for you have failed, and you have stolen that which should never have fallen into your hands. Do you now understand why I did not want you to depart? Brave and bold you are, as are all of our kind, but you are also weak, just as Haradan once was. His curse is now also yours. Unknowingly, you have bound your fate to that of the Dark Lord of Um-Atra. When he falls - and he shall fall, I tell you this - so too shall you. Do not try to deceive me, for I know all that you have done. I felt it - felt him - when he left Iushvhatu in your grasp. The stone of Vecahr's staff, Prince of the *Blaecwên*, the Black Men, the greatest and most powerful servant of Urehel. And he will stain your pure soul and strip you of your will.

But there is still hope. All is not yet lost. Cast it away - into the wide sea, far from yourself, before it takes hold of your mind! It grieves me deeply to watch one of my beloved children fall into shadow, and yet I could not prevent it. But you shall be forgiven if you mend what you have broken."

Mylias gazed down at Aleth for a long moment, her words spoken, leaving nothing more to say. Then, she turned to Anwar, and he, too, heard her enchanting voice within his mind.

"I sense a growing longing deep within your heart since you entered my woods, and a deeper sorrow still. But your sorrow, at least, I can ease, for that is why you have come to me. Your longing, however, I cannot quell, Rehuil's descendant. I foresee that it cannot be soothed by anything mortal or of this earth. It is the radiance of my forests that stirs this desire - I see it in your eyes - yet even this beauty will one day fade."

Then, Mylias spoke aloud once more, her voice clear and strong. "But think no more of it for now. Perhaps, if you find at last what you have sought for so long, your longing will be forgotten for a time."

She turned her gaze to the side, and both Anwar and Aleth followed her eyes.

Two figures stood still and motionless, bathed in the blinding white light of the sun. Only as they slowly approached did the dazzling brightness fade, revealing their true forms to the others. One was small, with dark, curly hair, a little button nose, and large, expressive ears. The other was taller - though still much shorter than Mylias and the rest - and slender, with long, flowing black hair that shimmered like silk. She gazed at the young man with a deeply joyful smile.

At the sight of the girl, Anwar broke into tears of joy, rushing to embrace his sister, whom he had feared dead. Overwhelmed with relief, he could barely believe that she was truly alive and well. "Mara," he choked out, his voice breaking with emotion. "How wonderful it is to see you alive. I cannot find words to express how boundless my joy is. We were told of your death, and that news shattered all hope in Dinambad, especially within our family. Though I never truly believed it in my heart, I feared it might be true. But our father - he believes it, and his sorrow is unbearable. I beg you, you must come home with us and ease his grief before it's too late, before it consumes him - and us all with it. Return with me and bring an end to this dreadful pain!"

Mara hesitated. Something deep within her whispered that she should stay, and that made the thought of leaving more difficult. Yet she knew she needed to go. "I will come with you. I have been away from home for far too long. I long to see our father and our brothers again. But I will only go if Ardil is willing to come with us as well." She glanced down at the young Wusel beside her. "Will you come with me?"

Ardil's eyes lit up with joy. "May I? That's wonderful! I will go wherever you go, Mara, if you would have me with you."

Mara smiled warmly. "Then all is well."

Mylias now turned her gaze to Mara. "Do not forget, a long road still lies ahead of you. But the time for it has not yet come. And perhaps, if fate should turn in our favor, the need for such a journey may never arise. I cannot say for certain what will unfold. Though I foresee much, only a small part of it may come to pass. Dark days lie ahead for both of us - that is certain." She stepped closer to Mara, placing her hand gently upon her forehead. "*Dinna beneaer amin miht.* You are now blessed with my strength. Use it wisely and with caution. It will not aid you in battle but rather help you to avoid one. And never forget, even light needs the darkness to shine. Farewell, Althûbeael."

She then turned to Ardil and looked kindly down at him. "And you, my young friend, bearer of such a heavy burden - do not dwell too much on it. Every creature in this world becomes a prisoner of their own thoughts if they allow themselves to be ensnared by them. Your fate is uncertain to me, but that does not mean it is ill-fated. There is still hope for you - for all of us, in the end. Use this knowledge with wisdom and confidence. Farewell, Ardil of Nanglorin!"

And so, with hearts full of mixed emotions, the four of them set out on their journey.

ᚩ

Late in the evening, they made camp in the hilly lands of Ostlad, near the southernmost edge of Morabidan, already beyond the borders of Anros, under a cluster of towering stones. Beneath them, they sought shelter from the biting wind and cold. Aleth kept watch by a small, flickering fire, unmoving and silent. Meanwhile, Anwar, Ardil and Mara lay wrapped in dark grey cloaks of the Aedan, a farewell gift from Lady Mylias, trying to catch some sleep.

Only after Anwar and Ardil had fallen into restless slumber did Mara quietly rise and seat herself beside Aleth, close to the warmth of the fire.

"You should rest," Aleth cautioned, stoking the embers. "You will need your strength."

"I have slept far too long since my departure from Dunhir," Mara replied with a sorrowful tone. "I do not wish to sleep anymore. The darkness robs me of my strength and my mind." Her gaze fell upon the flickering flames, and with a shudder, she recalled the black shadow that had assailed her and Ardil in Nanglorin. "Terrible creatures I have seen - a dark monstrosity, a hideous being of unspeakable power. It came as far as Nanglorin, in the far northwest, at the foot of Tin Nangroth, seeking to claim the Stone. Poorly was Dartur advised when he chose me as Ardil's protector, for I nearly failed in my task. I would have perished in the ruins of the cellar, and all his efforts would have been in vain. Ah, if only he were here. I long for his counsel now more than ever. But he is not, and where he might be, I cannot say - if he still is at all. I fear greater perils lurk in Westhawen than he imagined. His plans did not seem to unfold as he had hoped, for even as he left Dunhir, he was forced to take the dangerous road through Cûmer."

"What of Arensted, the Pass of Elwech?" Aleth asked. "Would it not have been wiser to take that path? Safer and shorter it is. Why did he go eastward?"

"I do not know." Mara drew her knees close to her chest. "But when I crossed that pass, I struggled greatly. Not without reason is it called the Snow Pass, for never have I seen such a dreadful blizzard as the one that raged there. And I heard voices on the wind, voices I knew. I was tempted to follow them, but..." She sighed. "Had I done so, I would surely be dead now." For a moment, she fell silent. Then, gazing into the fire, she continued, "I saw tracks on the northern slope, faint yet fresh, no older than half a day. But the strange thing about them was that they led only so far and then turned back, descending northward into the mountains. They should have waited for me. It would have been better.

I cannot protect anyone. How could I? Why must I walk this path and not another?"

"Nothing in life happens without reason," Aleth said softly. "And nothing is given to us without purpose. Each of us is burdened with only what we are capable of bearing, and you, Mara - I am certain of this - are stronger than you believe. I would gladly have your hope and your courage, for despite your fear, I see a light in your eyes, a reflection of your heart's steadfastness. But my heart is empty, and I will never feel as you do."

Mara's gaze drifted to Anwar as she spoke. "Your heart is not empty, nor is his, for he has given it to you. Can you not see it, or do you choose not to? Anwar loves you. And I rejoice for you, for he is the wisest and kindest of my brothers - not as childishly naive as Diam, nor as bitter, cold, and stubborn as Enwir. His love for you is true, even if he does not readily confess it. But it is so. None knows him better than I, and it is no accident that our father chose him to search for me."

"Love must indeed be a wondrous thing, to make you shine so," Aleth said, attempting a smile. "All I know of it is now lost to me, and though I expected that loss, it still brings me great pain. But I shall not dwell on sorrow. I cannot." She forced another smile. "Tell me of him, this Lord Aric. I would like to hear more of the man who has won your heart."

Mara smiled softly, her heart warming at the thought of Aric. "He is unlike any man I have ever known in Miénast. Brave and fiercely strong, though often wild and unrestrained, like a beast driven by blind fury. Yet his heart is pure, full of loyalty and love for his king and his home-land. He lost much in his childhood - his father fell in battle, and his mother later died of a broken heart." Her voice trembled with sadness. "I hope he knows I am still alive. I long to see him again, even if only once more - even if it is the last time. But he has other worries now. His king is dead, and I fear war will soon come to Anros. I feel it. And who knows how all this will end? Yet still, I do not abandon hope that I will one day stand before him once more."

"Surely you will," Aleth said. "And if it brings you comfort, the Blue Stone has been found - by his sister Aasa, no less. She gave it to Aric, as Lady Mylias had instructed. So, he knows you live. Sometimes, when one gazes deep enough into the Stone, they can see something that fills them with hope and courage. Surely, he has seen you within it. And now, my heart longs all the more to gaze into it myself, for my hope has all but withered since my return from Iushvhatu." Unconsciously, her hand reached into her pouch, and she drew forth a black stone, turning it over in her fingers. "The dreadful shadow of Um-Atra found me too when I stood before the Lord of Iushvhatu, the greatest of Urehel's servants. With other dark creatures, he departed from his high tower at the foot of the mountain, making his way northwest. I escaped only by breaking his staff and taking this." She opened her palm, revealing the stone - a relic of the ancient sorceries given to those who served the Lord of Um-Atra, to enhance their power. "I did as Haradan once did."

Mara leapt to her feet, horrified. "And like Haradan, you will be destroyed by it! Not for nothing was the black Alyarel called Haradan's Curse - and this, Aleth, is now yours." Unknowingly, she had echoed the very words Lady Mylias had spoken to Aleth. Fear gripped her as she stared at the small gem in Aleth's hand. "Then it is true, and the rest of what I saw in Faldar shall also come to pass. A terrible war will descend upon Mahlrit, and my poor cousin will perish in agony." Mara's face grew deathly pale. "And Urehel's Stone will return to Um-Atra." Overwhelmed by terror, she struck the stone from Aleth's hand, and it tumbled into the roaring fire.

The flames surged, rising to a tremendous height, and within them, a figure began to form—a great man crowned with a sharp-edged helm. He stretched forth his fiery hand toward Mara, his maw wide, roaring with a thunderous voice. A piercing scream shattered the stillness of the night, echoing through the trees, fields, and across the towering rocks - growing louder and more numerous as it reverberated back. When the figure vanished from the flames, Aleth reached into the blaze with her bare hand and retrieved the stone. It was neither hot nor damaged by the heat, remaining entirely whole.

With feverish haste, Aleth tucked the stone away again.

The night's horrors had roused Anwar and Ardil from their slumber, and they sprang to their feet, peering into the darkness in alarm. "What is happening?" they asked in unison. A sense of dread overcame Anwar, suspecting that it had something to do with the danger Rável had warned Aleth about.

"They are here," Mara said, her face contorted with fear. "The Blaecwên." She retrieved her swan-hilted sword from among her brother's belongings, drawing the gleaming blade from its sheath. In the firelight, it shone with a menacing glint as she stood, poised for battle.

With a gust of wind that nearly extinguished the fire, four towering shadow-figures, draped in long, tattered black cloaks, their obsidian armor hidden beneath, advanced from all sides. Fear and dread preceded them. Avoiding the fire, they circled the group and unsheathed their jagged swords, each fixing their gaze solely upon Aleth. One of them, taller than the rest, stepped forward, though it was not the same one from whom Aleth had snatched the stone - none bore staves. He extended his hand toward her with greedy intent, seeking to reclaim what she had stolen.

An ominous silence hung over them.

Aleth did not move.

Suddenly, Aleth thought she heard a voice - a low, piercing voice that spoke only to her, commanding her in a chilling tone to use the stone's magic. She fought against it with all her strength, but a searing pain coursed through her body. Anwar, seeing the torment in her eyes, grabbed her and pulled her away from the outstretched hand of the shadowy figure.

The Blaecwên howled with a deafening, bone-chilling wail, forcing all four to cover their ears. Aleth collapsed to her knees, weakened. Anwar knelt beside her, holding her with concern. The shadowed figures raised their jagged blades high, ready to strike both Aleth and the man beside her down.

But Mara, with a sudden resolve, plunged her hand into the fire and drew forth a burning brand, waving it fiercely at the dreadful creatures. "Back!" she cried with commanding fury. "Back into the shadows, or you will face the unbridled might of the Immortals!" Raising her free hand toward the sky, a silver beam of light descended, piercing the darkness and illuminating the night as though it were day.

With agonized shrieks, the Blaecwên fled in terror of Mara's power, vanishing into the darkness.

Mara let the burning brand fall to the ground, breathing heavily. The strength gifted to her by Mylias was greater than she had ever imagined - perhaps too great for her to wield again. "We must leave at once," she commanded, her voice fierce with anger as she began to pack her belongings. "Now!" she barked at Aleth, Anwar, and Ardil, who crouched behind the rocks, trembling. Her voice was so filled with wrath and menace that even the three of them feared her. "The sooner we are far from here and reach Dinambad, the better."

She extinguished the fire and strode toward her horse.

Anwar lifted Aleth, her arm draped over his shoulder, helping her to stand. Hastily, they gathered their few belongings and followed Mara.

Ardil trailed behind them silently, cowed and uncertain. Never before had he witnessed Mara's power, and he had never imagined she could be capable of such deeds. He was so awestruck that he forgot everything else around him, lost in confusion.

Before mounting her steed, Mara gripped Aleth's arm tightly and spoke with grave urgency. "Destroy that thing, or it will destroy you! Cast it into the sea, as Lady Mylias commanded, or I foresee a grim and sudden end for you." She then hoisted Ardil into the saddle of her horse, mounted behind him, and rode off with haste.

Aleth remained silent, pondering what she should do. Throwing the stone away seemed foolish - it was powerful, and she desired its strength to combat her enemies. After some time, she too mounted her horse and followed Anwar, led by Mara into the dark unknown.

6

A veil of sorrow and grief still hung heavily over the once grand and joyous hall of the Lord of Dinambad.

Prince Ráhad stood with his eldest and youngest sons at the heart of the chamber, deep in counsel, as they deliberated their next course of action. With each passing moment, hope dwindled. Anwar and Aleth had not yet returned, Finmar could provide no word of their quest, and of Mara, there was no sign of life. Slowly, they all began to accept the bitter truth: the princess was likely lost, truly dead.

"I tell you, Father," Enwir began, "we must ride to Libentya and take our stand there, for surely the enemy's first blow will fall from that direction. We cannot afford to leave the old watchpost unmanned and in the hands of our foe."

"The supreme command of Miénast's army still rests with your uncle Dinhad," replied Ráhad, his voice weighed with despair. "And as long as he holds the reins of power in the capital, he will do nothing. And neither can we act against his will."

"His folly will be the death of us all!" Diam raged, his anger barely contained. "Where is this Haládan they claim to be the heir to the throne? The situation could scarcely be more dire, and yet he remains absent when we need him most."

"The heir alone will avail us little," Enwir said grimly. "But if we had this thing everyone has spoken of in recent days, we might stand a chance at victory. The Dark Lord would never expect us to strike him down with his own weapon."

"You are mistaken," the Prince replied. "That is precisely what he expects of us. It is for this very purpose that Dinhad sent your cousin Torhael north - to bring Urehel's Stone to Miénast. And to prevent this evil from taking root, I sent your sister as well. But the plan Othorin devised for her has failed, and I have sent my poor, innocent child to her death." A deep sorrow gripped him, and his eyes fell mournfully to the floor.

In that very moment, the great door of the hall swung open, and a cool wind swept in, filling the chamber with fresh air. With it came the stirrings of hope, for Mara entered swiftly, followed by Anwar, Aleth, and the young Ardil. Together, they hurried to stand before Mara's father and brothers.

The heavy shroud of death and grief lifted in an instant as Prince Ráhad beheld his daughter, thought long lost to the grave. Overcome with emotion, he wept and embraced her tightly. Her brothers, too, greeted her with tears of joy, and soon they laughed together, their spirits soaring. The dark days, it seemed, had been swept away by Mara's mere presence, as though she had banished all sorrow with her return. Once again, light filled the hall, bright and carefree, as if no shadow had ever darkened its walls.

A grand feast was then prepared in honor of Mara, and with great joy did all the lords and ladies gather in the dining hall, delighting in the many splendid dishes served before them. They ate and drank heartily, laughing as if all the bitter sorrows of the past had never been.

When at last the plates were cleared, the brimming flagons drained, and the sweet desserts all devoured, and when the cooks and stewards had swept and cleared the table, the lively merriment began to wane. The lightheartedness gave way to a more somber tone, and Mara began to recount to her family the many things she had witnessed since her departure. She spoke of the battle near the borders of the Ghostwood Morabidan, where she had been gravely wounded and fled into the depths of the forest, believed dead, only to be saved and brought to Faldar by Aranel.

"You must see it with your own eyes," said Anwar, his voice filled with wonder, and his eyes gleaming with the memory. "The Silver Forest. Never again shall you behold anything more beautiful than that enchanted place, where the trees grow taller and more radiant than anywhere else in the world. Alas," he sighed, "I was warned by the Wise Lady to beware, but it is too late now. A longing has awakened within me, and nothing shall ever quench it."

"Should the days grow brighter and fairer again, and we live to see it, I will take you to Faldar, my friend," said Aleth, offering him a gentle smile. "There you may sate your longing as much as you desire."

Anwar's face lit up with joy. "I shall hold you to that when the time comes."

Ráhad observed his son and Aleth, and when he realized how fond Anwar had grown of the Aedin, his heart swelled with happiness, for it had been far too long since he had seen his children so full of joy.

But Enwir, standing nearby, was not so pleased. To him, there was no place more beautiful than Dinambad by the wide sea, and he could not easily bear anyone thinking otherwise - least of all his own brother, with whom he had grown up and fought side by side in many battles. The thought that Anwar would rather live in the land of these immortal, long-eared Aedan than remain with him darkened his already troubled heart. He had already lost his sister to her love for Anros; now he feared he might lose his brother as well. But he held his tongue, for he did not wish to quarrel on this day. After all, it was a day of celebration - the happiest they had known in a long time.

Mara then continued her tale, speaking of High-Aedan Elfor, father of Ealdir, the founder king of Tanuhal, and first and eldest of the House of Haládan. She recounted with trembling limbs the attack of the dark shadow in Nanglorin, from which she and Ardil had barely escaped with their lives. "It was one of the Blaecwên, as we later discovered," she added, pausing as though she were trying to shake off the icy chill the memory sent through her.

"Are you alright?" asked Diam with concern.

"It is nothing," she replied simply, and then she spoke of Ardil and the other Wusel she had met in the northwest, telling of their curious fondness for food.

For a while, they all sat in silence.

At length, Anwar spoke, though his voice was heavy with sorrow, and his face mirrored his somber tone. "Before we reached Faldar, we stopped in Westhawen," he began, his voice faltering as though he could scarcely bring himself to speak the words. He stared down at the table, exhausted. "We received ill news there." He looked up at his father. "King Henric is dead." Each word was like a dagger to him. "We were not told how it happened, and we had no chance to offer our condolences to his daughter, Fala, who is now queen."

Ráhad went pale. He had known Henric for many years and held him in great esteem, as if he had been his own brother. Then, with a pained expression, he looked at his children one by one. "Men are dying, not only in Anros, leaving sorrow in their wake. Your cousin, Torhael, has fallen as well." A hush fell over them all, and tears welled in their eyes.

"No," cried Anwar, his voice trembling. "When?"

"We do not know," Ráhad answered gravely. "Fria found him nearly thirteen days ago. His broken body was carried down the Elwech. His bloodstained and torn cloak, with its golden trim, was the first sign of that dreadful discovery."

Aleth's heart ached deeply, and the thought of being forever parted from her beloved Torhael tormented her. Though she had feared this moment for some time, she had not wanted to believe it. But now it had come to pass - her dear Torhael was gone forever. And in that instant, a dark fire was kindled within her, slowly and unnoticed, casting a shadow over her spirit, leaving her vulnerable to the will of the Enemy in her moment of greatest weakness.

"A darkness is creeping over our land, swallowing all light in its murky gloom," said Ráhad, his voice heavy with sorrow. "Much has transpired since you left us, Mara - much that is grievous, and little that is good. The only good thing that has come of this day is your safe return. For that, I am glad and more hopeful for what lies ahead. Dinhad has sent out heralds with orders to gather all available men and bring them to Mahlrit. An attack is expected there, and Dartur, who has now arrived, confirmed Dinhad's worst fears. I must do what I can. I will soon depart. It grieves me that I may leave Dinambad forever, without seeing my daughter again. But now that you are here, I can go with a heart full of hope, not weighed down by sorrow."

"What does Dinhad plan to do?" Mara asked. "Has he sent for aid from Anros?"

"Anros?" Enwir scoffed with disdain, his eyes darkening. "We need no help from those savages of the East."

"Silence!" Ráhad rebuked him sharply, though he quickly calmed as he turned to his daughter. "He sent a messenger to Anros a few days ago. I pray it is not too late. We are in dire need of their support. But will they come? So much time has passed, and so much has happened since the two kingdoms were sundered."

"They will come," Mara said with certainty.

"And how do you know that, little sister?" Enwir asked, his tone mocking. "Have you suddenly gained the gift of foresight, like those web-spinners in their silver witch-woods?"

"No," she replied, paying no mind to his venomous tongue. "But the Wise Lady Mylias granted me a brief glimpse into her dreams, and I saw many things. Things that I had long feared, things that fill me with dread, but also some that give me hope. Anros will come." She turned to her father. "Fala will not abandon us."

"Good. That is good news, however strange the means by which it comes. But I will believe you." Ráhad rose to his feet. "There is much for me to do before I leave for Mahlrit."

Diam stood up quickly. "Let me come with you, Father. Every hand that can wield a sword will be needed if the enemy dares attack our fair capital."

Anwar stood just as swiftly. "If my younger brother goes, then I will go too, Father. For Miénast."

"Then I shall go as well," said Enwir, standing tall. In his pride, he towered over his two brothers, both in might and stature. "I would be ashamed if my younger brothers fought bravely while I stayed behind in safety."

"No," Ráhad said firmly. "Anwar and Diam will go with me. But you, my eldest son, must remain. I cannot and will not leave Dinambad unguarded and leaderless. What if we win the battle in Mahlrit, only to return to a home destroyed, with all the women and children slain? You are my heir, Enwir. One day, you will stand in my place as Lord of Dinambad. That is why you must stay." He then turned to Mara, who had risen from her seat. "And you as well. I will not risk sending you away again, my daughter. Stay here, and stay safe."

Mara bowed with a grateful smile. "Once, such words would have angered me, avar, and I would have been bitterly disappointed. But today I am glad, and I thank you, for I am weary from my long journey. The thought of entering another battle no longer stirs my heart."

Ráhad smiled at her in satisfaction and left the hall. Anwar and Diam followed him, while Enwir, fuming, stormed away, leaving Mara alone with Aleth and Ardil.

"What will you do now?" Aleth asked.

Mara took a few steps to the side, gazing into the distance. "Sleep," she said with a smile of relief. "I want to sleep, in my own bed, in peace, without the burden of the dangers that lurk outside."

"Mara!" Aleth cried, leaping to her feet. "The shadow in the North grows ever stronger. Soon it will cover the world in darkness. And you would do nothing? Lady Mylias gave you a portion of her boundless power - I witnessed its might with my own eyes. It was given to you to use, not to hide behind thick walls. The High-Aedan have hidden long enough. Will you stand by and watch as your loved ones die - your father, your brothers, and even Aric? Will you send them all to their deaths while you do nothing?"

The princess turned to face the Aedin. "It is no longer in my hands. Lady Mylias gave me a portion of her power to protect myself, should it be needed. No battle could I win with it. Did you not hear her words, Aleth, or did you choose not to? I know what else she told you. She warned me about you, and I did not believe her - until now. Your reckless theft in Iushvhatu has put us all in danger. The Blaecwên were after you, not Ardil." She paused. "I know what you plan to do, but I tell you it will fail. That thing was created by Urehel's power, and much of it remains within it - along with his will." She glanced at Aleth's clenched fist, which held the sorcerer's stone of the black mage in a pained grip. "To possess one of these stones is dangerous, whether it is a sorcerer's stone of the Blaecwên or one of the Alyarel." She looked sharply at Aleth. "Whether its power is used for good or ill matters not, Deoricar. You cannot use Vecahr's stone. Its dark power will deliver you to the Dark Lord in the North - and me with you. Neither of us is meant to wield such stones, nor any great power."

"What do you know of such things?" Aleth sneered and stormed away.

"*Ennaw din nanthrae*," Mara called after her, and Aleth froze. "*Eltha ithraën*."

Pondering Mara's words, Aleth left the hall in silence.

"What did you say to her?" Ardil asked, slightly intimidated yet fascinated by the beauty of her words.

Mara sighed but gave him a gentle smile. "You do not wish to know."

"I do," he insisted, eyes wide with curiosity. "That's why I asked."

"I am weary, Ardil." She stretched tiredly. "Let me tell you another time, please."

"Very well," the young Wusel sighed, a little disappointed.

17

Mara did as she had spoken. She lay down to rest in her own bed, and after so many days of fear and sorrow, it was a balm to her weary soul to finally find some peace in the safe and familiar haven of her home. Not in a long while had she slept so soundly and deeply.

Yet, that peace did not last for long.

At first, she dreamed of a gentle summer evening, where she walked along the coast with her friends. But suddenly, the sky darkened, and thick, black clouds swept across the shining sun. A fierce wind arose, and the calm waves swelled into raging torrents, crashing violently upon the shore. Now, she stood alone, and for a brief moment, she halted before the surging waters, for she thought she heard a voice calling to her from the depths of the sea.

"*Dinna i ferr*, Althûbeael. *Serhaedin dir maech andir arimaren*," spoke a deep, resonant voice, its powerful sound carried by the wind over the waves of Ymbsetta. "You are in danger," it cried again in Haldron. "Save your family and your heart."

Before Mara could move, a great wave crashed upon her, sweeping her far away. All around her, the world turned dark, empty, and cold.

After what seemed like a deep plunge into an endless abyss, she saw a faint glimmer of light above her. The sun shone in thin rays through the heavy clouds, casting a dull glow. Before her stretched a wide, barren plain, once covered with green grass and fields of wheat, potatoes, and other crops, now trampled, ravaged, and destroyed. Smoke rose from several places, veiling the land in thick gray mist. Here and there, Mara could make out black-clad creatures, hunched and limping across the fields, armed with torches and jagged blades, clad in heavy iron armor.

Suddenly, a horn sounded. Its blast was bone-chilling, filled with dread, and as it rang out, it seemed to sweep away the fog that hung over the plain.

Before Mara's eyes, the grand capital of Mahlrit appeared, its white-gray marble gleaming faintly in the dim sunlight. The clear glass of its windows and high terraces reflected the pale gray of the sky. Like a young forest of spears, the shining weapons of countless creatures rose high, arrayed in long ranks across the fields before the city.

Once more, the horn sounded. Catapults were drawn back, loaded, and aimed, and then hurled with tremendous force toward the city's sturdy stone walls. The defenders swiftly answered, launching ballistae and smaller projectiles upon the foes. Many stones fell harmlessly, but some struck true. Siege towers and battering rams were pushed closer to the walls by giant, troll-like creatures. The soldiers atop the ramparts fired arrows in vain, for the creatures were heavily armored, and even where their gray, leathery skin was exposed, it was as if they were carved from stone. The arrows simply bounced off them. They looked like monstrous trolls, but were far larger and more powerful, with two massive, curved horns jutting menacingly from their heads.

"Forward!" cried the commanders of the Celkûn. Among them were some even larger and more fearsome than the others.

Mara watched in horror as the battle raged before her. She stood in the midst of the chaos, powerless to act. As she tried to flee, the scene blurred before her eyes. Fog and darkness swirled around her, yanking her violently into another vision.

Now, she was surrounded by riders on all sides - great men with dark, braided hair hanging down over their shoulders. They were armed with gleaming spears, round shields adorned with golden designs, broad swords, and slender black-oak bows. Like an impenetrable wall, the riders thundered past her. At their head rode Queen Fala herself, her golden hair gleaming beneath her helm in the dusky light. Close behind her, flanked by the house guard, Aric rode with his men.

The riders of Anros were tall and broad, but two among them stood out. The one riding directly behind the queen was nearly a head taller than Aric, who was himself among the tallest of the men of Anros. His hair was short and lightly curled. The other, following close behind Aric, was much smaller and slighter than the others, his long, dark-blond hair flowing freely beneath his round helm - an unusual sight for the riders of the wild.

"Aasa!" Mara recognized her easily as she rode past.

The mighty host of Anros charged straight into the largest of the Celkûn, trampling many beneath their horses. But many men and steeds fell to the enemy's savage counterattacks, and the host dwindled swiftly.

The Nemar - troll-like, towering giants - grouped together, blocking the riders' path, wielding great hammers and axes. A powerful blow struck Queen Fala, hurling her and her steed far across the plain. She landed, broken and near death, amid shattered shields and torn banners. While the largest rider, who had been behind her, rallied the troops for another charge, Aric leapt from his saddle, sword in hand, and in a frenzy hacked his way toward the dying queen and the Nemar that loomed over her. In blind, burning rage, he slew the beast, which was more than three times his size.

Aasa rode closer, watching the scene unfold with deep sorrow. But at that moment, two Celkûn seized her from behind, dragging her from her horse. She cried out in terror, and Aric, hearing her, turned. But in his distraction, he did not see the blow coming. A Celek drove the sharp point of his axe into Aric's back.

Mara screamed in horror.

Aric collapsed to the ground, and nearby, Aasa was struck down by the enemy creatures. In a short span of time, the line of Andor, the royal house of Anros, was utterly wiped out, leaving Anros without king or heir.

Again, the horn sounded.

But this time, it came from the west, its call bright and full of hope. In the distance, the white banners of Dinambad fluttered, bearing the majestic swan, adorned with silver and gold. A force of riders, fewer than before but accompanied by many foot soldiers, approached swiftly. At their head rode Prince Ráhad, with his sons Anwar and Diam flanking him on either side. Without hesitation, they charged into the fray with a loud, resounding cry.

But they had come too late.

Too many men of Anros had already fallen, and the few defenders left on the walls and within the city had been nearly all slain.

Now Mara saw her cousin Fria, limping and wounded, stumbling out from the city. Her eyes were cold and vacant as she passed by Mara's side, throwing herself at the Celkûn with the last of her strength. She had entered the battle with only a handful of men, and it had been her doom.

As Mara watched helplessly, seeing her cousin fall, then her father and brothers slain by the enemy, she collapsed to her knees, weeping and crying out in despair.

Suddenly, everything went dark, and a chilling cold enveloped her. Before her rose a towering figure, advancing with slow, heavy steps. Upon his head was a crown of iron, its long, sharp spikes fused to a thick, metal helm. His long cloak billowed in the wind, seeming to burn with a fierce, fiery glow, while his dark eyes gleamed with the frozen light of ice.

"Althûbeael," he spoke in a harsh, gravelly voice that sent a shudder through the air. "At last, we meet." His words were spoken in a terrible, alien tongue, cruel and strange, yet somehow Mara understood him as if he spoke in the common speech. "They are all dead now - all whom you loved and cherished. Your foolish uncle revealed far more to me than was necessary. I might even thank him for that. In the end, he did exactly as I had foreseen. And they all died because of you. I can feel the great pain within you, devouring you slowly until nothing remains but a shadow of yourself." He stepped closer. "Would it not be wiser to sur-render and join me? Together, we could share in each other's power. I can offer you all that you desire. Your every wish, I can fulfill - if only you join me and return my stone." He stretched out his hand greedily. "Give it to me! I know you have it. Your uncle told me so. Return it."

"Never," she said boldly, rising to her feet. "I would choose death and any torment imaginable before I ever aid you, Urehel."

He roared with fury, bitter rage swelling within him. He seized her by the collar, and a searing flame, followed by freezing cold, shot through her body. For a moment, she was paralyzed, unable to breathe.

But at last, she wrenched free and staggered back, bent with pain. Yet fearlessly, she stood once more, raising her hand in defiance. "You have no power here!" she cried, her voice full of warning. A bright white light enveloped her. "Return to the shadows from whence you crawled, creature!"

Blinded by her radiance, Urehel stumbled back, shielding his eyes from the light with his hand.

"*Decere arcrae althû au lewa!*" Mara cried, her voice thundering with a mighty force that shook the ground beneath her. The brilliant light around her grew, driving away all darkness, until everything was bathed in blinding white.

"Do not celebrate too soon," Urehel snarled. "Here you may have triumphed, but in your capital, Mahlrit, I shall strike harder still. All that you have seen will come to pass, while you hide behind the walls of your greedy harbor city. Do not think your safety will last. Once Miénast's capital is destroyed, I will come for you. No matter how powerful you are, you will fall, just as all who came before you."

"Begone!" Mara cried in anguish. "None of what you speak will come to pass. Your words are worthless here. *Decere revar i craer*!"

"Mara! Mara!" Ardil's panicked voice cut through the darkness. He knelt beside her, frantically shaking her from her nightmare.

Trembling all over, she bolted upright, gasping for breath as if she had run a great distance. The terror of the dream only began to fade when she saw Ardil beside her.

"You were dreaming," he said, breathing a sigh of relief as he leaned back against the headboard. "And you were shouting. You were speaking in some strange tongue - nothing I've ever heard before, though I've been here long enough. I came as soon as I heard your first cry and tried to wake you, but it wasn't easy." He looked at her directly. "Did you see him? The Dark Lord from the North?"

"Urehel? Yes, I saw him, and much more besides. But I do not wish to speak of it further," she said wearily. "Yet, though the nightmare was dreadful and draining, I have gained something of value from it." She looked down at Ardil. "The Enemy knows much - more than is good for us - but not all. And not all of it is true. He believes I possess the stone, the black Alyarel - the one you found. And for that reason, if I remain here, he will strike at Dinambad. I must leave, and quickly."

"But where will you go? Will you take me with you? Honestly, I'd rather not leave. It's so beautiful here - so beautiful that it makes me forget the dangers outside."

"Fear not, you may stay as long as you wish, provided war does not reach every corner of the land. I will go alone. Whether it is wise or not, I cannot say, but I must go to Mahlrit - Dartur is there, and I need his help more than ever."

"This is far from wise," came the voice of Adraéth, who had entered unnoticed through the open door. "No matter how you twist it, but it is no worse than if you were to remain here. Yet in these days, you should not go anywhere alone. I will go with you. And do not dare try to stop me. I made a vow long ago, and I will honor it, come what may."

Mara smiled with relief. "Good. I am glad to have you with me. You are more than welcome on all my journeys."

"But I don't want to be left behind!" cried Ardil in dismay.

"You wished not to leave Dinambad, did you not? That wish will be granted. It is an honor, for you are the first of your people to enter our fair harbor city, and as a princely guest, no less," said Mara. "Besides, a battlefield is no place for a Wusel. I cannot risk bringing you, along with the stone, so close to the Enemy. Urehel must believe I possess the Al-yarel - but it shall not truly accompany me to Mahlrit. Here, you are safe. Urehel does not know you are here, nor that you have the stone. That will not change. So, stay! Perhaps we shall see each other soon. I hope it will be so." She smiled hopefully. "Come to the capital if we are victorious. My brother Enwir will be there too. I will tell him to bring you."

Ardil lowered his head sadly. Though he did not like the idea of Mara leaving him, he understood that it was likely for the best.

"Come, Ardil!" Adraéth said sternly. "The morning is still young. We should all rest a few more hours before the sun rises - if it even rises at all in these dark days."

The boy climbed out of bed reluctantly and left the room with the Aedin. Before Adraéth closed the door behind him, he turned and gave Mara a look of deep concern.

That troubled gaze lingered in Mara's mind throughout the night, leaving her with the uneasy feeling that she was making a grave mistake.

Sleep would not return to her before the morning, for with every passing moment, the decision to leave Ardil behind seemed more and more a terrible choice.

6

On a small, secluded balcony facing the sea, Mara leaned against the stone railing and gazed down at the crashing waves, which thundered as they shattered against the high cliffs below.

Adraéth approached, standing silently beside her for a while. "You seem uncertain still, unsure of what course to take," she said at last. "So let me offer you counsel, for time does not stand still. The longer you delay, the more quickly it will turn against you. Decide swiftly! But here is my advice: attend first to the danger that now lurks among us, and I do not mean the boy. Another threat has returned with you, one far graver. You know this well. You've already seen its effects with your own eyes. Why did you not refuse her return here?"

"How could I?" Mara replied with a heavy sigh. "Aleth is my friend. I cannot dictate where she may go and where she may not. Even if I could, she would not listen to me. What power have I to stop her?" She paused. "Yes, I saw that sorcerer's stone. And yes, I told her to destroy it or at least cast it away. But whether she will do so, I cannot say."

"She will do nothing," Adraéth replied darkly. "For she does not comprehend the peril of that power. To her, the stone is no threat. Only when it is too late will she realize what she has done. By then, she will be powerless to change it. You must speak with her again. She trusts you still, even if only you."

"I've already told her all that I could," said Mara, frustration tinging her voice. "But she listens to me no more, no matter how I speak or what words I use. Still, I hope that she will make the right choice."

"Aleth is weak," Adraéth continued gravely. "She always has been. I have known her for countless years. In her youth, she often wandered, and always alone. Who knows what dark depths she has glimpsed in those long travels? It is not without reason that the High Lady banished her from Faldar. There is more to Aleth than meets the eye, and that troubles me greatly - for it could mean the ruin of us all. If it comes to pass, all that we have fought for against Urehel will be in vain."

"What are you saying?" Mara asked, a sense of dread creeping into her voice.

"There were three sorcerers who came to Sedäa in the year 95 of the Second Age - autumn, I believe, if my memory does not fail me. Two of them you know: Dartur and Angborn. Angborn now calls himself Vec-ahr, the black sorcerer, Lord of Iushvhatu, and the mightiest of the five immortal Blaecwên.

The fate of the three was decided in the Caedyr. Only Dartur returned alive - at least, that is what we all believed for many years. He had watched with his own eyes as Angborn and the third sorcerer, Tielir, fell beside him. But they were not truly dead - at least, not Angborn. He joined the Enemy, and as a reward, he was given great power. That same power Aleth now possesses - at least a portion of it. I speak of the stone she stole from Vecahr, crafted with the strength of the black Alyarel, along with four others borne by the Blaecwên." Adraéth paused, her breath catching for a moment. "As for Tielir, no one knows what became of her. Her fate has remained a mystery. But had she joined the Enemy, we would have learned of it by now. Yet, for many long years, there has been no word of her, and she has slowly faded from memory - until Aleth returned from one of her many wanderings to Faldar.

Lady Mylias possesses great power and can see much, as you know from your time in her realm. She saw Aleth in her visions, surrounded by death and ruin. And so, Aleth was banished, perhaps in the hope that Mylias' visions would not come to pass. But it seems we were all mistaken in this."

Adraéth turned her gaze directly upon Mara. "Aleth is Tielir - or so I believe, and so Mylias foresaw. She is reborn in her, for it is the only way she could have escaped Vecahr unscathed. On the wrong side, she is an unpredictable force, for Tielir was powerful - far more so than Vec-ahr could ever be, even with or without his sorcerer's stone. She was always the strongest of the three sorcerers. She must not fall into the hands of the Enemy, or our doom is certain."

Mara lowered her head in despair. "What am I to do now?" she asked quietly. "For years, I thought I knew Aleth well, but it seems I have been utterly mistaken. Yet I cannot harm her, nor do I wish to."

"I do not ask you to harm her," Adraéth said softly. "Whether Aleth or Tielir, both were kindhearted, at least at the beginning. Speak with her! I beg of you. Perhaps you can persuade her, though I have failed. She trusts you still, even if she will not always listen to you."

6

In the early morning, though the threatening shadow creeping from the North cloaked the land, hiding the dawn, a great host assembled before the city gates. Mara stood beside Enwir as they accompanied their father and brothers, Anwar and Diam, to bid them farewell. As she counted, she noted five hundred brave men, their standards bearing the golden insignia of Dinambad: two gleaming swords crossed beneath the proud white swan. With words of hope, luck, and a wish for glorious victory, they sent them on their way.

Yet Mara could not help but gaze upon the army with growing concern. It was a small company, resplendent in full armor upon gray horses, with barely five hundred footmen behind them, dark-haired and gray-eyed, taller than many men of Miénast. But for a true battle, it seemed far too few. 'Five hundred?' she thought. 'So few? This will never be enough. I can only hope the riders of Anros are numerous enough that these five hundred will suffice.' Anxiety stirred within her as she feared she might never see her father and brothers alive again, for the memory of her dreadful nightmare loomed larger with every passing moment, inching closer to becoming reality. Yet she forced herself to smile, waving them off with what she hoped was a reassuring expression.

Once they were far enough away, Enwir turned to her. "You are thinking the same as I," he said as they made their way back into the city. "Five hundred men won't come close to being enough, not after what our uncle has told us. All of Vhatu is teeming with those wretched creatures and trollish beasts. What good will a measly five hundred do against that? A drop in the ocean compared to Urehel's vast horde."

"Much as I hate to admit it," Mara replied, "it looks as grim as you say. But I will not yet give up hope. The host of Anros will be large, surely. Many brave and swift riders dwell in the wide, wild grasslands - perhaps enough to claim victory with their help."

"I wish I had your hope," said Enwir, uncharacteristically refraining from his usual scorn for the men of Anros. "All I see now is death and despair, and that shadow." He looked up at the darkened sky. "It makes everything worse. I can do nothing but watch as they all march to their deaths, for I see little chance of victory. Now I finally understand how you must have felt all these years - trapped, unable to act. I understand you better now. It is a cruel thing to be forced to wait, helpless, not knowing what will come next."

"That feeling will soon pass," Mara said gently. "The battle will be fought. Until then, we can do nothing but hope for the best."

"Perhaps you are right, little sister," Enwir conceded. "And who knows, perhaps one day the sun will shine as bright as it once did, without shadow or fear. I will trust in that so long as you do. And to think, I never imagined I would willingly listen to the words of my younger sister and realize that she is wiser than anyone I know. Your words give me strength, and they lessen the weight of this darkness that surrounds us. How glad I am that you remained here with me. Never should you dwell anywhere else, for your presence brings me hope and comfort. I would not know what to do without you. You are like a warm ray of sunlight, and without you, all would be cold, dark, and endlessly empty."

Mara remained silent as they walked together into the lord's palace, her heart full of mixed emotions. Rarely had she seen her typically aloof and distant brother speak with such warmth and honesty, and it filled her with both joy and sorrow - for he did not wish her to ever leave him.

'But what of Aric?' she wondered. Must she remain in Dinambad, separated from him for the rest of her life? The thought was too dreadful to bear. Yet she loved her brother as well and could not bring herself to break his heart. She would rather shatter her own into a thousand pieces, hoping in pain that one day Aric would forget her. After all, there were many fair women in Anros. Surely, he would find another soon enough. But even this thought brought her no comfort.

She hoped fervently that she would never be forced to choose between Aric and her family, for it was a choice she would ponder for the rest of her days and longer still, never able to find a solution that would bring her peace.

Then a thought struck her: perhaps Aric could come to her, if she could not go to him. But would he leave his beloved homeland for her? Was his love truly so great? If it were, one of her burdens would be lifted, for another commander could be found to take his place in Suthawen. Yes, that thought pleased her far more. And yet, she continued to ponder, unable to rest easily.

But all these thoughts she had to set aside for now, for there were far more pressing matters at hand.

૦

Aleth stood upon the high pier, staring out over the sea, gripping the small stone tightly in her hand. The shadow from the North had grown so thick and impenetrable that the sky appeared as though it were already twilight, though it was not yet midday.

Slowly and cautiously, Mara approached her from behind. "Aleth," she said softly, "the time has come. Cast it into the sea now, or I shall do it for you."

Aleth did not turn. "Why?" she replied. "Why throw away such a powerful weapon when it could be used? That would be truly foolish."

"I beg you, heed my words! That stone brings danger. You must be rid of it, or it will destroy you."

"No!" Aleth cried, spinning around to face her. Her expression was twisted, and the warmth had drained from her eyes. "The stone is mine!" She drew her sword and advanced on Mara. "You just want it for yourself. Admit it! The Bariltincu, the black Alyarel, and the power of Lady Mylias are not enough for you, are they? But I will not give up the stone. It fell into my hands by fate, and it belongs to me alone." She raised her sword, striking without hesitation.

Mara barely managed to parry the blow with her Swanblade, stepping back in horror. "Aleth, I don't want to fight you. Stop this!" She ducked quickly, dodging another wild strike. "Look at what that thing is doing to you. It's making you attack your own friend!"

"Friend?" Aleth spat bitterly, moving in for another strike. "Some friend you've been. You sent me to my death, knowing full well what awaited in Iushvhatu. The stone was the only thing that saved me."

"You chose to go there yourself," Mara said, her voice strained as she deflected blow after blow, retreating toward the stairs. "It should have been me. That was my task, not yours. But you insisted on going in my place, to protect me. And now look at what you're doing!"

"Silence!" Aleth roared, grabbing Mara by the collar. "This is all your fault. You sealed my doom - and now yours as well!" She shoved Mara violently, sending her tumbling down the stone stairs. "I've had enough of your lies," Aleth shouted, storming down after her. She stopped a few steps away, glaring at Mara. "For all the pain you've caused me, Princess of Dinambad and rebirth of a mighty ancient one, you will pay dearly. Everything you hold dear, I will take from you." With a wicked smile, she ran her fingers over the stone - and in an instant, she vanished.

"No!" Mara cried, struggling to her knees. "Aleth! Don't! If you do this, he will see you!"

But Aleth did not hear her.

She had entered a kind of twilight realm. Everything around her was gray, dim, blurred, and distorted. Yet she was still in Dinambad. The once-glorious city now appeared barren, abandoned for thousands of years. Next to her, a bright figure knelt, glowing with pure light.

"Please," Mara's voice echoed faintly. "Stop! They can find you this way."

But it was too late.

A shrill, hideous wailing pierced the air, echoing through the outer gates of the city. The people fled in terror, barricading themselves inside their homes. A darkness blacker than night descended upon the white harbor city, and with it came the five dread Blaecwên, the Black Men. They stormed through the streets until they stood before Mara and Aleth, their vile eyes fixed upon them.

Mara rose, trembling, and stepped in front of them, her face set with courage. "Leave my homeland!" she cried. The few who had not fled watched in awe as she stood bravely before the shadowed beings.

"My stone has called us," rasped one of the Blaecwên. "It wishes to return to its lord in his realm. But it will not go alone."

"No," Mara said, dread rising in her chest. "You will not take her with you. You will have to go through me first."

"Foolish child," the creature hissed. "Give us the stone and its new bearer, or both of you shall die."

"Never," Mara said firmly, gripping her sword with both hands and holding it before her chest, ready for a battle she feared would be her last.

At that moment, a small company of guards rushed from the prince's palace, led by Enwir, his own gleaming Swanblade drawn and ready.

"What a terrible sight," Enwir exclaimed, halting in shock. "Drive them from our city!" he commanded his knights.

"No!" Mara shouted. "Wait!"

And then she heard it - a deep, piercing voice, filled with malice and power, that cut through the very air.

"Deoricar, Shadow-Wanderer," the voice intoned, cold and dreadful, audible to all around. "Though stolen, the stone is now yours, for your power is greater than many. Return to your new home and become our supreme commander by my side. And I will reward you greatly. All that you desire shall be yours, and more. It is time to repay the wrong done to you when you died without cause. Come to us, my dear friend. But first, finish what you have begun. Kill the child of light."

As the voice faded, Aleth reappeared. She still held the stone tightly in her hand, but now she seemed larger, more terrible, and in her eyes, a dark fire burned. There was no goodness left in her. She raised her sword high and advanced on Mara, who stood frozen, unable to move.

In the last moment, Enwir lunged between them, striking at Aleth with his sword. Had he not intervened, Aleth would have slain his sister without hesitation. But Aleth laughed and attacked Enwir with such ferocity that he fell to the ground, gravely wounded.

"Enwir!" Mara cried in anguish. At last, the spell was broken. In a panic, she rushed to her brother and knelt beside him.

"Now die, both of you!" Aleth shrieked, her voice twisted, resembling the harsh cries of the Blaecwên. She raised her sword for a final, deadly blow.

In that instant, Adraéth leapt forward, raising her bare hand. A blinding beam of light burst from her, striking Aleth and the Black Men like a thunderbolt. With a terrible scream, they all fled the city.

Mara looked at Adraéth in shock and gratitude. She had never known of her servant's power, and it seemed far greater than anything she had ever witnessed.

"I am so sorry. Please forgive me," Mara wept over her brother, tears streaming down her face. "This is all my fault."

"You are not the one who dared to steal the mightiest sorcerer's stone from Vecahr," Adraéth said with a sigh. "And Aleth, I fear, has now become one of them. Urehel will surely use her as another of his puppets. And she will be a powerful piece in his game. But when he is finally destroyed, so too will the power of his five stones fade. And all that will remain of Aleth is an empty shell. As long as she serves Urehel, she will fall with him when he falls."

"Then she will die?" Mara asked, her voice trembling. "I cannot allow that."

"It has already happened," Adraéth replied sadly. "The Aleth I knew would never have raised a hand against you. She held you dear, Mara - more than anyone, even herself."

Ô

Enwir sat upright in a small chamber, surrounded by healers and maidens tending to him with care. Mara sat beside him on a wooden chair, while Adraéth stood quietly at her side.

"It won't be enough," Mara said gravely. "There's no way they can achieve victory with so few men."

"What would you have me do?" Despair was written plainly on Enwir's face.

"Send all the men you can spare to Mahlrit."

"I cannot leave the city unguarded." Enwir's face was growing pale. "What if those dreadful shadow creatures return?"

"They will not dare come again," said Adraéth. "For two reasons: first, they have reclaimed their stone, and second, they have gained Aleth as an ally. They will be needed elsewhere now."

"Finmar's army is still here," Mara added. "If you send a portion of the guards with him, they'll have nearly two hundred men."

"Very well, I'll send Finmar," Enwir said, resigned. "If that satisfies you."

"There is one more thing." Mara's voice was filled with urgency as she looked at her brother. "Let me go with him! I must go to Mahlrit."

"No." Enwir struggled to rise from the bed, groaning in pain before sinking back down. "So, you can get yourself killed?" he gasped weakly. "Why do you long for death, sister? What can it give you that life cannot?"

"You misunderstand me. I do not seek to join the battle - that I promised Father, and I intend to keep my word. I must go to the city itself to prevent a terrible fate. Dinhad will die - there is nothing I can do to stop that, even if I wished to. But Fria must not fall with her father. Let me go to Mahlrit. I must prevent that. Or does the life of our cousin mean nothing to you? Amras is dead, and Torhael as well - but Fria is not, and I intend for her to live a long time yet."

"If I let you go, Father will not be pleased," Enwir warned. "He will punish me for disobeying his orders."

"Tell him I fled," Mara said. "He'll believe it – for it wouldn't be the first time. And if I meet him, I'll say the same, to ease your conscience."

"That will ease it only slightly," Enwir said with a sigh. "But I do not wish to lie to Father."

"Then let's call it a slight distortion of the truth," Adraéth interjected. "And to reassure you, I will accompany Mara."

"That does calm me," Enwir admitted, relief in his voice. "I've seen your powers with my own eyes, and I know my sister will be safe with you by her side." He turned to Mara, his expression somber. "Then go. But please, be cautious and do not reveal yourself to the Enemy. The Princess of Dinambad would be a great prize in the hands of the Dark Lord, and you know Father would do anything Urehel demanded to see you returned unharmed - no matter the cost. Even if it meant killing the heir to the throne, he would do it without hesitation." His gaze darkened with sorrow. "Losing you would be his undoing. And mine as well. So, please - be careful."

"I will," Mara replied gratefully, kissing her brother gently on the forehead. "With Adraéth at my side, nothing will harm me. Thank you, dear brother, for trusting us." She rose and, with Adraéth following, left the room.

"You could have told him the full truth," Adraéth said as they walked outside. "Your brother deserves to know everything."

"What good would that do him?" Mara replied. "It would only make him more fearful. And he would grow to distrust Ardil, who must stay here with the stone - in safety and out of Urehel's sight. The fewer who know, the better. Surely, you understand that."

"I do understand, child," Adraéth said calmly. "But your brother should still know that the Enemy believes you have his stone."

Mara halted, turning quickly to face the Aedin. "So, he can worry about me even more than he already does?" She sighed. "No, that would not be wise." Then she continued walking. "Sometimes, ignorance is a blessing," she said over her shoulder, as Adraéth quietly followed.

18

The battle on the fields before Mahlrit raged fiercely as the army of two hundred riders, led by Finmar and accompanied by Mara and Adraéth, arrived. The sky was fully darkened, casting an eerie and foreboding atmosphere over the land.

Mara and Adraéth rode in gleaming armor, adorned with the emblem of the white swan and crossed swords upon their breastplates, their helmets polished to a high sheen. They were nearly indistinguishable from the noble knights of Dinambad. Only by closer inspection could one see that they were more slender and delicate than the tall, broad warriors who followed behind them.

Before them lay a scene of horror, one that mirrored the dreadful vision Mara had seen in her dreams. Fear gripped her heart.

"We cannot linger here," Adraéth said uneasily. "Finmar!" She cast a commanding glance at the young leader. "Take us to the city gate as agreed!"

Finmar nodded and, with a cry, spurred his horse forward. His riders followed in tight formation, cutting down any foe that dared stand in their way. Mara and Adraéth rode safely in their midst, unnoticed as they crossed the battlefield and reached the city gates, already shattered and swarming with Celkûn and other dark creatures that stormed into the city, mercilessly slaughtering all in their path.

There, Adraéth ordered Finmar and his forces to assist in the bloody battle where they could, and they turned southward, where they found Lord Ráhad, his retinue greatly diminished. Only his sons and a handful of knights remained by his side. Relief washed over him as he saw Finmar and his men arrive to aid them.

Meanwhile, Mara and Adraéth hastened toward the upper rings of the city.

"Dartur!" Mara called as she spotted the sorcerer among the few remaining city guards. She rode up to him with Adraéth. "Where is my uncle?"

"He's in the tower above," Dartur answered, his voice hurried. "Good that you've finally come. The old fool could use some kind words from you."

"I'll have no kind words for him if what I've seen proves true," Mara replied, glancing around. She saw only a small group of men gathered around the sorcerer. "Is this all? Are there no more left to defend the city? Where are the riders of Anros?"

"They were meant to arrive at dawn," Dartur said grimly. "That was the plan. Where they are now, I do not know. But they *will* come - that much is certain. Tharon remains with them, Huandar's heir, and he will not abandon his kingdom." His gaze fell upon Adraéth, and his expression shifted to one of surprise and relief. "Your intervention is late, but perhaps not in vain."

"Late?" Adraéth laughed, her voice brimming with joy and light. For a moment, it was as if the sun had found a way to pierce the thick clouds. "I have never been late, old friend. I have wandered this world for countless years without aging, and yet now it feels as though time is slipping away. I've longed to speak with you again, and when this is over, we shall have that conversation, Othorin."

With that, she and Mara rode swiftly up the cobbled streets of the capital, moving from one district to the next, until they finally reached the highest ring, where a grand fountain stood amidst a patch of green, bordered by stone-paved pathways. They dismounted and hurried toward the building behind it.

Two men in gleaming black armor stood at the door, barring their way with crossed spears. Mara removed her helmet, allowing her long, shining black hair to spill over her shoulders. "I am Mara, princess of Dinambad, daughter of Prince Ráhad and niece of Lord Dinhad," she said in a commanding tone. "I demand entrance to Fheran's Tower."

The guards, awestruck, immediately stepped aside and opened the gate for her, bowing deeply in submission. Mara strode inside swiftly, with Adraéth close at her heels, impressed by the young princess's authority.

"Where is Dinhad?" Mara called into the empty throne room, her voice echoing off the high stone walls. "Where is the Keeper of the King's Crown of Miénast?"

"Lord Dinhad is in one of the chambers at the top of the tower," a small figure replied. He wore the armor of Mahlrit's household guard and stood in a corridor beside a stairway leading upward. As Mara and Adraéth moved toward the stairs, the figure drew a short, blunt sword and blocked their path. He stood as tall as he could, but even so, he barely reached the women's waists. "As the guard of the lonely tower, I cannot let anyone pass. The Keeper is with his daughter, who has returned gravely wounded," he said, sighing. "She is very near death."

"You have no idea how close she truly is to death, boy, if you do not let us through," Mara said angrily. "Do you not know who stands before you?"

"Oh, I know very well," the small man snapped back. "A rude girl with no eyes in her head. For I am not a boy, but a Wusel, a Halfman from the fair land of Nanglorin." He straightened with pride.

Mara stepped back in shock. "From Nanglorin?" she echoed, recalling something. "Are you Aldur, Ardil's father?"

"Yes, I am," he replied, his eyes gleaming at the mention of his son's name. "Is he well? How do you know him? What trouble has the little fool gotten into now?" His face suddenly paled. "Oh no, something has happened to him, hasn't it? I should have taken that thing with me. Oh, my poor boy. He's still so young."

"He is well," Mara said quickly. "Ardil is in my homeland, safe for now - safer than here, at least. I brought him there. Dartur wanted me to go to him. Whether I've done as he hoped or not, I cannot say. Much has happened since then, and not all of it as I intended. But I could not prevent everything I wished to."

"Mara," Adraéth urged, "we must get to Fria quickly."

Mara's face grew stern again, and she glared at Aldur. "Will you still not let us pass, Halfblood? Must I take your head, though I would rather not harm you?"

Aldur stepped aside hastily. "Please, don't kill me. I'll let you pass. I fear the Keeper is not in his right mind anymore."

Grateful but in great haste, Mara nodded to him and rushed forward with Adraéth, racing down the corridor and up the stairs. Aldur followed as quickly as his short legs would allow, driven by his insatiable curiosity.

6

Mara flung the door to the chamber open in a fit of impatience and stormed inside. She came to a halt, horrified by the sight before her: her uncle Dinhad sat slumped on a simple stool beside the bed where Fria lay, fevered and drenched in sweat. Her condition was dire.

Dinhad was so lost in his grief that he did not notice the uninvited guests.

Adraéth gently pushed Mara aside, rushing to Fria's bedside, where she knelt and placed a worried hand on the young woman's burning forehead. She whispered Fria's name softly.

Aldur slipped into the room, coming to stand a few steps away from Mara.

Dinhad suddenly rose in anger. "Begone, witch! No one is permitted to come here!" His eyes fell on Aldur. "Did I not give you a simple task? One single duty, and even in that, you've failed me. Death shall be your reward for this treachery." He reached for the old sword hanging by his side and moved toward the Wusel.

"It's not his fault," Mara said, stepping between her uncle and Aldur to shield the halfman from harm. "If you seek to punish anyone, let it be me. Perhaps it is time for you to wield that rusty sword again, even if it must be against your own niece. But spare Aldur - he defied your orders for your own good. If vengeance is what you seek, strike me down instead. I can bear it."

Aldur's eyes widened in astonishment as he realized this girl was the niece of the grim Keeper. He marveled at how someone with such merciless kin could be so kind and fair.

Dinhad stopped abruptly in the middle of the room. A deep pain filled his heart as he gazed at his niece, for her face reminded him of his beloved wife, Aminas, Mara's aunt, who had passed away years ago. Her death had left a wound that never healed. "Mara," he said, his voice heavy with sorrow. "You've come too late - whatever you intended to save is lost. Fria is as good as dead, just like my sons, Amras and Torhael. And, like my dearest Aminas." His grief-stricken gaze hardened. "Ah, the torment your lovely face brings me, for I see her in you.

Each time I look into your eyes, my heart shatters anew. Now that my line is all but extinguished, and I remain alone, all hope is gone. And now you appear to deepen my misery."

"Fria is not dead," Adraéth said, turning to face them. "She lives, but her life hangs by a thread. Without the proper medicine, she won't survive much longer. This bed is no place for her - we must move her swiftly to the chambers of the healers. There, perhaps, she can still be saved."

"Do not touch my daughter!" Dinhad shouted angrily, stepping toward Adraéth. "Take your hands off her, witch."

Mara followed him, grabbing his arm to hold him back. But in his anguish, Dinhad spun around, breaking free of her grasp and striking her hard across the face. She fell to the ground, and for a moment, even Dinhad seemed shocked by his own action.

Dazed, Mara lay on the cold stone floor, slowly sitting up. Aldur rushed to her side, his face filled with concern as he knelt beside her.

"Guards!" the Keeper bellowed. A moment later, half a dozen armed men in the armor of the city's watch entered the room. "Throw them out! And woe betide you if you ever let them in again. As for you, Aldur Halfblood, return to your post at once, and do not dare disobey me again, or I'll send you to the frontlines of the battle, where fate will decide your punishment."

The guards helped Mara to her feet while they dragged Adraéth away from Fria. Together, they hauled both women out of the room and threw them roughly onto the stone-paved courtyard outside the tower, slamming the gate shut behind them with a resounding crash.

Silent and defeated, Mara rose and walked to the wall, gazing out over the ruined city toward the battlefield below, where the enemy's vast armies swarmed like a dark tide. Columns of black smoke rose from various parts of the city, acrid and choking.

As Adraéth came to stand beside her, a loud horn sounded in the distance, echoing from the south.

Marching along the foot of Tin Uael was a vast host, tens of thousands of men on great grey and brown warhorses, forming in perfect ranks. The banner of Anros was unmistakable. A mighty shout rang out, and the riders charged into battle, crushing foes beneath the hooves of their steeds. Many enemies were felled by arrows, spears and swords.

Though it was a moment of hope, Mara could not rejoice. The arrival of the soldiers from Anros only brought dread, for now, what she had seen in her dream might yet come to pass.

"There is still hope," Adraéth said softly, noticing Mara's despair. "Though it may be faint, it is enough not to give up now. Come! There is nothing more we can do here, but the healers may still need our help." When Mara did not move, Adraéth gently placed a hand on her shoulder and said, "Do not think I am unaware of your fears, child. What you saw was only a trick to deceive you. Would you now rush into battle to prevent what might happen?" Mara nodded weakly. "That is exactly what Urehel wants. He still believes you possess the Alyarel. What do you think will happen if you fall on the battlefield and the stone ends up in the hands of our enemies? That is his goal. He won't care which of the seven Alyarel he obtains. Do not be led astray, as your uncle has been. But he bears no fault - Dinhad is weak. He has lost two beloved sons, and the death of his wife broke him long ago. You must not fall into the same trap, Mara. Forget what you saw. Now, come."

In silent torment, Mara followed Adraéth down the street until they reached a large building near a small, blooming garden, where they entered.

ϭ

"Inuriel," said Adraéth, stopping alongside the princess in a wide hall where numerous makeshift beds had been set up. Lying in those beds were many wounded men from all across Miénast, tended to by too few healers and medics.

The old woman turned slowly from a patient who lay unconscious, his breastplate bearing the symbol of the snow-capped peak of Mâhl, obscured by blood and grime. "Ah, Adraéth, it's you. But how did you make it into the city? Out there, on the fields - now burning and trampled beyond recognition, fields that once yielded such rich harvests, if they ever will again - a fierce battle rages. Well, it hardly matters how you managed to get here, for I am very glad that you are. Your skilled hands are sorely needed, as you can plainly see."

Her gaze shifted to Mara, who stood nearby, looking small and broken, lost in her troubling thoughts. "And who is this girl? One of your apprentices, perhaps? If so, it would do her well to be put to work immediately - there is plenty that needs doing. What's the matter with her? Can't she speak? Have you brought me a mute? No matter, speech isn't needed here. All she has to do is stitch wounds and clean injuries. Surely, she can manage that, can't she?" Inuriel looked Mara over once more. "What an odd child. She looks strange to me with that silent stare. And then, on top of everything, she's strapped into that ghastly armor - no more flattering on you either, my friend. A woman in battle? And such a young, pretty girl, too? No wonder she looks so broken and wounded. Who knows what horrors this poor thing has already faced? Come with me, you two. Remove those dreadful suits of armor. I'll find you something more fitting - you'll fare better without being trapped in that rigid metal."

Inuriel motioned them to follow and disappeared around a corner into a small dark chamber. She returned shortly, handing them a few garments. "Hurry up, now. There's a lot of work waiting for you both. This needless war has brought many casualties, but even without the battle, we've been overwhelmed with work ever since the days have turned so dark. It's that dreadful shadow hanging over the land. I can't help but wonder where it's come from and why it's happening now. A great storm is heading our way, I fear."

"That's no storm," Mara finally broke her silence, and the old woman turned to her with wide eyes. "The shadow comes from Um-Atra, and it has only one purpose - to darken the hearts of men and drain all hope from them. That his foul creatures can see better in this darkness, giving them an advantage over us, is but an unintended boon for him."

"Oh, heavens!" gasped Inuriel. "The poor girl can speak after all! And what a lovely voice she has - like the song of a cheerful bird. But you speak of terrible things. Who is this 'him' you speak of? Who is in Um-Atra?"

"No one of importance," Adraéth interrupted quickly. "No one whose name is worth speaking aloud."

"Well, if you won't tell an old wise woman, then keep it to yourselves. But it astonishes me that one so young knows of such horrors, things unknown even to me. Now that you've proven you can indeed speak, girl, tell me your name. I have a feeling I've seen you somewhere before, and I'd like to know who you are."

"You wouldn't know her, Inuriel," Adraéth cut in swiftly before Mara could respond. "She's not from here. Your eyes must be deceiving you. Her name is Ielyanna. She is indeed one of my apprentices, and the most skilled and clever of them all."

"Ielyanna, is it?" Inuriel frowned, studying Mara as though still uncertain. "Well, then. Quickly, now - take off that heavy armor. We'll have it set aside for you, though I hope you won't need it again. Time is short, and the many wounds here won't heal themselves." With that, she walked away, leaving Adraéth and Mara alone.

"Ielyanna?" Mara looked at her companion, confused. "Why did you lie to her? And what kind of name is that? It sounds strange to me. It's a wonder that woman, who speaks so many words, didn't see through your deception."

"It's for your own protection," Adraéth replied. "Inuriel has a loose tongue. Imagine if she learned who you truly are. It wouldn't take long before your father found out. Is that what you want? As long as we can avoid it, he must not know you're here."

"But why Ielyanna? What does that even mean? Couldn't you have chosen a name more fitting for me?"

"Soon enough, you'll see that no other name fits you better," Adraéth said with a sigh. "For it's a name you were once called long ago, in a different life, a life long since passed." She sighed again. "But now is not the time to explain all of this to you, child. Take off your armor and help tend to the wounded!"

○

The battle on the fields before Mahlrit raged fiercely. Relentlessly, enemy troops poured into the city, for at dawn that morning, the second gate had also been breached. Time and again, Dartur called out words of encouragement to the city's guards, and together they managed - though with increasing difficulty - to push their foes back. But then the wizard's hopeful shouts fell silent, for he had to hurry away, up into the city's highest ring, to the Tower of Fheran, for now only he alone could prevent what Mara had failed to stop.

But it was already too late.

Fria staggered out through the gate, half-dazed by too many useless medicines and other herbs. She struggled down the cobblestone road, followed by half a dozen watchmen.

"Fria!" Dartur called out, running toward her. But the wounded woman passed by him as if she could not even see him. "Fria! What madness is this?" The wizard had to shout, and at last, Dinhad's daughter stopped.

Slowly, with great effort, she turned to face him. "Madness?" she repeated, as if she hadn't quite understood him. "Is it madness for a young commander to march into battle? Or is it not rather a necessary duty? For me, it is surely the latter." She turned her back on the old man and continued her march, her loyal soldiers following.

"You will not return alive if you go now," Dartur warned.

Fria did not turn around. "I do not intend to," she said coolly, and pressed on.

But Dartur could not let her go so easily, and he hurried after her. "What foolish nonsense has your father filled your head with?" he asked. "You are walking straight to your death. Fria, listen to me! Do not throw your life away so carelessly."

"You don't understand," said the commander, not pausing in her steps. "I must do as my master bids, whether it is folly or not. It is not for me to decide, only to carry out."

"Your deep grief is blinding you, child," Dartur said angrily. "Do you wish to end up like your brothers? Your death will not undo what has happened. It will not bring Torhael and Amras back."

Suddenly, Fria stopped and stepped close to the wizard. Her gaze was hard and filled with fury. "What do you know about it, you foolish old man?" she snarled. "About my pain? My bitter torment? My fears?" She grew a little calmer. "No, you know nothing. You are just an old man with no family, no past. I would have gladly gone north in Torhael's place, but he talked me out of it. He assured me it would be a pointless, boring journey. I would love nothing more than to know what truly happened to my brother." Her eyes, heavy with suffering, filled with tears. "Why is he dead, and you are not?"

Dartur hesitated for a moment, regarding the young woman thoughtfully. "Much has happened since Torhael's departure," he began at last, "and little of it was ever intended. But I cannot undo what has been done. Such is the way of things. But as for his death - do you truly wish to know the whole truth? Sometimes it is better not to learn everything."

"Nothing you could tell me about my brother would shock me."

"You are mistaken. There is much I could say that would leave you astonished."

"Then speak, old man!" Fria growled. "There is still a battle to be fought, and we intend to win it."

"You will see no victory if you go now. You will die."

"That is what I want," Fria said, her voice filled with anguish. "What else do I have left in this wretched life? My mother died a cruel death two years ago. Amras took his own life because of it. Now my eldest brother - the one I always looked up to, the one I admired and trusted - is gone, and he has left me alone with my father. But what good is a father who does not love me? In his eyes, I am but a lesser, weaker child who will never achieve the glory Torhael and Amras won for themselves. I will never be the daughter my father wished for. And what's worse, he blames me for my mother's death. And perhaps he is right, for I feel a terrible guilt. So, what is left for me in this life? Everything I loved and cherished is now far away, beyond my reach, and I can only join them through death. So do not hold me back from my fate, Othorin! It is inevitable. We all must die - better sooner than later."

"Do not cast your life away simply because it seems dark and empty to you now," Dartur urged. "There is still much in this world to discover and experience. You have not lost everything, Fria."

"I've lost too much," she replied, taking a deep breath. "Farewell, Dartur. You were a loyal friend and mentor to me for many years. Now, whether by fate or choice, our paths part. Perhaps we will meet again someday in another place." She turned away from the wizard and walked on, her watchmen following closely behind.

Dartur stood still, watching them go. "*Lewawel*, Fria," he muttered sorrowfully.

6

Of all that transpired in the besieged city, Mara knew nothing. In the halls of the healers, at the middle ring of the city, the doors rarely remained closed for long. Wounded men were constantly being brought in, their injuries growing worse with each passing moment. Mara was overwhelmed with work. Soon, she forgot her sorrow, and all her worries were pushed aside, for in the chaos, there was no room for such thoughts in her mind.

She knelt beside a young man from Anros. His breastplate bore the engravings of two large horse heads, gazing at each other in profile, beautifully adorned. His hair was long and dark blonde, braided into two thick plaits. He bore a striking resemblance to Aric, though Mara did not notice, so absorbed was she in her task.

Still somewhat dazed, he opened his eyes and groaned as he sat up to better see the young woman tending to him. Suddenly, a sense of recognition dawned upon him. "I know you," he said, looking at her. Mara glanced at him briefly, offering a gentle smile before returning her focus to the grievous wound on his leg, working diligently to stop the bleeding and cleanse the injury.

"You were in Suthawen with Lord Aric," the young man continued. "I saw you standing on the high balcony, your bright eyes shining, and your black hair gleaming like silk." Mara did not respond to his words, continuing her care of his wound. "You are the Princess of Dinambad," he exclaimed suddenly, as though a veil had been lifted from his eyes. "You are the one to whom Aric gave his heart."

At this, Mara looked up at him, her eyes silently filling with tears, yet she remained silent.

"You are alive," the man said joyfully, his excitement causing him to try and sit up, though his painful wound kept him bound to the bed. "This will surely bring him great joy. Your loss was a bitter blow for the poor man. He has already lost so much in his life. We all thought it cruel that he should lose you too. How overjoyed he will be to see you again!"

"If he ever sees me again," Mara said quietly, pausing in her work. The man looked at her, puzzled. "So many men have already fallen. And for everyone we lose, two more of the enemy take their place. I see no good end to this battle unless unexpected help arrives. But who could still come to our aid? All the brave men who can fight are already on the battlefield. Oh, how I wish I could do something - something truly helpful - rather than sit here stitching wounds and patching up holes, like some frightened old woman who can do nothing else. I am still young and strong, and I have courage. I want to do more than this."

"Do you not see how important your work here is?" the man asked. "How many of these wounded would have succumbed to their injuries, never returning to their families, had you not cared for them? You wish to do more? Is this not enough?"

Mara cast her gaze around the room, seeing the many injured men lying in narrow beds or crouching on the floor beside them, groaning in pain and some near death.

"Is this not enough, noble lady?" the man continued. "Out on the battlefield, you would only find death. Is that truly what you want? To die? How can someone so young, so untainted, long for death when her whole life still lies ahead of her? Is there truly nothing in this world, however barren and cruel it has become, that can still hold you back from dying? Is there nothing left worth living for? You have not yet lost everything."

"You are right." Mara's thoughts inevitably drifted to Aric, and her troubled heart filled once more with a flicker of hope.

The man studied her closely. "He loves you dearly, you know," he said, sensing that her thoughts were indeed on Aric. "And the hope that you will one day be with him is what gives him the strength to endure this terrible darkness."

"You seem to know Lord Aric quite well," the princess noted. "If you can speak of his hopes and feelings."

"I grew up in Suthawen. My father, Dimlac, and his father, Arid, were friends from a young age. Also, my father married Arid's sister, Aorel. So, Aric is not only a good friend but also my cousin."

"And do you have a name, son of Dimlac and Aorel, nephew of Arid and cousin of Aric?" Mara asked with a slight smile. "For it seems you already know mine, and now I know the names of your parents and kin, but not your own."

"Forgive me." He looked startled. "I am Anlac. Until recently, I served in the king's guard. But after my father fell in battle, I became captain of Suthawen's cavalry, leading Aric's household forces."

A look of horror crossed the young woman's face. "But if you are here, where is Aric? Is he now standing alone on the battlefield? Oh, my heart grows heavy."

"No, he does not stand alone. The army of Anros is large and mighty, filled with brave and strong warriors who stand by him and our queen with unwavering loyalty. And Tharon, the Haládan, is with him too. When we crossed the Ush, our vanguard was ambushed by enemy forces lying in wait at Uswang. They nearly struck down our queen, who was surrounded by foes. But Tharon and Aric broke through, slaying nearly all the enemy themselves. That Haládan is a master swordsman. And though Aric is his equal, he could not be in better company."

Suddenly, the heavy door was thrown open, and four guards carried in a seemingly lifeless body on a stretcher.

Mara let out a horrified cry and leapt from Anlac's side, rushing toward them. "Aasa!" she cried, gently brushing the tangled, blood-streaked hair from the woman's face. Her skin was deathly pale, her body battered, and her flesh already cold.

Inuriel hurried over, gently pushing Mara aside to examine the motionless woman. "Quickly," she called to a healer nearby. "Fetch bandages and all the herbs we have left." The healer ran off at once.

Adraéth approached and stood beside Mara. "See? She lives. And without your intervention, she is in good hands, and soon Aasa will recover."

"With the few herbs we have left, her chances of recovery are slim," Mara said sorrowfully. "Her physical wounds may heal here, but I sense a shadow upon her soul, and against that, there is no cure." Discouraged, she turned and walked back to Anlac.

"How terrible," Anlac mourned. "The noble maiden of Anros lies there. We all feared this when she rode alongside our queen into the Stone Lands. Yet none of us dared to dissuade her from fighting in the battle. Oh, how dreadful. First, King Henric is taken from us, and now his niece lies here. Darker have the days grown - darker than we had ever feared."

"She is not yet dead," Mara said, filled with sorrow. "But it will take a miracle to save her now."

Suddenly, they heard shouts and cries coming from the battlefield, echoing up into the city. But these were not the cries of despair - they were cheers of joy and triumph. The battle was over, and the men of Miénast and Anros had finally won. The capital had held, and the enemy forces had either been slain or had fled.

"Perhaps that is one such miracle," Anlac said, a small smile breaking through his pain. "At least for me. The battle is over, as I hear. And though it was a costly victory, a victory it remains."

"We cannot rest long on these laurels," Mara said gravely. "Um-Atra has not yet been defeated, and the Dark Lord will not delay in avenging this bitter loss. When he strikes again, it will be like the great flood that sweeps away the sand of the shore in a raging storm." Her heart grew heavy once more, filled with fear for the uncertain future.

An older woman approached the two and gently pulled Mara away from Anlac. "Child," she said, her face hidden beneath a hood that cast a shadow over her features. "Come! There is something you must see." Without waiting for Mara's response, the woman led her away. They passed through a narrow side door and emerged outside, where they stopped behind the gardens, from which they could view the street leading to the healers' chambers. "Look here," the woman said, pointing to a group of men, all dressed differently and of varying heights, walking along the road.

Leading the group was Dartur, moving with difficulty and hunched, yet still in a great hurry. Beside him walked a man whose face was hidden beneath a hood, and his armor was concealed by a gray cloak. But for a brief moment, Mara caught sight of the hilt of a finely crafted sword. This cloaked figure was unusually tall, nearly as tall as Dartur. Following behind them were Lord Ráhad, Queen Fala, and Aric - all unharmed, though weary and drained from the long battle.

"Your miracle unfolds before you," the woman said to Mara. "Your father is safe, as you can see, and so are your brothers. I have already spoken with them. Now lay down your needless worries, my child. We have won. You should allow yourself some joy in that, even if it will not last long."

As the five figures disappeared through the door into the building, Mara turned to the woman. "You didn't bring me out here just to show me that my father is well. Why am I really here? And who are you? Reveal your face. I do not like speaking with a stranger whose intentions are unknown to me."

The woman laughed warmly and pulled back her hood. Beneath it was the face of an older woman, finely shaped, slender, and still beautiful, with hair as smooth and black as Mara's, though streaked with gray and white.

"Do you not recognize your own family when she stands before you, my dear child?"

"Aunt Ilbeth!" Mara cried in delight, throwing her arms around the woman. "How wonderful it is to see you!"

Ilbeth looked her niece over with an appraising gaze. "You've grown since I last saw you," she laughed. "But that's no great feat. You were just a small child back then. Truly, it brings me great joy to see you again at last. When I look into your bright eyes, I see the face of your dear Aunt Aminas. You have grown into such a beautiful young woman - more beautiful than I ever could have imagined." She smiled. "But surely you know why I brought you out here? Think, what would have happened if your father had seen you with the healers? What would he have said? How would he have reacted to find you here, in the midst of a devastating battle? Don't look at me like that - I know many things that have happened here. Knowing my stubborn little brother as I do, I suspect he ordered you not to leave his beloved harbor city. And knowing you, my dear niece, you disobeyed that order and came here anyway. Though you've done much good here, I doubt he will be pleased to find you."

Mara turned pale with fear. She hadn't even thought of that. "Oh no. I broke my promise to him. Shame on me."

"Now, now, my child." Ilbeth pulled her niece into a compassionate embrace. "You acted with good reason. But your father will likely not see it that way. So, it would be wise to avoid him here in the city for now. Come, let us take a walk instead." She took Mara's arm and led her down the street. "Aren't you curious about the hooded man walking beside the old wizard? Or do you already know who he is?"

"I can't say for certain, but I suspect it was Tharon. I caught a glimpse of his sword, and it looked valuable and finely crafted. I hope it was him. Who else could it be?"

"Anyone and no one," Ilbeth replied with a smile. "You are not entirely wrong. It is indeed Tharon, though in truth, he is no man. For he never was. Tharon is, in fact, a woman. Brave and strong, like you. And her true name is Thariel. But the people here will call her Ealdariel when they see her - Ealdir's heir, they say. And that will be the name she bears when she takes the crown, for it was foretold."

"You've traveled far," Mara observed. "In all these years since you left. But why did you leave? Was it because of Aminas?"

"Yes." Ilbeth stopped and looked at the girl, her expression somber. "I left because of her, but I would have gladly stayed for you. But your father never understood that, I'm afraid. He accused me of fleeing when I last visited you. But I could no longer live in the place where your aunt's longing had led her to her death. She loved Dinhad dearly, and her children, Torhael, Amras and Fria. But in that barren, stony capital, she withered like a freshly cut flower, for she also loved the sea. And she died from her unfulfilled longing for the Great Sea's endless horizon." She began walking again, and Mara followed. "Have you ever wondered why your father has always been so determined to keep you from leaving Dinambad? He feared you might suffer the same fate as Aminas. And in his endless fear, he doesn't see that all his worries may come true if he keeps you trapped in the harbor city any longer."

Mara stopped suddenly, thoughts of Aric flooding her mind. A fierce longing surged within her, and she had to summon all her strength not to run back to him into the healers' chambers.

Ilbeth placed a hand on her shoulder and said softly, "Though it should be a beautiful thing to give your heart to a man and feel true love for him, I can see that it causes you great pain. But why, I wonder? Who is it, Mara? And why can you not find joy in it? Love should be a joy, not a torment."

"It has been a joy only rarely," Mara said sadly. "But those few moments, I would not want to lose. Yet now it has indeed become a torment, and I wish my heart were empty and free of all this sorrow, for I love a man whom I am forbidden to love. He is merely a commander, not a nobleman or a king. In my brothers' blinded eyes, he is worth no more than a lowly stable boy."

245

"But what is he worth to you?"

"Everything." Mara was on the verge of tears. "Everything, and more. And yet it seems not to be enough. I am forbidden to love him, and so I will love no other."

"Oh, my dear child," Ilbeth said with a warm smile. "Do not give up so easily. So much is happening in these days that everything could look different by tomorrow. Come!" She led the girl further down the street. "Do not torment yourself so, for much can still change. Love can be painful at times, but sometimes, it is the most beautiful thing that can happen to someone."

◖

At last, they arrived at the Cobbler's Street, as the road within the first city wall was called, and there they had to climb over large heaps of rubble from the destroyed wall before entering an old inn. The common room was dimly lit, and there were few guests inside. In one shadowy corner sat two men - tall and slender, with long, shining dark hair. As the women approached, the men rose from the table and turned toward them.

With a joyful cry, Mara ran into the arms of her brothers, Anwar and Diam. They looked weary and weak, but they were otherwise unharmed.

"When we heard you were in the city, we had to see you, to make sure you were truly safe," said Anwar. "But how did you get here?"

"I came with Finmar and Adraéth," Mara replied. "But how much time has passed since then, and how long I have been here, I cannot say with certainty."

"If Father finds out, sister, he will be furious," said Diam.

"He won't find out," Ilbeth interjected. "At least not yet. And when a few days have passed, he will believe she only arrived after the battle."

"I just hope your plan doesn't fail, Aunt," Anwar said, before turning to his sister. "But tell me, did Aleth not come with you? Was it only Adraéth? Has she stayed behind in Dinambad? I am deeply worried about her. She has changed so much since her return from the darkness of Iushvhatu. And that black jewel terrifies me."

Mara lowered her head sorrowfully. "Aleth is gone. Far from Dinambad now, I fear, though I don't know where she is - or even if she still exists anywhere at all."

"What are you saying?" Anwar asked, his brow furrowing with concern. "Does it have something to do with that stone?" He sighed in despair. "She didn't cast it away, did she?" The poor man was now filled with deep anguish.

"I'm sorry," Mara said softly, seeing the pain so clearly in her brother's eyes. "The Blaecwên came to Dinambad and took her with them - where, I do not know. But wherever the Black Ones have taken her, she is no longer the Aleth we knew. The woman who fled with them was someone else. I see no future left for her."

Anwar turned away from her, stepping aside, consumed by terrible grief, needing to be alone in his suffering.

Mara moved to follow him, to offer comfort, but Diam held her back. "Let him be," he said. "There's nothing you can do or say that will ease his pain."

"I wish that I could."

"How can you help him when you cannot even ease your own torment?" Diam asked his sister gently. "We wanted to see you here, not only to bring you joy but so that you might find it again yourself. Yet you still think of him constantly. Oh, my dear sister, I wish you all the happiness in this world. And you have my blessing, for whatever it may be worth. Today, I fought side by side with Aric, and he proved himself time and again. He possesses many great qualities, and they are plentiful. Rejoice, Mara, for Father was there too, and he owes Aric his life. I am certain now that Father will not think ill of him - Aric is braver than many of our boldest men. Once peace is restored, Father will bless the two of you, I am sure of it."

Mara's eyes lit up with excitement. "Tell me what happened on the battlefield."

And Diam obliged, recounting in great detail everything he had experienced, from his arrival in Mahlrit a few days ago to the day of the battle. He smiled as he saw hope filling his sister's face when he spoke of the arrival of the riders from Anros.

19

Toward evening, after the final counsel of the captains had taken place outside the gates of Mahlrit, near some half-collapsed farmsteads, a herald was sent with an urgent message into the city. He hastened up to the second ring of walls and entered the chambers of the healers, where he encountered Mara, though he was instructed to address her by another name. "Lady Ielyanna," he said, "I come with a message from the highest captains."

"Speak," she replied, curious.

"You are requested to come with me. I am to bring you to them - or rather, to one of them. No, actually, two of them, for Dartur will also be present. The other is Tharon, the Haládan, the heir to the throne, who urgently wishes to speak with you. So, hurry, and veil your face, so you are not recognized."

The young woman set everything aside, fetched a cloak, pulled its hood low over her head, and swiftly followed the man.

In the darkness of the night, the beleaguered capital seemed less grim, and the numerous ruined houses and walls were hardly visible. They passed through the shattered and wide-open city gate and walked straight across the battle-scarred field toward a few half-destroyed buildings, where only a few torches or candles flickered. They entered one of these ruins, the foremost and the least damaged of all, and stopped before two figures who stood with their backs turned toward them in the center of the room.

To the left stood Dartur, unmistakable in his grey and brown robes, leaning wearily upon a narrow table. To the right stood a tall, stately figure - whether man or woman was unclear - clad in a somewhat shabby armor. Around the waist, fastened to a belt, hung a beautifully ornate sword that gleamed in the candlelight.

Only when the two turned to face them did the herald leave the dwelling, and Mara lowered her hood. At the same moment, the figure besides Dartur revealed her true face.

"Fair are the daughters of Rehuil - fairer even than many of the noblest of the Aedan," the strange woman said, smiling kindly. "Greetings to you, Marániel of Dinambad."

When the girl realized who stood before her, she fell to her knees in reverence, her eyes cast down to the ground. Although it had been Faran, the guardian of the order she had met in Menyána, who once bore the strange ring, it was now Thariel who wore it on her finger. And there was no doubt - it was Ealdir's ring, passed down to his son Endir, and then through many generations to the King of Tanuhal, later of Miénast. Thus, it became clear to her that Faran had not been merely a simple guardian, just as the woman standing before her was none other than Thariel, the rightful queen of the Kingdom of Men.

"Rise," Thariel bade her, her voice as gentle as the flowing of a quiet stream. "There is no need for the noble Princess of Dinambad to kneel in the dust before a humble guardian of the order."

Mara looked up into her kind eyes, then slowly stood and said, "You are no mere guardian, my lady, but my queen - whether you choose to claim that title or not. You are the heir of Huandar, and you must lay claim to the crown. Mahlrit is leaderless. My uncle, the Keeper of the city, has fallen into madness, and his daughter is dying - if she is not dead already. And yet, instead of taking your rightful place, you camp here in ruins, though all the dignity of kingship is yours. They call you Ealdariel, my lady - and not without reason, for you will give us all hope. But what hope can you truly offer if you will not enter the city and instead choose to remain here?"

"All things will happen in time, as they must," said Thariel. "But first, there are more pressing matters to attend to - even for you."

Dartur then stepped forward. "You did not come to Mahlrit by chance - though it was a dangerous and reckless decision. You were led here by a power greater than any that has ever ruled Sedäa. You are destined for great deeds. The stone I gave you was meant to aid you on your journey. But I see you no longer carry it. What has happened?"

"It was lost," Mara answered. "But it was found again. Lord Aric carries it now, I hope. There is little more I can do at this point. I am sent here and there only to speak. What use is the Blue Stone to me now? It is safer with Aric."

"Perhaps," the wizard replied, "for what lies ahead for all of us - including him - will not be easy."

"Tomorrow evening, we will set out northward, to Um-Atra," Thariel said. "Aric will go with us, as will your father."

"Is that why you summoned me, my queen? I am already overwhelmed with work in the city, and every minute I spend here could mean another wounded man dies."

"Are you not glad to finally speak with me?" Thariel asked.

Shame washed over Mara. "Of course, my lady, I am glad. But I do not understand why I am here."

Thariel stepped closer and took her cold hands in her own. "My journey is nearing its end, but yours is only beginning, Child of Light. I wish to give you hope for the road ahead. Will you accept it? Or would you rather let your sorrow consume you? Mara, I feel the pain in your hands and see it in your eyes. I have traveled far and learned much of healing over the years. I was even able to heal a grievously wounded warrior - Aasa, the fearless maiden of Anros, who would not stay behind in the battle against the enemy. Her contributions to the fight were great, but she was sorely hurt, far worse than you. Yet even I cannot heal the wounds you bear, for they are many and deep. You have seen something in the darkness of night, a terror that clings to you, and it is so great that even I cannot drive it away. Nor can I heal your broken heart. But in this, I understand your fear, for I share it. Look at me! I do not give up, for love alone is stronger than anything else in this world - even stronger than death. I understand your sorrow all too well, and I share it with you. The man I love now fights his own battles, and who knows what fate awaits him? But you are still young, and your life lies ahead of you. Do not give it up because you fear what may come." Thariel smiled warmly. "I will return, and the man you love will too. Then I will take the crown and claim my inheritance. So it shall be, I tell you, and you shall find joy again. That is my wish for you. Now return to the city and do your work as best as you can. And when I return, the sun shall shine for you once more."

At this, Mara smiled gratefully. "I thank you, my queen. Truly, your words give me hope. I wish you luck on your journey. May all happen as you say, and then I too shall be happy again." She bowed and left.

Dartur quickly followed and stopped her just outside the walls of the dwelling. "There is one more matter I must speak to you about - Aleth. She has fallen under Urehel's power and now serves him. But you likely already know this."

"Adraéth said she would die when Urehel falls. Is that true?"

"That is uncertain," the wizard replied. "She has not been under the enemy's will and dark power for long. It is unclear what will become of her. But one thing is certain: the goodness in her is dead, and now she is filled with hatred and greed. If she survives, you must destroy her."

"I cannot do that," Mara said, horrified. "Aleth is my friend. You cannot ask me to kill her. I would sooner strike down a sister than her. Please, do not ask this of me."

"If you do not, she will kill you first. And before that, she will mercilessly destroy your family and all those you love. You must find her. The sooner, the better. The longer you wait, the harder it will be. The power of the stones has not yet faded. Use it and destroy Aleth. Let Adraéth go with you; she can be a great help and support. But hurry, Mara! When Urehel is vanquished, the power of the seven stones will fade, and they will become nothing more than beautiful relics. Then you will face Aleth alone, without the Alarmár to aid you, since you chose to leave it with another for its protection, while she still wields great power. You must find her. Go now! Immediately."

With these words, Dartur sent the princess back to the city, his heart heavy with concern. He feared that she would not do what he had commanded. But he knew that sooner or later, whether she wished it or not, she would have no choice.

Mara returned to the chambers of healing and after her work was done for the day, she sat alone in the quiet chambers of the healer's hall, the soft flicker of a lone candle casting long shadows on the stone walls. The day had been long, filled with tending to the wounded and trying to lift the spirits of the weary soldiers who had survived the fierce battle at Mahlrit. Mara's thoughts were restless, swirling with questions and half-formed answers that offered no peace.

Her mind drifted to Thariel, the queen-to-be, the rightful heir of Miénast. Mara remembered the first time she had seen her - though at the time, Thariel had not revealed her true identity. She had been

Tharon then, a mysterious figure, tall and strong, who had fought along-side them all, hidden behind the guise of a man. The memory of that first meeting tugged at Mara's mind. Why had Thariel disguised herself so? Why had she taken on the name of a man when she was destined to be queen?

Mara pondered the question, her fingers absently tracing the edges of her cloak. Thariel was no ordinary woman; her strength, her leader-ship, and her resolve were unmatched. But surely, there was more to her decision than mere practicality. Was it to protect herself? To shield her true identity from those who might seek to harm her? Or perhaps it was to move unnoticed in a world where women - no matter how noble or skilled - were often not granted the same respect or authority as men, especially in matters of war.

"Tharon," Mara whispered to herself. The name seemed to belong to a shadow, to someone forged in secrecy, a guise that allowed Thariel to walk among warriors without drawing suspicion. But what must that have been like for her, to hide her true self? To wear the face of someone else while knowing that the weight of a crown and a kingdom's future lay on her shoulders?

Mara sighed softly, her heart heavy with a newfound sympathy for the queen-to-be. Thariel had carried the burden of her lineage, of her destiny, and yet, she had hidden it beneath a man's name, beneath ar-mor that spoke of war rather than of the throne. There was strength in that, but there was also sadness. It was a sacrifice, one that spoke of the difficult path she had walked, alone in her secret, until the time had come for her to reveal herself as Thariel, rightful queen of Miénast.

But then there was Faran. Mara had not seen him for many moons, not since that day in Menyána when he had worn Ealdir's ring. The ring, once the symbol of a great king, had passed through many hands, and Mara had come to learn that it had been destined to be worn by the one who would unite the people of Miénast in their darkest hour. And yet, it was not Faran who now held that legacy, but Thariel. The memory of Faran, the quiet, watchful guardian who had seemed to know more than he ever said, gnawed at her thoughts.

Where was he now? Mara wondered, and why had he not come with them to Mahlrit? Why had he not stood with them in the final battle against Urehel? The last time she had seen him, he had been a figure of calm authority, a man who seemed to carry the weight of ancient wisdom on his shoulders. He had worn Ealdir's ring, the symbol of kingship, as though it were his birthright, and yet... Thariel now wore it.

Had Faran given it to her willingly? Or had there been some other force at play? Mara could not shake the feeling that there was more to Faran's absence than met the eye. He had been a figure of great importance in her journey, but now he was nowhere to be found. Perhaps he had known all along that the ring was never truly his to keep, that it had always belonged to Thariel, the true heir. Or perhaps he had some other tasks, something that kept him away from the battlefields of men, but no less vital to the fate of the world.

Mara rose from her seat and walked slowly to the window, gazing out at the now peaceful city of Mahlrit. The streets, though scarred from the siege, were quiet. The light of the moon cast a pale glow over the land, and for a moment, she let her thoughts drift to Faran, wondering if he, too, stood somewhere beneath this same sky, watching and waiting.

Why had he chosen to remain apart from them? Could it be that he had known his part in the story was over, that the mantle of leadership had passed to Thariel? Or was there another, more pressing task that had called him away - something he had not yet revealed, something that still hung in the balance?

Mara felt a shiver run down her spine. There were still so many questions left unanswered, so many paths left unexplored. Thariel had stepped into the light, revealing her true self at last, but Faran remained a shadow, a mystery that haunted the edges of her mind. Whatever his reasons for staying away were, she could not help but feel that they had not yet seen the last of him. Faran had always been a figure of secrets and quiet power, and such men rarely vanished without leaving a trace.

And so, as she stood there, her thoughts swirling with the uncertainties of the past and the mysteries of the future, Mara resolved to be patient. Thariel had revealed herself in due time, and perhaps Faran, too, would return when the time was right. But for now, the world was slowly healing, and Mara knew that she had a part to play in helping it recover.

The road ahead was still long. Thariel would need her strength, as would her people. And perhaps, one day, the answers to her questions would come - whether through Faran's return or through the unfolding of destiny itself. But until then, Mara would wait, ever watchful, and ever ready for the next chapter in their story.

○

Many days had passed since the united army of Miénast and Anros, led by Thariel, Dartur, Lord Ráhad, Queen Fala, and Aric, had set out northward toward the iron gate of Um-Atra. No news had come from them, and so no one knew where they might be by now or if it was all over and they had all been slain.

In Mahlrit, none were aware that this very day would mark the fall of Urehel. Yet he had not been vanquished, and in these very hours, his vast war-host was launching a ferocious assault against the army of men.

Mara wandered, lost in thought, through the beautiful gardens within the second ring of the stone city. She had spent many days in the chambers of the healers, tending to and caring for wounded soldiers. But whenever she had a spare moment, she would walk through the blooming gardens, finding solace in the vibrant display of delicately scented flowers.

Several times, she had crossed paths there with her brother Diam, who had remained behind to lead the city in place of Dinhad. Fria had fallen in the battle, and her father, blinded by grief, had thrown himself into the fray with his daughter's sword, leading inevitably to his own death. Their bodies were laid side by side in Finian's Tower, the palace of the king, where many of the city's people came to pay their respects and mourn their loss. Now, Diam was the Keeper of the Crown of Miénast, taking on the responsibilities of their uncle, leaving him little time to visit the gardens.

Mara sat on a bench, gazing northward. Though she could not see much from there, she sensed a looming power stretching over the land. Dartur's words echoed in her mind. Days had passed since he had spoken them, but in all that time, Mara had not once left Mahlrit. She had no desire to seek out Aleth, hoping instead that with Urehel's fall, her friend's tormented life might also come to an end. She could not bring herself to destroy Aleth, and thus, she had not tried - and nothing had happened yet. So, the princess continued to hope that she might never have to face her friend again.

So deep was she in thought that she failed to notice a young woman with hair white as snow and golden as the sun's light approaching her.

"Aasa!" Mara cried when she finally noticed her, springing to her feet and embracing her with joy. "It's so wonderful to see you well again. You look much better. I spent many hours at your bedside while you slept, deeply worried for you. How glad I am now to see you, healthy and strong."

"Had I known sooner that you were here, I would have come much earlier," Aasa said with a faint smile. "The news of your death, which reached us a few weeks ago, brought us great sorrow. But I never truly believed it to be true."

"I know," Mara replied. "And I also know that you were there and found the blue stone."

"I did. And I gave it to Aric."

"I thank you," said Mara, walking with Aasa by her side through the gardens. "The stone is safer with him, and he will protect it. You need not worry."

"Need not worry?" Aasa stopped, looking at Mara with a concerned expression. "When we received the message of your death, I was deeply troubled for my brother. You did not see how much he suffered, Mara. No matter what I said to him, I couldn't ease his pain. If I hadn't found the stone, I fear he might have died of a broken heart." Then, suddenly, she smiled. "But now you are here, and you live. I am so glad. Tell me, will you go with him to our homeland when he returns?"

"Nothing would make me happier, if I am permitted - and if he still wishes it."

"There is nothing my brother would want more than for you to go with him."

Mara's face brightened with hope. "It does me good to hear that, especially in these dreadful hours."

At that moment, Adraéth approached them hastily. "Mara," she said in a stern tone, "it seems you've lost track of time. Inuriel is beside herself with fury. You must return at once. We are short of hands and have too many wounded. Please, come now."

Before Mara could even say farewell to Aasa, Adraéth tugged her away and swiftly brought her back to the chambers of the healers.

Inuriel had been waiting all along to give Mara a piece of her mind. "At last, you're here, Ielyanna. You're lucky Adraéth found you so quickly. Shame on you, foolish child. We give you food, drink, and a warm bed, and on top of that, you're paid generously for your work. As punishment, today's wages and those for the next three days will be withheld, and for the coming days, you'll get no more than a simple breakfast."

"I don't want your money or your food," Mara retorted angrily. "I have more than enough wealth of my own. I don't need your charity. Don't you know who I am?"

"Hold your tongue, child!" Adraéth interrupted swiftly. "Calm yourself. Go and do your work."

"You'd best listen to Adraéth, girl, or this will end badly for you. No one dares shout at me, least of all a foolish, clumsy apprentice. But what else should I expect?" Inuriel sneered. "You came into my house wild, and even I haven't managed to tame you. You're far too young and have no idea how life truly works. Foolish and immature, with not an ounce of respect or gratitude."

"Keep your ignorant tongue in check," Mara commanded, her voice cold and threatening. "I have walked on the brink of death through harrowing pain, seen creatures shaped from shadow and death, cruel beyond imagining. Do not presume to call me immature. I am no foolish apprentice, despite what Adraéth has led you to believe. I'm only here so my father won't find me, and to lend what little help I can. Forgive me if I took a moment to gather my thoughts - for they are many. If you knew even a fraction of what lies before me, you would think twice before daring to utter a single word against me. My name is not Ielyanna. I am Mara, daughter of Ráhad, Lord of Dinambad."

Inuriel stared at Mara in shock, but after a moment, she broke into scornful laughter. "What? You expect me to believe you're the Princess of Dinambad? I don't think so. That spoiled, pampered noble child would never set foot in a place like this, working in filth and poverty for a pittance. Don't you dare lie to me again, foolish girl. Now go and do your work."

Mara seethed with rage, biting back all the things she wanted to say to the old woman. But it wasn't worth the effort. She let it go and walked away.

"These young ones today," Inuriel said, turning to Adraéth. "They don't know their place anymore. You should be much stricter, my friend, so that this Ielyanna, or whatever her real name is, learns what discipline means." She shook her head as she left, muttering angrily about the girl.

6

The sun had not risen for many days now. Thick, oppressive clouds rolled endlessly across the sky, and the shadow of Urehel, the Dark Lord, had long since smothered the light. For weeks, the armies of Miénast and Anros had marched north, their spirits dwindling as they drew closer to the cursed fortress of Um-Atra. At the front of them rode Thariel, the rightful heir to the throne of Miénast, clad in armor tarnished from battle but with a fierce gleam in her eyes. By her side rode Dartur, the brown wizard, his age-old wisdom hidden behind wearied features, and Fala, now queen of Anros, her golden hair dulled by the grime of war. At the head of their forces rode Aric, steadfast and true, his banner flying high, his gaze ever watchful for the coming storm.

Before them loomed Um-Atra, the fortress of Urehel, surrounded by jagged, blackened rocks and shrouded in perpetual twilight. The ground seemed to pulse with darkness, and a foul wind blew from the gates, carrying with it whispers of despair. Thariel, though young, felt the weight of ages pressing upon her. This was not merely a battle for her kingdom - it was a battle for the world. Should Urehel prevail, all hope would be lost.

As they approached, the gates of Um-Atra creaked open with a hideous groan. From within poured Urehel's legions - great, monstrous beings forged from shadow and flame, their eyes burning with malice. They charged across the field, a black tide against the weary, but determined forces of men.

"Steady!" Aric shouted, his voice cutting through the din. His men stood firm, swords and spears ready, but even the most battle-hardened among them felt a flicker of fear as the enemy bore down upon them.

Thariel raised her sword high, the blade shimmering with an ethereal light in the murk. "For Miénast! For the light that has not yet died!" she cried, her voice carrying over the battlefield like a beacon of hope.

The armies clashed with a thunderous roar. Steel met steel, and cries of battle filled the air. Thariel fought at the front, her sword cleaving through the dark creatures with a skill born of necessity. Beside her, Aric fought valiantly, his sword flashing like lightning, and Dartur moved among the fray, casting spells to shield the soldiers and hurl bolts of magic at the enemy.

But no matter how many fell, more of Urehel's creatures surged forth from the fortress. Their strength seemed endless, and the light in Thariel's heart began to falter. She could see the strain on the faces of her comrades, the tiredness in Aric's eyes, and the deepening lines on Dartur's brow.

Suddenly, the battlefield was torn asunder by a deafening roar. The earth split, and from the chasm rose Urehel himself, a towering figure cloaked in shadow, his armor black as night and his eyes burning with a terrible, ancient fire. His voice was like thunder, shaking the very foundations of the earth.

"You dare defy me, child of men?" Urehel bellowed, his words dripping with contempt. "I have ruled this land long before your ancestors were born. You are but a flicker of flame, and I am the eternal night."

Thariel felt the full weight of Urehel's presence bear down upon her, but she did not falter. "You may be eternal, Urehel, but so is the light that stands against you. I am no mere child - I am the heir of Miénast an Nyarost, and I will see you fall!"

Urehel's laughter echoed across the battlefield, a cold, terrible sound. "Then come, little queen, and see if your light can withstand my darkness."

Thariel charged at Urehel, her sword glowing with a blinding light. Behind her, Aric and Fala rallied the soldiers, pushing back the tide of darkness that threatened to overwhelm them. Dartur, his staff held high, began to chant ancient words of power, drawing upon the forces of the earth to aid them in this final battle.

As Thariel's blade met Urehel's, the clash sent shockwaves through the air. The force of it nearly knocked her from her feet, but she held firm, gritting her teeth as Urehel bore down on her with the full weight of his malevolence. His sword, a massive, jagged thing of darkness, hissed and crackled as it struck again and again at Thariel's defenses. Each blow was like the strike of a hammer, and it took all of Thariel's strength to parry them.

"Do you feel it?" Urehel hissed. "The weight of despair? It is inescapable. You cannot defeat me, child. You are alone."

But Thariel was not alone. Aric fought his way through the chaos, his eyes locked on them. With a mighty shout, he leaped into the fray, his sword crashing against Urehel's side, momentarily drawing the Dark Lord's attention.

"Your time has passed, Urehel!" Aric shouted. "You cannot stand against us all!"

At the same moment, Fala let loose a volley of arrows, each one gleaming with a faint, magical light. They struck Urehel's armor, and though they did not pierce it, they slowed his movements, giving Thariel and Aric the chance they needed.

Dartur raised his staff, summoning a great wind that howled across the battlefield. With a booming voice, he called upon the ancient powers of the earth, and the ground beneath Urehel's feet began to tremble. Cracks appeared, and from them burst roots of the oldest trees, wrapping around the Dark Lord's legs, trying to drag him down.

"Now, Thariel!" Dartur shouted. "Strike now!"

With a cry of defiance, Thariel raised her sword high, its light shining brighter than ever. She leaped forward, her blade aimed straight at Urehel's heart. Urehel snarled, trying to shake free, but the roots held him fast, and with a final, desperate effort, Thariel drove her sword into his chest.

"You fools," Urehel rasped, his voice carrying the weight of ancient malice, though his once mighty form lay shattered, diminished. His eyes burned with undying hatred, his breath shallow but defiant. "This is not the end. The shadows do not die so easily." The words dripped with a venomous promise, as though even in defeat, his soul was bound to darker forces, waiting to rise again.

For a moment, time seemed to stand still. Then, with a terrible scream, Urehel's form exploded in a burst of shadow, his body disintegrating into a cloud of dark mist that was carried away on the wind.

As the darkness fled, the sky began to lighten. The clouds, which had so long hung over the land, broke apart, and a golden light spilled across the battlefield. The sun, which had been hidden for so long, rose again, casting its warm rays over the broken earth.

Thariel, her body aching and her breath ragged, stood in the light of the new dawn. She looked around at her companions - Aric, bloodied but alive, Fala, leaning on her bow but smiling, and Dartur, the old wizard, his eyes filled with quiet pride.

"It is over," Thariel whispered, her voice thick with emotion. "Urehel is defeated."

The battlefield was still. The forces of darkness had fled, and the men of Miénast and Anros stood victorious, though many had fallen. But in that moment, all could feel it - the shadow was lifted, and hope had returned to the world.

Thariel turned to Aric, her heart filled with relief and joy. "We did it," she said softly.

Aric smiled, exhaustion etched into his face, but his eyes were bright. "No, my queen. *You* did it. You led us to this victory."

Thariel shook her head. "I did not do it alone."

Dartur stepped forward, resting a hand on her shoulder. "No great victory is ever won alone," he said quietly. "But it was your strength, Thariel, that guided us here. And now, the light returns."

Together, they looked to the horizon, where the sun rose in full, glorious splendor, banishing the last remnants of the dark clouds. The war was over. Peace, though hard-won, had come at last.

And with it, a new era dawned.

Still fuming, Mara knelt beside Anlac's bed, carefully changing the bandages on his leg. The deep wound had nearly healed, and the young man's face had regained some color.

"That old woman is awful," Anlac said.

"You heard that?" Mara glanced up at him.

"It was impossible not to, Ielyanna," he replied, frowning. "What a strange name, but it has a certain beauty to it. It suits you in an odd way. Still, I don't understand why she refuses to believe you."

"Look at me," Mara said with a sigh. "I'm wearing old clothes, covered in dirt and blood. What princess would choose to look and live like this?"

"Fine clothes don't make a princess," Anlac responded. "I'd love to see the look on Mistress Inuriel's face when she finds out you truly are the Princess of Dinambad."

Mara smiled at the thought. "That would be most amusing."

Suddenly, Ilbeth burst into the chamber, her voice filled with excitement. "Look! The shadow—it's gone!"

Mara quickly stood, hurrying to the window. She threw open the shutters and gazed out into the dazzling white daylight. Indeed, the shadow from the north had vanished. Though smoke rose in the distance, the rest of the sky was a brilliant blue, with the sun shining brightly in all its glory.

"What do you see, Mara?" Anlac asked, shifting painfully in his bed to get a glimpse outside.

"It's over," Mara said softly, and it was as though a heavy burden had lifted from her shoulders. "I can see the sun again, the beautiful blue sky. The dark clouds are all gone." She turned, her face radiant with joy and relief. "They have won. The dark lord Urehel is defeated." She ran to her aunt and embraced her, overjoyed. "At last, it's over."

"How wonderful," Ilbeth beamed. "I'll tell the others at once. Oh, how happy I am! The queen will return soon. We must decorate the city for her arrival. Her coronation will be a grand festival, one that no one will forget. Come, Mara, help me get everything ready in time."

"I can't," Mara replied. "There's still so much work to do here, and Inuriel isn't exactly pleased with me."

"I understand," Ilbeth nodded. "I'll find someone else to help with the preparations. But make sure you attend the coronation, child. Everyone will be there." Smiling warmly, Ilbeth left the room.

Mara's joy, however, began to wane. A troubling thought crossed her mind, though she kept it to herself as she returned to Anlac and carefully wrapped a clean bandage around his leg.

"You are going to the coronation, aren't you?" Anlac asked, noticing the doubt in her eyes. "I'm sure Aric will be there. Don't you want to see him again?"

"Oh, I do, more than anything," Mara said softly. "But if everyone is going to be there, as my aunt says, that means my father will be there too."

"Well, you'll finally be able to prove to Mistress Inuriel who you really are."

"That doesn't concern me anymore," Mara said with a sigh. "What worries me is that if my father sees me, he'll be furious. He doesn't know I'm here, and I don't want him to find out."

"There will be so many people that he probably won't even notice you," Anlac assured her. "Trust me, it will be a grand, crowded day. People from all the valleys and villages in the mountains are coming to greet their new king. Among them, you'll surely go unnoticed. You really should go."

Mara thought over his words, realizing he might be right. She then found herself wondering how her long-awaited reunion with Aric might unfold—if he could even spot her amidst the throngs of people.

20

The grand armies of Miénast and Anros marched triumphantly back towards the city of Mahlrit. After the long and grueling battle at Um-Atra, the soldiers returned as victors, the dark reign of Urehel shattered and his forces scattered. The once shadowed sky was now a brilliant, clear blue, and the sun shone down upon the battered soldiers as if it, too, were celebrating their victory. The people of Mahlrit awaited them, eager to greet their returning heroes and to witness the coronation of their new queen, Thariel, as the rightful heir to the throne of Miénast.

Thariel rode at the head of the army, flanked by the great leaders who had fought beside her: Dartur, the wise and ancient brown wizard, Queen Fala of Anros, and Aric, the brave captain who had proven his worth time and time again in battle. Behind them marched the soldiers of Miénast and Anros, their banners flying high, their armor gleaming despite the scars of war.

Mara watched from the walls of Mahlrit, her heart swelling with pride and relief. She had feared for her father, Prince Ráhad of Dinambad, who had also fought alongside Thariel and the others. Though he had been injured, he rode with the victorious army, alive and well. As the gates of the city opened and the army entered, the citizens of Mahlrit cheered, their voices rising in unison to welcome their champions home.

Preparations for the coronation had already begun. The city, though scarred by war, had been adorned with colorful banners and garlands of flowers. The streets were swept clean, and the scent of fresh blossoms filled the air. In the central square, a grand dais had been constructed, where Thariel would be crowned as queen before the assembled nobility and people.

In the chambers of the royal palace, Mara stood before a polished mirror, her heart racing with anticipation. She wore a gown of deep blue, embroidered with silver threads that shimmered like stars. It was a gift from her aunt Ilbeth, who stood beside her, adjusting the delicate fabric with care.

"You look radiant, my dear," Ilbeth said, smiling warmly. "Today is a day of great joy. You should allow yourself to feel it."

Mara smiled, though her thoughts were elsewhere. She could not stop thinking about Aric, the man who had been at the center of her heart for so long. She wondered if he would be at the coronation, if he would see her, if he still thought of her after all that had happened.

Inuriel, the stern and pragmatic healer who had once scolded Mara so harshly, entered the room. Despite their past disagreements, she had softened in the days following the battle, recognizing the strength and nobility in Mara.

"You mustn't keep the queen waiting, child," Inuriel said, though there was no bite in her words. "It is a day for celebration, not for lingering in thoughts. Now, go. The ceremony is about to begin."

Mara nodded and, with Ilbeth by her side, made her way to the grand square, where the coronation was to take place. The crowd had already gathered, filling the streets with excitement and anticipation. As Mara took her place among the nobles and dignitaries, she saw familiar faces: Queen Fala of Anros, regal and composed, with her cousin Aasa by her side. And there, standing tall among the assembled warriors, was Aric. Her heart leapt at the sight of him, though she quickly looked away, afraid that her feelings might be too transparent.

The ceremony began with the ringing of bells, and the crowd fell silent as Thariel stepped onto the dais. She wore a gown of white and gold, simple yet magnificent Dartur stood beside her, his hands raised as he spoke the ancient words of the coronation rite. His voice, though old, was strong and clear, and it carried over the gathered throngs like the wind itself.

"As it was in the time of Ealdir, so it shall be now," Dartur proclaimed. "Thariel, daughter of Erchad, you are the chosen heir, the rightful queen of Miénast and the falling kingdom of Nyarost. With this crown, you shall guide your people into a new age of peace and prosperity."

With solemn grace, he placed the crown upon Thariel's head. The crowd erupted into cheers as Thariel stood tall, the weight of her new responsibility settling upon her shoulders, but her face was calm, serene. She raised her hand, and the people quieted once more.

"I accept this crown," she said, her voice carrying across the square. "But I do so not for myself, but for all of you. We have faced great darkness, but now, we shall rebuild. Together, we will restore both Miénast and Nyarost to their former glory. Let this day mark the beginning of a new era."

The crowd cheered once more, and Mara felt tears of pride well up in her eyes. Thariel had proven herself to be a true queen, one who would lead with wisdom and strength. But as the ceremony came to a close and the crowd began to disperse, Mara's thoughts returned to Aric. She knew he was there, watching, and her heart ached to see him again.

As if summoned by her silent yearning, Aric appeared beside her. His presence was quiet, yet powerful, and Mara's breath caught in her throat as she looked up at him. His hair was tousled by the wind, and though his face bore the marks of battle, his eyes were warm as they met hers.

For a moment, neither of them spoke. Then, without a word, Aric reached into the pouch at his belt and withdrew something small and delicate. It was Mara's necklace - the one Aasa had found. He held it out to her, his hand trembling ever so slightly.

"I believe this belongs to you," Aric said softly.

Mara's hand shook as she took the necklace from him, her fingers brushing against his. She looked up at him, her heart pounding in her chest, and she felt the words she had longed to say rise up within her. But the weight of them was too great, and she found herself unable to speak.

Aric, too, seemed to struggle with his emotions. His eyes, so full of warmth and tenderness, betrayed the depth of his feelings. He wanted to tell her - needed to tell her - how much she meant to him. But the fear of losing her, of saying too much, kept the words locked behind his lips.

"I..." Mara began, but her voice faltered.

"I know," Aric whispered, his hand lingering on hers for just a moment longer before he withdrew it. "I know."

They stood there in silence, the world around them fading into the background. The joy of the coronation, the celebration of the people - it all seemed distant, overshadowed by the intensity of the moment between them. They had been through so much, fought through so much darkness, and yet, here they were, standing on the edge of something new, something both terrifying and beautiful.

But neither of them could bring themselves to say the words that hung between them. The fear of losing what they had, of risking the delicate bond they shared, kept them both silent. And so, with a soft smile and a lingering glance, they parted ways, each carrying the unspoken weight of their love in their hearts.

As Mara watched Aric disappear into the crowd, she clutched the necklace to her chest, knowing that one day, they would have the courage to speak the words that had gone unsaid. But for now, they would wait - two souls bound by love, yet held apart by fear.

Prince Ráhad had found his daughter at last. His stern face, weathered by years of leadership and battle, was set in a scowl. He had not seen Mara since before the war, when he had commanded her to stay behind in Dinambad. Yet here she was, standing in the heart of Mahlrit, defying the very orders he had given her.

As he approached, the noise of the celebration seemed to fade, leaving only the tension between father and daughter. Mara saw him coming, her heart racing with both dread and anticipation. She knew the scolding that awaited her.

"Mara," Ráhad said in a low, angry voice. "I gave you a direct order to remain in Dinambad. What madness possessed you to come here, to the heart of a war, when I commanded you to stay safe?"

Mara met his gaze, her heart heavy with the weight of her decision. "Father, I came because I could not sit idle while our world fell apart. You may call it madness, but I call it duty. I needed to help where I could."

"Help?" Ráhad's voice was sharp with disbelief. "You risked your life, your future. Do you not understand the peril you placed yourself in? Have you no respect for the orders I gave you?"

Mara held her ground, though she could feel the sting of his words. "I do respect you, Father, more than you know. But I had to be here. I could not hide in safety while others fought and bled for our future."

For a long moment, Ráhad was silent, his face taut with anger and something else - a deeper emotion he could not yet name. His daughter had grown stronger, more determined, than he had ever realized. She had a fire in her eyes, a strength of will that reminded him so much of her mother. And it frightened him, for he knew what it would mean.

But before he could respond, Mara's gaze shifted, drawn away from her father for just a moment. Across the hall, Aric stood near the newly crowned Queen Thariel. Their eyes met, and in that fleeting instant, the world around them seemed to fall away. There was a depth in that look, a silent connection that spoke of something unspoken but undeniable - a love that had been forged in the fires of war and tempered by the weight of responsibility.

Ráhad saw it too. He followed his daughter's gaze and saw the way Aric looked back at her. It was not just admiration or fleeting affection. It was love - deep, unwavering love. The kind that could not be hidden, no matter how much one might try.

For a moment, Ráhad's anger wavered. He saw the truth in their eyes, the bond between them. He had heard rumors of Mara's connection to the commander of Anros, but now, seeing it with his own eyes, he realized that his daughter's heart had found its home - not in Dinambad, not even in Mahlrit, but in Anros, with Aric.

He felt a pang of sorrow, knowing what this would mean. He had always imagined that Mara would remain in Dinambad, by his side, helping him rule their people. But he could see now that her heart yearned for something else, for someone else. She was no longer the girl he had sought to protect, but a woman who had found her own path.

And yet, he could not bring himself to say it. Not yet.

Ráhad turned back to his daughter, his face softening ever so slightly, though his voice remained stern. "You have always been headstrong, Mara, but you are still my daughter. You defied my orders, and that cannot go unanswered. But... we will speak of this later."

Mara looked at him, a mixture of relief and confusion in her eyes. She had expected a harsher rebuke, but there was something in her father's tone that suggested he was holding something back. She opened her mouth to speak, but the words failed her.

Ráhad glanced once more toward Aric, who had now turned away, speaking with others at the coronation feast. He knew that, in time, he would have to let her go. She would not be happy in Dinambad. Her place, her happiness, lay elsewhere - perhaps in the distant fields of Anros, where Aric's heart beat only for her.

But tonight was not the night for such a revelation. Tonight was for celebration, for joy. Ráhad would wait. He would hold onto her for a little while longer, even if he knew that the day would come when he would have to let her go.

"Come," he said at last, his voice softer now. "We have a feast to attend. Let us not linger in anger on a day like this."

Mara hesitated, then nodded, grateful for the reprieve. She cast one more glance toward Aric before following her father into the grand hall, where the light of a new age was just beginning to dawn.

○

The grand throne room of Mahlrit was heavy with the weight of expectation. Since her coronation, Queen Thariel had opened her court to the people of Miénast, who came from near and far to present their pleas, grievances, and hopes for justice. It was a duty she did not take lightly. The dark days of Urehel's reign were over, but their shadow still lingered in the hearts of many. Some came seeking aid, others forgiveness, and a few were brought forward in chains, accused of misdeeds committed in the chaos before Urehel's fall.

Seated on her high throne, Thariel wore a simple crown, her calm gaze surveying each petitioner as they were brought before her. She was known for her wisdom, though her decisions were sometimes harsh. Beside her, Dartur, the old wizard, stood as an advisor, his expression somber as he observed the proceedings. His eyes missed little, and his voice was a steady guide in matters of judgment.

One by one, the people came forward.

A farmer from the outer reaches of Miénast, his face lined with worry, knelt before her. "My Queen," he began, his voice trembling. "During the dark days before Urehel was slain, my land was ravaged by marauders. My family is starving, and my crops will not grow in the scorched soil. I beg for your aid."

Thariel listened quietly, her hand resting on the arm of her throne. "You have suffered much, as have many," she said, her voice thoughtful. "The land will heal, in time. I will send aid to your village to help rebuild, but the soil must rest, as must you. Take this time to restore your strength."

The farmer wept with gratitude, and Thariel signaled for him to be led away, provisions already arranged for him and his people.

Next came a group of soldiers, accused of abandoning their post during the final siege. They knelt before the queen, their heads bowed in shame.

"Your cowardice nearly cost the lives of those who fought bravely," Thariel said, her voice hardening. "But the times were dark, and fear is a powerful force. For your failure, you will work in service to the people you abandoned, helping rebuild what was lost because of your actions. Only then can you begin to earn back the honor you cast aside."

The soldiers, pale and humbled, accepted their punishment without a word.

Thariel continued to hear the pleas of her people, meting out justice with a balance of mercy and severity, until at last, a figure entered the throne room who caught her attention more than the others. Mara, the Princess of Dinambad, stood before her, her head held high but her heart heavy with the knowledge of what was to come. She had known this day would arrive, yet it did not make the moment any easier.

Her father, Ráhad, had sent her to face judgment for her disobedience, for defying his orders to remain in Dinambad and instead coming to Mahlrit, risking her life in the heart of the war. Mara had not fought in the final battle against Urehel; it was her father who had stood with Thariel, earning great honor for his bravery. But Mara felt none of the pride that others might assume was hers. She had broken her father's trust, and in doing so, had distanced herself from the man she loved most.

As she knelt before the queen, the weight of her guilt bore down on her.

"Marániel, daughter of Ráhad, come forward," Thariel said, her voice carrying through the room.

Mara rose to her feet, though she kept her gaze low, her hands clenched at her sides.

"You stand before me not as the Princess of Dinambad," Thariel continued, "but as a citizen of this realm, who disobeyed the orders of her father and placed herself in danger. What say you to this?"

Mara looked up, meeting Thariel's gaze. "I ask not for any special treatment, my Queen. My father's deeds are not my own. It was he who stood by your side in the battle, not I. I have done nothing to deserve the honors others have given me. I defied my father, and for that, I am willing to accept whatever punishment you deem fit."

A murmur rippled through the court. The daughter of Ráhad, asking for punishment? It was unheard of for one of her station to seek such humility.

Thariel studied Mara closely, her eyes narrowing in thought. "You would have me treat you as any other?" she asked, her voice quiet but stern.

"Yes," Mara replied. "I am not above the law."

Thariel was silent for a long moment, and then she spoke, her tone firm. "Very well, then. You shall face a task, not as a princess, but as one who still has much to prove."

Mara's heart skipped a beat. She had expected punishment - perhaps exile, perhaps confinement - but not this.

"A task?" she asked, her voice trembling slightly.

"Yes," Thariel said. "Aleth still lives."

The name sent a cold shiver through Mara. Aleth, once her friend, now a twisted servant of Urehel's dark power. It was rumored that Aleth had been taken by the dark forces, her heart turned to shadow. Even after Urehel's defeat, Aleth had escaped, her whereabouts unknown, but her power growing.

"You know as well as I that she is a threat to us all," Thariel continued. "She has grown more dangerous with each passing day. I cannot spare more men to search for her, but you... you will find her. And you will end this threat."

Mara's blood ran cold. She had feared this moment, feared that she would be called upon to confront Aleth. "My Queen," she whispered, "I am not strong enough. I will fail."

Thariel's gaze softened, but only slightly. "You doubt yourself because you have not yet faced the true test of your strength. The Mara who knelt before me is not the same woman who will stand before Aleth. You have power, more than you know. It is time you embraced it."

Mara wanted to protest, to argue that she was not ready, that Aleth was too powerful, but deep down, she knew that Thariel was right. She had come this far, and now, she had to go further.

"Take Adraéth with you," Thariel added. "She will be your guide. But the final blow... that will be yours to deliver."

Mara felt her heart tighten. To face Aleth was one thing, but to strike her down, to kill someone who had once been like a sister to her - that was something she did not know if she could bear.

"I... I don't know if I can do it," Mara admitted, her voice small.

Thariel stood, her presence commanding as she approached Mara. She placed a hand on her shoulder and spoke softly, though her words were filled with strength. "You will find the strength when the moment comes. You are not your father, Mara. His deeds are not yours. But you have your own path to walk, and this is the first step."

Mara swallowed hard, her thoughts racing. How could she defeat Aleth? How could she strike down the person she once cared about so much? But she knew she had no choice. The safety of the realm depended on it.

"You must go," Thariel said, stepping back. "And may the light guide you, for you will need it."

With a heavy heart, Mara bowed deeply to the queen and turned to leave the throne room. The path ahead of her was fraught with danger, and doubt gnawed at her soul. But somewhere, deep within, a flicker of determination burned. She would face Aleth. And though she feared what would come, she knew that she could not run from this fate.

She only prayed that she would find the strength Thariel believed she possessed, before it was too late.

6

Aric's heart raced as he made his way through the winding streets of Mahlrit, his steps heavy with both determination and fear. For days, he had wrestled with his feelings, trying to summon the courage to say what had weighed on his heart for so long. But now, with Urehel defeated and the dark days behind them, there was no more time for hesitation. He knew what he wanted - Mara, the woman he had loved from the moment he first laid eyes on her.

His hands trembled slightly as he reached the entrance to the chambers of healing, where he believed she would be. The echoes of his steps reverberated off the stone walls as he strode through the halls, each moment feeling like an eternity. He could see her face in his mind - those bright eyes filled with strength and vulnerability, the black hair that flowed like silk down her shoulders, and the way her smile could warm even the darkest of days.

Today was the day he would tell her. No more waiting. No more doubts.

As he approached the room where the wounded were being tended, Aric slowed his pace, drawing in a deep breath. He imagined how he would say it. 'I love you, Mara. I always have. Will you come with me, to Anros? Will you let me be by your side for the rest of our days?'

The words sounded so simple in his head, yet he feared they would never leave his lips if he hesitated for even a moment. His heart swelled with a mixture of anticipation and dread as he pushed open the door.

Inside, the room was filled with the scent of herbs and the low murmurs of healers tending to the wounded. Sunlight streamed in through the high windows, casting soft light over the beds where injured soldiers rested. But Mara was nowhere to be seen. Instead, by one of the beds, stood Adraéth.

The tall woman turned as Aric entered, her eyes sharp and knowing. She had the air of someone who could see straight through to the soul, and her presence, though not unkind, was always unsettling.

"Aric," she said, her voice calm but edged with something unreadable. "What brings you here?"

He faltered for a moment, caught off guard. "I... I came to find Mara," he admitted, his voice rougher than he had intended. "I need to speak with her."

Adraéth tilted her head slightly, her eyes narrowing as if measuring his resolve. She let a moment of silence hang between them before answering. "She is not here."

A wave of confusion passed over Aric. "Not here? Where is she?"

Adraéth crossed her arms, her expression becoming more serious. "She is with Queen Thariel."

The name sent a jolt of unease through Aric. His mind raced. "With Queen Thariel? Why? What is happening?"

Adraéth sighed softly, her gaze softening, as if she understood more than she was willing to say. "Mara is facing her punishment for disobeying her father's orders. You know she came here to Mahlrit against his will. Queen Thariel is not unkind, but justice must be served."

Aric's heart sank. He had heard whispers of Mara's defiance, but he had hoped that it would be overlooked after all they had endured. "What kind of punishment?" he asked, his voice tight.

"I do not know the queen's judgment," Adraéth replied. "But Mara is not one to ask for leniency. She has asked to be treated as any other citizen, despite her father's deeds and titles. She may be in greater trouble than you realize."

The weight of those words hit Aric like a blow. His thoughts spiraled as he imagined Mara, standing before Thariel, perhaps in shame or defiance, her fate hanging in the balance. He had to speak to her. Now. Before it was too late.

"You must act quickly, Aric," Adraéth said, her voice low but urgent. "If you truly want to speak to her, if you truly want to tell her what lies in your heart, then you should go now. Queen Thariel's judgment may set Mara on a path from which she cannot return."

Aric's chest tightened, his fear now palpable. He had waited too long already. Too long to tell her that he loved her. Too long to ask her to leave the burdens of royalty behind and come with him to Anros, to live a life of peace and love. What if she was sent away? What if her punishment separated them forever?

"I... I should go," Aric said, his voice barely above a whisper. "But what if it's too late?"

Adraéth's eyes softened, a rare moment of kindness in her usually steely gaze. "It is not too late yet. But you must hurry. She is stronger than she knows, but even the strongest need a hand to hold them steady. Go to her, Aric. Tell her what you came here to say."

His pulse quickened as he nodded, determination flooding his body. He had come too far to turn back now. The fear that had held him in silence for so long melted away in the face of the urgency Adraéth's words had awoken in him.

Without another word, Aric turned and left the healing chambers, his heart pounding in his chest. He could not lose her. Not now, not ever. There was too much left unsaid, too much left to be shared between them.

As he raced through the corridors of Mahlrit, towards the chambers where Queen Thariel held court, one thought echoed in his mind: 'Mara, wait for me. Just wait a little longer.'

For he had found the strength, at last, to tell her the truth - he loved her more than words could ever say, and he wanted nothing more than to spend the rest of his life by her side. He only hoped he was not too late to tell her.

Aric hurried through the dim corridors of Mahlrit, his heart pounding in his chest. His mind was filled with one singular purpose: to reach Mara before it was too late. The echo of Adraéth's words spurred him forward, pushing him past the dread that gnawed at him with every step.

He reached the entrance to the throne room, the grand wooden doors standing tall and imposing before him. His hand moved to push them open, but before he could, two familiar figures stepped into his path - Enwir and Anwar, Mara's older brothers.

Enwir, the eldest, who only arrived a few days earlier, stood with arms crossed, his face grim and stern. Anwar, beside him, was equally resolute, though there was a flicker of something softer in his eyes as he looked at Aric. Both were dressed in the formal garb of their station, yet their expressions made it clear that they weren't here to celebrate or welcome him.

"Aric," Enwir said, his voice cold and commanding, "you shouldn't be here."

Aric blinked, confusion flooding his thoughts. "I need to see Mara," he said, stepping forward, but Enwir held up a hand, stopping him in his tracks.

"You can't see her," Enwir continued. "She's inside, being judged by Queen Thariel. It's not a time for interruptions, and certainly not from you."

A knot of fear twisted in Aric's stomach, but he refused to back down. "I have to talk to her. I need to tell her-"

"She doesn't want to see you, Aric," Anwar cut in, his tone less harsh than Enwir's but no less firm. "She told us herself."

Aric's breath caught. He stared at Anwar, struggling to comprehend the words. "What... what are you talking about? Why wouldn't she want to see me?"

"Because you bring her nothing but pain," Enwir said, stepping closer, his gaze sharp as steel. "She may have feelings for you, but that's not enough. It's never been enough, Aric. You come from a wild and dangerous land. Your world is nothing like ours. Mara belongs to Miénast, to Dinambad. She could never leave her home to go to Anros, to live in those rough, untamed lands."

"That's not true," Aric said, his voice shaking with disbelief. "She told me-"

"She told us," Enwir interrupted, his tone hard, "that she can't bear the thought of leaving the stone lands behind. She can't abandon her people, her family, or her duty. It may hurt her to admit it, but she knows it's the truth. Her heart is with Miénast, not with you."

Aric's chest tightened, doubt flooding his mind. "No," he whispered. "She wouldn't - she wouldn't say that."

Anwar stepped forward then, placing a hand on Aric's shoulder, though his grip was firm. "She told us not to let anyone inside, especially not you. You have to leave her be, Aric. Let her find her own way. She's in pain, and your presence only makes it worse."

The words struck like a blow. Aric's mind reeled, fighting against the lies he was being told but finding no strength to counter them. He had seen the love in Mara's eyes, felt the connection between them. But now, standing before her brothers, hearing their words, doubt crept into his heart like a dark shadow.

"She..." Aric began, his voice breaking. "She loves me."

Enwir's expression hardened further. "Maybe she thought she did," he said, his tone ruthless. "But love isn't enough to change who she is. Mara is the daughter of a noble house, a princess of Dinambad. She has responsibilities far greater than a fleeting romance with a soldier from a distant land. She belongs to her people."

Anwar's hand squeezed Aric's shoulder gently, as though trying to comfort him. "We've told you the truth, Aric. She made her choice, and that choice is Miénast. You need to accept that and move on. Go back to Anros. There's nothing for you here."

The weight of their words crashed down on Aric, suffocating the hope he had clung to. Every instinct in him screamed to push past them, to find Mara, to hear her say it herself. But what if they were right? What if she truly couldn't bear to leave the stone lands behind, no matter how much she cared for him?

For a moment, he stood frozen, torn between the love he felt for Mara and the reality her brothers presented. His heart screamed for him to fight, but doubt gnawed at his resolve.

"You should go, Aric," Enwir said, his voice quiet now but no less commanding. "Leave her to her fate."

Aric's gaze flickered to the closed doors of the throne room. His hands clenched into fists at his sides, his body trembling with the weight of the decision before him. Every part of him ached to see her, to tell her how he felt, but her brothers' words echoed in his mind.

Without another word, Aric turned away from the doors, his heart heavy with sorrow.

As Aric finally disappeared into the shadows of the hall, the tension between Enwir and Anwar began to mount. The grand doors of Queen Thariel's throne room loomed behind them, closed and silent, as though bearing witness to the unspoken conflict between the two brothers.

Enwir stood tall, his jaw clenched, watching Aric's retreat with cold determination. Anwar, on the other hand, stared at the floor, his arms crossed tightly over his chest, his face a mask of uncertainty. The lie they had told weighed heavily on him, and it was becoming impossible to ignore.

"Did we really need to do that?" Anwar finally muttered, his voice low but laced with doubt. "He didn't deserve that."

Enwir turned to him, his eyes sharp and unforgiving. "Yes, we did, Anwar. You saw the pain Mara was in. Every time she looks at him, it tears her apart. We had to protect her from that."

"But what if..." Anwar began, shaking his head, unable to finish the thought. "What if we're wrong? What if we just made things worse?"

"We didn't make things worse," Enwir snapped, stepping closer to his brother. "We saved her. If we'd let him in, let him see her - who knows what she would have done? She might have gone with him to Anros, left everything behind for a dream that would only bring her more heartache."

Anwar's face twisted with guilt. "But Mara should be the one to decide that, not us."

"And you think she's in any condition to make that decision right now?" Enwir's voice dropped, his tone harsh. "She's overwhelmed, exhausted, torn between her duty to Miénast and whatever feelings she has for that man. If we hadn't stepped in, she would have followed him, and you know it."

Anwar was silent, chewing on his lip as Enwir's words sank in. Deep down, he knew there was some truth to what his brother was saying. He had seen the look in Mara's eyes whenever she spoke of Aric - how her heart ached for him, but how that longing also seemed to deepen the chasm of doubt inside her.

But something still felt wrong.

"I don't know," Anwar murmured after a long pause. "It doesn't feel right, lying to her, lying to him. If she loves him - really loves him - maybe that's enough. Maybe... maybe she deserves to be happy."

Enwir's expression hardened, his brows drawing together. "You think he can make her happy? You think that wild life in Anros, with no certainty, no stability - wouldn't that crush her? She was born in stone halls, Anwar. Raised in Dinambad. She's a princess. That world out there... it would destroy her."

Anwar sighed, his shoulders slumping as he ran a hand through his dark hair. "Maybe. Or it' is what she needs. Maybe it would set her free."

"Free?" Enwir scoffed, shaking his head. "She's needed here. In Miénast. Father would never allow her to leave, and even if he did, it's not the life for her. You know that."

Anwar looked up at his brother, his eyes conflicted. "And what about love? Doesn't that matter? Do you really think we're doing the right thing, keeping them apart?"

Enwir hesitated for the first time, his resolve faltering under the weight of Anwar's question. For a brief moment, doubt flickered in his eyes. But then he shook his head, steeling himself once more. "We're doing what we must. What's best for her. Even if she can't see it now, she'll thank us one day."

"Will she?" Anwar asked quietly, doubt still clinging to his words.

Enwir's jaw tightened. "She will. When she's stronger, when she's seen what her future holds here, she'll understand. And when she looks back, she'll realize we saved her from a life of regret."

Anwar let out a long breath, his heart heavy with the burden of their actions. He wanted to believe Enwir, wanted to trust that they had made the right choice for Mara. But the guilt gnawed at him, and he couldn't shake the image of Aric's face - crushed and defeated - as he walked away.

"Maybe," Anwar said at last, his voice low and uncertain. "But I still don't feel right about it."

"We did what had to be done," Enwir said firmly, turning away from his brother and glancing at the doors to Thariel's throne room. "Now we wait. Mara will understand, in time. And Aric... he'll move on."

Anwar nodded slowly, though the weight of their lie still sat heavy on his chest. He wasn't sure he believed Enwir, not fully. But for now, he would go along with it. They had to protect their sister, even if that meant keeping her from the one thing that might make her truly happy.

And deep down, Anwar wondered if they had made a terrible mistake, one that neither of them could undo.

6

Enwir now stood alone before the grand doors of Queen Thariel's throne room, his posture rigid and his face clouded with the weight of the deception he had just woven with Anwar. The hall was quiet now, the earlier tension having dissipated, but within Enwir, a storm still raged. He had convinced himself that what they had done was for the best, but the guilt clung even to him, gnawing at his conscience.

The doors creaked open, breaking the silence, and Enwir straightened instinctively as Mara stepped through. Her face was pale, her expression tired and contemplative. She had just faced Queen Thariel's judgment, and it was clear that the ordeal had left her emotionally drained.

"Enwir," she said softly, her voice carrying the weight of exhaustion. "What are you doing here?"

For a moment, Enwir's resolve wavered. His sister's vulnerability was plain to see, and he hated the thought of causing her more pain. But he knew what had to be done. He couldn't let her hope linger - hope that would only break her further in the long run.

He swallowed hard, his throat dry, and took a step toward her. "Mara," he began, his voice gentle but firm, "there's something I need to tell you. Something about... Aric."

At the mention of Aric's name, Mara's eyes lit up, a faint glimmer of hope flashing in her weary expression. "Aric? What is it? Where is he?"

Enwir hesitated, but only for a heartbeat. "He asked me to speak to you," he lied, his words cold despite the effort to soften them. "Aric wanted me to tell you that his feelings for you aren't as strong as you might have thought."

The color drained from Mara's face, and she blinked, as if trying to process what she had just heard. "What...?" Her voice trembled, disbelief hanging on every syllable.

"He told me," Enwir continued, forcing himself to maintain his composure, "that he believes he deserves a woman from the wilds. Someone who suits him better than a noble princess from the stone lands. He said you... you wouldn't understand his world, that you belong here, in Dinambad, not out there."

Mara's gaze faltered, her eyes searching her brother's face for any sign of untruth, but Enwir's expression was unreadable. He had practiced this lie in his head enough times that it now came easily, though each word felt like a dagger in his chest.

"He said that?" Mara whispered, her voice breaking.

Enwir nodded. "He did. And..." He drew in a deep breath. "He has already left Mahlrit. He returned to Anros, and he won't be coming back. He despises the stone lands, Mara, our cities. He... couldn't stay here any longer."

For a moment, time seemed to freeze. Mara stood motionless, her heart breaking beneath the weight of Enwir's words. It was as if the world had collapsed around her, leaving her standing on the edge of a great, empty abyss. She had clung to the hope of seeing Aric again, of speaking with him, of understanding what their future could be. But now... that hope was gone.

She felt hollow, as if all the light had been drained from her. Aric, the man she had given her heart to, had left. And worse still, he had chosen to abandon her, believing she did not belong in his world.

Enwir could see the devastation in his sister's eyes, but he pressed on, knowing it had to be done. "Come, Mara," he said, his voice gentle now. "It's time for us to return to Dinambad. We need to go home."

Mara didn't respond. She simply stood there, staring at the ground as her mind tried to make sense of the pain she felt. Slowly, numbly, she nodded.

Without another word, Enwir turned and began to walk down the hall. Mara followed him in silence, her steps heavy with sorrow. The great stone walls of the palace seemed to close in around her, and her heart ached with every step she took away from the throne room, away from the place where she had believed, even for a brief moment, that she might find happiness with Aric.

But now that dream had shattered.

As they reached the outer corridors, Enwir glanced back at his sister. Her face was blank, her eyes distant. She had always been strong, always determined. But now, she looked like a shadow of herself, lost in a sea of pain.

"I'm sorry," Enwir said softly, though he wasn't sure whether the words were for her or for himself.

Mara said nothing, and they continued in silence, the halls of Mahlrit echoing with the quiet footsteps of a princess whose heart had been broken, and a brother who had sacrificed the truth to protect her - whether it was the right thing to do or not.

6

The night was deep, and the stars glittered brightly beside the blue-hued moon in the clear sky. A peaceful stillness lay over the city, the kind of calm that followed the storms of war. Yet, in the heart of Mara, no such peace could be found. She walked silently beside Enwir, her steps slow and heavy as they descended the cobbled street. In her hand, she clutched the Blue Stone tightly, as if fearing it might slip away, knowing it was the key to a fate that weighed heavily upon her soul.

Suddenly, a frantic voice shattered the silence.

"Mara! Mara!" Ardil, the young Wusel, came dashing up the main road of Dinambad, his face pale with panic. Breathless, he stumbled to a halt in front of them, struggling to catch his breath as terror gripped him. "The Stone... it showed me something... She... she's calling for it!"

"She?" Enwir asked, his brow furrowing in confusion. "Boy, what are you talking about?"

Ardil's wide eyes reflected the fear that consumed him. "Aleth... I saw her. But it wasn't her, not truly. She was... monstrous. She burned like fire and froze like ice. She's coming for you, Mara. She's coming to kill you." His voice trembled as his whole body shook with fear.

Mara's heart clenched. She motioned for Enwir to leave them alone, her voice steady despite the storm brewing inside her. As soon as her brother was gone, she knelt before the trembling Wusel and placed a gentle hand on his shoulder, her eyes softening as she spoke. "What did you see, Ardil? Tell me everything."

Ardil struggled to form the words, still haunted by the vision. "It was her - Aleth, and yet, not her. She was... terrifying. There was fire in her eyes, but coldness in her soul. I saw it. She wants you dead. We must act quickly!"

"Did the Stone show you this?" Mara's voice hardened. "I warned you not to use it!" A sudden wave of guilt washed over her, her thoughts spiraling into despair. "How foolish I've been... If only I had done what Dartur asked of me sooner, we wouldn't be in this dire situation. Oh, what a selfish fool I've been." She muttered to herself, her voice thick with self-loathing. "I was too consumed by other thoughts - by him. My foolish heart... I wish I didn't have one."

Taking a deep breath, she turned back to Ardil, her tone urgent now. "Where is she? Did you see anything else? We don't have time to waste."

Ardil's voice shook as he recalled the dreadful vision. "It was dark where she was - deep beneath a mountain, I think. There were tunnels, vast caves, winding corridors..." His eyes widened in sudden realization.

"The Tin Nangroth! She's there, where I found the Stone. But why would she return? The Stone is here... with you."

Mara's mind raced. "Was she alone?" she asked, her heart pounding with dread.

"No," Ardil replied, his voice breaking. "There were creatures with her... five of them. One was much larger than the others, and they all looked as terrifying as the monster that attacked us in Cottingen."

Mara's gaze softened as she saw the distress in the boy's eyes. "I'm sorry you had to endure that," she said gently, regret filling her voice. "You've been braver than most, Ardil. But what you've seen is crucial. We must be prepared."

Ardil nodded, still shaking, but relieved that he wasn't alone in this terror. "But what could she want there?" he asked. "There's nothing left in Tin Nangroth. The Stone is here with you."

"There must be something else," Mara mused, standing up, her thoughts racing. "We will find out tomorrow. Tonight, we must rest. Whatever comes, we need our strength."

She extended her hand to Ardil, helping him rise. "Come," she said softly. "Let's try to get some sleep, though I doubt it will be easy."

As they continued down the street, Ardil's young voice broke the silence again. "Have you seen my papa?" he asked, his tone filled with childlike hope.

"Aldur? Yes, but that was before the battle. Since then, I'm not sure where he is." Mara's voice was calm, though she knew the uncertainty weighed on the boy.

"He's with Dartur... but I haven't seen him since," Ardil said, his voice faltering. "What if something's happened to him?"

Mara smiled gently, squeezing his shoulder. "Do not worry, Ardil. If something had happened to your father, we would know. The guardians of Menyána are watching over your home. Dartur would have made sure of it."

With these words, a fleeting thought of Faran suddenly crossed her mind. In that moment, she seemed to understand why he had not journeyed to Mahlrit alongside Thariel and Dartur. It must have been his duty to guard the Halflings of Nanglorin from the looming peril.

Ardil's worry did not vanish, but Mara's words seemed to offer him some comfort. Yet, as they walked further into the quiet night, the weight of what lay ahead pressed on her. Aleth, twisted by darkness, awaited her in the Tin Nangroth, surrounded by creatures born from the same evil that had nearly destroyed them all.

She glanced at the Blue Stone in her hand, its once comforting glow now a reminder of the terrible responsibility she bore. She had hesitated too long, allowed herself to be distracted by her own fears and desires. Now, the fate of her friend - and possibly her world - rested on a confrontation she wasn't sure she could win.

As they made their way toward the shelter of the city's walls, Mara felt the burden of destiny settle upon her once more.

21

In the quiet, predawn hours, Diam hurried into the stables of Mahlrit, his movements swift and urgent. He saddled his horse with a steady hand, though his thoughts were anything but calm. The heavy, creaking doors of the stable groaned open again, causing him to pause. Through the soft morning light, a bent figure shuffled toward him. Diam's gaze turned wary, his hand instinctively tightening on the reins. But as the figure drew closer, recognition dawned, and a flicker of relief crossed his face. It was Dartur, his gray robes trailing along the ground, his eyes weary yet sharp as ever.

"You're leaving?" Dartur's voice cut through the stillness, though it carried no accusation - only curiosity as his gaze swept over Diam with a piercing intensity.

"I know my sister is preparing to leave Dinambad again," Diam replied, his jaw tightening. "And I intend to ride with her. She should not face what lies ahead alone."

Dartur studied him for a moment, a small smile tugging at the corners of his mouth. "Does she know of your plans?" he asked, though there was a knowing gleam in his eyes.

Diam set his shoulders. "She will not approve, but I care not for her disapproval. I will accompany her, whether she wishes it or not."

The old wizard chuckled softly. "Indeed, I would expect no less from you," he said, his tone warm despite the weight of what he knew lay ahead. "But alas, I cannot join you, for my path diverges elsewhere."

Without further explanation, Dartur reached into the folds of his robe and drew forth a small shiny object, pressing it into Diam's hand. The wizard's fingers closed firmly over Diam's, ensuring the object remained within his grip. When Diam opened his palm, his breath caught in his throat - there, resting against his skin, was the white Stone of Creation, Vaagos Alyarel.

"Why are you giving this to me?" Diam's voice trembled with both awe and trepidation. The stone was ancient and powerful, far beyond anything he had ever touched.

Dartur's gaze softened, though his voice remained grave. "I no longer need it, for where I must now tread, the Alyarel will do me no good. But it will serve you well on the journey ahead. There is great need for all seven stones to be reunited, and though I cannot walk with you, I trust you will see it done. I, too, have tasks to fulfill, but this - this, Diam, is now your burden."

"I thought that with Urehel's destruction, the power of the Seven Stones had faded. What use could I have for this simple gemstone? It will not aid me on the path ahead."

"It will," Dartur replied gravely. "The power of the stones cannot be extinguished by any means - not even by their destruction, which is near impossible, even for one such as I. The once unbridled force of the Seven, the very essence that shaped this world, has indeed been diminished, its brilliance dimmed, but it has not perished. The White Stone, of this I am certain, will lend you its aid on your journey."

Diam stared at the gemstone, disbelief and uncertainty warring in his heart. "Why me?" he asked, his voice barely above a whisper. "I am no great hero, no wizard or warrior of renown. What makes me worthy of such a burden?"

"You fought bravely at Um-Atra," Dartur reminded him, his eyes gleaming with an ancient wisdom. "You stood beside me when many faltered. I know who you truly are, Diam, even if you doubt yourself. You possess a strength of will that few can match. And I need someone who can resist the call of power, who will use the stone wisely and only in the direst of needs. I only hope I have chosen wisely."

Diam looked up sharply. "What do you mean by that?"

A weary sigh escaped Dartur's lips, his age and the weight of many years suddenly more evident. "I have set you on this path, and your brother Anwar on another. I fear I may have asked too much of him. He is to take Ardil back to their homeland, where they will await your arrival. Their journey will be safer, for they travel westward, while you will take the more perilous route over the Arensted. The enemy's eyes will be upon you, for they believe you carry the Black Stone, and thus they will hunt you relentlessly."

Dartur's voice darkened, his expression grave. "You must move with caution, for many dangers will lie in wait. When you pass through the Sunlit Mountains, make for Nanglorin. They will expect you there.

But be warned, Diam - this path is not an easy one, and much will rest upon your shoulders."

For a long moment, the two stood in silence, the gravity of the situation sinking deep into Diam's bones. He felt the weight of the stone in his hand, a symbol of both hope and doom, and wondered if he could truly bear it. Dartur's words echoed in his mind - he was no hero, no wizard with ancient power at his command. How could he be the one entrusted with such a task?

But before he could voice his doubts, Dartur placed a hand on his shoulder, the touch gentle yet filled with purpose. "You are stronger than you know," the wizard said quietly. "And the world needs you now, perhaps more than it ever has."

Without waiting for a reply, Dartur turned and, with surprising swiftness for his age, departed the stables. The sound of his footsteps echoed softly, mingling with the early morning birdsong as he vanished into the dawning light. Diam was left alone, staring down at the white stone, his mind swirling with uncertainty and fear. Yet beneath it all, a flicker of determination began to grow.

Diam mounted his horse, the weight of the Alyarel pressing against his chest, and set his gaze toward the horizon. The road ahead was fraught with peril, but he would walk it, not for glory or power, but for his sister and the world they both fought to protect.

6

The early morning sun cast a soft golden glow over the city of Mahlrit, but it could not lighten the mood that had settled over the camp of the men of Anros. Queen Fala stood at the head of her people, overseeing the final preparations for their return home. Around her, the soldiers moved with practiced efficiency, tightening saddles, packing supplies, and speaking in hushed tones. Among them was Aric, who moved with a quiet determination, yet his thoughts were far from the mundane tasks at hand.

Aric had not seen Mara since the last dark days of the war. The hope of reuniting with her and returning to Anros together now felt like a distant dream. His heart was heavy with unspoken words, but duty called, and he could not wait in Mahlrit forever.

Just as they were preparing to ride out, the great gates of the city creaked open, and a figure stepped through. The soldiers halted their preparations, eyes turning to the familiar form of Dartur, the ancient and wise brown wizard, leaning on his staff as he approached with the weariness of one who had carried the burdens of many lifetimes.

"Queen Fala, Aric," Dartur's voice was grave, and it echoed in the morning stillness. "I come with dire news. You cannot leave yet. The war is not over."

Queen Fala, regal and composed, stepped forward to meet the wizard. "What do you mean, Dartur? Urehel is defeated. The land can begin to heal. Why do you bring such words when we should be returning to Anros?"

Dartur's eyes darkened, and his voice was filled with an ancient sadness. "Urehel's fall was but one step in the greater battle. His defeat was not the end, for there are darker forces still at work. Mara was tasked with finding and stopping Aleth, but she has failed. Aleth is no longer herself - she is Tielir, one of the most powerful sorcerers who ever lived, reborn into the world of shadows."

Aric's heart clenched at the mention of Mara's name. His mind raced with the implications of Dartur's words, but he said nothing, waiting for the wizard to continue.

"Tielir has but one purpose now," Dartur went on. "She seeks to find Beliach, Urehel's most trusted and powerful servant, who was defeated long ago, before even our fathers' fathers were born. His body was lost to time, but rumors have persisted - rumors that his remains lie hidden deep beneath the mountains of Tin Nangroth, near Nanglorin."

Fala's expression hardened. "If Beliach is truly as powerful as you say, why has no one sought to recover him before now?"

"Because," Dartur said, his voice low and ominous, "few believed the rumors to be true. It was said that Beliach's remains were guarded by the darkest magic, that his soul could not be resurrected without the power of the Alyarel."

Aric's thoughts turned to Ardil, the young Wusel who had stumbled upon the black Alyarel while exploring the ancient mines. "You mean... the stone that Ardil found?"

"Indeed," Dartur nodded gravely. "The black Alyarel of Urehel was with Beliach, hidden beneath the mountains, waiting for one who could wield it. Tielir seeks to bring him back, to breathe life into his remains and awaken the terror that once nearly consumed this world. And she, in the fullness of her power, shall no longer have need of the Black Stone, for she now possesses a gem of her own. The one she wrenched from the grasp of the highest of the Blaecwên, a prize stolen from shadow and flame, and now bound to her will. It is hers, claimed by dark right, a jewel of terrible might, and through it, her dominion deepens, and her strength knows no bounds."

Fala's eyes narrowed. "If Tielir succeeds, she will not stop at mere destruction. She will seek to conquer, to rule over the lands of men and Aedan alike, and Beliach will be her weapon."

Aric felt a cold dread settle in his chest. "Then she seeks to use Beliach to finish what Urehel could not - to enslave all free peoples."

Dartur nodded solemnly. "Tielir's desire is power, and Beliach will give her the strength to command the forces of darkness. Together, they will raise armies that will sweep across this world like a plague. We cannot allow her to succeed."

Aric's heart pounded in his chest, and for a moment, the world seemed to close in around him. Mara had failed in her mission, but he could not let her bear the burden alone. "What must we do?" he asked, his voice steady, though fear gnawed at his resolve.

Dartur's gaze softened as he looked upon the young warrior. "You must go to Tin Nangroth, Aric. Find Tielir before she awakens Beliach. Destroy her gemstone if you can, and if not... ensure that it does not fall into her hands again. You and Queen Fala may be the last hope to stop the rising darkness."

Fala looked to her soldiers, their faces grim but determined. "We will go," she said, her voice filled with the strength of a queen. "If Tielir seeks to bring ruin to this world, she will find that Anros does not bend so easily."

Aric nodded, though the weight of the task ahead of him felt immense. His thoughts drifted once more to Mara, and he wondered where she was now, if she was safe. He had to believe she was. He had to.

As Dartur turned to leave, he paused and looked back at Aric. "Remember this, young one: the fate of this world rests not only in your strength of arms but in your heart. Tielir's power is great, but the love of those who fight for freedom is greater still. Hold fast to that, and you may yet prevail."

Aric felt the wizard's words settle deep within him. He would fight, not just for the world, but for Mara - for the chance to build a future with her, free from the shadows of darkness.

As Dartur disappeared into the shadows, Queen Fala turned to Aric, her eyes filled with resolve. "We leave for Tin Nangroth at once."

Aric nodded, gripping the hilt of his sword. The journey ahead would be perilous, but he would face it with unwavering courage. For Mara. For Anros. For the world.

And so, the men of Anros, led by their queen and their fiercest warrior, rode out from Mahlrit, their hearts heavy with the knowledge that the war was far from over. But they rode with purpose, knowing that in the deep, dark caverns of Tin Nangroth, the fate of all that was good hung in the balance.

6

The pale light of dawn filtered through the heavy curtains of the chamber in Dinambad, casting a soft glow upon the stone walls. Mara sat by the window, her gaze lost on the horizon, where the sea lay still and vast, but her heart was troubled, weighed down by fears that she could no longer suppress. The city was silent, but within her mind, chaos reigned. The shadow of the past events, the looming threat of Aleth, and the uncertainty of what lay ahead gnawed at her spirit.

She clenched her hands around the armrests of the chair, feeling powerless. The Blue Stone, cold and gleaming in her palm, seemed like both a burden and a promise - one she did not fully understand. What truly lay ahead for her? What dark forces were stirring beneath the earth and beyond the mountains?

A gentle knock broke her thoughts. Mara turned her head slightly as the door creaked open, and Adraéth entered the chamber, her face calm but her eyes carrying the weight of many battles and long years of wisdom. The elder woman stepped closer, her presence a stark contrast to the gloom that had taken hold of Mara's heart.

"You seem troubled, child," Adraéth said softly, standing by Mara's side, her voice like the wind that whispers through ancient forests. "More than you've ever been."

Mara did not respond at first. She turned her gaze back to the sea, but the tension in her body betrayed the storm within.

"I am scared," Mara whispered, her voice trembling with a vulnerability she rarely let others see. "I have never feared so much in all my life. I fear what is to come, what dark force Aleth has become, and... I fear for the truth that I do not yet know."

Adraéth watched her in silence for a moment, her eyes soft with understanding. She knelt beside Mara, placing a hand on the young princess's knee. "Fear is natural, child. Especially now, when shadows still move where we thought light had won. But you are strong - stronger than you think."

Mara shook her head, tears welling in her eyes. "You say that, but I do not feel strong. I feel lost, as if I am standing on the edge of an abyss, and one more step will plunge me into darkness. I want to know the truth, Adraéth - about what truly dwells in the old mines of Tin Nangroth. What are these shadows we face?"

Adraéth's expression darkened, her eyes taking on a weight that only those who have seen too much can carry. She rose and walked to the window, gazing out at the same horizon, as if gathering her thoughts from the depths of her long memory.

"Are you certain, Mara, that you wish to know?" she asked quietly, her voice edged with caution. "The truth is not a gentle thing. If you seek it only to ease your fear, you will not find solace. The truth may offer understanding, but it will also reveal more terror than you can imagine."

Mara clenched the stone in her hand tighter, her knuckles white. She hesitated. Her heart longed for the truth, but something deep within warned her that knowledge could be as great a burden as ignorance.

"I thought if I knew... if I knew what I must face, it would make me stronger," Mara admitted, her voice barely above a whisper. "But if the truth is darker than my fears, what hope do I have?"

Adraéth turned, her gaze piercing through Mara's uncertainty. "Hope, child, lies not in knowing everything but in knowing what you must do when the time comes. If I tell you all, you may be haunted by it for the rest of your days. But if you must know... I will not withhold it."

The silence that followed was heavy. Mara swallowed, feeling her heart race. She opened her mouth to speak, but no words came. She realized she was not ready - not for the whole truth, not for the horrors that lay hidden in the depths of the old mines, where even the bravest feared to tread.

"I... I don't want to know everything," Mara finally said, her voice shaky. "I'm scared enough as it is. I thought knowing would give me courage, but perhaps... it would do the opposite."

Adraéth nodded solemnly. "It is a wise decision, child. The darkness beneath Tin Nangroth is older than the world you know, and it holds secrets that should remain buried. You are right to fear it, for the power that stirs there is not something that can be faced lightly."

Mara's breath caught in her throat. She had known fear before, but this... this was something darker, something ancient and terrible. She lowered her head, her fingers brushing against the cold surface of the Blue Stone.

"But..." Adraéth continued, her tone softening, "there is something you must do before you leave, Mara. Something that may be harder than facing the shadows."

Mara looked up, confused. "What is it?"

"You must say your goodbyes to Aldir," Adraéth said gravely. "For the road you now walk is perilous, and it is uncertain whether you will return."

Mara's heart clenched. Aldir... her trusted companion in Dinambad. She had always thought he would be there, always. The thought of leaving him, possibly forever, cut deeper than any blade.

"I don't want to say goodbye," Mara whispered, her voice breaking. "I don't want to leave him behind."

Adraéth knelt again, taking Mara's hands in her own. "I know, child. I know it is hard. But the path you must walk is your own. And sometimes, we must leave those we love behind, not knowing if we will meet again. But if you do not say goodbye, it will weigh upon your heart, and that is a burden you cannot afford to carry."

Mara's tears fell freely now. She had faced many trials, but this - this felt like the hardest one yet.

"I don't know if I can do it," she said, her voice trembling.

Adraéth smiled softly, her eyes full of compassion. "You can. And you will. Because you must. Say your goodbyes, and then, when the time comes, face the darkness with all the strength I know you have."

With a heavy heart, Mara nodded. She knew what she had to do, but that did not make it any easier. The road ahead was filled with shadows and uncertainty, but for now, she would hold onto the light of those she loved, and that would have to be enough.

◐

The sun was sinking low over the horizon, casting long shadows across the land as Queen Fala of Anros stood by her horse, looking out toward the west. Beside her stood Aric, his face set with quiet determination, his hand resting on the hilt of his sword. Around them, the warriors of Anros readied themselves for the journey home.

The victory over Urehel was a triumph, but Fala knew that their battles were far from over. Word had reached them that new dangers stirred in the north, in the deep caverns of Tin Nangroth, and Fala and her warriors were resolved to ride into those shadowed lands. But first, they needed to return to Westhawen, to prepare for the long and perilous journey ahead.

As they prepared to ride, the air grew still, a heavy, unnatural silence settling over the land. The horses, once calm, began to shift nervously, their ears flicking and their eyes wide with unease. Fala's instincts, honed over years of warfare, sharpened. She glanced at Aric, who had already drawn his sword, his gaze fixed on the darkening horizon.

"They're here," Aric muttered, his voice low but steady.

Fala turned her gaze to the east, where the grassland rose in gentle hills. A shadow moved in the distance, followed by another, and then many more. Dark shapes, moving quickly, almost unnaturally, toward them. The Celkûn had found them.

Fala's grip tightened on the reins of her horse, her heart quickening. The Celkûn, the twisted, monstrous servants of Urehel, had not all been destroyed. They had retreated into the shadows after their master's fall, but now, like wolves in the dark, they had returned, hungry for vengeance.

"Prepare yourselves!" Fala called out to her warriors, her voice carrying strong and clear across the camp. "They are coming!"

The men of Anros responded immediately, forming a line of defense, their shields raised and swords drawn. Aric took his place at Fala's side, his eyes scanning the approaching horde.

The Celkûn came swiftly, their twisted bodies lithe and powerful, their armor blackened and cracked from countless battles. Their eyes burned with a cruel, hateful light. In moments, they were upon the warriors of Anros.

The clash of steel rang out, echoing through the air as the two forces collided. The Celkûn fought with wild ferocity, their claws tearing at shields, their spears thrusting with deadly precision. The warriors of Anros, though outnumbered, held their ground, their discipline and skill honed through years of defending their homeland from every manner of foe.

Aric fought like a man possessed, his sword a blur of motion as he parried and struck. He felled one of the Celkûn, then another, his movements precise and deadly. But for every one he cut down, two more seemed to take its place. His arm ached, his breath came in ragged gasps, but he did not falter.

Fala, atop her horse, moved like a force of nature. Her sword flashed in the dying light as she carved a path through the horde, her presence rallying her men even as the Celkûn pressed their attack. Her eyes burned with the fire of a queen who had faced darkness and had come out victorious - but even she knew that this battle was one of survival, not of victory.

Hours passed, and still the battle raged on. The warriors of Anros fought valiantly, but the relentless tide of the Celkûn seemed unending. The ground beneath their feet was slick with blood, both of their enemies and their own. The night had fully fallen now, and the battlefield was lit only by the pale light of the moon and the occasional flash of steel.

Aric's strength was waning. His arm felt like lead, and every breath he took burned in his chest. He glanced toward Fala, who was still fighting, though her movements had slowed, the exhaustion evident even in her.

"Hold the line!" Aric shouted to his men, rallying those nearest him. "For Anros! For the Queen!"

His words gave them strength, and for a moment, it seemed as though they might push the Celkûn back. But then, from the darkness, a new terror emerged.

A towering figure, larger than any of the Celkûn they had faced, strode onto the battlefield. Its skin was like iron, its eyes glowing red with malice. It carried a massive warhammer, which it swung with terrifying strength, crushing any who stood in its path.

Fala's eyes widened as she saw the creature approach. "A champion of Urehel," she whispered, recognizing the dark magic that clung to the monster. "Aric, stay with me!"

Aric turned just in time to see the creature advancing. His heart sank. This was no ordinary foe. The beast was powerful, perhaps more so than any enemy they had yet faced.

But there was no time for fear.

Fala spurred her horse forward, charging at the beast with a battle cry that echoed across the field. Her sword met the creature's hammer in a clash that sent shockwaves through the air. The force of the blow nearly unseated her, but she held firm, striking again and again.

Aric rushed to her side, his sword slashing at the creature's legs, trying to bring it down. The beast roared in anger, swinging its hammer in wide arcs, forcing them back.

The battle seemed hopeless, but neither Fala nor Aric would give in.

With a final, desperate effort, Fala drove her sword into the creature's side, and Aric followed with a swift strike to its neck. The beast let out a deafening roar before collapsing to the ground, its massive form shaking the earth beneath them.

For a moment, there was silence. The Celkûn, seeing their champion fall, hesitated, their assault faltering.

"This is our chance," Fala gasped, her voice hoarse from exertion. "Press the attack! Drive them back!"

With renewed strength, the warriors of Anros surged forward, cutting down the remaining Celkûn. One by one, the creatures fell, their dark forms vanishing into the night as the men of Anros fought with the fury of a people defending their homeland.

Finally, after what seemed like an eternity, the last of the Celkûn lay dead, and the battlefield was still.

Aric stood amidst the fallen, his chest heaving, his sword slick with blood. His body ached, but they had survived. They had won.

Fala dismounted her horse, her face weary but determined. She surveyed the battlefield, the losses heavy, but her people still stood.

"We must return to Westhawen," she said quietly, her voice filled with resolve. "There is no time to waste. The north awaits us, and we must be ready for whatever comes."

Aric nodded, though his mind was already on what lay ahead. The battle had been won, but the war was far from over.

$$\mathbf{\mathfrak{o}}$$

In the quiet morning of Dinambad, the city lay bathed in the soft golden light of the rising sun. Mara walked through the familiar streets, her heart heavy with the weight of the decision she had made. Her path was set, her journey inevitable. But there was one last farewell she had yet to make, a parting that weighed upon her more than she cared to admit.

She found Ardil waiting for her in the garden of the palace, standing under the ancient willow where they had shared many quiet moments together. His small form, once full of boundless energy, seemed diminished by the grief that clouded his gentle features. His dark eyes, so full of life, now carried the weight of a heart broken by the knowledge of her departure.

"You're leaving," he said quietly as she approached, his voice small and strained. It wasn't a question - it was a truth they both had to face.

Mara nodded, unable to meet his gaze. "I must," she replied softly. "The danger grows, Ardil. Aleth is still out there, more powerful than before. If I do not stop her, who will?"

Ardil clenched his fists, his small hands trembling. "And you think it's right to leave me behind? After everything we've been through together?" His voice cracked, and the pain in his words pierced Mara's heart.

She knelt beside him, placing a hand on his shoulder, her eyes filled with sorrow. "I wish it didn't have to be this way. You know I would take you with me if I could. But this journey is too dangerous, Ardil. Aleth is not what she was, and what lies in Tin Nangroth..." She trailed off, shaking her head. "I can't ask you to come with me into that darkness."

Ardil bit his lip, fighting back tears. "I've faced danger before. I've been with you through so much, Mara. Why can't I go with you now?"

"Because I won't risk your life. Not this time," she whispered, her voice barely above a breath.

For a long moment, they stood in silence, the only sound the rustling of leaves in the gentle morning breeze. Finally, Ardil reached into his tunic and pulled out a small, black stone that shimmered faintly in the sunlight. Urehel's Alyarel - the stone of the Dark Lord himself, the very object that had nearly brought ruin to their world.

Mara recoiled slightly at the sight of it, her breath catching in her throat. The dark aura surrounding the stone was faint, its power weakened after Urehel's fall, but it was still there - an ominous presence that made her blood run cold.

"You need to take this," Ardil said, his voice trembling as he held out the stone. "You'll need it now more than ever. I... I can't keep it. Not anymore. I don't have the strength."

Mara shook her head, backing away. "No, Ardil. I can't. That stone is cursed. Its power may be diminished, but it's still too dangerous. Even now, it could destroy the will of whoever wields it. I won't let it twist you, or me."

"You don't understand," Ardil insisted, his voice rising with ur-gency. "I've seen things, Mara - things that are coming. Aleth is more powerful than we ever imagined. She doesn't need Urehel's Alyarel an-ymore. She has something worse now. But you-" He thrust the stone toward her, his hand shaking. "You need this. Without it, you don't stand a chance."

Mara stared at the black stone, her heart pounding in her chest. She could feel the weight of it, the dark pulse of its power calling to her, tempting her. She remembered all too well the stories of those who had wielded such stones, how they had been consumed by their power, their will bent until they were nothing more than shadows of themselves.

"I can't," she whispered again, her voice trembling. "I can't control it, Ardil. No one can. Not even Dartur could use it without being tainted. How could I hope to resist it?"

"You're stronger than you think," Ardil said, his voice breaking as tears welled in his eyes. "Stronger than any of us. Please, Mara. Take it. I trust you. I... I can't bear the thought of you going into this battle with-out something to protect you."

Mara hesitated, her heart torn. She saw the desperation in Ardil's eyes, the love and fear he held for her. He was right - Aleth was a force beyond their understanding, and without some kind of aid, Mara would be walking into her doom. But the thought of holding Urehel's Alyarel, of using the power that had once nearly destroyed the world, filled her with dread.

Finally, after what felt like an eternity, she reached out and took the stone from Ardil's hand. It was cold to the touch, unnaturally so, and a shiver ran down her spine as the dark energy of the Alyarel seeped into her skin. She could feel its pull, its insidious whisper at the edges of her mind, but she forced it back, pushing away the fear that threatened to overwhelm her.

"I'll take it," she said softly, her voice steady despite the storm rag-ing inside her. "But I promise you, Ardil - I will not let it consume me."

Ardil nodded, though his eyes were filled with sorrow. "Just come back to me," he whispered, his voice barely audible. "Please. Don't leave me behind forever."

Mara leaned down and kissed the top of his head gently, her heart aching. "I'll come back," she promised, though she wasn't sure if she believed her own words. "No matter what happens, I'll find my way back."

She stood, clutching the Alyarel in her hand, and turned toward the stables, where her horse awaited. As she walked away, the weight of her task pressed down on her like a mountain. Behind her, Ardil watched, his heart breaking as he saw her go, knowing that this might be the last time he ever saw her again.

And with every step she took, Mara felt the darkness of the Alyarel grow heavier in her hand, a constant reminder of the battle yet to come, and of the uncertain path that lay before her.

⟳

The early morning light bathed the ancient stone walls of Dinambad in a soft golden hue. The city still lay quiet, its people resting in the brief peace that had returned after long and troubled days. But for Mara, there was no peace in her heart. She walked through the streets alongside Adraéth, her thoughts weighed heavily with the burden of the journey ahead. They were leaving Dinambad, bound for the dangerous northern lands, where an ancient evil stirred once more.

As they neared the great gates of the city, Mara's gaze fell upon the massive walls, the stronghold that had sheltered her people for generations. Her footsteps grew heavier with every step, knowing this may be the last time she would see her homeland. She glanced over at Adraéth, the tall, mysterious woman who had stood by her side through many dark trials. Though Adraéth's face remained calm, Mara could sense the same unease within her.

When they reached the gate, they found Diam waiting for them. He stood tall, his dark hair tousled by the wind, and beside him were three horses, saddled and prepared for the long journey. He smiled at his sister, but there was a sadness in his eyes, one that mirrored her own.

"You're ready, I see," Diam said, his voice steady, though Mara could hear the tension beneath it.

Mara stopped short, shaking her head. "Diam, you can't come with us. The journey ahead is too perilous. Aleth is no longer who she once was. The darkness within her grows stronger, and the lands we travel to are fraught with ancient dangers. I won't risk your life."

Diam's brow furrowed, but he held his ground. "You won't go without me, Mara. I've fought beside you before. I've seen the darkness we face, and I won't let you face it alone."

Mara's gaze softened, but her resolve remained firm. "I know your heart is strong, brother, but this is not a battle we can win through strength alone. Aleth's power now is unlike anything we've faced. And the northern lands... they hold secrets far darker than you realize. I cannot bear to lose you."

"I understand the danger," Diam said, his voice low and determined. "But Dartur entrusted me with something." He reached into his cloak and withdrew a small, glowing stone, pure and white as freshly fallen snow. It shimmered with a faint light, even in the morning sun. "Vaago's Alyarel," he said softly. "Dartur gave it to me. He said I would need it on this journey, and that its power, though weakened, would aid us."

Mara's eyes widened at the sight of the stone. She recognized it immediately - the White Stone of Creation, one of the seven ancient stones that had shaped their world. It was a relic of immense power, a stone that held the essence of life itself. She had not expected Dartur to give such a powerful artifact to her brother.

"Why would the wizard give you this?" Mara whispered, her hand hovering near the stone. "This... this is a great responsibility, Diam. It's power is beyond any of us."

Diam nodded. "I don't fully understand why he gave it to me, but I believe there is a reason for everything Dartur does. He said it would guide us when the time came, that its light would show us the way when the darkness grows too thick to see."

Mara's heart wavered. She was always protected by her older brother, and now he was asking to walk into the heart of danger with her. But the sight of the Alyarel in his hand filled her with a strange sense of hope. It was true that the power of the stones had not faded completely, even with Urehel's defeat. Perhaps, in this stone, there was a glimmer of light they could use against the shadows that pursued them.

Adraéth, who had been silent until now, placed a hand on Mara's shoulder. "He is right, Mara," she said quietly. "The White Stone could be the key to our success. And Diam... he carries a strength within him, one that even you may not fully see yet."

Mara hesitated, looking between her brother and the stone. She could feel the burden of her choice settling on her shoulders. To take him with them was to expose him to the worst dangers of the world, but to leave him behind might rob them of the strength they needed to succeed.

Finally, after a long moment, Mara sighed and nodded. "Very well," she said, her voice heavy with the weight of her decision. "You may come with us, Diam. But you must promise me this - no matter what happens, you will not let the power of that stone consume you. You are my brother, and I will not see you lost to the same darkness that took Aleth."

Diam smiled, a warmth in his eyes that hadn't been there before. "I promise, little sister. I will not let it consume me. We will face this together."

Mara took a deep breath and reached for the reins of her horse. "Then let us go. The north awaits, and time is not on our side."

With that, the three of them mounted their horses, and as the gates of Dinambad creaked open before them, they rode out into the wild lands beyond the city. Ahead of them lay the mountains, the vast forests, and far away the ancient mines of Tin Nangroth, where Aleth waited, cloaked in shadow, her power growing with every passing day.

The road would be long and filled with peril, but now, with the light of Vaago's Alyarel in their hands and the strength of their bond as siblings, Mara allowed herself a fleeting hope that perhaps they might yet overcome the darkness that threatened to engulf them all.

22

The long ride back to Suthawen had drained Aric's spirit. His men, hardened by battle but weary from the endless march, followed in silence. The shadow of war clung to them, and although their queen, Fala, had pressed north toward Westhawen with a fraction of their strength, Aric knew he could not follow, not yet. His heart was too heavy, and his soul too wounded. He needed to return home, to Suthawen, where he could gather new strength, reinforce his army, and perhaps - just perhaps - find a moment's peace.

The city of Suthawen, nestled within the highlands of Anros, came into view beneath the setting sun. Its old stone walls stood tall, though weathered by time, and the great hall at the city's center loomed as a testament to its enduring legacy. Aric had been raised in these lands, and they were as much a part of him as the blood in his veins. But as they rode through the gates, he could not shake the feeling of loss that gnawed at him.

Inside the city, the people greeted him with weary smiles and words of praise, though their faces held the same exhaustion that had settled over his heart. Among them stood Rían, who became steward of Suthawen in his absence. She was a woman of striking beauty - tall, with raven-black hair and sharp green eyes. She had taken on the mantle of leadership with grace and strength, tending to the needs of the city while Aric led his men to war. But there was something in her gaze that unnerved him, a subtle intensity that he had never seen before.

As he dismounted his horse, Rían stepped forward, her voice laced with something too sweet to be genuine. "You've returned, Aric. Alone." She paused, her eyes searching his face. "I feared... I feared you might not come back at all."

Aric nodded, his heart too burdened to find words. He glanced at his men, who began disbanding to tend to the horses and find rest.

Rían's gaze lingered on him, and as they moved to the great hall, she walked beside him, her voice low and questioning. "And Mara? Where is she? Surely you did not leave her behind?"

At the mention of Mara's name, something deep within Aric stirred - pain, guilt, longing. His jaw tightened, but he could not find the strength to defend the woman he loved. The words stuck in his throat, like a shadow binding him.

"Ah," Rían said, her tone turning bitter, "so she remains behind, then. Perhaps she has other ambitions? A princess of the stone lands like Dinambad, raised among nobles and kings, might find the wild lands of Anros too untamed for her delicate tastes."

Aric frowned but still said nothing. He should have stood up for Mara, for the love that had once burned so fiercely in his heart. But he felt weak, drained, as if some unseen force weighed down upon him. He had left Mara behind, had allowed the distance to grow between them, and now he felt that weight crushing his will. Rían's words felt like venom seeping into his thoughts, clouding his mind. He shook his head, struggling against the strange pull he felt toward her.

"Mara..." he began, but his voice faltered, "Mara has her own path to walk."

Rían's lips curled into a slight smile, one that did not reach her eyes. "You speak as though she has chosen to abandon you, Aric. But perhaps it is for the best. Here, you are needed. Here, your people look to you for strength, not to her."

Aric felt a strange haze falling over his thoughts, as if Rían's words were beginning to make sense. Mara was far away, lost in the turmoil of her own battles, while he stood here, in the city that had been his home, surrounded by those who needed him. Rían stepped closer, her hand brushing lightly against his arm.

"Anros needs you, Aric," she whispered, her voice soft, almost tender. "The people trust you. More than they trust Fala. If she falls in the mountains of Tin Nangroth, who will lead them? Who will protect Anros if not you?"

The words struck a chord within him. He had always been a leader, always someone his people could turn to in times of crisis. But the idea of becoming their king - it was not something he had sought, yet now, the thought of it began to take root in his heart. Could he truly abandon them, knowing what lay ahead? Could he let Fala march into the north without him, risking her life in a fight against a darkness even Urehel could not vanquish?

"You could be king," Rían continued, her voice soft but insistent. "The people would follow you. They already look to you for guidance, not Fala. She is their queen, yes, but it is your name they call in the streets. And Mara... she is not of this world. She belongs to the stone cities of Miénast, not to Anros. You are of these lands, Aric. You were raised here, and only you can understand what these people truly need."

Aric closed his eyes, struggling to clear his mind. He knew Rían was only a mortal woman, one without any magical power or enchantment. Yet her words felt like a spell weaving around his heart, binding him in a way that felt unnatural.

"Rían," he said, his voice rough, "this is madness. I'm no king."

"Not yet," she whispered, her green eyes gleaming with something unreadable. "But you will be. It is your destiny. The people of Anros know it, and deep down, you know it too. Stay here, Aric. Lead your people. Forget about Mara. She is not one of us."

Aric wanted to protest, wanted to fight back against the strange power Rían held over him. But his heart was weak, his resolve shattered. He could feel his love for Mara slipping away, buried beneath the weight of duty and the strange pull of the woman before him.

"Stay," Rían said again, her hand now resting on his chest. "Suthawen is your home, and Anros needs its king."

Aric stared at her, feeling a deep sense of betrayal - betrayal of his own heart, of the love he had sworn to protect. But in that moment, he felt lost, unable to fight against the tide pulling him away from Mara, away from his past.

"Perhaps you're right," he said at last, his voice heavy with doubt. "Perhaps... my place is here."

Rían smiled, a triumphant glint in her eyes. "It is."

And so, as the night fell over Suthawen, Aric felt the weight of his choices settling upon him like a shroud, unsure if he had made the right one or if he had been led astray by a voice sweeter than reason and a promise he wasn't sure he truly wanted.

◯

Anwar stood at the gates of Miénast, watching as the sun dipped below the horizon, casting a deep golden light across the land. He had waited for this moment, knowing that his mission was more than just duty - it was a promise kept. Beside him stood Aldur, the Wusel from Nanglorin, Ardil's father, who had been lost amidst the turmoil of war. It had taken time to find him, but now the journey back to Dinambad could begin. Father and son would be reunited, and Anwar would ensure they returned home safely. But their road was long and full of uncertainty.

As they set out on the journey, the air was crisp, filled with the scent of pine and earth. Finally, they arrived at Dinambad. The towering walls of the city loomed before them, but the air felt lighter here, as though the weight of the past had been lifted. Inside the city, Ardil was waiting, pacing anxiously. When he saw his father, his eyes widened with disbelief, then filled with tears.

"Papa!" Ardil cried, running forward to embrace the old Wusel. Aldur, though wearied by the journey, hugged his son tightly, his voice choked with emotion.

"My boy," Aldur whispered, "I feared I might never see you again."

"And I you," Ardil replied, his voice shaking. "But now you're here, and everything will be all right."

Anwar watched the reunion with a mixture of relief and melancholy. His mission was not yet over - there was still the journey to Nanglorin, where father and son would finally return home. But for now, he gave them their moment, standing quietly beside them.

After a brief rest in Dinambad, they set out once more. The path they followed was hidden, known only to a few. Instead of traveling through Anros, where dangers might still lurk, Anwar had chosen a secret route - a passage straight to the north, through the ancient woods of Folares, which lay to the north of Dinambad.

The trees of Folares were tall and regal, their leaves shimmering in hues of emerald and gold as the wind whispered through them. Anwar had heard legends of these trees, said to be enchanted, guardians of the hidden paths that led to the forgotten corners of the world. As they ventured deeper into the forest, the weariness of the past months seemed to fall away. Aldur, though aged and tired, appeared more at peace as they walked beneath the ancient branches, his eyes filled with wonder at the beauty around them.

"These trees," he said softly, his voice full of reverence, "they remind me of stories my grandfather told me as a child. Of a place where the earth still remembers its first breath, where life itself is woven into the leaves and the roots."

Anwar smiled, though his heart was heavy with the weight of his mission. "Folares is a place of healing," he said, "but it is also a place of secrets. Few come here now, and fewer still find the ways through."

As they continued, their path took them through the hidden passageways that led beneath the mighty mountains of Tin Uael. The mountains loomed above them, their peaks shrouded in mist. Few knew of the secret passageways that cut through them, but Anwar had learned of this route from ancient maps and old tales. It was the safest way north, away from the dangers of open roads and prying eyes.

The passage was narrow and dark, the air cool and damp. The sound of their footsteps echoed off the stone walls, and the flickering light of their torches cast eerie shadows around them. Yet there was a strange calm in the darkness, a quiet solitude that allowed Anwar to think, to reflect on the task that lay ahead.

"We're almost there," Anwar said after many hours of walking. "Soon, we'll reach the other side."

When they emerged from the passage, the sight that greeted them was one of sorrow and devastation. The city of Rist lay before them, burned and broken. Once a place of beauty and power, it was now little more than charred ruins, a memory of what had been. Smoke still rose from the wreckage, though the fires had long since died out.

Aldur gasped at the sight. "Rist... I had heard tales of its fall, but I never imagined it could be so... destroyed."

Anwar nodded, his face grim. "This is what happens when the darkness touches a place. But we must pass through. The path to Nanglorin lies beyond."

The city was eerily silent as they moved through the ruins. Anwar led them carefully, his senses alert for any sign of danger. The air was thick with the scent of ash and decay, and the silence felt heavy, oppressive.

"This city once stood as a beacon," Anwar murmured, "but now it lies in ruin, like so many others. We must press on."

They continued their journey, hearts heavy with the weight of what they had seen. The road ahead was long, and they did not know what awaited them in Nanglorin. But Anwar knew that they had to keep going, to return Aldur and Ardil to their home, and to face whatever darkness still lingered in the north.

As the mountains of Tin Uael faded into the distance behind them, Anwar could not help but feel that their journey was far from over. Though Urehel had fallen, a deeper, more insidious threat still loomed, and it was up to them to face it - together, as they walked into the uncertain future that lay before them.

6

In the quiet, empty streets of Suthawen, the midnight hour cast long shadows upon the cobblestone paths. The wind whispered through the narrow alleys, cold and silent, as if the city itself was holding its breath. Suthawen slept, but not everyone rested peacefully.

Rían moved with careful steps, her dark cloak wrapped tightly around her slender form, hiding her face from any curious eyes. She had arranged this meeting in the deepest hour of night, far from the prying gaze of anyone who might suspect her. Her heart beat steadily, though there was a coldness in her that matched the night.

At the corner of an old, abandoned market square, a figure waited. His form was obscured by shadows, a hood concealing his features. Even in the darkness, there was something unsettling about him, a presence that sent a chill through the air.

Rían approached the man without hesitation. "You came," she said softly, her voice low but steady.

The stranger gave a slight nod, stepping forward just enough so that the dim light from a distant lantern flickered across his face, though it revealed little. His eyes, however, gleamed with a strange intensity. "I always come when called, Rían," he replied in a deep, rasping voice. "What news of our... plan?"

Rían glanced around the empty square before meeting his gaze. "Aric grows weaker by the day," she said, her voice filled with quiet satisfaction. "His heart is divided, torn by his feelings for that girl from Dinambad - Mara. His love for her has made him vulnerable, easy to manipulate. I've sown the seeds of doubt in him, fed his insecurity. It will not be long before he abandons thoughts of her entirely."

The stranger's lips curled into a twisted smile. "Good. Very good. Love can be a useful weapon when wielded properly. And you, Rían, wield it with the precision of a blade."

Rían allowed herself a small smile of triumph, though her eyes remained cold. "He trusts me now. In his heart, he knows that I am the one who has always been there for him, not Mara. I have convinced him that Anros needs him more than she ever will, that he was born to lead, to rule. The people already look to him for strength, not Fala. And when the time comes... when the queen falls... I will be there at his side, as his queen."

The stranger's smile widened, his voice dripping with dark amusement. "You play a dangerous game, Rían. But then again, you always have. I remember how you dealt with Finian."

At the mention of the name, Rían's smile faded, replaced by a cold, calculating expression. Her voice dropped to a whisper. "Finian was a fool. He had everything - power, blood, the love of the people. But he refused me. He cared for nothing but his vision of being the perfect prince, the noble leader of Anros. I was nothing to him, a mere distraction. So, I removed him. It was simple, really. A sudden fever, a few whispered rumors, and Finian was gone."

The stranger chuckled softly, his voice barely more than a growl in the shadows. "You were clever then, Rían, and you are clever now. But remember, Aric is not Finian. He may not be as idealistic as his cousin was, but he is no fool."

Rían's eyes hardened. "Aric is a broken man. His love for Mara is his greatest weakness. He longs for something he can never have. I have made sure he understands that the wilds of Anros are his true home, and that the people need him far more than any foreign princess ever could. He will stay. And in time, he will realize that I am the one he needs, not her."

The stranger studied her for a moment, his gaze sharp and calculating. "And what if Queen Fala does not fall in Tin Nangroth? What then?"

Rían's eyes gleamed with cold ambition. "Then I will find another way. Fala is strong, but she is not invincible. The war is far from over, and danger lurks everywhere. If the battle does not claim her, something else will."

The stranger was silent for a moment before nodding slowly. "You have thought of everything, it seems."

Rían lifted her chin. "I have waited long enough. Finian was supposed to be my chance, my path to power. But he was too blind to see what I could offer him. Aric, however, is different. He is broken, and I will mend him. He will fall for me, and when Fala is gone, I will rule at his side."

The stranger's smile returned, dark and cruel. "You have always been ruthless, Rían. That is what I like about you. But be careful. Love is a dangerous thing to toy with. If Aric ever discovers the truth about Finian... or about your plans for Fala..."

Rían's eyes narrowed. "He will not. He believes me. And soon, he will believe in nothing else."

The stranger stepped back into the shadows, his form disappearing into the darkness. "Then let us hope your plans succeed, Rían. For your sake."

As the man melted away into the night, Rían stood alone in the cold square, her thoughts racing. Aric was hers to mold, hers to control. The pieces were falling into place, just as they had with Finian all those years ago.

But this time, she would not fail. This time, she would take the throne that had always eluded her, and no one - neither Mara nor Fala - would stand in her way.

○

The morning sun bathed the landscape in a golden hue as Anwar, Aldur, and Ardil traveled north along the Ferry Road, the gravel crunching softly beneath their boots. The road was quiet, stretching far toward the distant crossing that would take them over the great lake Nyar. Aldur, the elder Wusel, rode quietly on the back of a small horse, while his son Ardil walked close by, his young face lit with curiosity and occasional fear. Anwar led the way, ever watchful, his hand never far from the hilt of his sword.

The air was crisp, the kind that spoke of the untamed wilds they ventured deeper into. But even in this serenity, Anwar felt an unease tugging at his senses. The threat, though unseen, was palpable.

"The crossing should be just ahead," Anwar said quietly to the two Wusel. His sharp eyes scanned the horizon, every shadow under the hills examined with care.

"Good," Aldur muttered, his face tired from the long journey. "My bones are weary from this endless ride. The north awaits, but it seems further away with every step."

Anwar nodded but said nothing more. His instincts were finely honed from years of battle and survival. And now those instincts screamed at him, though he could not see the source of his discomfort. There was something wrong, something lurking.

Soon, the road dipped into a narrow valley where the ferry crossing over the great lake Nyar appeared before them. The lake stretched far into the distance, its dark waters shimmering in the early sunlight. The ferry itself was a sturdy wooden raft with thick ropes anchoring it to the banks, operated by a few ferrymen who looked hardened from years of navigating these treacherous waters.

Anwar led Aldur and Ardil onto the ferry, and the ferrymen began to push them slowly across the wide, still lake. It seemed peaceful enough, but Anwar's sense of danger grew stronger.

"We should be on guard," Anwar whispered to Ardil, who looked up at him with wide eyes. "Stay close to your father and me. Something stirs in these lands."

Ardil swallowed hard and nodded, his small hands gripping his father's saddle anxiously.

As they reached the northern shore of the lake and disembarked, the world seemed suddenly quieter. The wind was still, the birds that had been singing along the ferry road now silent.

"We'll continue along the road for a while longer," Anwar said, his voice tense, "but stay ready. I don't like this silence."

For another hour, they walked along the winding path. But Anwar could feel it - something was wrong, terribly wrong. And then, without warning, he made a decision.

"We leave the road," he commanded, turning sharply to Aldur and Ardil. "We need to travel through the hills. There's danger close, though I cannot see it."

"But why?" Aldur asked, though his tone carried no challenge - only concern.

"I feel something," Anwar said, his voice low. "Something watching. We must move where we won't be seen."

With no further explanation, Anwar guided them off the road and into the rolling hills that flanked the great forest. They moved carefully, Anwar's eyes scanning the landscape for any sign of movement. The hills provided cover, but also brought the unknown. Every shadow felt like a possible ambush.

They had not been traveling for long when suddenly, out of the thicket, a group of Celkûn burst forth from the shadows. Savage and relentless, the Celkûn were twisted, dark creatures of the night, corrupted beyond recognition. Their eyes glinted with malice, and their jagged weapons caught the light in a menacing gleam.

"Run!" Anwar shouted, drawing his sword in one swift motion. The Wusel, though small in stature, moved with surprising speed, and they darted into the hills as fast as they could.

The Celkûn were on them in moments, their guttural cries filling the air as they charged in pursuit. Anwar slashed at one of the creatures, but more poured out of the shadows behind it. His heart pounded in his chest as they raced over the uneven terrain.

Aldur, though old, kept pace as best he could, but Ardil, his younger legs moving swiftly, was in danger of being overtaken.

"Stay close!" Anwar called, pushing himself to run faster, his sword gleaming as he swung at another Celkûn, narrowly avoiding its blade.

The hills stretched on before them, but the Celkûn were relentless. They knew these lands well, and it was clear that they had been tracking the travelers for some time. Every step felt more desperate, the path ahead uncertain.

"We won't outrun them for long!" Aldur gasped, his breath coming in ragged bursts.

Anwar's mind raced. There was no time for fear, only action. "Into the trees!" he shouted, steering them toward a dense thicket that rose ahead. The cover might buy them time, or at least confuse the Celkûn long enough to gain some distance.

As they darted into the thicket, Anwar turned to see the Celkûn crashing through the undergrowth, their eyes wild with hunger for the kill.

"Keep moving!" Anwar urged. His muscles burned, but he pushed forward, leading Aldur and Ardil through the trees, their only hope to lose their pursuers in the forest's maze-like depths.

But as they ran deeper into the woods, Anwar knew the battle was far from over. The Celkûn were cunning, and they would not stop until blood had been spilled. Anwar's heart pounded with the weight of responsibility - not just for his life, but for the two Wusel, who were now depending on him for their survival.

Whatever happened next, he would have to stand his ground.

6

The sun hung low in the western sky as Queen Fala and her retinue of warriors finally returned to Westhawen. The long journey had left them weary, but the sight of the city brought a sense of both relief and urgency. Westhawen stood tall, its wooden palisades shimmering in the fading light, but a heavy weight hung over Fala's heart. The threat of Aleth and Beliach, still lurking in the shadows, grew ever nearer.

Beside her rode Aasa, her cousin, silent but equally burdened by the knowledge of the battles yet to come. Her hair, tousled by the wind, framed a face lined with concern. Though Aasa was a brave and capable warrior, her thoughts were consumed by her brother Aric, who had not yet returned from Suthawen.

As they approached the gates of Westhawen, two tall figures with long silver hair stood waiting at the entrance, their serene faces betraying a quiet power. These were the Aedan, the ancient people of Faldar, who traveled across vast lands only in the gravest of times. Fala recognized them at once - Aranel and Rável, siblings of great renown. Their presence was both unexpected and foreboding.

Queen Fala dismounted her horse, her tired legs steadying beneath her. Aasa followed suit, casting a curious glance toward the Aedan as they approached.

"Queen Fala of Anros," said Aranel, bowing slightly, his hair gleaming in the golden light. His voice was calm, but there was an urgency in his eyes. "We have traveled far from Faldar to bring you a gift, though we wish it were under different circumstances."

Rável stepped forward, his movements as graceful as a leaf in the wind. In his hands, he held a small, ornately carved wooden box. As he opened it, Fala saw three gleaming stones inside, each glowing faintly with its own unique color.

"The Alyarel," Rável said quietly, his silver eyes locking onto Fala's. "The Red, the Brown, and the Green. Taken from Mylias, Elfor, and Thergil, long hidden from the world. They are yours now, for the fight you must soon face."

Fala's breath caught as she looked at the stones - the Red of Mylias, filled with the ancient fires of love and creation; the Brown of Elfor, rooted in the earth's deepest wisdom; and the Green of Thergil, radiating the strength of forests untouched by time. These were no mere trinkets, but three of the seven most powerful relics in existence, tied to the very fabric of the world.

"The three of the Seven," Fala murmured, her voice barely above a whisper. "I did not expect to hold such power in my hands."

"Nor did we," Aranel replied. "But the shadow that rises now is unlike anything we have faced in many ages. Aleth, once your ally, has fallen into darkness. Worse still, Beliach stirs in the depths. You will need all the strength you can gather for the battle to come."

Aasa, standing beside her cousin, felt a chill at the mention of Beliach. The very name invoked dread. "We have heard rumors of his return," she said softly, her voice steady but grim. "If Aleth succeeds in reviving him, our world will fall into ruin."

"That is why we came," Rável said. "The Alyarel may be your only hope against such a threat."

Fala closed the box gently, her mind swirling with the weight of what lay ahead. She could feel the power of the stones even through the wood. But despite the gravity of the moment, a new concern tugged at her.

"Where is Aric?" Fala asked suddenly, looking at Aasa. "He was supposed to meet us here before we ride north, but there has been no word from him."

Aasa's eyes narrowed with worry. "He has not yet returned from Suthawen. It's unlike him to delay without sending word. Something must have happened."

Fala frowned, her concern deepening. Aric was not the kind of man to abandon his duty or ignore a summons. The thought that he might be in danger gnawed at her, but she couldn't delay preparations for the looming threat.

"I will ride to Suthawen and find him," Aasa said, determination sharpening her features. "You must prepare for the battle ahead, but I cannot wait idly while my brother's fate is uncertain."

Fala nodded, her hand resting briefly on Aasa's shoulder. "Go then, but take caution. If anything seems amiss, do not hesitate to return. We cannot afford to lose you both."

Aasa gave a curt nod, her heart heavy but resolute. She turned and strode toward the stables to prepare her horse, the weight of her mission pressing down on her.

As Aasa departed, Fala turned to the two Aedan. "We must prepare, and quickly," she said. "Aleth and Beliach will not wait for us to gather our strength. We must be ready to face them when they strike."

Aranel and Rável exchanged a glance before Aranel spoke. "You are wise to prepare, Queen Fala. But remember, the Alyarel are not to be used lightly. They can turn the tide of battle, yes, but they also come with great risk. Be wary of their power."

"I will," Fala promised, though in her heart she knew the decision to use the stones would not be easy. But she also knew that the world hung in the balance, and they could not afford to hold back in the face of such evil.

With that, the preparations began. Fala's men, still weary from their last battle, were summoned to train and prepare for the coming fight.

Armor was mended, weapons were sharpened, and scouts were sent out to monitor any movements of the enemy.

But even as the preparations continued, Fala could not shake the feeling that something was amiss. The absence of Aric weighed heavily on her mind, and Aasa's departure only deepened her anxiety. If Aleth and Beliach were gathering their forces, they would need every ally they could muster.

As the day faded into night, Fala stood on the walls of Westhawen, staring out over the darkening landscape. The wind whispered through her hair, carrying with it the scent of salt and distant storms. Somewhere, far to the north, Aleth was preparing her dark rituals. Somewhere, deep beneath the mountains, Beliach's spirit stirred.

And somewhere, in the shadow of Suthawen, Aric remained absent, his fate uncertain.

23

The Celkûn were close, their guttural voices echoing off the craggy rock walls of the pass as Anwar, Aldur, and Ardil ran through the narrow, twisting paths of the hills. They could hear the heavy footfalls of their pursuers - brutal hunters who would show no mercy once they caught up.

"We can't keep running forever," Anwar muttered under his breath, casting a quick glance over his shoulder. Aldur, the older of the two Wusel, was panting heavily, his small legs struggling to keep pace. Ardil, younger and spryer, ran just ahead, but the fear in his wide eyes was unmistakable. They were exhausted, their bodies battered by days of relentless travel, and now the Celkûn were closing in.

Suddenly, the path ahead narrowed even more, leading to a sheer cliff. A dead end.

Anwar stopped abruptly, his chest heaving as his heart sank. "No..." he whispered, scanning the rocky ledge for any possible escape. But there was none. Behind them, the Celkûn were drawing nearer, their howls growing louder and more triumphant. It was only a matter of time before they would be upon them.

Aldur stumbled to a halt beside him, wheezing heavily, while Ardil clutched his father's arm, terror etched on his young face. "We're trapped!" Ardil cried, his voice breaking with panic.

Anwar glanced at the Wusel beside him, knowing that defending them alone against a pack of Celkûn was hopeless. But he would fight to the last breath if he had to. "Stay behind me," he ordered, his voice firm despite the dread gnawing at his heart. "No matter what happens."

The Celkûn emerged from the shadows of the pass, a horde of savage figures with grotesque, snarling faces. Their black armor gleamed dully in the fading light, and their weapons - curved blades and jagged spears - dripped with malice. They moved forward slowly, savoring the terror of their prey.

Anwar raised his sword, preparing to fight, when suddenly, a sharp whistle cut through the air, followed by the sound of hooves and the clash of steel. Out of nowhere, figures in grey and green appeared, descending upon the Cclkûn with the speed and ferocity of a storm.

The Guardians of the Order had arrived.

Leading them was Faran, tall and imposing, his presence commanding even amidst the chaos. His eyes glinted beneath his helm, and his sword flashed as it cleaved through the Celkûn ranks. The battle was immediate and fierce, the sound of steel ringing out as the Guardians engaged the enemy in a deadly dance of blades.

Anwar wasted no time. With renewed hope, he surged forward, his sword slicing through the air as he joined the Guardians in the fray. The Celkûn were relentless, their attacks brutal and unyielding, but the Guardians fought with the skill and precision of warriors born to battle.

Amidst the melee, Anwar found himself fighting side by side with Faran. "Just in time," Anwar shouted, his sword clashing with the blade of a snarling Celkûn.

Faran grinned grimly, parrying a blow. "I sensed you might need some assistance. But where is Mara? I had hoped she would be the one to bring the two Wusel back to Nanglorin."

Anwar ducked beneath a spear thrust, taking a Celkûn down with a swift strike. "She's not here," he said, breathless. "My sister is on a much darker path. She's going after Aleth... and Beliach."

Faran's expression darkened, though his movements remained fluid and deadly. "Beliach," he muttered, his eyes narrowing as he blocked a savage swing. "I had feared as much. The rumors are true, then."

"Too true," Anwar replied, slashing at another Celkûn. "Aleth seeks to revive him, to bring about a darkness even greater than Urehel's reign."

For a moment, Faran's focus sharpened, his face tightening with the weight of this revelation. He fought with renewed vigor, cutting down Celkûn left and right, his blade a blur. "Mara must succeed. If Aleth and Beliach unite, all will be lost."

The battle raged on, fierce and desperate. Blood soaked the ground as Guardians and Celkûn clashed in a brutal struggle for survival. Anwar fought like a man possessed, knowing that the stakes were higher than ever. He slashed and parried, every breath a battle, every swing a struggle for life. Meanwhile, the Wusel huddled together behind a rock, fear gripping their hearts as they watched the chaos unfold.

The Guardians of the Order, though fewer in number, were unmatched in their skill. With great loss and sacrifice, they began to push the Celkûn back, their enemies falling one by one. But the cost was high. Bodies of Guardians and Celkûn alike littered the battlefield, and the air was thick with the stench of death.

At last, with a final cry of defiance, the last of the Celkûn fell. The field was silent save for the ragged breaths of the survivors. Anwar, bloodied and weary, lowered his sword. His body ached, but relief flooded through him as he saw Aldur and Ardil unharmed.

Faran wiped his blade clean, his face grim. "It's done," he said softly, though the weight of what lay ahead still pressed upon him.

Anwar approached him, his face pale and drawn from the fight. "Mara knows the dangers she faces, but I fear she may not be strong enough. She's going to face Aleth and Beliach, and the powers they wield..."

Faran sheathed his sword, his expression grave. "Mara is stronger than she knows, but the road ahead of her is dark. If Aleth truly is Tielir, and Beliach rises again, it may take more than strength to defeat them. It will take hope. And sacrifice."

Anwar nodded, his heart heavy with worry for his sister. He had fought many battles, but none compared to the war she was about to face. "She will not be alone," he said quietly, more to himself than to Faran. "We will not let her face this darkness alone."

Faran placed a hand on Anwar's shoulder. "No, we will not. But for now, take Aldur and Ardil back to Nanglorin. Ensure their safety. Their part in this is not over, but they must live to see it through."

Anwar glanced back at the two Wusel, who were still trembling from the ordeal. He gave them a reassuring nod, then turned to Faran. "And you?"

"I will do what I must," Faran said, his voice low but resolute. "I will find Mara. And I will help her finish what she has started."

With that, Faran turned, leading what remained of his Guardians into the shadows, their forms vanishing into the mist like ghosts.

Anwar watched them go, his heart aching for what was yet to come.

◌

The wind howled through the high walls of Suthawen as Aasa rode in, her heart heavy with the burden of her mission. The long journey from Westhawen had left her weary, but her determination to find her brother, Aric, and bring him back to their queen had not wavered. The threat of Aleth and Beliach loomed on the horizon, and Aasa knew that Fala would need all the strength Anros could muster for the coming battle. But there was another reason Aasa had come, a more personal one - Mara.

She dismounted her horse at the entrance to the grand hall, her boots echoing against the cobblestone floor as she made her way inside. The great wooden doors creaked open, and Aasa's heart nearly stopped as her eyes fell upon the scene before her.

Aric, her beloved brother, sat on the old wooden throne that once belonged to their ancestors, his hair falling in waves over his broad shoulders. But he was not alone. Standing beside him, leaning in close, was Rían. Her hair shimmered in the dim light, and her smile was soft, almost predatory, as she spoke to him in a voice too low for Aasa to hear. There was something intimate about their posture, something Aasa hadn't seen in her brother since... since Mara.

A surge of anger and disbelief washed over Aasa as she took a step forward, her voice cutting through the room like a blade. "Aric!"

Both Aric and Rían turned to face her, surprise flashing in Aric's eyes before a strange coldness settled over him. Rían's smile remained, but it had turned sharper, more calculating.

"Aasa," Aric said, his voice calm but distant. "What are you doing here?"

Aasa clenched her fists at her sides, her heart racing with confusion and anger. "I've come to bring you back. Fala needs you. Mara needs you."

At the mention of Mara, a flicker of something crossed Aric's face, but it was gone as quickly as it had come. He shook his head, his tone resolute. "Mara doesn't want to see me. She made that clear."

Aasa frowned, taking a step closer. "What are you talking about? Mara loves you. She has always loved you."

Rían's voice slipped in, smooth as silk. "Aric has told you, Aasa. Mara asked her brothers, Enwir and Anwar, to tell Aric to leave her alone. She doesn't want him anymore."

Aasa's anger flared. "That's nonsense! I don't believe it. Mara's love for Aric is as strong as ever. You know this, brother! Why are you letting her go?"

Aric stood from the throne, his face hardening as he faced his sister. "Mara doesn't love me anymore, Aasa. Enwir and Anwar both told me the same thing - that she begged them to make sure I stayed away from her. They said she's chosen the stone lands over me."

"She would never say that!" Aasa snapped, her voice breaking with the weight of her frustration. "This is a lie, Aric. Mara's heart belongs to you, and you know it. Don't let Rían fill your head with these lies!"

Rían's smile faltered, but only for a moment. "Careful, Aasa," she said softly, her eyes gleaming with amusement. "Aric has made his choice. He's a leader now. He belongs here, in Anros, with his people."

Aasa's eyes burned with fury. "This is her doing, isn't it?" she said, pointing at Rían. "She's trying to blind you, Aric. Don't you see what's happening? She wants you for herself!"

Aric's jaw tightened, and for a brief moment, doubt flickered in his eyes. But Rían stepped forward, resting a hand on his arm, and the moment was gone.

"You don't understand, little sister," Aric said, his voice low and filled with weariness. "I'm needed here. The people of Anros trust me. They rely on me. Fala will be fine without me. I have a duty to stay."

"Fala needs you!" Aasa cried, desperation creeping into her voice. "The war is far from over. Aleth and Beliach are still out there, and we cannot fight them without you."

Aric's gaze darkened. "If Fala falls, someone must be here to take up the mantle. The people of Anros need me, not just as their captain, but as their future king."

Aasa felt as though the wind had been knocked out of her. "King?" she whispered, her voice trembling. "Is that what this is about? You think you should be king?"

Rían's voice was a whisper of venom. "Fala's time will come, Aasa. And when it does, Anros will need a leader - someone the people trust. That someone is Aric."

Aasa shook her head, unable to believe what she was hearing. "This isn't you, Aric. This isn't who you are."

But Aric's face remained stony, his resolve unshaken. "I'm sorry, sister. But I can't go with you. Not this time."

Tears of frustration welled in Aasa's eyes. "You're making a terrible mistake. Mara-"

"Enough!" Aric's voice boomed, the sudden anger in his tone startling Aasa into silence. He looked away, the weight of his decision clear in his eyes. "If you continue with this, I'll have no choice but to lock you up. I won't allow you to disrupt what needs to be done here."

Aasa recoiled as if struck, disbelief and heartbreak mingling in her chest. "You would imprison your own sister for telling you the truth?"

"I would do what I must to protect Anros," he said coldly.

Aasa took a step back, shaking her head. "Then I'll leave. But you're wrong, brother. You're wrong about everything."

With one last look at her brother, Aasa turned and fled from the hall, her heart breaking with every step. She would return to Westhawen and tell Fala everything. The brother she had once known was gone, lost to the darkness that had seeped into his heart.

As she rode away from Suthawen, tears blurred her vision. Aric had been blinded, not by magic or spells, but by ambition and the whispers of a woman who sought power for herself. Aasa's only hope now lay with Fala - and with the distant, flickering chance that Aric would realize the truth before it was too late.

◐

The cold night wrapped the camp in a shroud of silence, broken only by the soft breathing of Aldur and Ardil as they slept beside the crackling fire. Anwar sat alone, his eyes heavy with exhaustion, his body weary from the long journey north. They were close to Nanglorin now, their destination almost in sight, but a sense of unease had settled in his heart. The air felt thick with tension, as though something unseen lingered just beyond the reach of the firelight.

Anwar lay down on the hard ground, pulling his cloak tighter around his shoulders. His thoughts wandered to Mara and the weight of the task she carried. He feared for her - feared what lay ahead, and what would become of them all. Slowly, his eyelids grew heavier, and sleep claimed him.

But it was not the restful sleep he needed.

Anwar found himself standing in a dark and twisted landscape. The air was thick and suffocating, the sky a swirling mass of storm clouds, and the ground beneath his feet cracked and burned as though it had been scorched by some terrible fire. A shadow loomed in the distance, its form familiar and terrifying all at once.

"Aleth?" he called, his voice trembling in the eerie stillness.

The figure moved toward him, but it was not Aleth who emerged from the shadows. It was someone else - someone far more terrifying. Her form shifted, flickering between the woman he had once loved and something far more sinister. Her face was no longer soft and familiar, but twisted and cruel, with eyes that burned like molten fire. Her hair was a cascade of silver flame, and her skin shimmered with a dark, unnatural light.

"Aleth is gone," she said, her voice a seductive whisper that seemed to echo in his mind. "I am Tielir now."

Anwar recoiled, his heart pounding in his chest. He tried to take a step back, but his feet seemed rooted to the ground, as though the very earth had risen to trap him.

"Come to me, Anwar," Tielir purred, her lips curling into a smile that sent a shiver down his spine. "We could be together again. You loved Aleth once, didn't you? You could love me now."

Anwar shook his head, his throat tightening with fear. "No... Aleth is gone. You are not her."

Tielir laughed, a cold and cruel sound that echoed in the dark sky above them. "Aleth may be gone, but I remain. And I am stronger now - stronger than she ever was. We could rule this world together, Anwar. You and I. Just think of it: power beyond your wildest dreams. We could shape this world in our image, mold it as we see fit."

Anwar clenched his fists, fighting against the wave of emotions that surged within him. He had loved Aleth once, with all his heart. But the woman standing before him now was not her. She was something else, something darker, something evil.

"I won't join you. You may wear Aleth's face, but you are not her. You are a monster."

Tielir's eyes flared with anger, but the smile never left her lips. "A monster?" she said softly, her voice dripping with mockery. "You wound me, Anwar. I offer you the world, and this is how you repay me? Think of what we could accomplish together. All the kingdoms of men, Aedan, and creatures beyond would bow before us. We could create a new world, a world of our own design. You need only say the word."

Anwar's heart raced. There had been a time when he would have followed Aleth anywhere, done anything for her. But that time was long gone, and he knew that what stood before him now was a twisted shadow of the woman he had once loved.

"I can't," he whispered, his voice trembling. "Aleth is dead."

Tielir's smile faltered, and her eyes burned with fury. "She's not dead," she hissed, stepping closer. "I live in her place. I am stronger than she ever was. You *will* come to me, Anwar. You *will* bow before me."

Her presence seemed to wrap around him like a vice, her power seeping into his mind, pulling at his thoughts, his desires. Anwar struggled to hold on, but her voice was everywhere - calling to him, whispering promises of power, of love, of everything he had ever wanted.

"Come to me," Tielir said, her voice wrapping around his mind like chains. "We could rule this world together. You know you want it."

Anwar's vision swam, and for a brief, terrifying moment, he felt himself slipping. The part of him that had once loved Aleth, the part of him that had wanted to be with her forever, stirred deep within him. But then he remembered her face - Aleth's true face, kind and gentle, so different from the twisted visage before him now.

With a roar of defiance, Anwar tore himself free from Tielir's grip, his heart racing with fear and anger. "You are not Aleth!" he shouted. "And I will never join you!"

Tielir's face twisted with rage, her eyes burning like embers in the darkness. "Fool," she snarled. "You think you can resist me? I am Tielir, the greatest sorceress this world has ever known. You will kneel before me, whether you wish it or not."

But before she could speak again, the world around Anwar began to fade, her voice growing distant as the dream unraveled.

With a gasp, Anwar awoke, his heart pounding in his chest, sweat dripping from his brow. The fire had burned low, and the sky above was still dark. Aldur and Ardil slept peacefully beside him, unaware of the battle that had just raged within his mind.

Anwar sat up, his breath coming in ragged gasps. Tielir's words still echoed in his mind, her promises of power and control tugging at the edges of his thoughts. But he knew the truth - he had to. Aleth was gone, and whatever dark force now wore her face had to be stopped. He couldn't give in to the temptation she offered, no matter how strong the pull might be.

With a heavy heart, Anwar looked out into the dark night, his mind troubled. The path ahead was treacherous, but he had made his choice. He would fight against the darkness, even if it meant facing the ghost of the woman he had once loved.

6

The night was still and cold, the stars twinkling like distant memories above, casting a pale light on the barren land. In the middle of nowhere, Mara, Adraéth, and Diam too sat beside a small campfire. The warmth of the flames fought against the chill, but it did little to ease the weight on their minds. Their journey north had been long and difficult, and though they rested, their thoughts remained restless, heavy with the dangers that lay ahead.

Mara, her gaze fixed on the flickering fire, finally broke the silence. "Adraéth," she said softly, her voice carrying a trace of hesitation, "there's something I've been meaning to ask you, ever since you called me by that name... Ielyanna. Why did you call me that? And what does it mean?"

Adraéth, who had been sitting quietly across from her, stirred at the question. Her eyes, which had been lost in thought, lifted to meet

Mara's. For a moment, she said nothing, as though weighing her answer carefully. Finally, with a deep sigh, she began to speak.

"Ielyanna," Adraéth said, her voice low and measured, "is a name from a time long before the world as we know it came to be. It is a name bound to ancient history, to the roots of all things - Farham, the world itself, and the seven High Aedan who shaped it with their own hands."

Diam, who had been staring into the fire in silence, glanced up at this, intrigued. Mara leaned forward, her curiosity piqued.

"The seven High Aedan," Adraéth continued, "were the first beings of creation, the architects of our world. They were Vaago, Urehel, Thergil, Argeniel, Mylias, Elfor, and Laeva. Each of them wielded a powerful gemstone, the Alyarel, seven stones that held within them the essence of creation itself. With these stones, they wove the very fabric of Farham - the mountains, the oceans, the sky, and the stars."

Adraéth's gaze flickered to Mara, a glimmer of ancient knowledge in her eyes. "Urehel," she said softly, "was not always the dark force he became. No, he was once one of the brightest among the High Aedan, perhaps the most brilliant of them all. Though he was the one who created the darkness, it was not born out of malice. Darkness, in the beginning, was simply a balance, a necessary counterpart to the light, as night balances day."

Mara's heart tightened as she listened. She had known of Urehel's evil, of his endless thirst for power, but to hear that he had once been something else, something better, felt like the unveiling of a great and terrible secret.

Adraéth's voice softened further, almost reverent. "And Urehel... He once knew love. He fell deeply in love with Aviél, the youngest daughter of Mylias, who was the Lady of Growth and the one who shaped life itself in Farham. Aviél was radiant, a being of pure light and beauty, and she saw in Urehel something few could - a heart capable of love, of tenderness, even if it was shrouded in shadow.

And they had a son," Adraéth continued, her gaze darkening. "A boy they called Beleal. For a time, it seemed that the union between light and darkness had borne something pure, something good. But as Beleal grew, so too did the shadow within him. He began to thirst for power, to crave dominion over all things. He rejected his name, rejected his heritage, and took on a new name - Beliach."

Mara felt a chill crawl up her spine at the mention of the name. Beliach. She had heard it before, whispered in fear and reverence alike. He was the one who had brought unimaginable destruction to the world, the one who had been vanquished long ago, but whose shadow still haunted Farham.

"Beliach's evil was boundless," Adraéth said, her voice now laden with sorrow. "He sought to claim the Alyarel for himself, to bend the very stones of creation to his will. His ambition tore the world apart, sparking the war known as the Caedyr, the Great Slaughter. The remaing High Aedan - Vaago, Thergil, Argeniel, Mylias, Elfor and Laeva - united against Beliach and his growing legions of darkness. Urehel, once a creator, now found himself torn between the love he had for his son and the knowledge that Beliach had to be stopped."

Adraéth paused, the weight of the story heavy on her shoulders. "The Caedyr was a war unlike any the world had ever seen. Mountains crumbled, seas boiled, and entire realms were shattered. The High Aedan, even with all their power, struggled against Beliach. He wielded his own dark stone, a twisted mirror of the Alyarel, and his might was terrifying."

Mara's heart ached as she imagined the devastation of that ancient war, the clash of beings so powerful they could shape the world itself.

"Eventually," Adraéth continued, "Beliach was defeated, though at a great cost. His body was shattered, his soul scattered to the winds. But the wounds of that war have never fully healed, and the echoes of Beliach's power remain. It is said that his remains lie hidden deep beneath the mountains of Tin Nangroth, and that is why Tielir seeks them now - to resurrect the one who even Urehel could not fully destroy."

Mara shivered, gripping the edges of her cloak tightly around her. "But... what does this have to do with me? Why did you call me Ielyanna?"

Adraéth smiled faintly, though her eyes were sad. "Ielyanna was a name once given to a great figure in those ancient days. She was a warrior of the light, a protector of the High Aedan and their legacy. Her name means 'Bearer of Hope.' I called you by that name because I see the same strength in you. You, Mara, are a bearer of hope in these dark times."

Mara's chest tightened, the weight of Adraéth's words settling heavily on her. She did not feel like a bearer of hope. She felt small, overwhelmed by the enormity of what lay before her. The darkness was rising again, and she was being drawn into a battle far greater than she had ever imagined.

But as she looked at Adraéth, and then at Diam, who sat quietly beside her, she felt a flicker of resolve stir within her. The road ahead was fraught with danger, but she was not alone. They were in this together.

"So," Diam spoke up, his voice quiet but steady, "this battle we're heading toward... it's part of the same war, isn't it? The same war that began with Beliach."

Adraéth nodded. "Yes. The Caedyr may have ended long ago, but its shadow remains. And now, it falls to us to stop it from rising again."

"What became of the other High Aedan?" Mara asked, her voice laced with curiosity and a trace of unease. "Elfor, Thergil and Mylias remained in Farham, and Urehel, though all believed him defeated, lingered too. But what of Vaago, Argeniel, and Laeva? Where are they now? And why did Dartur possess Vaago's Alyarel?"

Adraéth looked at her, the flickering firelight casting deep shadows across her face. She sighed, a weariness settling over her as if the weight of ages rested on her shoulders. "You are full of questions," she said quietly. "I had hoped many would be answered by now, but it seems you seek the deeper truths."

She paused, gathering her thoughts, before continuing. "Laeva, the one who wielded the Blue Stone, did not survive the Caedyr. She fell in battle, slain by none other than Beliach himself. It was her death that turned the tide of that dreadful war, for her loss was a grievous wound to the Aedan, and even the earth mourned her passing."

Mara's breath caught in her throat. Laeva, a name spoken in reverence, a figure of unimaginable grace and power, slain by the very evil they now faced again.

"After Beliach was finally imprisoned," Adraéth went on, "bound deep beneath the mountains of Tin Nangroth where the shadows are thickest and the paths are lost to time, the High Aedan Vaago and Argeniel carried Laeva's remains. They returned to the Ahar, the higher beings that had created even the Aedan, the secret architects of this world and beyond. Vaago left his Alyarel behind, knowing it would be needed for the battles still to come. Dartur, in his wisdom, has safe-guarded it ever since."

Mara's heart quickened, a strange tremor running through her as Adraéth turned her gaze upon her, her eyes sharp as stars but filled with a weight of sorrow and certainty.

"But there is more," Adraéth said, her voice growing softer, almost a whisper carried on the night breeze. "You are not merely a bearer of hope, Mara. Ielyanna was not just a name I chose at random. Ielyanna was Laeva herself."

Mara felt the earth beneath her seem to shift, her mind reeling. "What... what do you mean?" she asked, her voice barely audible.

"Laeva's spirit was not lost when she perished in the Caedyr. Her essence, her power, was too great to fade entirely. She is reborn in you, Mara. You are her heir, the living embodiment of her light. This is why you feel the weight of this world so keenly, why the shadows seem to claw at your soul. It is because they fear you. And it is your task, as it was hers, to stand against the darkness."

Mara sat in stunned silence, her heart pounding in her chest, her mind grappling with the enormity of Adraéth's words. Laeva, the High Aedin of legend, whose wisdom and power were said to rival the heavens themselves, had been reborn in her?

Adraéth's voice broke the stillness, calm yet firm. "This is why Beliach must fall by your hand. It is the fate that has been woven for you since the dawn of time. You are bound to this struggle, just as Laeva was, and only by fulfilling this ancient task can the world be free from the shadow."

Mara looked at Adraéth, her eyes wide with fear and disbelief. "But I am not Laeva. I am just Mara. How can I possibly carry such a burden? How can I defeat a creature like Beliach, who has survived even the might of the High Aedan?"

Adraéth leaned forward, her gaze piercing, yet filled with a strange, fierce tenderness. "Laeva's strength dwells within you, whether you know it or not. The same power that once shaped the stars, that held the darkness at bay, is now yours to wield. You will not face this battle alone. But know this, Mara: you are not just fighting for yourself. You are fighting for all of Farham, for the light that must never fade."

Mara stared into the fire, the flames dancing like echoes of the power she could feel stirring within her, a power she had never understood but could no longer deny. And with it came the terrifying knowledge that the fate of the world, of all she loved, now rested on her shoulders.

The night remained still, with only the crackling of the fire breaking the silence. The weight of destiny had settled upon the three travelers, and neither could escape the knowledge that the fate of Farham rested in their hands.

Adraéth broke the silence again, her voice low and serious. "To kill Beliach once and for all, we need all seven Alyarel."

Mara's brow furrowed. She glanced at Diam, then back at Adraéth. "But... We only have three," she said, her voice tight with concern. "The black, the blue and the white. How are we to accomplish this if we are so far from gathering the rest?"

Adraéth looked at her with a calmness that belied the gravity of her words. "You are not alone in this," she replied, her eyes flickering with the knowledge she carried. "The stones of Elfor, Mylias, and Thergil are also making their way to the Tin Nangroth. They will be brought by others who know the stakes as well as we do."

Mara leaned forward, her heart pounding. "But we still lack one," she whispered, her voice almost trembling. "The yellow stone - where is it?"

Diam's expression darkened as he realized the same. "Without all seven, how can we stand against Beliach? If we're missing even one, he will rise again, stronger than before."

Adraéth's face softened, and for a brief moment, a hint of a smile touched her lips. Reaching into the folds of her cloak, she drew out a small pouch. From it, she pulled a brilliant gemstone - a golden stone that shimmered in the firelight, casting soft rays of light that seemed to banish the darkness around them.

"This," Adraéth said, holding up the yellow stone, "is the Alyarel of Argeniel."

Mara's breath caught in her throat, her eyes widening in disbelief. Diam stared at the stone as if it were a vision from legend. The yellow Alyarel, lost for so long, now lay before them, and it felt as if the very air had changed with its presence.

"Argeniel herself gave it to me," Adraéth continued, her voice soft, reverent. "She foresaw the coming of this day, knowing that her Alyarel would be needed again. I have carried it in secret for many years, waiting for the time when it would serve its purpose. That time is now."

Mara stared at the stone, her fear momentarily forgotten. "But why didn't you tell us before?" she asked, her voice small, as if the truth itself might crumble under the weight of her question.

Adraéth sighed and looked into the flames. "The time wasn't right. You needed to grow into this path, to understand the weight of the stones, the enormity of what we are facing. I could not burden you with everything all at once. But now... now we are nearing the end."

The golden light of the Alyarel reflected in Mara's eyes, and she felt a mixture of awe and dread. The stones, the seven Alyarel, the keys to shaping the world - they were almost within their grasp. Yet, she could not shake the feeling that the road ahead would be far more treacherous than any of them could imagine.

"We have all seven now," Diam said, his voice brimming with new-found determination. "Together, we can defeat Beliach."

Adraéth nodded solemnly. "Yes. But gathering the Alyarel is only the beginning. Beliach is no mere foe to be slain with steel. His power runs deep, bound to the very essence of darkness itself. Even with all seven stones, victory is not certain. We must be prepared to sacrifice everything."

Mara shuddered, her thoughts turning to the future. "What if I'm not strong enough?" she asked quietly. "What if I fail?"

Adraéth placed a hand on her shoulder, her eyes kind but firm. "The strength you need is within you, Mara. It has been since the beginning. The spirit of Laeva flows through your veins, and you carry her courage. You will not be alone in this fight, and the Alyarel will guide us."

Diam, still gazing at the yellow stone, nodded slowly. "We must trust in the path laid before us. If we falter now, all will be lost."

Adraéth stood, her eyes scanning the distant horizon as though she could already see the shadow of Beliach rising over the mountains. "Prepare yourselves. The time is coming soon. We will head to the Tin Nangroth, where the final battle will be fought."

And with those words, they all knew that the fate of Farham rested not only in the hands of the Alyarel but also in their strength, their unity, and their will to face the darkness one last time.

24

The journey had been long and grueling, but as dawn broke over the hills, Cottingen came into view. Anwar, leading the way, glanced back at the two Wusel behind him - Aldur, who looked wearied but determined, and young Ardil, whose eyes were heavy with exhaustion. Yet there was a sense of hope in the air, as if the long road behind them was leading them to something more than just a homecoming.

Cottingen was still a ruin in many places. The scars of war and destruction were even visible there. The once-lush fields had been trampled, the trees scorched by fire, and the houses of the small village were mostly heaps of rubble. But amidst the devastation, there was movement - a sign of life, of rebuilding. As they drew closer, they saw figures working on the remains of one particular cottage at the far end of the village. The sight of it made Aldur's heart quicken, for that was his home.

Ardil, too, felt a surge of emotion. Though the house was but a shell of what it had once been, the sight of it stirred memories of his childhood - the laughter, the warmth, and the love that had filled its walls. And now, after all that had happened, they had returned to this place. His heart swelled with both relief and trepidation. Was this truly home anymore?

As they approached the half-rebuilt cottage, a man stepped out from behind the walls, wiping his hands on his dirt-covered tunic. His face, though weathered by time and hardship, lit up the moment he saw Aldur.

"Son!" the man cried, rushing forward. It was Albin, Aldur's father and Ardil's grandfather, who had been laboring tirelessly to rebuild their home. He embraced Aldur tightly, and then, catching sight of Ardil, his eyes filled with tears. "My little boy, you're alive!" His voice broke as he knelt before Ardil, clasping him tightly. "I have been waiting for you both. So long have I prayed for this moment."

Ardil, overwhelmed by the reunion, could only nod, tears glistening in his eyes as he clung to his grandfather. The weight of the long journey, the battles fought, and the dangers they had escaped all seemed to fade in this moment of pure joy. For the first time in what felt like an eternity, the darkness that had gripped his heart loosened its hold.

"You've done well to survive, all of you," Albin said, looking up at Anwar with gratitude. "I returned from Dunhir not long ago. I feared I would never see you again. But I kept faith, and I began to rebuild our home, hoping you would return."

Anwar, feeling the heaviness of the moment, gave a modest nod. "The road was perilous, but we made it. And now, you are together again. That is what matters."

As Albin stepped back, the door to the cottage creaked open, and an elderly figure stepped out, leaning on a wooden staff. His hair was white as snow, and his face bore the deep lines of age and wisdom. But his eyes, sharp and bright, held the same spark of life they always had. It was Anfrid, the great-grandfather of Ardil, who had been thought dead by many in the village after the attack.

When Ardil saw him, his heart leaped with such joy that it felt as though it might burst from his chest. "Great-grandpa!" he cried, running toward him. All the sorrow and fear that had plagued Ardil on his journey melted away in an instant. There was no shadow of Urehel, no fear of Aleth - only the warmth of family and the sense of home.

Anfrid, smiling with a tenderness only age could grant, opened his arms and embraced his great-grandson tightly. "Ah, my boy," he said, his voice soft but steady. "You've come back to me. I knew you would."

Ardil's heart was full, and he felt lighter than he had in many months. It was as if the dark cloud that had followed him all this time had finally lifted. The memories of the battles, the fear of the unknown, all seemed to fall away in the light of his great-grandfather's embrace.

"I thought you were gone," Ardil whispered, burying his face in Anfrid's shoulder. "I thought I had lost you forever."

Anfrid chuckled softly. "I'm too old and stubborn to go just yet, lad. There's still much work to be done."

Ardil pulled back, wiping his eyes with the sleeve of his tunic. He felt a sense of peace he hadn't known for a long time, and for the first time, he could breathe freely. "I'm so glad you're here," he said, his voice still shaking with emotion. "Everything feels right again."

Aldur, standing nearby, watched the reunion with a proud smile. He had been carrying the weight of worry for his son and grandson for so long, but now, seeing them together with Anfrid, the worry fell away. This was what mattered. This was home.

Anwar, though he remained slightly apart, felt a sense of relief wash over him. He had promised to bring Aldur and Ardil home safely, and he had kept that promise. His heart, however, still lingered on the task ahead. He knew this peace, though beautiful, was but a momentary respite. But for now, he allowed himself to share in their joy.

Albin gestured toward the cottage. "Come, let's go inside. It's not much yet, but I've rebuilt the hearth. We can sit and eat together, as a family once again."

They all, including Anwar, entered the half-rebuilt home, and though it was still in ruins, the warmth of the hearth and the love between them made it feel complete. Ardil, sitting beside his great-grand-father, felt the weight of the world lift from his shoulders. The journey had been long and hard, but in this moment, he was at peace.

As they sat together, laughing and sharing stories, Ardil looked around at his family, his heart full of gratitude. The darkness that had taken hold of him was gone, replaced by the light of love and hope. And though he knew there were still battles to fight, for now, he was content.

For now, he was home.

As the hours wore on and the warmth of the hearth crackled softly in the background, Aldur, who had been silent for much of the evening, began to speak. His voice was low and heavy, as though the weight of his memories threatened to crush him under their burden. Yet the words came slowly, each one carrying the sorrow of ages.

"It has been long," Aldur said, his eyes distant, staring into the flick-ering fire as if it held the images of the past. "Too long, since the day we set out from Dunhir. I would not have thought that journey would cost so much." He sighed deeply, his breath trembling with the grief he could no longer conceal. "Much was lost along the way, and we faced not only the wildness of the land, but men - if one can call them such - who seemed more like beasts than anything of the kind."

The room fell silent as Aldur continued, his words now filled with a dark and heavy sorrow. "We ventured through the heartless lands of Cûmer, a place where even the wind feels cruel and the earth is barren of any kindness. It was there, in that forsaken land, that they found us - the Cûmeri, savage as wolves, and twice as cunning. From the moment we entered their domain, they sensed us, tracking our every step, as hunters do their prey."

He paused, as if the memories themselves pained him, and his voice grew quieter. "They followed our trail relentlessly, never letting us rest, until finally, they caught us. Their attack came swift and without warning, like a storm descending upon a fragile ship at sea. We fought, but their numbers were too great, their ferocity unmatched."

Aldur's eyes darkened as he recalled the terrible events that followed. "There was a warrior with us, from Mahlrit. Torhael was his name. Brave and noble he was, a man of great heart and strength. When the battle turned against us, when it became clear that we could not stand against the flood of Cûmeri, Torhael chose to make his stand."

A hush fell over the group as Aldur continued, his voice trembling with the weight of the memory. "He fought like no other, holding back the Cûmeri so that we might flee. But the price was his life. I can still see him, standing amidst the fray, his sword gleaming with the blood of his foes, yet he was overwhelmed by their numbers. We had no choice but to run, though it tore at our hearts to leave him behind."

Aldur's face twisted with pain, and he closed his eyes as if trying to block out the vision that still haunted him. "The last thing I saw as we fled was Torhael's body, limp and broken, thrown mercilessly into the cold, rushing river by the Cûmeri. They stood there, watching, their laughter echoing in the air as his lifeless form drifted away, carried by the current. The river ran red with his blood, and I thought to myself, that such a man deserved a better end."

The fire crackled, filling the silence that followed Aldur's words. Anwar, Ardil, Albin and Anfrid sat still, each lost in their own thoughts. For a moment, it seemed as though the weight of Torhael's sacrifice hung in the air, a silent tribute to a man who had given everything for those he barely knew.

Ardil, whose heart had lightened upon their arrival, now felt the heaviness return, as if the shadows of that day had followed them even here, to this place of warmth and light. He looked at his great-grandfather, whose hands trembled as they rested on his lap, and at his father, who had bowed his head in silent respect for the fallen warrior.

Anwar, too, was deep in thought. He had heard tales of the Cûmeri, wild and ruthless, but hearing it from Aldur, from one who had faced them and seen their cruelty firsthand, gave the stories a new and dreadful weight. He could almost see it - the chaos of the battle, the desperation in their flight, and the river, filled with the blood of the brave.

"It was not in vain," Aldur continued after a long pause, his voice now softer. "Though we lost Torhael that day, his sacrifice saved us all. We were able to escape, to live, because of him. But his death weighs on me still, for he was not just a warrior. He was a man of honor, a man who deserved to live."

Ardil looked up at his father, his voice barely above a whisper. "Do the Cûmeri still roam those lands?"

Aldur nodded grimly. "They are ever there, lurking in the shadows, waiting for those who stray too far into their territory. They are a people without mercy, driven by hatred and bloodlust. But we cannot let that deter us. We must move forward, for Torhael did not die for us to live in fear."

Anwar met Aldur's gaze and spoke quietly but firmly. "We will honor his sacrifice, Aldur. The memory of Torhael shall not be forgotten, nor the price he paid."

The old Wusel nodded, though his eyes remained clouded with grief. "Yes," he murmured. "We will honor him, though it brings little comfort. For now, we must carry on and hope that the journey ahead holds fewer sorrows."

And so, the night deepened, the fire burning low as Aldur's tale lingered in the air. Though the shadows of the past still clung to their hearts, there was a shared resolve among them, a quiet understanding that whatever trials awaited them, they would face them together. Torhael's death was not the end - it was the beginning of something greater, a story yet to be told, written in blood and sacrifice.

6

The air in Westhawen was thick with an unsettling stillness, as though the world itself held its breath. Aasa rode through the gates, her heart heavy, her spirit broken, as she made her way toward the queen's hall. The sun had just begun to set, casting a reddish hue across the sky, a color that seemed to mirror the grief in her heart. She had failed - failed to bring her brother Aric back to Queen Fala's side, failed to break the strange hold Rían had on him.

As Aasa entered the hall, she saw Queen Fala standing by the window, her sharp eyes scanning the horizon as if she could already see the dark lands of Tin Nangroth where their battle would take place. Fala turned when Aasa approached, her face stern but expectant.

"Where is Aric?" Fala asked, her voice cool but with an undertone of concern.

Aasa hesitated, her lips quivering with the weight of her words. "He will not come," she finally said, her voice breaking. "Rían has poisoned his mind. He... he is not himself. He believes Mara no longer loves him, that her brothers spoke the truth - that she wanted him to stay away."

The queen's eyes narrowed in fury. "Rían..." she hissed, the name dripping with venom. "I should have known she would weave her schemes again." Fala clenched her fists, anger surging through her veins.

But before Fala could say another word, a quiet footstep echoed in the shadows of the hall. A figure appeared, emerging slowly into the dim light of the torches. It was a woman, with a hooded cloak pulled over her head, her face hidden in shadow.

Aasa instinctively reached for her sword, but the woman lifted her hand in a gesture of peace, then slowly lowered her hood.

"Nariya!" Fala gasped, her voice tinged with both shock and anger. Aasa's eyes widened in disbelief.

Nariya, the woman everyone believed had run away after the mysterious death of Henric, Fala's father, stood before them. Her face was pale, her eyes weary but filled with sorrow.

"You!" Fala snarled, her rage burning hotter than ever. "You dare to show your face here, after all this time? After what happened to Finian and to my father?"

Aasa stepped forward, her hand still on her sword. "You caused their death! Why shouldn't we end you here and now?"

But Nariya, to their surprise, fell to her knees, her head bowed in submission. "I deserve your wrath," she said softly, her voice trembling. "But there is something you must know - something I have kept hidden for far too long."

Fala's eyes blazed with fury. "Speak, before I lose what little patience I have left."

Nariya's voice wavered, but she spoke nonetheless. "Finian and I... we were in love. Deeply, truly, from the moment we met. But then... then came Rían. She saw in him more than just a prince. She saw her chance for power, for the crown of Anros. Rían knew Finian loved me, but she believed she could turn his heart. And when she failed, when she realized Finian would never love her... she killed him."

The words hung in the air like a death sentence. Fala's breath caught in her throat, her mind racing with memories of her brother's untimely death. "You're lying," Fala whispered, though there was doubt in her voice. "It was you... everyone said it was you."

Nariya shook her head. "No. I loved him. I would never have harmed him. But Rían - she poisoned him. I saw it with my own eyes. I tried to stop her, but it was too late. She made it look like an illness, and I... I was too ashamed, too broken to tell the truth. After she had done the same to your beloved father I fled, and in doing so, I let everyone believe it was my fault."

Aasa's grip tightened on her sword hilt. "Why should we believe you now?"

Tears welled in Nariya's eyes as she met Fala's gaze. "Because I know Rían better than anyone. I know her ambition, her cruelty. She is the one who has poisoned Aric's mind, just as she poisoned Finian. And she will stop at nothing to seize control of Anros. I offer you my aid, Queen Fala, Aasa. Let me help you free Aric from her grasp before it is too late."

Fala's expression was unreadable, torn between the rage she felt toward Nariya and the weight of the truth that had been revealed. She glanced at Aasa, whose face was pale, her eyes wide with disbelief.

Aasa stepped forward, her voice low but urgent. "If what you say is true, then Aric is in greater danger than we thought. We cannot let Rían take him, not like she took Finian or Henric."

Fala's hand clenched around the hilt of her sword, her knuckles white. The weight of her decision pressed on her like a mountain. "You have given me much to consider, Nariya," she said coldly. "But if this is another one of your tricks-"

"It is not," Nariya interrupted, her voice steady now. "I swear it on Finian's memory. Rían will stop at nothing to rule. She will twist Aric's heart until he is no longer the man you know. If you let me help, I can guide you to Suthawen, and together, we can break Rían's spell."

Fala stared hard at Nariya, her heart torn between suspicion and the desire to believe the woman kneeling before her. Time was running short, and every moment wasted meant that Rían's grip on Aric tightened.

With a deep breath, Fala sheathed her sword and turned to Aasa. "We don't have time to waste. You will ride to Suthawen with Nariya and see if her words hold truth. But know this - if you find any sign of treachery, kill her."

Aasa nodded, though uncertainty still lingered in her eyes. "I will not fail you, my queen."

Nariya, still kneeling, bowed her head. "Thank you. I will not betray you."

Fala turned, her voice firm and commanding. "I have an army to lead to Tin Nangroth. The three Alyarel are in our hands, and our path is set. We march at dawn."

As Fala strode from the hall, the flickering firelight casting her shadow long across the floor, Aasa looked down at Nariya. "I still don't trust you," she said softly, "but for Aric's sake, I will give you this chance."

Nariya stood slowly, her eyes dark but resolute. "That is all I ask."

With that, the two women left the hall, ready to face the darkness that awaited them in Suthawen, while Queen Fala prepared her army for the battle that would soon decide the fate of their world.

◐

The cool, misty air of Anros still hung heavy around Mara as she, Adraéth and Diam passed over the border and onto the long, twisting road that led to the Darkwood. For hours, they had ridden in silence, the only sound being the occasional creak of leather or the steady footfalls of their horses over the uneven ground. The further north they ventured, the more Mara could sense it - the dark power growing stronger, pulsing like a heartbeat from the north. It was as if the shadows themselves whispered to her, filling her mind with a sense of dread that gnawed at her resolve.

But she kept her fears buried deep, locked behind a mask of determination. She could not show her fear. Not now. Not when the weight of so much rested on her shoulders.

"We'll be reaching the Darkwood soon," Adraéth murmured from beside her, her eyes scanning the horizon where the towering trees of the forest loomed like dark sentinels. "It is said the wood is cursed by ancient magic, that even the bravest warriors fear to tread there."

Mara tightened her grip on the reins. She had heard the stories too. Darkwood, a place where light barely pierced through the thick canopy, where even the birds refused to sing. But it wasn't the ancient magic that frightened her, for she walked through the woods before. No, it was something far more insidious - a presence, a darkness waiting for her, like a predator stalking its prey. Still, she pressed on.

"We'll be fine," Mara said softly, though the words felt hollow even to her own ears. She glanced at Diam, who rode slightly behind her, his face a mask of focus, the white stone of Vaago hidden safely within his tunic. She could tell he felt the tension too, but her brother was strong. Stronger than she had realized.

Together, they entered the Darkwood.

The shadows closed in around them almost immediately, swallowing the light and casting the world in shades of gray. The air was damp and thick with the scent of moss and earth, and every branch seemed to creak with a voice of its own. Mara's heart pounded in her chest, but she kept her face neutral. She would not let fear consume her now.

As they moved deeper into the forest, a rustling sound caught their attention. Mara's hand flew to the hilt of her sword, and Adraéth muttered a quiet incantation, ready to summon whatever magic might be needed. Diam stopped his horse, his sharp eyes searching the woods for any sign of danger.

Suddenly, figures emerged from the trees, their cloaks blending seamlessly with the shadows, their movements as silent as the wind. Mara's heart skipped a beat as she recognized the sigil on their armor -

the Guardians of the Order. And at the forefront of the group stood Faran, his stern gaze meeting hers.

"Faran," Mara whispered, lowering her sword but not her guard. The tension in the air was palpable.

Faran inclined his head slightly, his expression unreadable. "Princess Mara," he greeted, his voice calm yet firm. "We finally meet again, though I had hoped it would be under less dire circumstances."

Mara dismounted, her mind racing with questions, her heart filled with confusion. As the two groups joined together, she could no longer hold back the torrent of thoughts that plagued her.

"Why did you lie to me, Faran?" Mara asked, stepping forward. "You told me Tharon was seen in Anros, but it was always Thariel. And why did you wear Ealdir's ring, the ring that now sits on Thariel's finger? I want the truth."

Faran's eyes flickered with something unreadable - regret, perhaps, or sorrow. He exhaled slowly, his broad shoulders slumping slightly. "I owe you the truth, Mara," he said softly. "But you must understand, everything I did, I did for my sister."

Mara's brows furrowed in confusion. "Thariel?"

"Yes," Faran replied, his voice steady. "My true name is Tharon. But I prefer to keep the name Faran, for it has become a part of me, bound by the roads I have walked and the battles I have fought. It is the name I chose when I sought no crown, no throne, only the path of a wanderer and guardian. Let it remain so, a reminder of who I truly am beneath all else. And Thariel is my elder sister. The lie I told you was not meant to deceive, but to protect her identity, as well as mine. I was always in her shadow, as it should be. She is the rightful heir, the one meant to unite the lands of men. But in case she failed - if she had fallen to Urehel's darkness - she gave me Ealdir's ring and insisted that I wear it, so that I might take the throne in her place."

Mara stood silent, the weight of his words sinking into her. "But you didn't want the throne," she said slowly, understanding dawning on her.

Faran nodded. "No. I am no ruler. I am a Guardian, and that is where my heart lies. I returned the ring to Thariel because I believe it is she who must lead, not I. My sister is strong, stronger than any of us. She is the queen who can unite these fractured lands. That is her destiny."

They continued walking through the shadowed path of the Dark-wood, the canopy above so thick that only the faintest slivers of light pierced through the gloom. Mara felt the weight of the revelation pressing down on her, but a new question formed in her mind.

"If Thariel was always meant to be queen, why hide it for so long? Why keep this secret?"

Faran's eyes darkened. "Because our enemies are many, and not all would have accepted her claim. We needed to be careful, to protect her from those who would seek to destroy her before she could unite the lands. The ring was a safeguard, a way to keep hope alive, should the worst happen."

As they spoke, the forest seemed to grow quieter, as if the very trees were listening. Mara's mind churned with the weight of his words. She had always felt there was more to Thariel and Faran, a strength that went beyond the mortal realm, but now... now it all made sense.

"I understand," she said softly. "But Thariel has succeeded. She defeated Urehel, and the ring is hers. You were right to return it."

Faran's face softened, a hint of a smile playing on his lips. "Perhaps. But know this, Mara - though I will never wear the crown, I will fight to protect my sister's reign with every breath in my body. And I will fight to protect you, too. For you are as much a part of this as she is."

Mara's heart swelled with a mixture of gratitude and fear. She knew the battle ahead would be unlike any they had ever faced, but with Faran's help, she felt a flicker of hope.

As they ventured deeper into the Darkwood, the shadows lengthening around them, Mara looked at Faran with newfound respect. He was not just a Guardian - he was a brother, a protector, and a keeper of great secrets. And though his heart did not long for the throne, he was every bit as noble as any king.

Together, they would face the coming storm, and together, they would stand against the darkness that sought to consume them all.

6

At the break of dawn, as the first pale light crept across the sky, Queen Fala stood at the edge of the city, her gaze fixed northward toward the distant mountains of Tin Nangroth. The cold wind from the northern heights brushed against her face, carrying with it the scent of snow and stone, and the quiet promise of battle to come. Her army was stirring behind her, knights and warriors gathering their strength, preparing for the long march ahead, but Fala stood apart from them, lost in her thoughts.

In her hands, she held the three Alyarel - the Red from Mylias, the Brown from Elfor and the Green from Thergil. The stones gleamed faintly, their ancient power palpable beneath her fingers. Yet even with these powerful relics in her grasp, Fala felt the weight of loneliness settle over her like a shadow. She had borne the burden of leadership for so long, leading her people through dark days and endless battles, but in this moment, as the dawn slowly rose, she realized how deeply she craved something more than the weight of her crown.

Her mind wandered to Aric and Mara. She had seen the way they looked at each other - the unspoken bond between them that transcended words. It was a love so pure, so fierce, that it withstood the darkness and the countless dangers they faced. They had found in each other what Fala had always longed for - a soul that could walk beside hers, through light and shadow alike. But for her, there had never been anyone. No one had ever filled the hollow place in her heart, and the fear that it might never be filled gnawed at her.

She pressed the Alyarel closer to her chest, as though their warmth could somehow ease the ache of solitude. The Red stone pulsed softly, as if in answer to her thoughts, but it brought no comfort. Fala's heart was heavy with doubt. She was a queen, a leader of warriors, a beacon for her people, but in that silent dawn, she felt nothing more than a woman, alone on a road filled with uncertainty.

"I have my people," she whispered to herself, trying to steady her resolve. "I have my kingdom." But the words rang hollow in the quiet. She had long ago sacrificed any hope of personal happiness for the good of her people. She had believed, once, that she could live without love, that duty alone would be enough to sustain her, but watching Aric and Mara's love had kindled something long buried deep within her heart. She longed for that kind of connection, that deep bond, and yet she feared she would never find it.

As her army began to form ranks behind her, Fala turned and looked upon them - the warriors of Anros, brave and steadfast, ready to follow her into the heart of darkness. She was their queen, and they trusted her to lead them to victory. She would not fail them, not now, not when so much was at stake. But as she took up her reins and prepared to ride north, she could not shake the feeling that, in defeating the threats ahead, she might be sacrificing the last hope of ever finding the love she secretly longed for.

With a deep breath, Fala mounted her horse and looked once more toward the distant mountains. The journey to Tin Nangroth would be perilous, and the enemy they faced - Aleth, now transformed into the sorceress Tielir, and the dark forces of Beliach - were unlike any they had fought before. She knew the coming battle would test her in ways she had never been tested, but more than anything, she feared what it would cost her personally. Was she doomed to lead and never truly live? To rule and never be loved?

Pushing the thoughts aside, Fala raised her hand, signaling for the march to begin. The horses snorted, their breath visible in the cold morning air, and the soldiers set their jaws in grim determination as they prepared for the long road ahead.

The army moved forward, but Fala lingered for a moment, casting one last glance back at the city she was leaving behind. Westhawen shimmered in the dawn light, the place she had called home for so long, but now it felt distant, like a memory. In that moment, Fala realized that she was no longer the queen of a peaceful land - she was a queen of battle, a queen of war, and the path before her would be one of endless strife unless the final victory was won.

As they marched north, her fingers tightened around the Alyarel. The ancient power within them was her only solace now, but as the mountains loomed ever closer, she could not shake the feeling that she was walking into the unknown, not only for her people, but for herself. The dawn grew brighter, but Fala felt the weight of loneliness more keenly with every step. And in the quiet of her own heart, she feared that even if they won this war, she would still lose the one thing she wanted most - a heart to call her own.

⑥

The Darkwood loomed over them, ancient trees with gnarled branches tangled above, casting shadows that seemed alive in the fading light. The air was thick with the scent of damp earth and the rustling of unseen creatures moving through the undergrowth. Mara walked at the head of the group, her hand resting on the hilt of her sword, though her thoughts were far away, pulled toward the future battles she feared awaited her. Adraéth and Diam flanked her, their faces grim, while behind them, the Guardians of the Order marched in silent vigilance, their eyes ever watchful for the dangers that lurked in this darkened forest.

But among them, Faran felt a different kind of weariness. His eyes scanned the trees as they pressed deeper into the heart of the forest, but his mind was elsewhere, lost in a web of thoughts he could not easily escape. Outwardly, he appeared as steady and resolute as any of the Guardians, yet within, his heart was troubled.

Faran had long believed that he had found his purpose among the Guardians of the Order. The camaraderie of the warriors, their shared vows to protect the ancient secrets of the world, and the battles they had fought together had given him a sense of belonging he had once thought unattainable. In those early days, after abandoning any claim to the throne that might have been his, he had found peace in the simplicity of his new life.

Yet something had changed.

It had been subtle at first, an ache he couldn't name, but it had grown with each passing day. And now, as he walked close to Mara, he could no longer deny the hollow feeling that gnawed at him. It wasn't the thrill of battle or the call of duty that stirred his heart, but something far more profound and unsettling - something he saw in Mara's eyes every time she spoke of Aric.

Love.

A deep, undying love burned in her, even when she tried to hide it beneath the weight of her responsibilities. Faran had seen it before, in stolen glances, in the moments when her voice faltered as she spoke of him, in the way her gaze softened when she thought no one was looking.

It was the kind of love he had once yearned for but had convinced himself was beyond his reach. He had told himself that he had no need of such things, that his path was that of a Guardian, bound by duty and honor, but seeing Mara's heart laid bare had rekindled a longing within him that he could no longer ignore.

And so, as they moved through the Darkwood, Faran's heart ached with a pain he could not voice.

He feared that he would be alone forever, that his choice to leave the throne behind had not only set him apart from the world of kings but also from the world of love. He had believed that the Guardians were his true family, that their shared mission was enough, but now he questioned whether it was truly enough to fill the void inside him. Watching Mara suffer for her love, yet be strengthened by it, only deepened the wound.

He stole a glance at her as they walked. She was strong, unyielding, but he saw the weight she carried in her eyes. She had no choice but to march toward the danger that awaited them, and her love for Aric would give her strength to face it. But Faran... What did he have? Duty? A crown he had forsaken? A life of purpose, yes, but one filled with an emptiness he hadn't even known he possessed until now.

As they trudged on through the shadows of the forest, he felt his isolation more keenly than ever. The Guardians around him were brothers-in-arms, bound by sacred oaths, but they could not touch the part of him that longed for connection, for a love that would light the dark places of his heart. He felt adrift, caught between the life of a warrior and the yearning of a man who feared he might never find the one thing that mattered most.

Adraéth, walking just ahead, seemed to sense the shift in his mood. She slowed her pace and fell into step beside him. "You are quiet, Faran," she said, her voice soft in the thick stillness of the woods. "Your thoughts seem heavy."

Faran glanced at her, startled that she had noticed. "I am fine," he replied, though the words felt hollow even as he spoke them.

Adraéth regarded him with her keen eyes, the wisdom of centuries reflected in them. "Fine, perhaps. But you are troubled, are you not?"

He hesitated, his pride warring with the desire to unburden himself. "I've chosen my path, Adraéth. But sometimes, I wonder if it was the right one."

Her gaze did not waver. "Do you speak of the throne? Or something else?"

Faran clenched his jaw. "I speak of love. Of the life I could have had, had I not given it all up."

For a moment, Adraéth said nothing, her gaze distant. Then she spoke, her voice low and thoughtful. "You are not alone in those thoughts, Faran. There are many who feel the weight of their choices, who long for something more, even as they walk the path they were given."

He met her eyes then, searching them for understanding. "Even you?"

A shadow passed over her face. "Even me. We all carry our burdens, Faran. You are not the only one who feels the ache of loneliness."

The admission surprised him. He had always thought of Adraéth as unshakable, as someone beyond the reach of mortal fears and desires. But here she was, revealing a piece of herself he had never seen before.

"Then what do we do?" he asked, his voice tinged with bitterness. "What do we do with this loneliness, this... emptiness?"

Adraéth's lips curved into a sad smile. "We endure. We find strength in the bonds we have, in the duty we serve, and in the hope that one day, love will find us."

"Hope," Faran repeated, the word tasting foreign on his tongue.

"It is all we have sometimes," Adraéth said quietly. "But it is enough."

Faran said nothing more, but as they continued their march through the Darkwood, he found a small measure of solace in her words. Perhaps he was not as alone as he had thought. And perhaps, in time, he would find what he sought - not in a crown or a title, but in the love he had once believed was beyond his grasp.

For now, he would keep the name Faran, as a reminder of the man he had chosen to be. But in his heart, he knew he was still searching for something more. Something that might yet be within reach, if only he dared to believe it.

25

In the heart of the ruined city of Rist, where crumbling stone buildings stood as silent witnesses to a past long forgotten, a group of children played near the old fountain known as the Fountain of the Seven Children. Once a place of joy and laughter, it was now overgrown with weeds and vines, with the faces of the seven stone children adorning the fountain worn down by time and weather.

Among the group was Arwin, the young boy with a mop of dark hair and eyes filled with curiosity. He had grown up amidst the ruins, making the decaying city his playground, despite the lurking dangers. Today, however, something felt different. The air was heavy, and an odd stillness seemed to blanket the city, as if it were holding its breath.

Arwin's friends, oblivious to the strange atmosphere, climbed over the fountain, laughing and playing as they always did. One of them, a boy named Léon, hoisted himself onto the stone ledge of the fountain. He balanced precariously on the edge, his arms spread wide for balance.

"Watch this!" Léon called, his voice echoing off the ruined buildings.

As he swung his legs over and shifted his weight, his foot slipped and hit something - an odd stone on the side of the fountain. There was a soft click, almost too faint to hear, but Arwin heard it. His sharp ears caught the sound as something ancient, something forgotten, stirred beneath the fountain.

The ground beneath them trembled. From within the base of the fountain, a hidden drawer slowly slid open with a creaking groan, revealing something that had been lost to time. The children, startled, stopped playing and gathered around to see what had happened. But while the others stared in confusion, Arwin's eyes widened.

Inside the drawer lay a round silver frame, gleaming despite the dirt and dust that covered it. Seven oval notches, perfectly shaped as if to hold something precious, were carved into the frame, each one aligned with precision. Arwin instinctively knew that this was no ordinary object - it was something far more important, far more powerful.

He knelt beside the fountain, his heart racing, and gingerly picked up the silver frame. It was heavier than it looked, cold to the touch, and as he turned it over in his hands, he felt a strange energy hum within it, as though the very air around it pulsed with life. The seven notches seemed to call to him, begging to be filled, though with what, he could not yet understand.

Before he could inspect it further, a sound broke through the stillness - a sound that sent a chill down his spine.

It was the guttural growl of Celkûn.

They had come, as if sensing the discovery, their twisted and deformed bodies moving with unnatural speed through the ruined streets. Celkûn were foul creatures, more beast than man, their eyes burning with malice, their claws scraping against stone as they charged towards the children.

"Run!" Arwin shouted, his voice cutting through the sudden panic that gripped his friends. The other children didn't need to be told twice. They bolted, their feet pounding against the cobblestones as they fled through the ruined alleyways of Rist. The Celkûn closed in, their savage cries echoing off the broken walls.

But Arwin did not run.

He knew he should have followed the others, but something held him there, a fierce determination burning in his chest. He placed the silver frame carefully back into the hidden drawer and pushed it closed, the ancient mechanism sealing it away once more. He could feel the weight of destiny upon him, as though fate itself had guided him to this moment.

The Celkûn were almost upon him now, their monstrous forms looming ever closer. Arwin's hand instinctively went to his belt, where a small but sharp dagger was sheathed - the dagger that Mara had given to him not long ago. It was a gift, meant for protection, though Arwin had never truly expected to use it. Until now.

He drew the blade, the silver glint of the dagger catching the fading light. His grip was steady, though his heart raced with fear and adrenaline. He had never fought before, but something in him - a spark of bravery, of defiance - would not let him flee. Mara had entrusted him with this weapon, and he would not disgrace her trust.

The first of the Celkûn lunged at him, its yellow eyes gleaming with malice. Arwin sidestepped quickly, the creature's claws missing him by inches. With a swift movement, he slashed at its arm, the dagger cutting deep into its hide. The creature howled in pain, recoiling from the unexpected blow.

But there were more, and they were closing in fast.

Arwin knew he couldn't hold them all off. His small form was dwarfed by the Celkûn, their sheer numbers overwhelming. But still, he stood his ground, his dagger ready, refusing to back down. If this was to be his last stand, then he would face it with courage, just as Mara had taught him.

The Celkûn circled him, snarling and snapping their teeth, their eyes gleaming with hunger. Arwin tightened his grip on the dagger, his breath coming in short, sharp bursts. The weight of the battle pressed down on him, but he did not falter. Not yet.

Somehow, he suddenly felt a surge of strength, his resolve hardening. The Celkûn lunged again, and Arwin met them with a cry of defiance, his blade flashing in the dim light. The battle had only just begun, but in his heart, he knew he would not fight alone.

6

When Aasa and Nariya finally arrived in Suthawen, their horses tired and worn from the long journey, the sun hung already low in the sky. The town, with its crumbling walls and wind-whipped streets, felt eerily quiet, but a sense of urgency gripped both women as they dismounted. They had ridden quickly from Westhawen, hoping to reach Aric before it was too late.

Aasa's heart was heavy with worry. She knew her brother well, knew how strong his loyalty and love had always been for Mara. But now he had been cold, distant - almost as if he was no longer the same man who had fought beside Queen Fala. She feared what they might find.

As they approached the main hall of Suthawen, the doors creaked open, revealing a sight that made Aasa's heart drop. There, standing close together in the center of the room, were Aric and Rían. They were speaking softly, their heads bent toward each other, and there was a warmth between them that Aasa had never seen before. Rían's hand rested lightly on Aric's arm, and his expression was one of tenderness.

Aasa's chest tightened, anger flaring inside her. "Aric!" she called, her voice shaking with emotion.

The man looked up, surprise flashing across his face before it was quickly masked by indifference. "Aasa? Why have you returned?"

"Fala has already left," Aasa said urgently, striding forward with Nariya at her side. "She's heading to Tin Nangroth. She needs you, Aric! If you don't go to her, she will die!"

Aric's gaze flickered, but Rían was quick to interject, her voice soft yet insidious. "She doesn't need him, Aasa. You're being dramatic. Aric is where he belongs - here, with his people."

Aasa could feel the venom in Rían's words, the way she twisted the truth. "You're wrong! Open your eyes! It's Rían! She's poisoning your mind, Aric!"

But he, blinded by whatever spell Rían had cast over him, stepped closer to Aasa, his face twisted in anger. "Don't you dare speak about her that way! You know nothing, Aasa! It was Nariya who killed Finian and King Henric. And now she's brought you here to destroy me, too!"

Nariya, who had been silent until now, stepped forward, her voice shaking with fury and desperation. "It wasn't me, Aric! It was Rían! She poisoned Finian because she wanted the throne. She's been lying to you this entire time!"

Rían's eyes gleamed with cold amusement as she watched the scene unfold, her grip tightening subtly on Aric's arm. "Lies," she hissed. "Nariya has always been jealous, always trying to twist things. Don't listen to her, Aric."

Aric's expression darkened, his hand moving to the dagger at his side. "I've heard enough!" he growled, his anger boiling over. "You'll never speak about Rían like that again!"

Aasa felt her heart pound in her chest as she realized what was about to happen. "Aric, no!" she cried, stepping forward to stop him. But he was too fast. With a snarl, he drew his dagger and lunged toward Aasa.

But Nariya, her instincts sharp and quick, threw herself between them. The blade sank into her side with a sickening thud, and she gasped, collapsing to the ground. Blood pooled quickly around her as Aasa knelt beside her, her face pale with shock.

"Nariya!" Aasa screamed, pressing her hands against the wound to try to stop the bleeding. But Nariya's eyes were glassy, and her breathing was labored.

Aric stood there, the dagger in his hand, his face pale and confused, as if the reality of what he had just done was slowly sinking in.

"Rían has poisoned you," Nariya gasped, her voice weak but filled with a fierce determination. "She killed Finian, and now she's trying to destroy you. You must-" She coughed, blood trickling from her lips. "You must see the truth, Aric... before it's too late."

Rían, still standing beside Aric, feigned horror, her voice dripping with false concern. "Oh, how tragic. Nariya, always so reckless. I told you she was dangerous, Aric."

Aric blinked, his hand shaking as he looked at Nariya's fallen form, then at Rían, who was now wrapping her arms around him, her voice soothing, her touch intoxicating. "You did what you had to, my love."

But Aasa wasn't done fighting. "Aric, listen to me!" she shouted, her voice filled with urgency. "Fala is in danger! If you don't follow her, she will die. You can't stay here, blinded by Rían's lies!"

Aric's eyes flickered with uncertainty, but the grip Rían had on him was too strong. He shook his head, his face hardening once more. "I won't leave. Fala will have to fight without me."

Aasa's heart broke as she realized that Aric was lost, that Rían's magic had twisted his mind so deeply that he no longer saw the truth. With tears in her eyes, she gently cradled Nariya, who was slipping further into unconsciousness.

"Take them to the old prison," Aric ordered coldly, stepping back. "I don't want to see them again."

The guards moved quickly, dragging Aasa and the bleeding Nariya away from the hall and towards the dark, forgotten prison beneath Suthawen. Aasa's heart ached, knowing that Aric was no longer the brother she knew, no longer the man who had once stood beside Fala and Mara.

Ò

Mara rode silently alongside Adraéth, Diam, and Faran with a small group of the guardians of the Order trailing closely behind them. The ancient trees of the Darkwood towered above, their dense canopy filtering the pale northern light. The air was thick with tension, every step of their journey heavy with the knowledge of what lay ahead. The north, the dreaded Tin Nangroth, where darkness gathered, and the ultimate battle was drawing near.

As they pressed on, Mara felt a strange sense of unease creeping over her. Her heart, which had always been brave, now trembled with a nameless fear. She glanced at Adraéth, whose sharp eyes scanned the woods for any danger, and at her brother Diam, who rode beside her with quiet determination. But it was Faran's solemn face, burdened by his own inner conflict, that caused her to turn inward.

Suddenly, a cold shiver ran through her body, and a flicker of light danced before her eyes. At first, she thought it was the play of shadows in the trees, but then the light began to swirl, taking shape before her as a vision unfolded.

She gasped, her breath catching in her throat.

In the vision, she saw Aleth - her once dear friend, now lost to the darkness - standing at the heart of a desolate land. Around her, the sky burned crimson, and the earth was split open, releasing dark tendrils of smoke and fire. Aleth was not alone. Her hands moved in strange patterns, weaving ancient and terrible spells. Before her, a towering figure began to rise from the cracked ground, his form monstrous and terrifying. It was Beliach, the bringer of ruin. His blackened skin glistened like obsidian, and his eyes burned with malevolent power.

Mara could feel the air thicken with evil as the vision showed Aleth's success - Beliach, fully resurrected, unleashing a devastating war upon the world. The skies darkened, and armies of twisted creatures, led by Aleth and Beliach, marched across the lands, razing cities and leaving nothing but death in their wake.

She reached out instinctively, trying to grasp at the vision, to stop it somehow - but it was only the beginning.

The scene shifted violently, and now Mara saw Queen Fala, noble and fierce, standing with her men in the northern plains. They fought valiantly, but their efforts were in vain. Fala's men were outnumbered, and the enemy overwhelmed them. In the chaos, Fala herself was struck down, her blood staining the snow-covered ground. Her men followed soon after, their bodies falling lifelessly around her. The last image Mara saw was Fala's broken form lying amidst the carnage, her hand clutching her sword even in death.

Mara's heart clenched, tears threatening to spill as the vision shifted again.

This time, it was Mahlrit - the once-proud city, now under siege. She saw the towering walls crumbling as dark forces swarmed through its streets, leaving death and destruction in their wake. At the heart of the city, in the throne room, Thariel, the newly crowned queen, and Dartur stood defiantly. They fought with all their strength, their powers unleashed in a desperate attempt to defend the city. But it was not enough. Mara watched in horror as the dark forces overwhelmed them, and in one swift, brutal moment, both Thariel and Dartur were struck down. Their lifeless bodies lay together, the last bastion of hope in Mahlrit destroyed.

"No..." Mara whispered, her voice trembling. "It can't be."

But the vision was relentless.

The final flicker of light twisted before her eyes, and she saw Aric - her beloved Aric. But something was wrong. He was not the man she remembered. He stood beside Aleth and Beliach, his face cold and hard, his once-kind eyes now filled with darkness. His armor gleamed in the flickering firelight, blackened and cruel. Mara's heart shattered as she watched him raise his sword, not in defense of the innocent, but as an instrument of destruction.

Beside him stood a woman, her face hidden beneath a shadowed hood, her hand clasped tightly in Aric's. She whispered something to him, her words dripping with malice, and Aric nodded, a twisted smile on his lips. He was no longer the man she loved - he had become an ally of Beliach and Aleth, consumed by the very darkness they sought to destroy.

Mara's hands shook, her heart aching with sorrow and disbelief. She couldn't accept it, didn't want to believe that this was his fate.

"Aric..." she gasped, her voice barely a whisper, "No..."

As the vision faded, the world around her came rushing back, the trees of the Darkwood closing in on her once more. Her breath was ragged, her chest tight with the weight of what she had seen. She could feel her legs trembling beneath her, and she reached out to steady herself, gripping the reins of her horse with white-knuckled hands.

Adraéth turned sharply toward her, sensing the change. "Mara, what is it? What did you see?"

She shook her head, unable to find her voice for a moment. When she finally spoke, her words were strained. "I saw... Aleth. Beliach. They-" her breath hitched, "They are going to destroy everything. I saw Fala... dead. Thariel and Dartur, slain in Mahlrit. And Aric-"

Her voice broke, and she couldn't continue.

Adraéth's eyes darkened, and she reached out to place a hand on Mara's shoulder. "The future is not yet written," she said softly. "Visions can be warnings... but they are not always absolute."

Mara shook her head, tears brimming in her eyes. "But it felt so real. It felt like it was all happening right now."

Faran, who had been riding ahead, turned back toward them, his expression somber. "The enemy's power grows stronger with each passing day. The darkness you've seen... it is the path we will face if we do not act."

Mara closed her eyes, trying to push away the lingering images of the vision. But the weight of it was too heavy. She couldn't shake the fear that, despite their efforts, they would all fail.

Aric. Her heart ached for him, the man she had once known. She could hardly bear the thought of him standing beside Aleth and Beliach, their ally in this war of destruction. But deep inside, she clung to a flicker of hope - a small, desperate hope that the future could still change.

For the first time, she felt truly afraid that she might not be able to stop it. And the thought of losing everything she loved filled her with dread unlike anything she had ever known.

6

The sky over Rist was stained with the crimson hues of a dying sun, casting long shadows over the once-proud city that now lay in ruin. Fala rode at the head of her warriors, the wind stirring her braided hair as her eyes scanned the devastated landscape before her. The air was thick with the stench of blood and death, a gruesome testament to the savagery that had taken hold of the land. The distant sounds of battle - clashing steel, desperate cries, and the guttural roars of the Celkûn - reached her ears, a chilling reminder of the horrors ahead.

Her heart tightened as she urged her horse forward, her soldiers of Anros quick to follow, their resolve hardening as the cursed city of Rist came into view. Broken walls and crumbling towers rose before them, casting jagged silhouettes against the fading light, and beyond them, the shadows of war danced in a macabre display. In the distance, the towering figures of the Celkûn loomed like dark phantoms, their monstrous forms sweeping through the battlefield with ruthless precision.

Fala did not hesitate. Her sword gleamed in the last light of the sun as she raised it high, the air humming with power and purpose.

"Forward, my brothers!" she cried, her voice carrying over the din of battle, clear and commanding.

Without waiting for a response, she spurred her horse into a gallop, leading her warriors with the fierce determination of a queen who would not falter. Behind her, the sound of hooves pounding the earth rose like a storm, and her men surged forward, their swords drawn and their hearts ablaze with loyalty.

The battle began in earnest as the vile and twisted Celkûn turned their attention toward the approaching riders. The clash was immediate and brutal, steel against steel, flesh against flesh. The warriors of Anros met the Celkûn with courage, but the enemy was fierce, their monstrous strength and savagery driving into the heart of Fala's forces. The air rang with the screams of the fallen, the grunts of exertion, and the sickening sound of blades sinking into flesh.

In the midst of the chaos, Fala's sharp eyes caught sight of something unusual - a lone figure, small and vulnerable, standing amidst the carnage. Her heart skipped a beat as she saw a young boy, no more than twelve summers, clutching a dagger in his small hands. It was a familiar weapon – the hilt of the dagger was unmistakably adorned with the white swan of Dinambad. The boy held it with trembling hands, his face pale, his eyes wide with terror and despair.

Fala's breath caught in her throat as her gaze swept over the scene. Bodies lay strewn around the boy - an older man, a woman, and another elder - all of them lifeless, their bodies torn and bloodied by the merciless onslaught of the Celkûn. Yet the boy stood his ground, his small form shaking as he defended the bodies of what could only be his family. His eyes, wide and glistening with unshed tears, darted between the advancing Celkûn and the fallen loved ones he could not abandon.

For a moment, Fala was frozen, her heart twisting painfully at the sight of such a young soul in the midst of so much devastation. The boy's gaze met hers for a fleeting second, and in his eyes, she saw the rawness of fear, the weight of loss, and a desperate, unyielding determination to protect what little remained of his world.

"By the stars," she whispered, her voice barely audible over the tumult around her.

But there was no time for hesitation.

With a fierce cry, Fala drove her horse toward the boy, cutting through the throngs of Celkûn with a swift, deadly grace. Her blade flashed in the dim light as she struck down one of the monsters that drew too close to the child, its hulking body crumpling beneath the force of her blow. The queen's men followed her lead, pushing deeper into the fray to form a protective line around the boy.

The child stood frozen, his small hands still clutching the dagger as if it were the last hope he had. Fala slid from her horse, her sword raised as she blocked a strike from another advancing Celkûn. Her arm strained as the creature's strength met hers, but she held fast, her muscles burning with the effort. She drove her blade forward, piercing the beast's thick hide and sending it toppling to the ground with a dying howl.

Panting, Fala turned to the boy, her heart breaking as she saw the bloodstained bodies he stood over.

"Child," she called to him gently, though the roar of the battle still surrounded them. "We will protect you. Come with us."

But the boy did not move. His lips quivered as he shook his head, his knuckles white as they gripped the dagger.

"My family," he whispered, his voice barely audible above the chaos. "I have to protect them... I have to..."

Fala's chest tightened, and for a moment, she saw not a boy, but the embodiment of all the loss and suffering this war had wrought. The futility of it all crashed over her, a wave of grief that threatened to drown her in its depths. But she could not falter. Not now. Not while there were lives still to save.

"We will not let them harm you," she promised, her voice steady, though her heart ached. "Your family... they are with the stars now. But you must live, child. Live for them."

The boy's eyes flickered with something - hope, perhaps, or a deep, quiet sorrow that went beyond his years. Slowly, hesitantly, he nodded, though he still clutched the dagger with trembling hands.

Before Fala could reach for him, another wave of Celkûn charged at them, their grotesque forms looming in the growing darkness. The queen raised her sword once more, her soldiers rallying around her, their cries of defiance rising into the night as they fought back against the monstrous horde.

But the boy did not flee.

He raised the dagger, his small hands shaking as he stood his ground beside the fallen bodies of his family. And though his heart pounded with fear, he fought, slashing at the legs of the Celkûn that drew too close, his bravery a spark of light in the overwhelming darkness.

Fala fought with all her might, her heart pounding as she saw the courage in the boy's eyes. She knew then that this battle was not just for the kingdom, but for every innocent soul caught in the maelstrom of war.

As the last of the Celkûn fell to the blood-soaked ground with a final, guttural cry, the battlefield of Rist fell into a haunting silence. The warriors of Anros, battered and bruised but victorious, stood amongst the fallen, their swords slick with the blood of the enemy. The air was thick with the acrid scent of smoke and death, but the cries of the monsters had ceased, and the night seemed to exhale a long-held breath of tension.

Fala stood with her sword still in hand, the silver blade glistening in the dim light of the rising moon. She breathed heavily, her chest heaving as the weight of the battle settled on her shoulders. The ruins of Rist lay in further shambles, their broken walls barely standing. Her eyes, however, were not on the ruin around her, but on the small figure of the child who stood where he had fought, still clutching his dagger.

The boy looked smaller now, as if the weight of what he had endured was too much for him to carry. His face was streaked with blood and dirt, but it was his eyes, wide and filled with sorrow, that tugged at Fala's heart. She sheathed her sword and made her way to him, her steps slow and deliberate, as if approaching a wounded animal. The boy stood motionless, his gaze fixed on the bodies of his family lying lifeless on the ground beside him.

"Child," Fala called softly, kneeling down to be at eye level with him, though her presence was one of quiet strength. "It is over. You fought bravely."

His eyes flickered towards her, but they quickly returned to the still forms of his family. His hand gripped the dagger tightly, as if it were the only thing tethering him to the world around him. Fala reached out and gently touched his shoulder, her voice low and filled with empathy.

"Who are you, young one?" she asked, her gaze soft yet firm. "What is your name?"

The boy hesitated, his small frame trembling slightly before he answered in a voice barely louder than a whisper. "Arwin. My name is Arwin."

Fala nodded, her hand remaining on his shoulder, a steady presence amidst the chaos. "And where did you get that dagger, Arwin?" she asked, her eyes falling to the bloodied blade still clenched in his hand.

Arwin looked down at the dagger, his lip quivering as fresh tears welled in his eyes. "It... it was a gift," he said, his voice breaking slightly. "From Mara. She gave it to me when she left the village. She said it would keep me safe, but... but I never thought I'd have to use it."

The queen's heart tightened at the mention of Mara's name. She knew the princess well, and now the weight of that parting gift seemed even heavier. This boy, so small and so innocent, had been thrust into a nightmare he never should have faced.

"Mara is wise," Fala murmured gently. "She trusted you with that blade for a reason. And you have proven worthy of her trust."

Arwin's grip on the dagger loosened, and for a moment, he looked as though he might collapse under the strain of everything he had witnessed. His voice, when he spoke again, was thick with sorrow.

"They're all gone," he whispered, his eyes returning to the bodies of his family. "My parents... my brother, Astuil... everyone in the village. They're all dead. I'm the only one left."

Fala felt a deep ache in her chest. There was nothing she could say that would ease the boy's pain, nothing that could fill the void left by the loss of his family. But she could not leave him here. He could not be left alone amidst the ruins, haunted by ghosts of the dead.

"You are not alone," she said firmly, her voice a quiet promise. "You cannot stay here, Arwin. This place is no longer safe. I will take you with me."

Arwin's tear-filled eyes looked up at her, searching for any sign of deception or false comfort. But Fala's gaze was unwavering, her resolve as strong as ever. Without waiting for a response, she gently pried the dagger from his trembling hands and slid it into her belt, keeping it close.

"Come," she said, standing and holding out her hand. "You will ride with me. I will protect you."

The boy hesitated only for a moment before he took her hand, his small fingers curling around hers. Fala led him to her horse, lifting him up and placing him carefully in front of her on the saddle. He seemed so fragile, so utterly lost, but she could feel the strength of his spirit, the quiet resilience that had allowed him to survive where others had fallen.

As Fala mounted the horse, she held Arwin securely, her arms a protective shield around him. She looked back at her warriors, their expressions grim but resolute.

"We ride north," she called to them, her voice strong and commanding. "We have lingered here long enough. The enemy waits for us in Tin Nangroth."

The warriors of Anros, battered but unbroken, formed ranks around their queen, their loyalty unwavering. They had lost much, but they still had their strength, their honor, and their queen.

As the army began to move, Fala turned her gaze forward, her thoughts heavy with the burden of leadership. The road ahead was treacherous, and she knew that darker days were still to come. But in her arms, the small boy stirred, and she knew that for him, she had to remain strong.

26

As the sun descended behind the distant mountains, casting the world in hues of crimson and gold, Mara and her companions arrived at the entrance to the ancient mines of Tin Nangroth. The yawning mouth of the mine, dark and forbidding, beckoned them inward. These were the Mijn Dvârg, the fabled tunnels once carved by the hands of the Dwarves, whose very name lingered in the fading annals of history, long after the race itself had perished from the world.

The air inside the tunnels was cold, damp, and filled with a silence so heavy it seemed the earth itself was holding its breath. As they ventured deeper into the labyrinthine passages, Mara found her thoughts drifting, questioning the fate of the Dwarves. What had driven their noble race to extinction? Why had their halls fallen silent, their once-great civilization crumbled to dust?

"Their own greed was their doom," came the voice of Adraéth, who could read Mara's troubled mind with ease. "They dug too deep, too far, ever hungry for more wealth. Without knowing, they carved their own graves. Some were buried beneath the weight of their own mines, suffocated by the depths they had carved, while others - those who delved here - awoke something ancient, something that had been sealed away since the dawn of time. The heart of the mountain held a terror meant never to see the light again, a force so dark it would bring ruin to all. Yet the Dwarves, in their blind avarice, freed it. And that was their end."

Mara's breath hitched at the thought, her heart heavy with the implications of the tale. But Adraéth was not done. "It was not fully awakened until the stone of his father found its way back to him - when Haradan, Huandar's weak-willed son, unknowingly led it here. And had young Ardil not found the Black Alyarel, it would have fallen into Beliach's hands, leaving us with no hope at all."

"Your legend is mistaken, Adraéth," said Faran, his voice low and steady as he stepped closer, the firelight casting long shadows across his face. "The Black Stone was not brought here by Haradan, nor was it by chance that it came to this forsaken place. Urehel himself placed it near the remains of his fallen son, Beliach, with a dark hope festering in his heart - that someday, someone would awaken him. For Urehel, mighty as he once was, could not. The power to do so had long slipped from his grasp."

Faran's gaze flickered with the weight of ancient knowledge as he continued. "After Haradan, in his reckless ambition, stole the Alyarel from Urehel, he wandered the world, consumed by the very power he sought to wield. For years, Urehel hunted him, but when he finally found him, Haradan was but a shadow - his spirit broken, his mind shattered by the weight of the stone's curse. Urehel reclaimed the Black Alyarel, but by then, it was too late. Haradan was no more than a husk, an empty vessel. And so, in a twisted act of desperation, Urehel brought the stone back to Beliach's tomb, placing it beside his son's remains, waiting - waiting for the day when Beliach would rise again and carry forth his dark legacy."

At these words, Mara felt a chill race down her spine. The very air around them seemed to grow colder, the weight of the revelation pressing heavily upon her. Her mind spun with the implications of what Faran had said, her breath catching in her throat.

Her voice, when it came, was a whisper edged with fear. "I pray we are not too late."

Her words hung in the air, fragile and desperate, as the shadows of Tin Nangroth seemed to close in around them.

"Ah, you've always been so fearsome," a voice rasped from the shadows ahead. Rough and cold, it sent a chill through the veins of all who heard it. From the darkness, a figure emerged, her broken body cloaked in shadow. It was Aleth - or rather, what was left of her.

Mara gasped, her heart aching at the sight of her old friend, now a twisted mockery of her former self. "Aleth?" she whispered in horror, struggling to recognize the woman she once knew.

"My name is Tielir now," the creature hissed, a wicked grin twisting her cracked lips. "Aleth is dead. All that remains of her is this decaying shell - fragile and crumbling. But as you can see, even this pitiful form won't contain me for much longer."

With terrifying speed, Tielir lunged at Mara, slamming her to the ground. The others barely had time to react as Tielir loomed over the princess, her shadowed form crackling with dark energy. Her body was like fragile porcelain, riddled with cracks from which a dark, swirling mist seeped out - like a blackened fog, it clung to her, writhing and twisting.

Adraéth, fierce and unyielding, raised her hand and sent a wave of force crashing into Tielir, throwing her back. Diam rushed to his sister's side, kneeling beside her with a look of frantic concern, while Adraéth gave chase, her hands alight with magical power.

But they were not alone. Vecahr, the foul leader of the Blaecwên, surged forward with his four lieutenants, dark lords of their own cruel domains. The battlefield erupted in chaos as the Blaecwên descended upon them. Faran and the guardians moved swiftly, engaging Vecahr and the lieutenants with all the grace and fury of their heritage.

As the battle raged, Tielir struck Adraéth with a vicious blast, sending her crashing into the stone walls. Diam, horrified, leapt between Tielir and the fallen Adraéth just as Tielir raised her hand to deliver the killing blow. Her twisted hand swung down with terrible force, but in that moment, Diam drew a gleaming stone from his pocket and thrust it forward.

A searing light exploded from the white Alyarel, Vaago's Stone, and Tielir recoiled, her tortured scream echoing through the tunnels. Her body shuddered as she was forced back, writhing in agony beneath the stone's blinding radiance.

Adraéth, dazed but alive, gazed up at her young savior.

Meanwhile, Mara stood slowly, her gaze moving over the battlefield as the tide of war surged around her. Every warrior fought with desperate strength, struggling against the overwhelming forces of their enemies.

"Go!" Adraéth shouted, her voice sharp with urgency. "Now! You know what you must do!"

Mara hesitated no longer. With a deep breath, she turned and ran deeper into the mines, the winding tunnels stretching out before her like a maze. She did not know where she was headed, but she knew one thing with terrifying certainty.

Beliach.

The name echoed in her mind as she plunged further into the darkness, driven by the knowledge that he was here, somewhere in these cursed tunnels, waiting. And she, like prey in the jaws of the beast, would find him.

6

In the dimly lit cell, Aasa knelt beside Nariya, her hands working quickly and carefully to tear strips of cloth from her own clothes to bandage Nariya's wound. Blood seeped through the makeshift bandage, and Nariya winced, though she tried to hide her pain behind a stoic expression.

"Stay still," Aasa whispered, her voice filled with concern. "This isn't deep, but it will still hurt. I need to stop the bleeding."

Nariya, pale but determined, managed a faint smile. "I've endured worse," she muttered, though her voice was strained. "But thank you. I wasn't expecting to get out of that alive."

Aasa tied the last knot on the bandage and leaned back, her face weary. "We're not out of it yet," she replied, glancing around the gloomy cell. "But we will be. We must."

As they sat in the flickering torchlight, a voice from across the small prison caught their attention.

"Planning to escape, are we?"

Both women looked up to see a man leaning against the bars of the cell directly across from theirs. His face was shadowed, but his voice was unmistakable - it was Anlac, Aasa's cousin. His arms hung through the bars as he gazed at them, an amused but sympathetic look on his face.

"Anlac!" Aasa breathed, her eyes widening in surprise. "What are you doing here?"

"Same as you, I imagine," Anlac replied with a wry smile. "Locked up for daring to oppose the wrong people. Rían has had her eye on me for a while now. Didn't take much for her to throw me in here after my last 'disagreement' with her."

"Disagreement?" Nariya asked weakly, though her tone was skeptical. "More like a betrayal."

Anlac shrugged. "I told her what I thought of her little games. She didn't appreciate my candor." He paused, then his expression grew serious. "But that's not important. What's important is that we get out of here."

Aasa glanced down the long, narrow corridor that led to the stairs, the only exit out of the dungeons. "And how do you suppose we do that?" she asked.

Anlac grinned, a mischievous glint in his eye. He glanced down at the floor of his cell, where an old, rusted hammer lay discarded in the corner. "I've had time to think about that," he said, leaning down and grabbing the hammer. "The hinges on these doors are weak. I figure if I can knock them loose, we'll have ourselves an exit."

Aasa's heart leapt with hope. "Do you really think it will work?"

Anlac nodded confidently. "We don't have much choice. And besides," he added with a wink, "I've gotten out of worse places than this."

He moved quickly, taking the hammer in hand and striking it against the hinges of his cell door. The sound was dull and muffled, but effective. With a few well-placed blows, the top hinge gave way, and the door sagged slightly on its frame.

Aasa and Nariya watched with bated breath as Anlac continued his work, his muscles straining with effort. The second hinge groaned as it loosened, and with one final strike, the door swung open with a creak.

Anlac stepped out of his cell, a look of triumph on his face. He moved quickly to Aasa and Nariya's door, glancing over his shoulder to make sure no guards were nearby.

"Hold still," he whispered as he set to work on their door. The sound of the hammer against the metal hinges filled the small chamber, but no one came to investigate. After a few tense minutes, the door to their cell gave way, and Aasa and Nariya were free.

"Let's move quickly," Anlac urged, motioning toward the stairs. "We don't know how much time we have before someone notices."

Aasa helped Nariya to her feet, though the older woman winced with every movement. They moved as silently as they could, creeping up the stairs one by one, the darkness pressing around them like a living thing.

As they reached the top of the stairs, the faint light of dawn filtered through a small window, casting long shadows across the cold stone walls. Anlac led the way, his footsteps careful but quick.

The hallway above was empty, but Aasa's heart pounded in her chest. She knew their escape was far from over, but for the first time since their imprisonment, she felt a glimmer of hope.

And with that, the three fugitives moved swiftly through the fortress, their hearts set on freedom and the fight that awaited them beyond the walls of the dungeon.

○

As dawn broke over the desolate landscape, the warriors of Anros marched steadily toward the shadowed entrance of the Tin Nangroth mines. When they reached the entrance to the ancient mines, a darkness seemed to linger around the mouth of the cave, as though the air itself hesitated to enter. Fala halted her horse and turned to face her men. Her gaze was sharp, decisive.

"Half of you will stay behind," she commanded, her voice strong. "Guard the boy. Arwin cannot follow us where we are going. The rest of you, with me."

The warriors of Anros nodded in unison, silent and resolute. Fala dismounted and walked over to Arwin, her armor clinking softly as she knelt beside him.

"You are brave, little one," she said, her voice softer now, though her eyes still held the weight of the battle ahead. "But this fight is not for you. Stay here. These warriors will protect you, no harm will come to you."

Arwin, clutching the dagger Mara had given him, looked up at her with wide, fearful eyes. "But... I want to help," he whispered, though his voice trembled with doubt.

Fala smiled faintly, brushing a lock of hair from his forehead. "You've already done more than enough. Protecting the memory of your family was the bravest thing I have ever seen. Stay here, Arwin. When we return, we will need your strength."

Reluctantly, the boy nodded, his small fingers tightening around the hilt of the dagger. With a final glance at him, Fala rose to her feet and motioned to the rest of her men. Without another word, they followed her into the mines, their footsteps echoing ominously against the cold stone walls.

Inside, the air grew heavy and damp, and the flickering light from their torches illuminated the ancient markings on the walls - runes left by the long-gone Dvârg. The silence was thick, but Fala could sense something - a deep unease that gnawed at the edge of her mind.

It didn't take long before the sound of battle reached them. Clashing steel and cries of pain echoed through the winding tunnels, guiding them deeper into the mines. Fala quickened her pace, her heart pounding as they neared the source of the conflict.

When they rounded a corner, they came upon a scene of chaos and destruction. In the dim light, Fala saw Adraéth locked in fierce combat with Tielir, her once-human form twisted into something monstrous, her body cracked like porcelain, leaking darkness from within. Nearby, Diam held the glowing white Alyarel, its light forcing Tielir back with every strike, but he was tiring. Faran fought beside them, his Guardians of the Order fending off Vecahr and the other Blaecwên, whose savage blows were relentless.

As they arrived, a deep tremor coursed through the very ground beneath their feet, a foreboding shudder that sent a chill through the air. The cave itself seemed to groan and shift, as if waking from some ancient slumber. From the shadows, the low, guttural murmur of Vecahr's incantations echoed ominously, his voice weaving through the stone walls like a creeping mist.

With each word that left his lips, the earth heaved and cracked open. From the darkened fissures, there rose abominations wrought from sand and stone, towering figures whose very forms were sculpted by the malice of Vecahr's dark magic. Their eyes - glowing with a terrible, fiery light - burned with pure malevolence, casting a crimson hue across the cavern.

A deep rumble filled the air as these creatures, forged from the bones of the earth, shuddered to life. Their limbs, jagged and unyielding, moved with terrifying force as they advanced. The ground beneath them trembled with each step, their stone bodies grinding like the turning of ancient millstones. Their gazes locked onto the intruders with a hatred that seemed to consume them entirely, as if their sole purpose was to destroy all that dared defy them.

With a brutal, unrelenting fury, they surged forward, striking with the weight of mountains and the swiftness of a storm. The very air trembled under the force of their attack, as dust and rock filled the air in a chaotic tempest. What had moments ago been an eerie silence, now roared with the clash of battle, as the warriors braced themselves against the onslaught of these primeval horrors.

Without hesitation Fala and her warriors plunged into the fray. The sound of steel on steel filled the air, mingled with the harsh cries of the enemy. Fala's men fought valiantly, pushing back the darkness with every strike.

Fala herself charged toward Vecahr, her eyes blazing with fury. He was larger than any foe she had ever faced, his skin as black as night and his eyes burning with malice. He raised his massive blade to meet her, but she parried the blow with a strength that belied her slender frame.

Their battle was fierce, each strike shaking the very ground beneath them. Vecahr grinned wickedly, his blows heavy and merciless, but Fala was swift, her movements precise. She fought with the desperation of one who knew the stakes, her blade flashing as she deflected his attacks and pressed forward.

Nearby, Diam, still clutching Vaago's white stone, staggered but held his ground. His strength was nearly spent, but the Alyarel's light continued to hold Tielir at bay. Adraéth, bruised and bloodied, was locked in a deadly duel with the sorceress, her magic weaving through the air in dark tendrils.

Then, without warning, a blinding flash of light rent the darkness, striking with such fierce brilliance that the very shadows recoiled in fear. And in that instant, as though consumed by the searing blaze, Tielir vanished - her form swallowed by the radiance, leaving behind not even a whisper of her presence.

The moonlight filtered softly through the narrow window of Aric's chamber, casting long shadows across the stone floor. He lay restless in his bed, the weight of exhaustion pulling at his eyelids, but his dreams were not his own. They were plagued by whispers - faint, but persistent - like a distant voice calling him from a place he couldn't quite reach. Rían's face swam in his vision, and though her presence comforted him, there was a disquieting edge to her smile, a shadow that he couldn't explain.

Suddenly, the creaking of the door stirred the silence. A faint rustle of feet upon the stone. Aric's eyes fluttered open, his body still weary from the night's restless sleep. A silhouette moved in the dim light. He blinked, struggling to make sense of what he saw. But before he could react, strong hands grabbed him, forcing him back into the bed.

"Stay down, Aric!" a voice hissed. It was Anlac, his face set in determination as he pressed the warrior's shoulders into the mattress with all his strength. Aric struggled, confused and half-dazed.

In the faint light of the moon, Aasa and Nariya slipped into the room behind Anlac, their faces tense with worry. Nariya's movements were slow and careful, still weak from the wound Aric himself had inflicted, but her resolve was unshaken. Aasa, her eyes flickering with both hope and fear, glanced at Aric, her brother, lying trapped beneath Anlac's grip.

"He's under her spell," whispered Nariya, clutching her side where the wound still ached. "We have to free him before it's too late."

Aasa stepped closer, her heart breaking to see her brother like this, twisted by magic. "Rían's poisoned his mind. We can't let him leave here like this... he's not the Aric we know."

Aric, though groggy, felt a surge of rage. He thrashed beneath Anlac's grasp, his strength slowly returning. "What... what are you doing here?" he growled, eyes narrowing as he struggled to rise. "Rían was right about all of you... traitors!"

Anlac tightened his grip, muscles straining. "We're trying to help you, cousin. You don't understand. She's not what you think-"

But before Anlac could finish, Aric broke free with a violent shove, sending the man staggering backwards. Aric was on his feet in an instant, moving like a caged animal that had just tasted freedom. His eyes, once clear and proud, were now wild with fury. He saw his sword - resting against the wall, just within reach. He lunged for it, seizing the hilt.

"Aric, no!" Aasa cried, rushing forward, but Aric swung the sword in a warning arc, forcing her back.

Anlac, unarmed except for the old hammer from the cell. He lifted it in defense, his knuckles white as he faced the deadly steel in Aric's hand. The room was filled with tension, the air thick with the threat of violence.

"Brother, please!" Aasa begged, her voice trembling. "This isn't you. You're not yourself!"

But Aric's face twisted in a snarl, his grip tightening on the sword as he raised it high. "You dare stand against me, my own blood?" His voice was sharp, laced with malice, as if the man they had once known had vanished entirely.

"She's controlling you, Aric!" Nariya shouted, wincing as she stepped closer. "Rían has poisoned your heart, twisted your mind. You have to fight it!"

The words barely reached him. His eyes burned with a strange, unnatural light, and he advanced on Anlac, sword gleaming in the faint light. Anlac's hammer looked pitiful in comparison, but he stood his ground.

"I won't let you hurt them," Anlac growled, positioning himself between Aric and the women.

Aric lunged, the sword coming down in a swift arc. Anlac parried with the hammer, but the force of the blow sent him reeling. He barely managed to keep the sword from cleaving into his shoulder. His arm shook under the strain, but he held fast, gritting his teeth as Aric pressed forward.

Aasa's heart pounded in her chest. She had to do something – anything - before her brother did something he would never be able to undo.

In desperation, she grabbed a vase from a small table by the bed. Without thinking, she brought it down hard on Aric's head. The vase shattered on impact, the sharp sound echoing in the small room. Aric's eyes went wide for a brief moment before they fluttered shut. He crumpled to the ground, his sword clattering beside him as he fell into unconsciousness.

The room fell silent, save for the shallow breathing of the three figures who remained standing.

Aasa knelt beside her brother, tears in her eyes, shaking as she looked down at him. "I didn't know what else to do," she whispered, her voice barely above a breath. "I just... I just wanted him to stop."

Nariya, pale but resolute, limped over to where Aasa sat. "You did what you had to. He wasn't himself, Aasa."

Anlac, breathing heavily, dropped the hammer to the floor. His hands shook from the exertion, but he forced a weak smile. "Let's hope... that was enough to break Rían's hold on him."

Aasa looked up, her face filled with worry. "And if it's not?"

Nariya's eyes darkened, and she placed a gentle hand on Aasa's shoulder. "Then we'll find another way. But we have to act quickly. Before Rían realizes what we've done."

They shared a look, each of them knowing that time was running short. Aric lay unconscious at their feet, and though the immediate danger had passed, the shadow of Rían's magic still loomed over them, threatening to drag Aric back into its grip at any moment.

"Let's bind his hands," Anlac said, "just in case."

Ô

As Mara rushed forward, darting wildly through the endless labyrinth of caves, her breath ragged with both fear and urgency, she suddenly found herself before a colossal gate. It stood ajar, already broken as though it had long been forced open by some unspeakable power. Yet above the shattered frame, in ancient runes, there was a clear inscription carved deep into the stone, weathered but legible still.

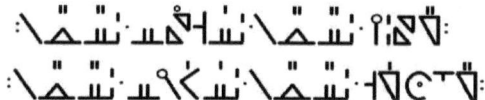

"Seweth tincath, seweth ahnel. Seweth trakath, seweth calquél," the young woman read aloud, translating the ancient words with ease, for they were known to her - fragments of an old verse. It was part of the fabled *Lay of the Seven Stones*, a poem passed down from generation to generation since the dawn of Sedäa itself. Its purpose was to serve as a grim reminder of the doom that Beliach had once unleashed upon the world.

These very words had once been his undoing. They had bound him, banishing him beneath the mountains of Tin Nangroth, sealing him away in the heart of the earth where it was hoped he would never again rise. The runes, etched in warning and defiance, were the last line of defense against an evil that could not be slain. For even then, in the days when the might of the High Aedan had stood against him, they could not kill him. No one could.

No one, save one.

So, it was told in the ancient legends, a whisper on the winds of time, that only a singular being could bring his end.

○

Aric lay unconscious, propped against the wall, his hands tightly bound with coarse rope. He looked peaceful, almost unaware of the battle that had just taken place within him. But Aasa, Nariya, and Anlac were anything but at ease.

They stood close together, tension palpable in the room. Nariya, weakened and pale from the wound she had sustained in their earlier encounter with Aric, leaned heavily against the wall, while Aasa paced the small space. Anlac stood firm, his eyes fixed on Aric, trying to make sense of everything that had transpired.

"We need to figure out how to break the curse," Anlac said, his voice gruff. He glanced down at the man who once commanded armies with unshakable strength but was now bound and defenseless. "Rían's magic... it's dark. There's something about her power we don't understand."

Nariya, clutching her side where her bandaged wound ached, nodded weakly. "She's not an ordinary sorceress. That much is clear. But where is she now? We haven't seen her since-"

Suddenly, the door creaked open behind them, the faintest whisper of movement cutting through the air. Unseen by the trio, Rían slipped into the room, her movements silent, predatory. Her eyes gleamed with malice, and in her hand, she held a dagger - its blade sharp and glistening in the morning light.

Before any of them could react, she lunged forward. The dagger flashed through the air with deadly precision, sinking into Nariya's back.

Nariya gasped, her eyes wide with shock as the pain radiated through her body. She staggered forward, clutching at her chest, the world spinning around her. Aasa cried out, rushing to her side, but Rían was already weaving her dark magic.

"You're all fools," Rían hissed, her voice cold and venomous. She stood tall, her dark hair cascading around her, and for a brief moment, the three saw it - a glint of light reflecting off a necklace she wore. A stone, dark as midnight, pulsed with a terrible power, hanging from the chain around her neck. The black stone seemed alive, its energy thrumming with ancient malice.

Aasa's eyes widened. "That stone... it's-"

"One of the Blaecwên's stones," Anlac finished, his voice trembling with the realization. "Given to them by Urehel."

Rían sneered, raising her hands. From her fingertips, tendrils of dark energy lashed out, striking Aasa and Anlac with brutal force. They staggered back, barely able to defend themselves as the dark magic threatened to overwhelm them. Anlac swung his hammer, trying to disrupt the magic, but the blasts were relentless.

Aasa tried to rise, but the weight of Rían's magic pressed down on her like an iron fist, pinning her to the floor. "You won't win, Rían!" she shouted, defiance in her voice, though she could feel her strength waning. "Aric... he will break free from you."

Rían's laughter echoed in the chamber, cold and mocking. "Aric? He is mine. And you, his sister, are but an obstacle. Soon, you'll all be gone, and he will be by my side, the rightful ruler of Anros."

She stepped forward, her magic swirling around her like a storm. Aasa and Anlac lay on the ground, bruised and bleeding, their bodies too weak to rise.

"You've fought valiantly," Rían said, her voice dripping with false sympathy. "But now, it's over."

She raised her hand to deliver the final blow. Darkness crackled in the air, swirling around her like a vicious wind. Her eyes gleamed with the twisted delight of victory. But before she could strike, a figure moved behind her.

Nariya, with the last of her strength, pushed herself up from the floor. Her breaths were shallow, her vision blurred by pain and exhaustion. But her will was unbroken.

In a swift, desperate motion, she reached for Aric's sword - still lying on the ground where it had fallen. With every ounce of strength she had left, she thrust the blade into Rían's back, burying it deep between her ribs.

Rían's eyes went wide with shock and disbelief. She gasped, her breath catching as the sword pierced her flesh. Dark magic swirled around her wildly, uncontrolled, as her grip on the powers she wielded began to falter. The black stone around her neck flickered, its light dimming.

With a final, desperate scream, Rían crumpled to the ground, the dark magic dissipating into the air like smoke. She lay motionless, her grip on Aric broken at last.

Aasa and Anlac slowly rose to their feet, their bodies aching from the fight. They looked down at Rían's lifeless form, her once-beautiful face twisted in pain and fear.

"We did it," Anlac breathed, relief flooding through him. He turned to Aasa with a faint smile. "It's over. She's dead."

But as they moved toward Nariya, their victory was quickly overshadowed by sorrow. Nariya lay on the ground, her face pale, her breaths shallow and ragged. The wound from Rían's dagger was too deep, too cruel.

Aasa rushed to her side, tears welling in her eyes. "Nariya... no."

Nariya smiled faintly, her voice barely a whisper. "It's alright... it had to be done."

Aasa held her, cradling her head in her lap. "You saved us."

Nariya's eyes fluttered closed, her final breath escaping her lips in a soft sigh. "I hope you can forgive me..."

And then she was gone.

The room fell silent, heavy with the weight of loss. Aasa bowed her head, her tears falling freely. Anlac stood solemnly by her side, his heart heavy with both victory and grief. Rían's curse was broken, but the cost had been great.

ᑯ

The sudden vanishing of Tielir sent a shiver through the gathered company. Adraéth stood frozen in shock, her eyes searching the space where the dark sorceress had disappeared moments before. Around her, the remnants of the battle still smoldered, and the heavy silence that followed seemed more dreadful than the clashing of steel. The ground beneath her feet still quivered as if it, too, recoiled from Tielir's sudden absence.

Adraéth's gaze swept the battlefield until it fell upon Fala. The queen of Anros, weary yet unbowed, stood among her warriors, clutching a bundle close to her chest. Three Alyarel - gifted to her by the Aedan of Faldar - gleamed in the faint light.

Adraéth's heart quickened, her shock giving way to urgency. She stepped forward swiftly, her voice barely above a whisper but filled with desperate conviction. "Fala," she called, her voice cutting through the murmur of tired soldiers. "You hold the remaining stones."

Fala turned, her eyes narrowing as she looked at Adraéth. "The stones will aid us," she said, her tone firm, but Adraéth shook her head, stepping closer, her face grave.

"All seven are needed," Adraéth insisted. "Without the full power of the Alyarel, Beliach cannot be destroyed. His resurrection is upon us, and we are too late. But there is still hope. You must carry all of them."

Fala blinked, the weight of Adraéth's words heavy upon her. She glanced down at the stones in her hands, their soft glow reflecting in her determined eyes. She looked around - at her warriors, still catching their breath after the fierce battle, at Adraéth, who had fought so valiantly alongside her, and then at the distant tunnels where Mara had disappeared into the depths of the mine.

Adraéth reached into her satchel, pulling out the Yellow Stone. Diam stepped forward then, the White Stone of Vaago cradled carefully in his hand. Its brilliance was soft and soothing. He offered it to Fala without a word, his eyes locked on hers with silent determination.

Fala hesitated, her breath catching in her throat. "Why me?" she asked, her voice faltering for the first time. "Why must I carry this burden?"

Adraéth placed a hand on her shoulder, her grip firm but reassuring. "Because you are strong, Fala. Stronger than you know. Mara cannot face what lies ahead alone, and you are bound to this quest. You've carried the weight of your people, led them through war and death. Now you must carry this."

Fala clenched her jaw, the weight of the Alyarel pressing down on her. She looked again to the tunnels, where the shadows grew deeper, knowing that the final battle with Beliach awaited them within. Without another word, she nodded.

Adraéth stepped back, her eyes filled with trust. "You are our hope now, Fala."

With the stones gathered, Fala turned toward the path that led into the heart of the mines, where Mara had disappeared. Her heart pounded, and she could feel the weight of the Alyarel - not just physically but spiritually. They thrummed with ancient power, each one resonating with its own purpose, each a part of a greater whole. Together, they could save the world - or doom it.

Without hesitation, she began to walk toward the darkness, alone, her steps resolute. Behind her, the others watched in silence as she disappeared into the shadows, leaving them behind with only the faint glow of the Alyarel lighting her path.

6

As the sun began to rise, casting its first pale rays through the cracked windows of the room, the air was thick with the remnants of battle and sorrow. Aasa knelt beside Aric, who lay still unconscious on the cold stone floor, his chest rising and falling steadily but unaware of the chaos and the terrible loss that had unfolded around him. She dipped a cup into the small basin of water on the table, her hands trembling slightly from both exhaustion and grief.

With a deep breath, she tipped the cup and poured the cool water over Aric's face.

The shock of the water jolted the man awake. He blinked rapidly, coughing slightly as he wiped his face, his mind slow to register what had happened. His eyes first found Aasa kneeling beside him, and then, as his gaze drifted across the room, they landed on the two bodies lying still on the floor: Rían, the woman he had trusted, and Nariya, the one he had doubted.

His confusion deepened. His head throbbed, and there was a fog in his mind as he tried to piece together the fragments of his shattered memory.

"What... what happened?" Aric's voice was hoarse, thick with confusion.

Aasa exchanged a quick glance with Anlac, who stood silently behind her, his face grim. Then, turning back to her brother, she spoke softly but with a firmness that pierced the silence.

"Rían put a spell over you, Aric." Aasa's voice was slightly trembling but strong. "She clouded your mind, poisoned your thoughts, made you believe lies. She twisted everything until you couldn't see the truth anymore."

Aric's brow furrowed as he struggled to remember, the weight of Aasa's words settling over him like a suffocating blanket. He looked again at Rían's lifeless form and then at Nariya.

"Nariya...?" Aric whispered, his voice breaking as he stared at her still body. "She... she saved me?"

"Not just you, Aric," Anlac interjected, his voice low but clear. "She saved all of us. Twice. When you were ready to kill us in your madness, she took the blow meant for Aasa. She gave her life to protect you and to break the spell that Rían had cast over you."

A hollow pit opened in Aric's chest, guilt and sorrow flooding in as he stared at the woman who had given everything for him. For a long moment, he couldn't speak, couldn't move. The memories of the last few days were a blur, but he could feel the weight of every mistake, every deception, pulling him down into a sea of regret.

Aasa placed a hand on his shoulder, grounding him. "Rían was a traitor," she said quietly. "She manipulated you. But you're free now, thanks to Nariya."

Aric clenched his fists, his heart aching with both shame and anger. How could he have been so blind? So easily swayed by Rían's lies? The fog was gone, and with it, the terrible realization of what had nearly happened.

"I was a fool," he muttered, his voice shaking with the strain of emotion. "I nearly destroyed everything."

"But you didn't," Aasa replied, her voice soft but unwavering.

Aric closed his eyes for a moment, taking a deep, steadying breath. When he opened them again, there was a renewed clarity, a determination that burned through the pain and confusion.

"We ride north," he said, his voice stronger now. "We ride to Fala, to the Tin Nangroth. The war is not over, and I owe it to Nariya to see this through. We will stop Beliach, no matter the cost."

Anlac nodded in agreement, already gathering his things. "We'll gather the men, and we'll ride with you."

Aric pushed himself to his feet, his body still aching from the fight, but his resolve was set. He stepped over to Nariya's still form, kneeling beside her for a brief moment. "I will not forget what you've done, Nariya. Your sacrifice will not be in vain."

With a heavy heart, he turned to Aasa. "I'm sorry. For everything."

Aasa gave a sad smile. "There's no time for apologies now, brother. We need to act before it's too late."

Aric nodded, his eyes flashing with newfound determination. Together with Aasa and Anlac, he made his way to the courtyard, where the rest of his men were already gathering. He wasted no time. In a firm voice that brooked no argument, Aric began giving orders.

"We leave immediately," he commanded, his men straightening at his words. "We are going to aid Queen Fala. The enemy gathers in the shadows, and we will not let them take our lands without a fight."

The warriors of Anros, who had followed Aric into countless battles, stood tall at his words, their loyalty unshaken. They could see the fire in his eyes, the strength in his voice.

Aric looked to Anlac, who stood ready, the old hammer still at his side. "You ride with me."

"Always," Anlac responded with a firm nod.

Aasa looked at her brother, the man who had once been lost to her but who was now free, thanks to Nariya's ultimate sacrifice. She knew there was no turning back.

The sound of steel and leather filled the air as the warriors prepared for what would likely be their greatest and most dangerous battle yet.

As the sun began its slow ascent, casting a warm glow over the horizon, Aric and his army thundered out of Suthawen, heading toward the north, while Aasa remained behind, waiting for her brother and her queen to return.

27

"You are too late," snarled a voice, bone-chilling and filled with malice, so terrifying that Mara froze in her steps, fear gripping her heart.

She glanced around but saw no one. "Where are you? Show yourself, coward!" she called boldly, her voice echoing off the cavern walls. "I know you're here."

"I am everywhere," the horrific voice replied, dripping with menace. "Not just in the flesh, but in the minds of many. I dwell within the hearts of men, wherever death and suffering reign. I am the fear that haunts them, the danger that shadows their steps. But not just in the hearts of frail mortals do I reside. My power brought down the dwarves, crushed them under the weight of their own greed. It was my hate, my hunger, that led them to their doom. And it will be the same for men, and for the Aedan - those who do not flee like pitiful weaklings to their immortal haven beyond the stars. But the children of the Ahar have always been cowards. Now, the time has come for them to reap what they have sown. They will pay for what they did to me. My father was old, weak. His failure was inevitable. But I-" the voice seethed with rage, "I will complete what he began."

"You are wrong," Mara countered, trying to deceive him. "Your father did not fail. In the end, he gave up because he realized he was wrong all along."

"Lies!" The man screamed, stepping out from the shadows. He stood some distance from her, glaring with a hatred that burned as fiercely as the fire in his eyes.

Mara's breath caught in her throat as she beheld her foe. Beliach was far more terrifying than she had imagined. His skin was blackened, cracked and brittle, as though he had been scorched alive. His eyes burned with flames, but his pupils were like shards of ice. His entire being was wreathed in fire and frost, swirling around him in a deadly dance of elemental fury.

"I speak the truth," Mara continued, her voice steady despite the terror she felt. "Urehel abandoned his cause and was forgiven. He now rests beside your mother, where he always longed to be."

At the mention of his mother, Beliach let out a tortured scream, filled with unspeakable agony. "Silence!" he shrieked.

But Mara pressed on. "She took her own life because of you. She knew what you would become."

"Yes!" Beliach bellowed, his voice a thunderclap of hatred. "Because you showed her!" He howled with fury, raising his hand high. In a flash, a sword of blazing fire formed in his grip, its flames licking hungrily at the air. He swung the weapon down toward Mara with deadly intent.

She dodged swiftly to the side, drawing the Swan Sword of her family from its sheath.

A fierce and merciless battle ensued between them, a clash of fire and ice, of power and grace. Though Beliach was stronger, far more powerful, Mara fought with speed and precision, matching his brutal might with her nimble strategy and unyielding will.

Their blades clashed with a sound like thunder, and the cavern around them trembled with the force of their struggle.

6

The remaining soldiers of Anros stood in a tense silence outside the entrance to the ancient mines of Tin Nangroth. Shadows from the setting sun stretched long across the rocky terrain, casting an eerie stillness over the waiting company. The faint sounds of battle echoed from deep within the mine, but here on the surface, all seemed deathly quiet. Arwin sat by the edge of a crumbled pillar, gripping the strange silver frame he had found back in Rist. The soldiers exchanged uneasy glances, their hands resting on the hilts of their swords, unsure of what might happen next.

Without warning, the ground beneath them began to tremble. The soldiers exchanged alarmed looks as the earth quivered, then groaned, and then violently shook. Stones and dust fell from the mouth of the mine, and the once-solid ground cracked open like an old scar, revealing an ancient and terrible truth long buried.

A low, dreadful moan rose from the depths. It was a sound of agony, of souls long forgotten, a cry that pierced the hearts of the living. The soldiers looked down in horror as from the fissures and cracks in the earth, skeletal hands reached upwards, pulling decayed bodies wrapped in tattered remnants of armor from the very ground they stood on. The darkness that surrounded the corpses was not mere shadow; it was a thick, consuming force, alive with malice.

One of the soldiers gasped, stepping back. "What... what is this?"

"The ground," murmured another, his voice trembling, "it's a grave... a grave for the dwarves. All the fallen who were lost in the depths of these mines."

Dozens, then hundreds, of dwarven corpses rose from the earth, their faces twisted in eternal torment. Their hollow eyes, flickering with terror and hate, locked onto the living soldiers. In silence, they charged.

The soldiers of Anros braced themselves, but nothing could have prepared them for what came next. The dead dwarves, once mighty miners and warriors, now moved with unnatural speed, their skeletal hands clutching rusted weapons that still gleamed with a sinister glow.

Arwin leapt to his feet, terror gripping him, yet his grip tightened on Mara's dagger. The soldiers of Anros, though brave, were momentarily paralyzed by the sheer horror of what they faced.

"For Anros! For Queen Fala!" cried one of the captains, snapping the men out of their fear.

The soldiers raised their swords and charged into the horde of undead. Steel clashed against bone and rusted metal, but the dead did not falter. The soldiers fought valiantly, but each fallen enemy was quickly replaced by another, as more and more dwarven corpses emerged from the earth, as if the very ground itself sought to drown the living in death.

The battle was chaos. Sword strokes that would have felled any living foe barely slowed the undead. Severed limbs and shattered bones seemed to mean nothing to them. The dead dwarves kept fighting, their eyes burning with the torment of their forgotten past.

One of the soldiers was dragged down by a skeletal dwarf, its bony fingers wrapped around the soldier's throat. His cries for help were lost in the din of battle as the life was choked from him. Another one, fending off two dead dwarves at once, was struck from behind by a rusted axe. He fell to the ground, his lifeblood pooling beneath him as the dwarven dead marched over him without a glance.

Arwin, standing at the edge of the battlefield, watched in horror as the soldiers were slowly overwhelmed.

Suddenly, a strange tremor stirred beneath his coat, faint at first, but growing with an insistent pulse, like a distant drumbeat. Arwin's hand instinctively reached for the source, and his fingers brushed against the cold, metallic edge of something he had nearly forgotten - the silver frame he had discovered within the depths of the well in Rist. He had taken it unnoticed in the chaos, its significance lost to him in the harrowing hours that followed, but now it seemed alive, vibrating with a power he had not sensed before, as if awakening to the gathering darkness around him.

He gripped the silver frame tighter, feeling a strange pull from the object. His mind raced. *This... this thing... it's connected to all of this, isn't it?* He remembered the eerie voice that had whispered to him when he first held it.

"Arwin!" a soldier called out to him, snapping him from his thoughts. "Run, boy! Get away from here!"

But Arwin couldn't move. He felt rooted to the spot, as if something deeper was compelling him to stay. And in that moment, he realized the truth: the silver frame held some connection to the dead dwarves, perhaps even to the darkness that surrounded them.

Suddenly, one of the skeletal dwarves lunged toward him. Arwin raised the dagger instinctively, his heart pounding in his chest. The undead creature's cold fingers reached for him.

Arwin, still clutching the silver frame, felt a surge of energy pulse through him. His body tingled with an ancient power, and for a fleeting moment, the undead seemed to hesitate, their hollow eyes flickering as if they recognized something in him.

The soldiers of Anros rallied, forming a protective circle around the boy, but the dead dwarves pressed on relentlessly. Arwin's mind raced, struggling to make sense of the power he felt from the frame. What is this? What does it mean?

In the distance, over the noise of battle, a horn sounded - faint but unmistakable. Reinforcements were coming.

But would they be enough?

Ò

"'Enough!" Beliach bellowed, his voice a storm of fury as he thrust the young woman from him with such force that she was hurled back, crashing against the jagged, unforgiving stone floor. He watched with twisted satisfaction as she groaned, struggling to her feet. "Must we truly fight for all eternity?" he sneered, a wicked grin spreading across his darkened face. "You and I - we are not so different. Both of us destined for greatness, yet trapped in these frail, mortal shells. But our souls, ah, our souls are boundless, more powerful than even death itself. We shall not fade, not even at the end of all worlds. Would it not be foolish for us to continue this endless war? Together, you and I, we would be unstoppable. The world of Sedäa - and more - would be ours for the taking. Think on it. We could reign as one... Laeva."

"Spare me your words," Mara replied coldly, her voice steady despite the pain. "Only a prisoner would offer such a bargain. But I am no fool to be swayed by you. You are a traitor, as you were before, and you always shall be. Perhaps I lost the last time we stood against each other, but today, it is not only Laeva who faces you."

Beliach's eyes darkened with contempt. "Who you are matters little to me. Mortal, Aedan or some lost spirit - it is all the same. No matter who or what you claim to be, you remain a human, and humans have always been weak, easily bent to the will of power."

"Just as you were," Mara retorted, her gaze unwavering. "Strip away all your dark sorceries, and what are you? A mere human, no greater than I or anyone else."

Beliach's laughter was a deep, sinister echo in the cavern. "We shall see about that." With a swift movement, the sword of flame in his hand transformed into a searing, burning whip, ablaze with terrifying light. He lashed out with it.

The first strike Mara barely dodged, but the second blow hit her with brutal force, sending her crashing once more into the rocky wall. The impact was so violent that for a moment, she feared she might lose consciousness, as the world around her dimmed into a haze. Her grip on her sword faltered, and with it, the two Alyarel fell from her grasp.

An eerie silence fell over the chamber. The blue and black stones rolled from Mara's hand and came to rest before her, glinting on the cold stone floor.

Beliach's eyes widened in raw greed and triumph, gleaming with malice. "I must admit," he said, drawing nearer with slow, deliberate steps, his gaze locked on the stones, "I had expected more from you. But haven't we all? Everyone whispered of your greatness, of how you alone would defeat me." His voice dripped with mockery. "And now look at you – broken and already as good as dead. You've forgotten one simple truth: to destroy me, all seven Alyarel are required. But to crush you - to extinguish your pathetic light forever - I need only one."

His gaze fell hungrily upon the black stone, lying within his reach. With a greedy hand, he reached for it, the air thick with the anticipation of finality."

6

The Blaecwên, with all their dreadful might, led by the fearsome Vecahr, drove Adráeth, Diam, Faran, the few remaining warriors of Anros and the guardians of the Order back with an unrelenting force. The onslaught was so fierce that they were pushed out of the mines, stumbling through the dark corridors until they found themselves outside at the entrance. But what awaited them there was a sight of unspeakable horror.

Hundreds - no, thousands - of skeletal warriors, their decayed forms still clad in rusted armor, their beards long and matted with dust and rot, surged upon the rest of Queen Fala's soldiers from all sides. These were no mere remnants of the fallen, but the cursed dead, bound by dark sorcery to serve Vecahr's will. Their empty eye sockets gleamed with an unnatural light, driven by the malice of centuries untold.

The clash of steel and the cries of battle filled the air, when suddenly, from the distant hills, the faint sound of a horn was heard again - a signal of hope. But even as it stirred their hearts, bringing the faintest flicker of salvation, the ground seemed to tremble with the approach of something far more sinister. The horn call drew nearer, swift and urgent, but the shadows of fate cast another stone upon the path of the weary defenders.

Amidst the chaos, like a storm of darkness given form, Tielir appeared in the very heart of the battlefield. Her presence was a force of death itself. With merciless precision, she cut down anything that dared stand before her. Warriors who had held their ground for hours now fell like leaves before a winter gale, their cries silenced by the cold, unyielding blade of the sorceress.

Adráeth, seeing the devastation she wrought, knew there was no choice but to face her. Stepping forward with grim determination, she raised her hands, her eyes locking with those of her former ally, now corrupted beyond recognition. A terrible silence fell for a moment, the battlefield itself seeming to hold its breath as the two figures, avatars of opposing powers, stood face to face.

And then, like a storm breaking upon a mountain, the two clashed. Magic and steel collided in a maelstrom of fire and shadow. Sparks flew as their blades met, the ground beneath them cracking and groaning under the weight of their battle. Tielir, her face twisted with fury and madness, struck with a force that would have shattered any mortal foe. But Adráeth, though weary, stood firm.

The battle between them was fierce and unyielding. Lightning arced through the sky as Tielir summoned dark powers, and Adráeth, calling upon the light of the Aedan, met her blow for blow. The air around them crackled with the energy of their struggle, each strike a clash of worlds - life against death, light against darkness.

But even as they fought, the war raged on all around them. The soldiers of Anros, harried on all sides by the skeletal horde, struggled to hold their lines. Fala's banner still flew, but her men were faltering under the relentless assault.

And all the while, the horn grew louder, the herald of something unknown, something that could turn the tide... or seal their doom.

On the distant horizon, figures emerged - many of them, their shapes dark against the fading light. The thunderous sound of hooves rumbled through the air, shaking the very earth beneath them like the coming of a storm. At the forefront, riding with an iron gaze and a spear gleaming in the twilight, was Aric. Close behind him, steadfast and un-yielding, rode Anlac. Like a surging tidal wave, Aric's army crashed into the heart of the battle, sweeping through the ranks of the enemy and cutting them down in their multitudes.

6

Beliach bent low, reaching for the stones at his feet. "In the end," he sneered at Mara, "you've disappointed everyone."

But before his fingers could touch even a single Alyarel, a mighty sword stroke sent him stumbling backward.

Queen Fala, her blade gleaming in one hand and the remaining Al-yarel clutched in the other, stood defiantly between Beliach and Mara.

"What?" he snarled in disbelief, his dark eyes narrowing as he re-gained his composure.

As Fala prepared herself for battle, Mara slowly rose, clutching the blue and black stones close to her chest, her heart pounding with fear and fury.

"Your end is near," Fala cried with a voice full of wrath, her eyes blazing like the fire of a thousand battles fought and lost.

Beliach laughed, the sound of it cold and venomous. "Two mere mortals?" he spat with disdain, his lips curling into a sinister grin. "And to make it even more absurd - two women? How pathetic! You can never defeat me." His voice thundered with cruel mockery as he hurled him-self at them with merciless power.

The battle began anew, with a fury unlike any the two had faced be-fore. Fala and Mara fought with every ounce of strength they possessed, wielding their swords with desperate grace and channeling the ancient power of the seven stones. But despite their valor, Beliach's strength was overwhelming.

Time and time again, he threw them to the ground, his dark, cor-rupted form seeming invincible. Whenever he sought to crush one of them beneath his might, the other would rise, deflecting his blows and drawing his wrath away. It was a relentless cycle of struggle - two mortal women pitted against an ancient force of darkness that had endured for eons.

Then, for a fleeting moment, Beliach stilled, as if he had sensed some distant tremor in the fabric of fate - something had shifted, a ripple in the threads of time. A dark and sinister laughter echoed from his lips, mockery burning in his fiery eyes. He turned his gaze upon Mara, his malevolent intent clear: to crush the last fragile tendrils of hope clinging to her heart.

"Do you feel it?" he hissed, his voice dripping with malice. "The pain festering within you, growing like a shadow in your soul."

"Enough of this madness!" Mara's voice was steady, though her heart trembled.

But Beliach only grinned wider, his eyes gleaming with cruel amusement. "Ah, how delightful," he mused, circling her like a predator. "I always thought one would feel it... deep inside, in the marrow of their bones, when their own flesh and blood perishes."

Mara frowned, confusion and dread creeping over her. "What are you talking about?"

"Your beloved brother. Anwar, was it not?" Beliach's voice slithered, relishing every word. "I can still taste his torment... the agony that gnawed at him, breaking him from within."

"Stop!" Mara shouted, her voice trembling with disbelief, unwilling to accept his words. "Lies!"

But Beliach's laughter grew louder, darker, filling the cavern like a storm of shadows. Raising his right hand, he summoned forth a vision - not an illusion, but a window into a distant reality, vivid and real. The air crackled with dark energy, and before them, an image formed.

There, atop a cliff in the desolate heights of Nanglorin, stood Anwar, alone. His once proud stance now broken, his eyes hollow and lost, brimming with tears. The sky above him wept with storm clouds, as though the very heavens mourned his sorrow. With a final, despairing gaze to the sky, he stepped forward. His body plummeted, vanishing into the abyss below, swallowed by the cruel earth.

"No!" Mara's scream tore through the air, her knees giving way beneath her as she collapsed to the ground, hands trembling as if trying to grasp something that had already slipped away. Her soul cried out in vain, but the image was unrelenting in its truth.

"Do you feel it now?" Beliach whispered, his smile twisted in grim satisfaction. "Does it wound you, deep within? I hope it does... for now you know what I feel. Every single moment. The unending pain. The bitter torment."

"It's not true... It can't be," Mara murmured, her heart refusing to accept what her eyes had just witnessed.

"Oh, do not deceive yourself, child," Beliach sneered, his voice sharp as a blade. "You know what I showed you has happened. And you know why." His laughter rang through the cavern like a death knell. "Love!"

Fala stepped forward, her voice thick with desperation. "Stop this madness!"

Beliach's gaze shifted toward her, cold and mocking. "Why should I?" he asked, his voice a venomous whisper. "Because you don't understand what love is? You yearn for it, don't you? With all your soul. But it is a fruit you will never taste. Not in this life. Not in the next. And you should be grateful, for love is the greatest weakness of all."

Fala's fists clenched, her knuckles white against the sword's hilt. But Beliach only smirked, his voice dripping with cruel wisdom. "Love has slain more than hatred ever could. It blinds, it weakens, it binds mortals in chains they cannot see. You, Fala, should count yourself fortunate that love has eluded you. It is a curse far more destructive than any sword."

Mara, her body shaking, gazed up at Beliach with tear-filled eyes, the weight of his words settling on her like a crushing stone. Her heart ached with the loss of her brother, with the cruelty of truth, and with the bitter sting of love, a force that had brought her so much joy, now twisted into her greatest torment.

But in the depths of her despair, a spark remained. Beliach's taunts, though sharp, had not extinguished the fire within her.

And yet again, Beliach's blows rained down upon them like the hammering of a relentless storm. Sparks flew from Fala's blade as she parried his every strike, her muscles aching, her breath labored. Mara fought beside her with all her strength, but despite the combined might of the seven stones, the weight of Beliach's malice was too great.

For nearly two hours they battled, their strength slowly waning. With each minute that passed, the hope that had once burned brightly within them began to flicker, dimming in the face of such overwhelming power.

As Beliach's laughter echoed through the cavernous halls, Mara felt despair creeping into her heart. They had come so far, but now, as the weight of their struggle pressed down on her, she realized with a growing sense of dread that something was missing - some vital piece of the puzzle needed to defeat this ancient evil.

She glanced at Fala, who fought valiantly beside her, both their faces etched with exhaustion and pain. Neither of them knew what it was that they lacked. They had the seven stones, the ancient relics of a forgotten age, and yet they could not overpower him.

Beliach stood tall and unyielding, the embodiment of hatred, of greed, of everything dark in the world. He seemed untouchable, a force too vast to be undone by mere mortal hands. And as the battle raged on, Mara's heart sank, for she knew they could not win like this.

Yet still, they fought.

$$\mathfrak{O}$$

It happened in the briefest of moments - Tielir, distracted and unaware, allowed Diam to seize from her grasp the black stone she had stolen from Vecahr. In that instant, the tide of battle shifted.

With blinding speed, the advantage passed to Adraéth, who, without hesitation, cast her foe down. And with a single, decisive thrust, she drove her sword through Tielir's body.

A deep rumble echoed through the vast halls beneath the mountain, like the ominous tremor of a coming storm.

Faran, locked in a fierce struggle with Vecahr, saw his chance. Mustering the last of his strength, he struck down the black sorcerer, severing Vecahr's head from his body. And thus, Vecahr, the dread master of dark magic, was no more.

Tielir collapsed to the ground, her once-malevolent form now broken and fading. The shadow in her eyes lifted, and what remained was Aleth - no longer the sorceress Tielir, but the woman she once had been, crumpled before them, her life ebbing away.

Adraéth knelt beside her fallen friend, her heart heavy with guilt as she gazed upon Aleth's dying form.

"Forgive me," Aleth whispered, her voice weak and fractured, as though the weight of the world pressed upon her. "What have I done?"

"You are not to blame," Adraéth replied softly, her tone laced with sorrow. "It was Tielir who used you, not you who acted of your own will."

"I wasn't strong enough," Aleth coughed, her breath ragged. "I failed... just as Lady Mylias foretold."

"No, Aleth." Adraéth's voice was thick with emotion, tears threatening to fall. "You were a pawn in her cruel game. There was nothing you could have done. Anyone else would have succumbed to Tielir's power. But now, you are free. Free from her, and free from the pain."

A faint smile touched Aleth's lips, yet her eyes soon darkened with fear and grief. "Anwar," she whispered, her voice barely audible. "He... he is gone."

Diam dropped to his knees beside her, his face a mask of disbelief. "What do you mean? Where is my brother?"

Aleth's strength was waning fast. "I can no longer sense him. His spirit has left this world."

"No!" Diam cried out, his voice choked with anguish. "That cannot be!"

"I am sorry," Aleth murmured, her voice trailing off. "It is..."

But her words were silenced as her final breath left her, and her spirit passed into the twilight. Aleth Deoricar had finally perished.

Ó

Arwin, burdened by more pain than his tender years should ever know, stood frozen in the cold, desolate darkness of the mines. Fear clutched at his heart, its icy fingers tightening with every breath he took. The past few hours, the past few days - everything had crumbled around him like the ruins of a forgotten age. His small body trembled, and his legs, once so eager to run through sunlit meadows, gave way beneath him. He collapsed onto the hard stone floor, his fragile form curling in upon itself like a leaf in the wind.

Tears streamed down his dirt-streaked cheeks, mingling with the dust of the ancient earth. He cried, not the gentle tears of a child who has scraped his knee, but the deep, heart-wrenching sobs of one who has lost everything—his family, his home, and the fragile sense of safety that had once cradled his innocent soul.

Before him lay two objects: the strange silver frame he had found in the well at Rist, and Mara's dagger. They glinted faintly in the dim light, cold and lifeless, surrounded by the same all-encompassing darkness that now threatened to devour the last remnants of his hope. The young boy stared at them, his vision blurred by tears, as if they were relics of a world that had slipped beyond his grasp.

In the distance, far deeper within the heart of the mountain, the sound of a fierce battle echoed. The clash of steel, the thunder of spells, and the inhuman roars of a godlike devil rang out - a war waged between forces far beyond his comprehension. Somewhere, two mere mortals - women of unbreakable will - fought against a power that should never have been awakened. But Arwin, huddled in the shadowed silence, felt so far removed from that world.

He was just a boy.

He didn't know what to do. He didn't know where to go. Every direction felt as hopeless as the next, each path swallowed by the oppressive weight of the earth above him. The mines, once merely dark, now seemed like the belly of some ancient beast, waiting to consume him whole.

Kneeling there, lost and utterly alone, Arwin's spirit shattered. The last fragile piece of hope, that faint flicker he had clung to in the darkest moments, broke within him like fragile glass. The light that once illuminated his dreams, the love that had once warmed his heart, flickered and died. There was no one left to save him. No mother's embrace, no father's hand to guide him through the night. The boy's sobs grew quieter, the weight of grief and terror pressing down upon him until his small chest could hardly bear it.

And in that crushing silence, as the boy wept for all the loved ones he had lost, for the home that would never again be his, the darkness around him seemed to grow deeper. There, in the depths of the mine, Arwin's soul teetered on the edge of oblivion.

His trembling hands reached out for the two artifacts lying before him, as though by their touch, they might offer him some guidance, some faint whisper of direction in the oppressive void that surrounded him. He clutched at them - Mara's dagger in one hand, the strange silver frame in the other - hoping that by holding them, some hidden strength would stir within his heart, some long-lost voice would guide him through the endless dark.

But there was nothing.

Only silence.

The heavy, suffocating silence of the forsaken deep pressed in on all sides, as if the very stones were holding their breath, waiting for him to break.

Arwin sighed, a sound so small it seemed lost in the vastness of the mines. His shoulders, which had once borne the weight of childhood's simple joys, now sagged beneath a burden too great for any child to carry. He knew it - knew in his bones that he could do nothing to stop the evil festering in these cursed depths. It was beyond him, beyond his reach, beyond hope.

But still, he stood.

His legs, though weak, found the will to rise. He took a breath, then another, and moved forward. The dagger's cold steel pressed against his palm, a reminder that though the world might abandon him, he could still fight, even if it meant fighting alone.

Suddenly, without warning, the ground beneath him shifted, a deep groan rising from the ancient stone as though the very earth had grown tired of holding itself together. The floor trembled, then cracked open. In an instant, the rock gave way, crumbling into a yawning abyss. Arwin gasped as the world beneath his feet vanished, and he plunged into the darkness below.

Down he fell, swallowed by the ancient hunger of the mines. The dagger and the frame remained clutched in his hands as he tumbled through the air, deeper and deeper into the blackened heart of the mountain. The void seemed endless, its depths cold and uncaring, and the faint light from the upper caverns soon disappeared from view.

He was alone. Alone in the darkness, falling, lost.

28

A violent shockwave tore through the plains, sweeping across the ancient, forgotten graveyard before the entrance to the mines. The earth trembled as if stirred from a deep slumber, and a great cloud of dust billowed into the air, swirling like a storm. For a moment, the world seemed to hold its breath, shrouded in uncertainty.

When the dust finally settled, the once-scattered remains of the dwarves were gone - as though they had never existed. Vanished were the bones and rusted armor, swallowed by the earth or perhaps by some darker force. All that remained were the four lesser Blaecwên, grim and shadowy figures, their malevolent presence now extinguished. They had been vanquished at last by the bravery of the guardians of the Order, whose courage had withstood the horrors of the underworld.

The warriors, battered and worn, allowed themselves a brief moment of rest. A peaceful stillness descended upon the battlefield, a fleeting calm that seemed to whisper of new hope. For the first time in what felt like an eternity, they could breathe without fear.

But the stillness was shattered as a murmur rippled through the men of Anros. Panic spread like wildfire among them, their voices raised in confusion and alarm. It was clear they had lost something - or someone.

"Where is the boy?" one of them shouted, fear tightening his voice. "He was with us just moments ago!"

Adraéth, standing nearby, turned swiftly toward the men, her eyes sharp and accusing. "A child?" she asked, her tone carrying a weight of disbelief. "What is a child doing in a place like this?"

One of the soldiers stepped forward, his face clouded with guilt. "Queen Fala brought him with us. We found him in Rist, near the great well. His entire family had been slain, butchered before his very eyes. She could not leave him behind, not alone."

At the mention of the well, Adraéth froze, her eyes widening in sudden realization. A chill ran through her, as if a shadow had passed over her heart. Without another word, she turned and darted back into the mines, her movements quick and determined, vanishing into the darkness that lay beyond.

Aric, who had been standing beside Faran and Diam, felt an unsettling certainty stir within him. He did not hesitate. Without a second thought, he followed her, his mind filled with an unshakable sense that something terrible awaited them in the deep, something tied to the boy.

Faran and Diam exchanged worried glances before they too ran into the abyss, their hearts heavy with uncertainty. They did not know what dangers lay ahead, but the urgency in Adraéth's actions and Aric's silent determination left them no choice but to plunge forward. Into the darkness, where ancient secrets and lurking terrors awaited them, they went - prepared for whatever fate would demand of them.

6

With every strike Beliach unleashed, the force of his blows drove Fala and Mara further back, and with each swing, he seemed to grow in size and might. It felt hopeless. He was too powerful. There was no denying it - his own father, Urehel, had feared his child. Urehel, once thought the pinnacle of darkness, had been but a shadow in comparison, defeated in a single, though long and grueling, battle. But Beliach - the embodiment of all evil that ever was and ever would be - could not be overcome so easily. Prophecy or no, Mara, even with the strength of Queen Fala beside her, could never hope to bring this creature to its knees.

A thunderous strike from Beliach sent the two women flying, crashing against the hard stone. The force of the blow was so tremendous that despite their desperate attempts to hold on, the seven Alyarel slipped from their grasp. Like silk, the stones slid through their fingers, tumbling out of reach, gleaming as they scattered across the ground.

Beliach's laughter echoed through the cavern, a bitter and terrible sound, for victory was close at hand. The Alyarel - those seven stones of unimaginable power - lay within his grasp. With them, he could subdue the world and reshape it according to his dark desires, as had been destined from the day of his birth.

He stepped forward, his eyes burning with cruel ambition, ready to seize the stones and claim the fate he believed was his. But as he reached out to take them, a sudden rumble from above sent a cloud of dust and debris crashing down. Hidden within the storm of rock and dirt, something fell, unseen at first - until the unmistakable sound of a body hitting the ground with a heavy thud shattered the moment of victory.

Beliach turned, his fiery eyes narrowing as a figure struggled to its feet. There, amidst the wreckage and swirling dust, stood Arwin. The boy's small form, trembling with fear and exhaustion, seemed pitiful against the towering demon before him. As Arwin lifted his head, his wide eyes took in the monstrous figure, its legs wrapped in fire and frost.

"A child?" Beliach sneered, his voice dripping with contempt. "How disappointing."

Raising his hand once more, Beliach prepared to strike, the air around him crackling with malevolent energy. With a cruel smirk, he swung his fiery blade down toward the boy, the sheer force of it threatening to crush him.

Desperate, with no other means of defense, Arwin raised the strange silver frame he had carried with him. His hands shook as he held it before him, a fragile hope that it might somehow protect him.

And then, something extraordinary happened.

As Beliach's fiery weapon made contact with the silver frame, an immense shockwave of power erupted from it, throwing Beliach back with such force that even he, the dark lord of terror, staggered. The mighty demon was sent reeling, confusion and fury flashing across his face as he struggled to comprehend what had just occurred.

Arwin, dazed but alive, slowly pushed himself up from the ground. As his vision cleared, he saw something remarkable. Surrounding him, lying on the ground in a radiant array of colors, were the seven Alyarel, glimmering in their full glory.

The boy stood, uncertain and overwhelmed by the magnitude of what had just transpired, but in his heart, a spark of hope rekindled - a hope that perhaps, just perhaps, all was not lost.

And in that fateful moment, the rest of the group arrived at the scene, their hearts heavy with the weight of the battle still to come.

Adraéth, her keen eyes falling upon Arwin, who stood amidst the scattered stones with the silver frame in his trembling hands, stepped forward with a sudden realization.

"That's it," she breathed, her voice filled with the solemnity of ancient knowledge. "Seven stones. Seven souls." She cast a quick glance at the others, urgency lighting her eyes. "Quickly now, there is no time to lose!"

Without hesitation, she darted towards the boy and, with a swift motion, reclaimed the yellow stone, its glow vivid against the shadowy backdrop of the cavern. Mara and Fala, still bruised from their desperate struggle, rose from the ground. Each reached for the stones closest to them - Mara for the blue, which seemed to hum with recognition in her grasp, and Fala for the brown, which gleamed like the rich earth.

Diam, his hand steady despite the turmoil around him, took hold of the white stone, the very same that Dartur had entrusted to him. Faran, the ever-loyal guardian, bent low and seized the green stone, his eyes flickering with resolve. Aric, still shaken from the spell that had once clouded his mind, clenched the red stone, its fire now in his hand, his gaze dark and determined.

In the midst of this gathering of power, young Arwin, his heart pounding with confusion and awe, looked down at the last stone - the black Alyarel, the most feared of them all. His hand wavered as he reached for it, the air around him thick with an ancient dread. Yet, something within him, perhaps the courage that had been born from his suffering, urged him forward. He bowed down, his small fingers closing around the dark gem.

As if the very earth had drawn breath, the silver frame began to shiver with a strange and potent magic. Its polished surface seemed to pulse, as though it knew that the moment of reckoning had come.

"Now!" Adraéth's voice rang out like the cry of a commander leading her forces into the final, desperate charge. With grim determination, each of them - stone-bearers all - stepped forward, their hearts united in purpose.

They moved as one, surrounding Beliach, who had just risen from the ground. His form, terrible and vast, loomed before them, flames of fury dancing in his eyes. Slowly, he gathered himself, preparing to unleash his dark wrath upon them once more. But even the ancient terror that was Beliach could sense the shifting of the winds. For the first time, he hesitated, his confidence faltering.

With a surge of unimaginable power, the seven stones flared in unison, their combined light growing brighter and brighter, like stars gathered in the heavens. A mighty wave of energy burst forth from them, crashing into Beliach with the force of a thousand storms. The dark lord, once untouchable in his wicked might, was thrown to his knees, his body trembling under the weight of the stones' collective strength. He struggled, but could not rise.

Above him, as though guided by some unseen hand, the silver frame lifted from Arwin's grasp. It floated in the air, its surface glowing with an ethereal radiance, and slowly, it placed itself above Beliach like a shield, shimmering with ancient magic, sealing him in place.

The seven stone-bearers, now standing in a circle around their foe, felt the very air around them hum with power. They could feel the stones in their hands vibrating with the energy of creation itself. The light they commanded grew so bright that it illuminated every shadow in the cavern, driving away the darkness as if the sun itself had been born within the depths of the earth.

Beliach, the dark god who had once sought to rule all, now knelt within that circle of light, bound by the power of the Alyarel, his strength sapped, his might undone. And as the radiant glow engulfed him, a final, brilliant light flared from the stones, illuminating every corner of the earth - bringing with it the hope of victory.

And with the light came salvation.

The dread power of Beliach, which had cast a shadow over all of Sedäa, was finally broken. His terrible form, once towering and full of wrath, began to fracture. His essence, like a shattered mirror, splintered into a thousand fragments, each piece burning with the heat of a blazing inferno and freezing with the chill of eternal ice. The echoes of his rage filled the cavern, but even they could not withstand the force of the seven stones.

What remained of Beliach was no more than a presence - an insubstantial whisper of malice, a lingering sense of dread. Yet even this, his final vestige, was drawn inexorably toward the silver frame. As though guided by the will of something far greater than any of them, the seven Alyarel - each bearing the weight of creation - lifted from the hands of their bearers. Mara, Fala, Diam, Faran, Aric, Adraéth and Arwin watched in awe as the stones floated through the air, their once vibrant light now dimming, their purpose revealed at last.

The stones, ancient and powerful, came together in perfect harmony. They slid into the silver frame as though they had always been meant to, each one finding its place with an undeniable certainty. Fire, earth, water, air, light, shadow and life - these primal forces united in a final act of cosmic destiny.

Then came the shockwave. It erupted from the very ground beneath them, shaking the world with its immense force. The walls of the ancient mines trembled as if the mountain itself had been struck by the hand of a god. Rocks tumbled from above, and the ground quaked with the fury of ages long past. Dust and debris filled the air, and the cavern, once a place of darkness and terror, began to collapse.

The silver frame, now holding the seven stones, fell to the ground with a dull, lifeless thud. No longer did it shine with the power of the Alyarel. Its brilliance had faded, and the magic that once coursed through the stones had been spent. The light of creation was extinguished, and what remained was but an empty vessel - silent, still, and void of its former glory.

Without hesitation, Arwin, whose small heart still carried the courage of one who had lost everything, reached out and seized the frame. It was cold to the touch, no longer imbued with the immense force that had once controlled the fate of worlds.

But there was no time for reflection. The mountain was crumbling around them, its very foundations giving way as the mines began to collapse into ruin. With quick, urgent hands, Mara grabbed Arwin, pulling him back from the edge of the abyss. The others - Fala, Adraéth, Diam and Faran - rushed to his side, forming a protective circle around the boy as the earth heaved beneath them.

"Go! Quickly!" Faran's voice, strong but strained, cut through the roar of falling stone.

Together, they fled, racing through the crumbling tunnels of the mine, the weight of their victory and the cost of their battle heavy upon their shoulders. Arwin clutched the silver frame to his chest as if it were the last relic of a vanished world, its weight both a comfort and a burden. The echo of Beliach's final defeat lingered in the air, but so too did the silence left in its wake - an eerie, hollow quiet, as if the world itself held its breath.

And as the last of them emerged into the light outside the mine, the entrance collapsed behind them, sealing forever the darkness that had once threatened to consume all of Sedäa.

Then, without a whisper of sound, the silver frame, once adorned with the seven stones of creation, began to dissolve. Slowly at first, its edges crumbled, the once-glorious relic of ancient power turning to dust before their eyes. Each particle shimmered with a faint, otherworldly light, as though imbued with the final breath of the stones' lost magic.

In silence, the dust lifted from the ground, rising into the air like the last sigh of a forgotten age. It floated upward, drifting on unseen winds, higher and higher, as if drawn by an unseen hand to a distant, sacred realm. The remnants of the frame and the stones, which had shaped worlds and borne the weight of destiny, ascended beyond the reach of mortal hands.

And as those who had witnessed the end of Beliach's reign gazed in awe, the particles soared ever upward, shimmering like stars lost in the light of dawn. It was as if they were being called home - to the Mencael, the eternal heavens, where the light of the Ahar dwelled, far beyond the realms of men and Aedan.

No word was spoken, for none was needed. The dust, filled with the essence of the seven stones, vanished into the sky, leaving only a lingering sense of peace. As the last trace of their power faded, it was as if the stones had returned to where they had first come into being, rejoining the cosmic fabric from which they were born. And in that quiet, sacred moment, the heavens seemed to welcome them home.

And though the seven Alyarel had perished, their essence was not wholly gone from the earth. Something of their ancient power lingered still, like a soft echo of the timeless forces that had shaped the world. Each of the seven stone-bearers, who had stood united to bring about the downfall of Beliach, bore now a subtle mark of that power - a single strand of snow-white hair woven amidst the dark locks upon their heads. It was a quiet reminder of their encounter with the divine, a faint reflection of the seven High Aedan, whose luminous white hair had been the mark of their near-unreachable majesty.

In that fleeting moment, as the dust of the seven stones ascended to the Mencael, queen Fala turned, and her eyes met those of Faran. It was as though the world paused, the chaos of the battle and the fading magic of the Alyarel falling away. Their gazes locked, and in that silent exchange, something deeper stirred, something beyond the power of words or even time itself. For in each other, they glimpsed what had been missing from their lives - the shared longing, the unspoken need, the untold sorrows they had carried through the years.

Fala, burdened by the weight of leadership and the emptiness of a heart never filled, saw in Faran the same solitude she had known for so long. And Faran, who had wandered with purpose but without peace, saw in the queen of Anros a kindred soul, one who understood the quiet ache of duty and the yearning for something more.

It was as though they had been destined to meet, two lives bound by a fate they had never foreseen, and in that instant, they found in the other what they had sought all their lives.

And thus, it was that Mara and Aric stood face to face, their eyes locked in a gaze that reached beyond the realms of sight, deep into the very essence of their souls. In that moment, nothing else in the world held any meaning - neither the whispers of those who had tried to sway them nor the shadows of doubt that had once lingered between them. All that mattered was this: they had found each other at last, beyond the trials of fate and the tumult of war.

Aric, with a heart now freed from the chains of past uncertainties, stepped closer. His hand reached out, trembling not from fear but from the depth of feeling that surged within him. Mara, her own heart beating in unison with his, met his touch without hesitation. The world seemed to still around them as they stood there, together at last.

And then, as if the heavens themselves had blessed the moment, Aric drew her into his arms and, with a tenderness that belied the storm of emotions within him, kissed her. It was no mere meeting of lips but a union of two souls, entwined in a bond that defied words. The passion of their love, long held at bay by fear and circumstance, now surged forth like a river breaking through a dam.

Those who beheld it - those who had fought alongside them, suffered with them, and hoped for them - felt their own hearts lift in pure, unbidden joy. For in that single kiss, there was a triumph greater than any won on the battlefield: the triumph of love, steadfast and true, against all odds.

And in that instant, the burdens of the world seemed lighter, and the shadows of the past faded away, for all who looked upon them felt, for a fleeting, wondrous moment, the undiluted joy of love fulfilled.

29

The path to the tomb of the Princes of Dinambad, where for many years the remains of Prince Ráhil II, the 14th Lord of Dinambad, along with his father Deluin and his grandfather Aranlad, had rested in solemn silence, was long and laden with sorrow. It was a journey of torment that Ráhad, Lord of Dinambad, and his children had no choice but to undertake. For no heart could remain unburdened when laying its own kin to rest - let alone one's own child or beloved brother.

Yet, though the grief pierced their very souls, and the cruel enemy had at last been vanquished, there was no avoiding this desolate day, nor the painful steps of this final journey.

And so, they bore Anwar, Ráhad's second-born son, on a bier adorned with flowers and wreaths, along the somber path that led deep into the tomb - a place that should have remained sealed for many more years to come. There, within the dim light of the ancient vault, Anwar was laid to rest for the last farewell.

Ráhad, with his remaining sons, Enwir and Diam, and his daughter Mara, stood beside the lovingly adorned bier, their hearts heavy and their breath shallow, as though even the air refused to offer solace.

Tears flowed freely, unchecked, for Anwar had been a prince beloved by all, a cherished companion and friend among the people of Miénast. His unexpected death weighed heavily upon the gathered throng, their hearts aching with the loss.

And then, a lamentation rose, borne on the gentle voices of the people - a song of mourning for the young prince who had fallen too soon, echoing through the ancient tomb like the whisper of time itself, a sorrowful tribute to a life cut short.

Beneath the skies of fading gold,
where once the waves of courage rolled,
there lies a prince, so brave and fair,
now bound within the cold night's care.

Oh Anwar, son of noble line,
your star has set before its time,
in battle fierce, your flame burned bright,
but shadows claimed your endless light.

The hills weep soft with misted dew,
for all who fought and followed you,
and in the hearts of Dinambad,
the songs of grief rise clear and sad.

Where once you walked, the earth now sighs,
beneath a thousand tearful skies,
the winds of Miénast call your name,
yet all remains, forever changed.

Your sword is still, your voice no more,
yet echoes ring from shore to shore,
for every heart that knew your grace,
now mourns the prince they can't replace.

Oh Anwar, rest in hallowed sleep,
while all who loved you, vigil keep,
until the dawn breaks clear and wide,
and we shall meet at heaven's tide.

The hours passed so slowly, dragging on as though they were days and months. Yet, as all things must, evening finally descended, and the last of the young fallen prince's friends paid their respects.

At the very end, his sister Mara stepped forward, carrying the swan-hilted sword that each of Ráhad's four children possessed, a symbol of their noble house. With trembling hands, she laid it gently in Anwar's cold grasp, along with a golden necklace that had once belonged to Aleth, which she had always worn around her neck. Mara closed his life-less fingers around the polished hilt of the well-worn blade. The swan-sword, a faithful companion in life, was now to guard him on the long road ahead, as it had once protected him in the world of Farham. It was her hope, and the hope of all who loved him, that Anwar might at last find the peace he had so richly earned. In this realm, his duty was complete.

Afterward, the bier was lowered into an empty, open tomb carved into the wall behind them. A solemn marble slab, adorned with ancient runes, was placed before the grave and sealed forever.

Thus, Anwar of Dinambad was laid to rest among his ancestors, and he would sleep there, undisturbed, in the halls of eternity.

As darkness finally descended and the last of the many funerals had come to an end, Prince Ráhad invited all his guests to a grand feast, for the day was not meant to be only one of sorrow. He knew in his heart that his son would have wanted it so. Of that, there was no doubt.

For every tear that had been shed, there was laughter to match it, filling the great hall with warmth and light. And though the grief of the day lingered, the late evening found its way to a fitting and heartfelt close, as sorrow and joy mingled like the fading echoes of an ancient song.

6

Aasa, captivated by the splendor of the harbor city of Dinambad, stepped outside the grand palace of the Prince. She descended the broad staircase and walked toward the fountain that stood at the center of the courtyard. The city, cloaked in twilight, was quiet, save for a few watchmen who stood their silent vigil. She found herself nearly alone, the stars above casting a soft glow upon her as she seated herself on a bench near the fountain, letting the memories of the past days flood her mind.

The cool night air carried a sense of peace, and the stars above seemed to reflect her thoughts. She sat for a time, lost in the stillness, when Enwir emerged from the palace. He paused at the top of the stairs, his gaze searching the courtyard as though seeking someone. His eyes found Aasa, seated by the fountain, and with silent steps, he descended the stairs and approached her. Without a word, he sat beside her, and at first, she did not seem to notice his presence.

"Rarely have I seen a more beautiful sky than tonight," Aasa finally broke the silence, her voice soft as she looked up at the heavens.

Enwir smiled gently. "In Dinambad, you may gaze upon the stars every night, whenever you wish."

His words caught her by surprise. She turned to look at him, expecting the stern, distant man she had known - one who had been cold and distrustful of Anros and its people. But the Enwir she saw now was different. There was no trace of disdain in his eyes, only a quiet gentleness that spoke of burdens he had long carried.

"Can you forgive me?" Enwir spoke at last, his voice low and sincere. "For all the harsh things I said about your land and your people? I was blinded by my fear for Mara, and in my worry, I could not see the truth - that her home truly belongs to Anros."

"Mara's home will always be where my brother's heart resides," Aasa replied, her voice firm but not unkind. She met his gaze steadily. "But I forgive you. You only sought to protect your sister."

A look of relief crossed Enwir's face, and for a moment, a soft smile graced his lips. Together, they sat in silence once more, watching the stars twinkle above and the lush gardens bathed in moonlight. The quiet moments stretched on, time seemingly forgotten.

"You are welcome to remain in Dinambad if it pleases you so," Enwir said after a while, his voice hopeful and warm. "It would bring me great joy to have the most beautiful woman in all of Anros here."

Aasa could not help but smile at his words, feeling her heart lighten with a joy that had been absent for so long. She gave him a gentle nod, her eyes twinkling with unspoken understanding.

Enwir, heartened by her silent response, moved closer, his arm resting gently around her shoulders, offering comfort and companionship under the vast expanse of the starry sky. Together, they found solace in the quiet, as if the weight of past sorrows had begun to lift, carried away by the soft winds of the night.

6

The days drifted by swiftly, like leaves carried upon a gentle breeze, and Mara, though she remained in Dinambad, could not escape the thought that the fateful day was drawing near - the day when Aric would come to stand before her father, Ráhad, to ask for her hand in marriage for her, and to take her to his homeland.

Yet, unaware of the quiet unfolding of fate, she did not know that this very day had come. The moment she had longed for yet feared in the depths of her heart was already upon her, carried in the footsteps of a man whose love had crossed mountains and seas to reach her.

As Mara stood upon the high balcony, her gaze lost in the boundless expanse of the sea, the wind softly playing with her hair, she remained unaware of the quiet footsteps that approached from behind. Finmar, ever careful and mindful of her solitude, drew near, his voice gentle but deliberate as he broke the silence.

"Lady Mara," he spoke, his words respectful yet carrying the weight of urgency. "Your father desires to speak with you."

For a moment, Mara did not stir, her thoughts still adrift upon the distant horizon. But the mention of her father's summons brought her back to the present, and she turned slowly, her expression caught between the serenity of the sea and the unknown message waiting to be delivered by her father's will.

Without hesitation, Mara followed Finmar, her steps swift yet measured, as they made their way through the grand archway into the heart of the palace. The echo of their footsteps resonated through the vast halls, where high columns rose like ancient trees, bearing the weight of stone and history upon their shoulders. The tapestries of her ancestors lined the walls, watching silently as she passed, each figure a memory of Dinambad's storied past.

Finmar led her onward, until at last they approached the stone throne, carved from the very rock of the mountains, standing tall and solemn at the far end of the great hall. There, amidst the flickering torchlight, awaited her father, Prince Ráhad, whose countenance held the wisdom of his lineage and the burden of many years of rule. Mara's heart quickened, though she kept her composure, sensing that the moment she had long anticipated was now upon her.

Beside her father stood none other than Aric, his presence commanding yet filled with a quiet desperation as his eyes sought hers across the hall. He was clad in a gleaming suit of armor, wrought with intricate designs, the silver and gold reflecting the torchlight like a radiant star. Every detail of his attire spoke of his noble lineage and the valor he had earned in countless battles, but it was not the armor that caught Mara's gaze - it was the look in his eyes. There, beyond the polished steel, lay a heart laid bare, waiting, yearning for the moment he had long dreamed of. His hands, though steady, betrayed the anxious hope within him.

"So, I suppose you know why I have summoned you?" Ráhad's deep voice echoed gently through the grand hall, though softened by the warmth of a father's love. His smile, though noble and steady, held a depth of understanding, as if he already sensed the storm of emotions swirling within his daughter.

Mara stood silent, her lips parted but no words escaped. She couldn't speak. Her heart, wild and untamed, beat so fiercely within her chest that she feared, for a fleeting moment, it might leap forth, betraying every guarded thought and secret hope. The weight of the moment pressed upon her like a great tide, and though her spirit longed to soar, she remained still, lost in the magnitude of what was unfolding before her.

"Lord Aric has asked for your hand in marriage," Ráhad spoke with a voice both tender and strong, his gaze resting on his daughter as though seeing her for the first time not merely as his beloved child, but as a woman standing on the threshold of a new life. "And by the light in your eyes, I now know that the answer I gave was the right one."

His words, though simple, carried the weight of a father's blessing, bound not by duty alone, but by a deep understanding of the love that had blossomed between his daughter and the noble warrior before him. It was as though the entire hall, the stone walls steeped in history and the air itself, held its breath in that sacred moment. Mara's eyes, wide and shining, were the only response needed - her heart laid bare before the two most important men in her life.

Suddenly, as though overcome by a flood of emotion too powerful to contain, Mara rushed forward, casting herself into her father's arms. Tears, bright as morning dew, filled her eyes and spilled down her cheeks - tears not of sorrow, but of pure, unbridled joy. Her voice trembled as she spoke, her words soft and full of love. "Thank you, *avar*," she whispered, the word for father in Aerin, the language of the Aedan, carrying the weight of her gratitude and affection, as though in those simple words she sought to convey a lifetime of meaning.

Ráhad, his own heart moved by the depth of her emotion, held her close, as though sheltering her from all the storms the world might yet bring.

At last, with a gentle yet bittersweet sigh, Ráhad loosened his embrace, though the warmth of his love lingered still. He took his daughter's hand and, with all the grace and solemnity befitting a lord of Dinambad, placed it into the waiting grasp of Aric. The young warrior, resplendent in his gleaming armor, bowed his head in silent reverence, knowing full well the trust bestowed upon him in that sacred moment.

Side by side, as though no force in the world could part them, Aric and Mara turned and walked from the great hall. The high stone walls, which had witnessed countless ages of joy and sorrow, now echoed with the quiet steps of a new beginning. Their path, though uncertain, was filled with hope, as they departed hand in hand, bound by a love that could weather even the darkest of fates.

As they descended the wide marble steps before the palace, their hearts light with the promise of the future, a sudden cry rang through the quiet of the evening air.

"Wait!"

The voice, strained with urgency, brought them to an abrupt halt. From the shadowed edges of the courtyard, a young boy came running toward them, breathless, his small frame trembling with the weight of unspoken sorrow. It was Arwin, the boy who had remained in Dinambad, ever at Mara's side, a steadfast companion in the face of so much loss.

His tear-filled eyes were wide with desperation as he placed himself before them, barring their path. "You cannot leave," he pleaded, his voice thick with the ache of abandonment. "Please." His words faltered, caught in the well of emotion that overtook him, and his hands trembled as they reached toward Mara, though he dared not touch her.

In that moment, Mara's heart broke for him, for she saw in his eyes the reflection of her own pain from so long ago - the unbearable fear of losing yet another loved one. Arwin, orphaned by war and tragedy, stood before them now, his chest heaving with sobs he struggled to contain. The last fragment of his fragile world was slipping away, and with it, his only hope of solace.

Tears filled his eyes, gleaming in the fading light like the stars that had so often comforted him in the darkness. "I cannot bear to lose you too," he whispered, his voice barely more than a breath.

"You shall not lose her," Aric said, his voice gentle yet firm, as he placed a comforting hand on Arwin's shoulder. A soft smile played upon his lips, though his heart, like Mara's, felt the weight of the boy's sorrow. In Arwin's tear-filled eyes, Aric saw the pain of a soul that had been ravaged by more grief than any child should ever know. "Wherever she goes, wherever we go, you will go as well."

Aric knelt before the boy, lowering himself to meet those mournful eyes that spoke of deep, unspoken wounds. His gaze was steady, filled with a kindness that reached beyond words. "You have lost much, far more than any heart should bear," he said softly. "But understand this, Arwin - you have been braver than even the mightiest of warriors. Without you, without your strength and courage, we would never have triumphed over Beliach. It was your resolve that helped turn the tide. You are as much a hero as any of us."

For a moment, Arwin's trembling hands gripped the edges of his tunic, his eyes flickering with doubt, as if he struggled to believe the words being spoken to him. The weight of his losses hung heavy in his mind, clouding the hope that Aric's words sought to kindle.

Aric smiled warmly, sensing the boy's uncertainty. "You belong with us now, Arwin. We are your family. And never again will you face such darkness or be left to wander alone in the shadows of grief. Those days are behind us, and the light of peace lies ahead."

Mara, her heart swelling with compassion, knelt beside Aric. She reached out, gently brushing away the tears from Arwin's cheek. Her touch was as soft as a summer breeze, filled with the tenderness only she could offer. "You are part of us now," she said, her voice like a melody of comfort. "We will never leave you behind, and we will never let you face this world alone again."

She took his small, trembling hands in hers, and in that moment, the world seemed to still, as if the very stars above paused in reverence to the bond now forged between them.